PRAISE FOR *The Everything Box*

"A rolling bouncy-house of a caper tale, *The Everything Box* abounds with quick-witted characters, snarky dialogue, and surreal analogies. If you haven't sampled Richard Kadrey's take on fantasy yet, this is a great place to start."

—Christopher Moore, *New York Times* bestselling author of *Lamb, A Dirty Job,* and *The Serpent of Venice*

"A manic and hilarious Venn diagram of Elmore Leonard, Dave Barry, and the Book of Revelation. The last time the end of the world in a novel was this funny, aliens destroyed Earth to build a hyperspace bypass through it."

—Matt Wallace, author of *Envy of Angels* and *Lustlocked*

"This book has everything I need in a book, and some things I didn't know I needed. I couldn't stop laughing at the freelance poltergeists, inept angels, doomsday devices, mooning werewolves (. . . mooning werewolf. I just got that), and small-time career criminals in way over their heads. Highly recommended."

—Mur Lafferty, author of *The Shambling Guide to New York*

"[Kadrey's] books are a romp . . . and they go down like cold lager on a hot afternoon."

—NPR Books

"The story is fast-paced, very funny, and exceptionally clever. Kudos to this author!"

—*Suspense Magazine*

"Hilarious, exciting, poignant, romantic, horrifying, and absurd in the very best way."

—New York Journal of Books

"A supernatural comic caper that reads like one of the late Donald Westlake's Dortmunder novels sprinkled with some fairy dust."

—*Kirkus Reviews*

"Kadrey's plot doesn't depend on magic; instead, magic is the broth bringing all manner of delicious ingredients together in this wonderful stew of a story. This unusual urban fantasy is a delight."

—*Publishers Weekly*

"Fans of the Sandman Slim novels as well as newcomers to the author will be thrilled by this fast-paced, smart-mouthed adventure."

—B&N Sci-Fi & Fantasy Blog

"[Kadrey] can make Hell funnier than you'd believe. . . . Raymond Chandler meets *Good Omens,* in which multiple doomsday cults, secret government agencies, and crooks of every description compete to retrieve the box, a perfect McGuffin, a Maltese Falcon with the power to destroy all of Creation."

—BoingBoing

"Kadrey's simultaneously glib and snide voice [peppers] his story with delightful turns of phrase. . . . *The Everything Box* is a fun read for all of the Kadrey-isms alone."

—*Locus*

"Richard Kadrey's work has often possessed a dark, satirical edge, but in *The Everything Box,* the San Francisco author allows himself to venture far into the realm of the outright silly. . . . Reminiscent of the comic novels of Christopher Moore, Neil Gaiman or Terry Pratchett"

—*San Francisco Chronicle*

"Mr. Kadrey's invention never flags. He always has another joke up his sleeve. Even if the joke is on us and our ability to drag the Heavenly Hosts themselves down to street level, and then corrupt them."

—*Wall Street Journal*

THE EVERYTHING BOX

ALSO BY RICHARD KADREY

Metrophage

Dead Set

Sandman Slim Novels

The Perdition Score

Killing Pretty

The Getaway God

Kill City Blues

Devil Said Bang

Aloha from Hell

Kill the Dead

Sandman Slim

THE EVERYTHING BOX

RICHARD KADREY

HARPER Voyager
An Imprint of HarperCollins*Publishers*

This is a work of fiction. Names, characters, places, and incidents are products of the author's imagination or are used fictitiously and are not to be construed as real. Any resemblance to actual events, locales, organizations, or persons, living or dead, is entirely coincidental.

Harper Voyager and design is a trademark of HCP LLC.

HarperCollins books may be purchased for educational, business, or sales promotional use. For information please e-mail the Special Markets Department at SPsales@harpercollins.com.

A hardcover edition of this book was published in 2016 by Harper Voyager, an imprint of HarperCollins Publishers.

FIRST HARPER VOYAGER PAPERBACK EDITION PUBLISHED 2017.

Designed by Shannon Nicole Plunkett

The Library of Congress has catalogued the hardcover edition as follows:

Names: Kadrey, Richard, author.
Title: The everything box : a novel / Richard Kadrey.
Description: First edition. | New York : Harper Voyager, an imprint of HarperCollins Publishers, [2016] | Description based on print version record and CIP data provided by publisher; resource not viewed.
Identifiers: LCCN 2015044325 (print) | LCCN 2015041562 (ebook) | ISBN 9780062389565 (ebook) | ISBN 9780062389541 (hardcover)
Subjects: LCSH: Angels—Fiction. | Thieves—Fiction. | End of the world--Fiction. | Paranormal fiction. | BISAC: FICTION / Fantasy / General. | GSAFD: Fantasy fiction.
Classification: LCC PS3561.A3616 (print) | LCC PS3561.A3616 E94 2016 (ebook)
| DDC 813/.54—dc23
LC record available at http://lccn.loc.gov/2015044325

ISBN 978-0-06-238955-8 (pbk.)

18 19 20 21 OV/RRD 10 9 8 7 6 5 4 3

To S. J. Perlman, early Woody Allen (not creepy recent Woody), Douglas Adams, and every heist and caper author and filmmaker ever. You made me want to write one of these stories and so I did. Now, though, I need a drink, so this is also for all the bartenders who got me off the cheap stuff, and especially that guy in Arizona (yes, Arizona) who made a mean Sazerac. You convinced me that whiskey didn't have to be downed neat and that absinthe was fit for human consumption. Like it or not, this one is for all of you.

"DON'T JUDGE A TACO BY ITS PRICE."

—Hunter S. Thompson,
Fear and Loathing in Las Vegas

THE EVERYTHING BOX

ONE

Earth. Four thousand years ago. Give or take.

THE ANGEL, MAJESTIC IN GOSSAMER ROBES, STOOD ON a mountaintop, taking it all in. The sky was clear and a few minutes earlier he'd been poking the carcass of a dead whale with a stick. The way he understood things, whales didn't normally spend a lot of time five thousand feet up the side of a mountain, which was probably why this one was so dead. It was the angel's first trip to Earth and everything was so exciting and new. Especially the destruction. A whole planet drowned. A damned clever way to clean up the whole "humanity mess." Of course, the flood made a different kind of mess, what with cities, people, and animals smashed willy-nilly across the land. And now that the rains had stopped, it was all getting a bit, well, ripe. But none of that was his problem. God got things rolling, and now he'd take care of the rest.

The angel raised his arms and unfurled his wings. They were large. Very large. Like a condor with a pituitary problem. The angel cleared his throat and spoke.

"Oh, humanity, heed the sound of destruction for your sins!"

"You don't have to shout. I'm right here."

The angel whirled around. The creature behind him was human.

A man. His hair was wild, like he hadn't combed or washed it in weeks. His face was streaked with mud and his filthy clothes were little more than damp rags.

"Sorry. I didn't see you there."

"Are you the one who's been fluttering around here the last few days?"

The angel smiled, standing a little straighter. Puffing his wings out even wider.

"Ah, you saw? Yes, that was me. I wasn't sure anyone had noticed. I was hoping someone might send an emissary. Is that what you are?"

"Sort of. People asked me to come up. I'm Tiras."

"Hello, Tiras. Very nice to meet you."

Tiras took a step closer. Having just crawled out of the mess of the semi-destroyed world below, he smelled like one of Lucifer's more pungent farts. The angel didn't say anything, partly because he was too polite and partly because he was holding his breath.

"Sounds like you're here to wipe out what's left of us," Tiras said.

"That's it in a nutshell. I wanted to speak to a representative who could pass the word along that—let me get this right—you're all awful, God is sick of you, and you should—what was it?—say your last prayers, beg for forgiveness, and all prepare to die horribly." The angel smiled at Tiras, proud of himself for remembering everything.

"The truth is," he said, "I wish we'd met a couple of days ago. Now I'm behind schedule."

Tiras nodded, glanced down the mountain and back at the angel.

"So, you're the angel of Death?"

The angel shook his head, a little embarrassed.

"I don't have that honor. In Heaven, I'm the celestial who bears the great golden quills, the silver Chroma, the holy vellums upon which the Lord God inscribes the fate of the universe."

Tiras's eyes narrowed.

"You're in charge of office supplies. You're the angel of office supplies."

The angel looked at him.

"That's a little reductionist, don't you think? Disrespectful, too, when you get down to it. You do understand that I'm a living representative of God on Earth, right?"

"What's your name?" said Tiras.

"I'm called Qaphsiel."

"And you're here to finish the rest of us off."

"Hopefully by tonight. As I mentioned, I'm a little behind schedule," said Qaphsiel brightly.

"Then let me give you a kiss from all of us left slogging around in the mud and dead things."

Tiras balled up his hand. Qaphsiel watched, fascinated. He'd read about this kind of thing. There was a word for it.

Tiras pulled his hand back and punched Qaphsiel in the nose. It hurt. It hurt a lot.

Fist. Yes, that was the word.

"What's wrong with you?" shouted Qaphsiel. "Hitting a celestial who sits at God's right hand?"

"Guarding the cabinet where they keep the quill sharpeners hardly makes you God's right-hand man."

"Well, it's a pretty big cabinet. And who are you to judge one of the holies?"

Qaphsiel took a step back when Tiras balled up his fist again.

The man said, "I should wholly kick your ass all the way back to Heaven for what you did."

Even though Qaphsiel's nose still hurt, he squared his shoulders and spoke in the loftiest tone he could muster.

"The flood wasn't my or any other angel's doing. It was God's. At the time, a lot of us didn't understand, but now, having met a human, I'm getting a pretty good idea why he did it."

The man stuck a finger in Qaphsiel's chest. That hurt, too. Were all humans this pointy and painful?

"You don't like me?" said the man. "What are you going to do about it? Take away my house and sandals? Oh wait, I don't have any because they all got washed away!"

Qaphsiel's eyes flashed with anger.

"Though I'm not the angel of Death, I've been charged by the Lord with finishing his work. The great flood was supposed to purge humanity from the Earth. Yet, some of you remain."

The man shook his head.

"Not that many. There wasn't much room in the boat."

"There are others, scattered around the world, on islands and high peaks like this. Enough to repopulate the world. That is why I'm here. I'm the Lord's hand in this matter. The wrath of God on Earth."

"You said you were in charge of paper clips."

Quietly, Qaphsiel said, "This is my chance for a promotion. Really. So yes, this isn't at all what I usually do, but destroying you people is getting more appealing by the minute."

The man smiled and backed away, holding up his hands in mock fright.

"What's your plan? Murder us with an inkwell? Stab us with a stylus?"

"No," said Qaphsiel. Storm clouds gathered overhead and the mountain turned dark. Lightning spiked across the heavens and crashed to the ground, exploding the rotting whale, sending a great blubbery rain down around them.

"Behold! The Apocalypse is nigh!" Qaphsiel shouted.

Tiras looked around, his eyes darting back and forth in their sockets like they were trying to figure out how to get away from the rest of him.

"Listen, Qaphsiel. I think maybe we got off on the wrong foot. No one's been sleeping or eating much, and I have this low-blood-sugar problem."

"Too late, wretched mortal!" thundered Qaphsiel, and the Earth rumbled beneath them. Tiras backed down the mountain away from the angel. Qaphsiel felt good. He felt powerful. Yes, he was going to enjoy obliterating these people and finally leaving office supplies behind.

He looked down upon Tiras and said in a voice that made the sky tremble, "Behold the instrument of thy destruction!"

Qaphsiel plunged his hand into the pocket of his gossamer robe . . .

. . . then his other hand into the other pocket. He patted himself down and looked in the silk bag he kept tied to his belt. It was empty. He turned in a circle, scanning the ground.

"Hmmm."

The object was gone. Qaphsiel looked down the mountain.

Humanity continued to crawl across the face of the Earth.

"Oh, crap."

TWO

Earth. The present.

ON A HOT MIDNIGHT IN LOS ANGELES, CHARLIE COOPER—Coop to his friends—hung suspended by a thin wire a few feet off the floor of Bellicose Manor's dining room, hoping he wasn't about to be eaten by a monster.

"Careful," whispered Phil.

"Of what?"

"Just careful. Don't want you to break a nail."

"That's really thoughtful. Now shut up."

Phil Spectre, freelance poltergeist, continued scrabbling around inside Coop's head. It felt like rabid ferrets were using his frontal lobe for a scratching post.

"Cut it out," said Coop.

"I can't help it. Your skull is so thick I get claustrophobic."

Coop—tall, sandy haired, in his mid-thirties—pulled himself slowly and steadily along the wire, careful not to touch anything. To his relief, Phil was quiet for a minute. Those few seconds let Coop concentrate on the job at hand. He looked around, and while he couldn't see the wall safe yet, he knew where it was hidden.

Bellicose Manor didn't stand so much as flop on a hilltop, like a giant Gothic carbuncle, in Benedict Canyon. The house wasn't an eyesore per se, but rather a soul-sucking nut punch to anyone who hung around the place too long without an invitation. This was by design, just one of the many magical defenses the Bellicose family paid for to keep the nice things they had in their house *in their house.* Anyone who was anyone had at least a few spells sprinkled around their place. How else would people know that they had things nice enough to steal? This idea had eventually trickled down to Hollywood hipsters and even some middle-class families. The kind that had a soft spot for government conspiracies and UFO conventions. You know the type, the ones crazy enough to believe that monsters and magicians actually existed and walked side by side with them down the Pop-Tarts aisle in Safeway. This paranoia led to a thriving industry in bogus wards and do-it-yourself witchproofing, proving once again that con men had been separating people from their cash since long before the first witch invited the first black cat for a ride along.

"Wendigos," said Phil suddenly. "I bet they have a Wendigo. Big place like this. Family has money. A vampire would be gauche. A hungry Wendigo, that's the way they'd go. It's probably right past the dining room table." He went quiet again. Then, "Or something with tentacles. Which do you hate more? I can't remember."

"Yes, you can."

"It's coming back to me. Is this a good time to discuss your fear of intimacy?"

Coop was sweating, and it wasn't just from exertion. His hand slipped and grazed the side of an antique wooden chair, one of several similar chairs surrounding an impressive dining room table. Bellicose Manor was stuffed to the ceiling with impressive bric-a-brac, most of which would kill you if you touched it the wrong way.

"Which part of you do you think the Wendigo will eat first?"

"Please. I'm asking you nicely," said Coop.

When he was twelve, Coop had checked out a book on emergency medicine from the school library specifically to see how many organs a human body could lose and live. It turned out that people needed pretty much everything they had, inside and out. Worse, Coop knew that Phil knew it, and when the poltergeist got bored or nervous it was hard to shut him up.

"Too bad people aren't more like lizards, huh?" Phil said. "Just regrow a spare leg or lung. But you can't. No, humans are good at growing bones, toenails, and cancer. That's about it."

The problem was, for all his pain-in-the-assness, Phil was actually good at his job. He'd pointed out many of the wards and electronic alarms protecting the mansion, and had even disabled a few so that Coop could break in. Now, if he'd just shut up, Coop would maybe get him an Employee of the Month cup.

Coop's fingers ached. The wire he was on was attached to the dining room's far wall with a claw made of cold iron, magicproof and cheaper than a silver one. Only Eurotrash and cowboys still used silver. What a waste of money, Coop thought. Still, someday it would be nice to have some extra cash to toss around on gear and a partner more reliable than a jumpy poltergeist.

"Please," said Phil. "If you had more money you'd still hire me, because you're too cheap to splash the cash for anyone else. Isn't that one of the reasons what's-her-name left you?"

"Leave my love life out of this and do your job. Look for traps."

Phil scrambled around some more. "Man, it's hot in here. Are you hot, too?"

"Shut up."

"Hey, pal. I'm your partner, remember, and I don't like your tone."

"You're fired."

"Duck," said Phil.

Coop lowered his head, just missing a nearly invisible glass needle hanging from a nearly invisible line right at eye level. "Okay. You're rehired."

"Goody. Now I can finally get that place in the Bahamas."

When he had his bearings again, Coop inched along the wire like a worm, in a skintight carbon-fiber suit that hid both his body heat and his breathing. Phil was right—the suit was hot as balls and smelled like sweat socks, but it did the trick. The room's heat and pressure sensors had no idea he was there.

Now if we could only finish this up and actually not be here, that'd be swell.

Easier thought than done. Bellicose Manor was well known in the criminal world for its curses and traps. That's why it was such a perfect place to rob. But it made things go slowly. And it was costing him a lot of money.

Phil charged by the hour.

"This better pay off big time," Coop said.

"That would be a nice change," said Phil.

After what felt like an eternity, Coop made it to the far wall. Before him was a large oil painting of a spectacularly ugly woman in a fuchsia ball gown. The Bellicose family claimed that it was a two-hundred-year-old portrait of the first Lady Bellicose back in Whereverthefuckland. Coop, however, had it on good authority that it was Grandpa Bellicose in a wig and party dress after losing a bar bet to Aleister Crowley. Coop touched the brass nameplate on the picture frame and the painting slid up into the ceiling to reveal a safe underneath.

"Well, that was disappointing," said Phil.

"Missing your Wendigo already?"

"A little. I mean, we've been here half an hour and still no carnage. And we haven't stolen anything. It's nerve-racking, you know? Mind if I sing?"

"Don't you dare."

Coop felt a tickling on the inside of his skull.

"It helps my nerves."

"Please don't sing."

"Fine," said Phil in a huff. "I'll hum."

Phil went into a hushed, tuneless free jazz number. Calling it noise would have given it too much credit. It sounded like claws on a blackboard, thought Coop, if the claws were chain saws and the blackboard was a busload of grizzly bears. Now that he was close enough, Coop could see why Phil had chosen this particular moment to turn his head into a karaoke bar.

In a darkly enchanted house like Bellicose Mansion, the term *wall safe* could mean a lot of things. In this case it meant a ten-foot reptilian snout with teeth the size of dragon fangs, which, in fact, was exactly what they were. The dragon growled at Coop uncertainly, like it didn't know whether to roast him or invite him in for a nightcap. Coop didn't like dragons.

"Neither do I," Phil said.

"Do you know what it is?"

"It's a dragon. Shit comes out one end and fire out the other."

"I mean what kind of dragon."

"Right. Sorry. It looks French. Rich jerks like French."

"Why?"

"They're loyal and vicious. Plus, did I mention it's a dragon? You might want to shake a leg."

"Good idea."

He pulled the portable alchemy kit from the utility sack at his waist. On other occasions, Phil had called it Coop's wicked witch fanny pack, but now he was too busy being terrified to say a word, which suited Coop just fine.

The dragon's growling changed, like it had decided that Coop was more of a petit four than a drinking buddy. As it opened its mouth, sucking in air to stoke its internal furnace, Coop held up the potion so it got a good whiff of the brew.

The dragon sneezed. Once. Twice. Then it yawned, showing even more horrifying lawn-gnome-size teeth and a tongue like a meat Slip 'N Slide, at the far end of which were the boiling guts of a Parisian hell beast. The dragon's eyes slowly began to close and it relaxed. A few seconds later and it was sound asleep.

"Nicely done," said Phil. "Too bad the critter's mouth is shut tight. You think you're going to Schwarzenegger those choppers open? You don't have the guns for it."

"You might have mentioned that before."

"I thought it was obvious."

"You're getting old, Phil. It's making you shaky."

"Yeah? And you're getting . . . shut up."

Coop ignored him and snapped a couple of tools off his belt. He jammed a minijack between the dragon's jaws, slotted the handle into place, and began to crank the mouth open.

"There you go, sport," said Phil. "Problem solved."

"I get tense when you call me clever. I know it's a trick."

"This is too nerve-racking. I hope you like Neil Diamond."

"I don't like *your* Neil Diamond."

Coop took out a flashlight and peered into the dragon's mouth as Phil hummed "I'm a Believer." There were lots of goodies scattered around in the monster's gob—gold coins, piles of cash, jewelry, guns—but Coop looked past all of that junk for something more valuable. Finally, he saw what he had come here for: a green file folder, closed with a red wax seal. Unfortunately, the folder was back by the dragon's molars, between a pile of Euros and a stolen Picasso. To Coop, it looked like a portrait of a woman after someone dropped a refrigerator on her head. That probably meant it was expensive. Too bad he didn't have room for it in his suit.

The poltergeist stopped humming. "Please tell me you didn't cheap out on the jack. I'd hate to see it fail and for those teeth to snap you in half. Actually, it might be kind of funny, but not while I'm in your head."

"I bought the best money could buy."

That my *money could buy, at least.*

They peered around the dragon's mouth for other traps.

"So you finally admitted it," Coop said. "You want me dead."

Coop inched forward on the line until his head was almost touching the dragon's front fangs. He pulled a collapsible gripper from a pocket sewn into his suit. He tested the trigger a couple of times to make sure the claw on the extendable arm worked.

"Not at all," Phil said. "I'm just saying that being eaten by a dragon might be karmic payback for being mean earlier. On your right. Near your elbow."

Coop looked right. A human eye floating in a bubbling potion was attached to a spray gun full of acid. He crawled underneath the eye's gaze.

"Thanks," he said.

"And the team is back together again!"

When he saw that the grip worked properly, Coop extended the arm and pushed it into the dragon's mouth as far as it would go. It was a good two feet short of the folder. He let his head drop onto his arms, knowing what he had to do.

"I don't want to jinx anything," said Phil, "but you're not really going to do this, are you?"

"I don't have any choice."

"Of course you do. Pack up and we go for waffles. My treat."

"Not tonight. I know I can do this. I have to."

"Oh, man. I'm definitely going to have to sing."

"Don't you dare."

Phil broke into a full-throated chorus of "Sweet Caroline."

Pushing himself off with his arms, Coop landed flat on the beast's tongue and slid forward, scattering piles of gold and diamonds, until he was knee deep in the dragon's mouth. Before he'd even stopped sliding, Coop thrust the claw forward and grabbed the folder, which he crammed into a Velcro pouch on the front of his suit.

"Are we dead yet?" said Phil.

"We're doing great."

Phil went back to his song.

"Except for the singing."

Moving backward out of the dragon's mouth was a lot harder than going in. He couldn't get a grip on the slippery tongue, so he had to worm his way back slowly, past the Bellicoses' other loot. He was almost out when he caught his leg on one of the dragon's front fangs and ripped through the suit, leaving a deep gash. The dragon growled sleepily as it tasted blood.

"Ah. I see what you meant. *Now* we're dead," said Phil.

Coop gave one massive push and shot out of the dragon's mouth hard enough that he almost missed the wire, grabbing it just before he touched the floor.

Slick as a human Skittle covered in dragon spit, cut, and exhausted, Coop inched his way back across the wire to the dining room door. He wasn't going to sleep tonight. Not for a couple of nights, probably, not with the image of the dragon's gullet so fresh in his mind. He considered using the rest of the sleep potion to knock himself out tonight, but nixed that in favor of a drink. Many, many drinks.

"I thought we weren't drinking anymore," said Phil. "Not after, you know. Which brings me back to your intimacy issues."

"I didn't drink until after. And you're my intimacy issue right now."

"Careful. I know some Sondheim, too, and I know how you love musicals."

"How's this? Give me sixty seconds to feel good over a job well done, okay?"

"Okay. But can I say one thing?"

"What?"

"You forgot your jack," said Phil.

Coop looked back at the dragon's mouth, where the jack glistened.

"Damn." He glanced back toward the door and the way out. "Forget it. With this payout, I'll buy another. I'll get a dozen."

"Damn. We are feeling good. Okay, it's waffles all around then."

Coop made it back to the door, dropped onto the hall floor, and packed up his gear.

Not bad, he thought. A tough job, but he got it done. He felt better than he had in months.

"You know," said Phil. "It's still a few hours until dawn."

Coop looked up at the walls. The Bellicoses were out of town at their summer place in whatever milder country the rich had decided to strip-mine this season. He and Phil had the place to themselves. Old masters hung in gilt frames on the walls. Antique Persian carpets covered the floors. Even the bowl holding a pile of wax fruit on a nearby table was gold. He shook his head.

"I was thinking the same thing, but no. The job went all right and now we're leaving."

"Buck, buck, buck," said Phil, doing a fairly convincing impression of a Rhode Island Red.

"Pipe down, Phil. I still have some professional pride left."

"You still think this one job is going to get your rep back?"

"Why not? No one has ever made it in and out of Bellicose Manor alive. Except for a couple of hiccups, things went just like I planned."

"Uh. No, they didn't." Phil cleared his throat.

Coop finished packing and looked up from the floor.

Damn.

"My snitch said this place would be empty for the whole week."

He felt Phil twirl around in his skull like he was looking for an ejection seat.

"Well, I'm gone," Phil said. "Good luck."

"Don't you dare."

Down the hall, a little blond girl in Wonder Woman footie pajamas stood and stared at them. She rubbed her eyes sleepily and squinted when she saw him, like she wasn't sure Coop was real. He froze, hoping that she'd keep one foot in dreamland until he had time to get out.

"Do you really think you're that lucky?" said Phil.

The little girl twitched. Something changed in her eyes. Coop knew it was the "Nope, you're awake" part of her brain finally kicking in. She dropped the glass of water and screamed. Coop stood and put a finger to his lips, hoping the sleepy kid might obey an adult simply out of habit. And she might have, if her face hadn't peeled open like a flesh banana, revealing a snarling red baboonlike mug.

"Oh, crap," said Coop and Phil.

Not a kid, Coop thought. A guard imp. There weren't supposed to be any left in the house, much less one in little-girl drag.

Coop reached into a pocket on his bloody leg and pulled out a packet the size of a walnut. The imp screamed again, its human disguise falling away completely. As it charged him, Coop threw the packet on the floor. A cloud of white smoke filled the corridor. When the fog cleared, three Coops stood side by side. Two of them took off running in different directions. The real Coop stood as still as a bacon-wrapped rat at a Rottweiler convention. Guard imps weren't known for their brains, and most were attracted to motion. But this imp just stood there.

"Oh, hell," said Phil. "We got the Stephen Hawking of imps. It's onto us."

"Shut up and let me think."

One of the extra Coops came back down the hall, looked around, and sprinted past them down the stairs.

It was too much for the imp. It finally ran after him, screaming like a banshee taking first place in an air-raid-siren sing-along contest.

"See you around, smart guy—"

Something snapped behind Coop and the whole house shook. He turned around just in time to see the dragon swallowing the last of his broken jack.

"The imp woke it!" screamed Phil. "We're double screwed! Do something, numb nuts!"

Coop ducked as the dragon blew a roiling blast of crimson fire over his head. The beast shook its shoulders, rocking the whole house. The wall started to crack as the monster pushed its way through and into the dining room.

"At least it's not a Wendigo," said Coop.

"You're not funny," said Phil.

"No, but I'm a good shot."

Coop took a flat lead conjuring coin from his alchemy kit and flipped it across the room. It spun through the air, striking the nameplate on the front of the painting. The frame dropped like a guillotine onto the dragon's neck, trapping it. It roared and shot out another jet of fire, but Coop was already down the corridor and out the same window he'd come in, shooting away from the house on the zip line he'd set up earlier. Phil whooped and jumped around in his skull.

"Suck on that, you monster assholes!" yelled Phil.

Coop was halfway across the manor grounds, heading for the stone wall that ringed the place, when he felt the zip line sag. He looked back and saw the imp sliding toward him down the line by one of its claws.

"Sorry, man, but those things eat poltergeists, too, and I'm not dressed for an evisceration," said Phil. "I'm out of here."

This time the poltergeist meant it, and Coop felt the sudden emptiness in his head that always followed Phil's exit to wherever it was he went when he vanished. He couldn't even feel angry for the guy deserting him. If he could desert himself right now, he would.

He looked back over his shoulder. The imp was close, almost close enough to grab him.

Coop reached into his suit and pulled out the secret weapon he kept for just such emergencies: a set of nail clippers. While the imp took swipes at his face with its free claw, Coop calmly clipped the tips of the ones holding onto the zip line. The imp, possessing just a little less brainpower than a wedge of cheddar cheese, didn't seem to understand what was happening and why it was slipping. Even when it began to fall it stared at its hand in wonder. Coop thought that he might have seen some kind of realization spread across the imp's face just before it hit the ground, but he was moving too fast to be sure.

When he was past the trees outside the wall, Coop squeezed the hand brake on the grip, which slowed him enough that he could jump off the line and hit the ground running. He headed straight for his car, parked at the end of a nearby cul-de-sac.

I'm gonna make it.

He didn't make it.

The car gave an encouraging beep when he pushed the button on his key ring to unlock the doors. The moment he got the driver's-side door open, though, lights from a semicircle of cars hit him. He had to put a hand up in front of his face to see what was happening. Red and white bars on a few of the cars pulsed like a jailhouse disco. Coop dropped his bag to the ground. Cops. At least a dozen of them.

They've been waiting for me this whole time.

At least Phil wasn't around to start another round of skull karaoke.

Two men in suits reached him first. They flashed badges, but Coop couldn't read them in the harsh light. He didn't need to. He knew exactly who they were. A couple of Abracadabrats: detectives from LAPD's Criminal Thaumaturgy squad.

The taller of the two shoved him back against the car, reached into the front pocket of Coop's suit, and pulled out the stolen folder.

How did he know what to look for . . . and where?

The detective broke the seal, thumbed through the papers, then showed them to his partner. The second detective looked them over, sighing at what he read. It occurred to Coop that he had no idea, beyond a folder, what he'd been hired to steal.

What the hell did I just give them? Missile launch codes? The formula for Coke? Abe Lincoln's porn stash? Whatever it was, he knew it was bad.

"Isn't someone supposed to read me my rights somewhere around now?" Coop said.

The shorter detective drew closer, shaking his head. Coop could finally see him when he stood in front of the light and blocked it. He was a squat man, roughly the shape and size of a mailbox, and, from the look on his face, with even less of a sense of humor.

"This is bad, Coop. Real bad," said the detective.

Oh, good. He even knows my name. This night can't get any better, thought Coop.

A uniformed Abracadabrat spun Coop around and handcuffed him, spun him around again to face the talking mailbox. The look on the cop's face slipped from utter disgust to amusement as he punched a button on his cell phone.

"Yeah," said the detective. "He's right here. Put the asshole on."

The mailbox held the phone up to Coop's ear. Coop didn't hear anything for a few seconds. Then someone started talking.

"Coop? That you? It's me, Morty."

Morton Ramsey. He'd known Morty since they were both six. Coop didn't have any magical skills at all, but Morty was a natural Flasher—he could open any lock, window, or door he encountered. The problem was, Morty was a lousy crook.

And right now, an even lousier friend.

"Hey. I'm sorry, man," Morty said. "They picked me up last night. It was my third strike. I had to give them someone. No hard feelings?"

The mailbox took the phone from Coop's ear and hung up. He raised his eyebrows at the thief.

"Anything to say, smart guy?"

"Yeah," said Coop. "Duck."

It burst through the trees, hissing and limping, heading straight for them. The detective turned around just in time to get a face full of imp, all teeth and what was left of its claws out, and really, really pissed. One of the uniforms shoved Coop facedown on the hood of his car, where he spent the next several minutes listening to a small army of L.A.'s finest trying to pull the creature off the screaming detective.

At least I get a floor show, he thought. Then, *They're going to blame me for this, too.*

Still, as he listened to the mayhem, he couldn't help but smile.

THREE

Eighteen months later.

OUT OF GUILT AND BASIC CROOK SOLIDARITY, MORTY got Coop the best lawyer he could afford, which basically meant he could dress himself and read the charges, but not much else. Coop didn't like Ferthington, the lawyer, the moment he laid eyes on him. The guy smiled when they first shook hands. Coop didn't trust lawyers who smiled too much. "Smiling lawyers are fatalists and you're the fatality," an old con had once told him. Looking at Ferthington's eyes, Coop felt like shark chum.

When he told him about it Morty opened his hands, groping for words. "Maybe it wasn't fatalism. Maybe it was irony."

"Oh, that's better. Ironic time passes much faster than regular time."

In the end, Coop didn't get the chair (not that he was going to). But the judge was friends with the Bellicose family and sentenced Coop to ten years' hard time.

Ferthington smiled as the bailiffs led Coop out of the courtroom. It wasn't fatalism or irony. It was the smile of someone not bright enough to know that he'd been as useful in court as a trout with a speech impediment. Coop started to shout something, but one of the bailiffs helpfully jammed a nightstick into his side, doubling him over and thereby saving him from the extra time the "attack" would have added to his sentence. *Maybe I should have gotten the cop for a lawyer,* he thought as he lay in the back of the prison bus, nursing a bruised kidney.

At least the other soon-to-be inmates were impressed that Coop had already been in a dustup with a guard, so they left him alone.

And while it wasn't the finest moment of his career, at least it covered up how entirely freaked out he was to be back in a bus on the way to jail.

The prison didn't have a name. Just GPS coordinates and a Viking rune that translated roughly as "Seriously, would you take a look at these dumbfucks?"

Inside, the jail was known as Surf City because of how close to the ocean it wasn't. Surf City was in the high desert and most of it was underground. This kept it out of the public and, more important, the press's eye. No need to feed the crackpot industry by letting regular saps get wind that, yes, magical thieves, sasquatches, and succubi were all real and on a bad day just as likely to steal your Prius as suck out your soul.

When Coop got the notice that he was going to be released after serving only eighteen months, it was a mystery to him, and he didn't like mysteries that involved his skin and bones. At first he thought the prison had gotten his file mixed up with some other con's, but when the warden convinced him that no, it was really Coop who was getting out, he kept his mouth shut and his eyes down, which meant a certain amount of banging into things, but better safe than sorry. Still, the whole thing bothered him. Even with good behavior, he should have been a good three years from a parole hearing.

In the two weeks between being told he was getting out and the time of his release, Coop went from puzzled to suspicious, back to puzzled, then even more suspicious, and finally, he settled into a nice long stretch of grim paranoia. Maybe he was a lab rat in a prison psych experiment and when he reached the gate to get out, the warden and all the guards would shout "April Fool's!" and drag him back to his cell.

"Good luck, Coop," said Rodney, his cellmate, as he was packing up.

"Luck? Why do I need luck? Did you hear something?"

"Relax," Rodney said. "It's just an expression, like 'see you around' or 'take it easy.' It doesn't mean nothing."

"Right," said Coop, trying to sound cool or, at least, a dignified level of panicked. "Nothing. But you didn't hear anything, did you?"

"Not a thing."

"Okay."

Rodney put out his hand to shake as Coop prepared to leave. Rodney was one of the many things Coop wouldn't miss about prison. It wasn't that Rodney was a bad guy. In fact, he was a fine cellmate. He knew when to keep his mouth shut and he never touched any of Coop's stuff without permission. Beyond that, Coop didn't know exactly what Rodney was and he was too polite to ask. He knew that before jail Rodney had haunted a swamp out by Cienega Grande and he got the feeling that he'd had some kind of drive-in horror-movie run-in with a vanful of idiot city kids over a spring break weekend. What Coop was most acutely aware of was that Rodney smelled like a garbage dump dry-humping a slaughterhouse in the large intestine of a sick elephant.

Coop stood there for a few seconds staring at Rodney's hand, just long enough that it become uncomfortable for both of them. Rodney was withdrawing his perpetually damp mitt when Coop reached out and shook it. Rodney beamed at him with his moss-colored teeth.

"Take care of yourself, Rodney," said Coop as he walked out of the cell.

He waited until he was at the end of the tier before sniffing his fingers. It was like his hand was made of liverwurst that someone had forgotten under a moldy sofa.

On his way out, Coop made sure to shake hands with every guard in his cell block.

Then, just like that, it was over and he was out. After all his paranoid fantasies, the walk out of jail was almost anticlimactic. He was outside the gate in the same blue suit he'd had on the day he'd been convicted. It was just a little baggier now.

Coop walked to the bus stop under the blasting desert sun and sat on the bench with a plastic bag that held all his worldly possessions. No one had told him how often the bus came by, but he wasn't going to move his ass until it did. He wished he'd been able to eat breakfast. Or dinner. But his stomach had been too jumpy and the last thing he wanted was to be sick on release day. Still, sitting there in his too-loose clothes, state-issued sneakers, and prison haircut, he'd never felt more like a loser con in his life.

A black Corvette sped up the two-lane road in front of the prison and squealed to a stop, leaving twin streaks of rubber on the asphalt. Half the body was Bondo-painted black in an attempt to match the rest of the car, which just made it look like it was slowly turning into an alligator.

"Hey, jailbird!" yelled the driver.

Coop lowered his head to see who was inside. The driver pushed a button and rolled down one of the side windows.

It was Morty. He was only a few years older than Coop, but already starting to go gray. He wore a red corporate-style pullover, chinos, and loafers. Coop thought he looked like the assistant manager at an Orange County Burger King. Morty beamed at Coop as he leaned over and opened the passenger door.

"Hop inside. I'll drive you to town, Jesse James."

Coop sat there for a minute before getting up. He started for the passenger door, stopped, and went around to the driver's side. Morty got out and opened his arms to hug him. The two men embraced. Coop moved them around a little so that Morty's back was to the prison, shielding him from anyone who happened to be watching from inside. When he was sure he was safe, Coop kneed Morty in the balls. Not hard enough to double him up. That would attract too much attention. Coop tagged him just hard enough that Morty dropped back down on the driver's seat seeing stars and trying to catch his breath. Coop went back around the car and got on the bus, which was just pulling up. As Morty watched him go, all he managed to say was "Urgh . . ."

[][][]

It was four hours back to L.A. The bus was empty except for Coop and a couple of cons he didn't recognize. Tough guys from one of the prison werewolf gangs, by the look of them. Coop stared out the window, watching the complete lack of scenery roll by, conspicuously not looking at the wolf crew, hoping they noticed his extreme inattention.

The bus dropped them on Seventh Street near Pershing Square. As it rumbled off, a blue Ford SUV pulled up, blasting black metal on the sound system. Coop didn't know what band, but he recognized the style because it sounded like a gorilla stuck in a clothes dryer. Between the shaggy, headbanger lycan driver, the haze of weed rolling out the side door, and the broken side window, the SUV could not possibly have looked more stolen. Coop had to admire the wolves' complete lack of giving a shit when he noticed that they'd noticed him noticing them. One of the gang who'd been on the bus stuck his butt out of the side door and dropped his pants, waving his human ass as the rest of the gang gave Coop the finger. The van sped off trailing a thick ganja fog, taking the gangsters away to party with friends, while Coop knew all he had going was a date with a single bed in a one-star hotel room, with overfriendly roaches and a TV stuck on the Weather Channel.

He heard a car honk from up the street. When he turned, Coop saw Morty in the Corvette about half a block behind him. He got out of the car and waited on the sidewalk, but didn't get any closer. As Coop walked over, Morty took a step back.

"Don't go getting all Rowdy Roddy Piper again," Morty said. "Who do you think got you out of jail early?"

"You got me in in the first place."

"And I got you out."

"How? You don't know anybody. I don't know anybody and you know even less people than me."

"That's because you're antisocial. You should get out more."

"I don't want to know people. They get you arrested."

Morty ignored the remark and looked around.

"Not the people I know. They get you unarrested."

Coop shook his head and turned to go.

"I don't want to hear it."

"You kind of have to," said Morty.

Coop stopped.

"Why?"

"That's how I got you out. I told him you were good for the job."

"You know what I'm good for right now?"

"What?"

"Not talking to you."

Coop jaywalked through traffic to a bus stop across the street. Digging in the plastic bag, he came up with enough change for the fare. When he turned around, Morty was right beside him.

"You just said it yourself, you don't know anybody. Where you going to go?"

"Away from you and your shifty friends."

A bus arrived and Coop started onto it, then stepped down.

"You have a cigarette?"

"Sure," said Morty. "Here. Keep the pack."

"Gee, the whole pack?" said Coop. "I guess this makes up for everything."

The door closed and the bus rumbled away with Coop on it.

FOUR

THE ANGEL STOOD IN THE DOORWAY OF A PORN SHOP on Seventh Street near Pershing Square reading a map. His stomach rumbled. He hadn't eaten anything in four thousand years. Worse, the plastic sandals he'd found in a Salvation Army discount bin pinched his toes. He had on brown corduroy pants worn smooth in spots so that they looked like a relief map of the Andes, and a green Windbreaker zipped up to his neck to hide his wings. Lucky for him, they'd confiscated his halo, or he'd have needed a hat, too. With the lack of food and the heat, Qaphsiel was sure that if he had to wear one more stitch of human clothing he'd have defected to You-Know-Who's side a long time back. Probably right after the Black Death swept across Europe and Asia . . . how long ago was it? Things were really looking up for him then. Whole cities laid waste. Flagellants running wild. Riots. Murders. Countries on the brink of anarchy. It looked like the human race was going to snuff it without him having to find the box after all. But then the unthinkable happened. The Plague died out. People got better. Just like after the Flood, the stinking, dirty survivors went on living and breeding and generally making a mess of the planet all over again. Some days, sunny ones like this when people looked so happy and non-extinct, it hardly seemed worth the effort anymore.

The map the angel held wasn't an ordinary one. First of all, it wasn't on paper, but a kind of semirigid ectoplasm. Shapes moved across its face, millions of squiggles, dots, spheres, and pyramids in four dimensions. Some shapes floated and others ducked below the flow, like cubist fish—a simple symbolic representation of the Earth, plus humans, supernatural creatures, and other celestial beings.

Qaphsiel was looking for something very specific. Something he hadn't seen in forty centuries. The lack of the object was why they'd exiled him on Earth in the first place. In the cool of the Earthly nights, when he slept in Griffith Park staring up at the stars, among winos and teenagers screwing in the scrawny drought foliage, he longed for the good old days in Heaven when he drank ambrosia and he and the other angels played games with star dust and DNA. His old friend Raphael—the archangel of healing—had invented the platypus that way, while Netzach had invented pulsars. Back when he was still allowed to play, Qaphsiel mostly stuck to star games, since the one time he got a really complicated DNA pattern to work, it turned out that he'd invented syphilis, and that hadn't been a hit with anyone.

Now, on top of everything else, there was something wrong with the map. Shapes, significant ones, were converging very near where he was standing, but when he looked up, all he saw were some werewolves in a van and a couple of men arguing by the bus stop. One of the men was in a threadbare blue suit and the other man looked like he might manage a Burger King. The one in the suit smelled like he spent too much time in swamps.

Qaphsiel shook his head. There was nothing for him here, no matter what the map said. He gave it a hard shake and headed north, wanting to get as far away from the swamp smell as possible.

FIVE

COOP HAD NO IDEA WHERE THE BUS WAS HEADED, BUT that was fine as long as it was away from Morty. He didn't really hate the guy, though he still felt that he owed him a lot more pain than the anemic little knee job outside the prison. No, a lot of why he wanted away from Morty was his luck situation. With getting out of prison, Coop was riding a very fragile line of luck, and he knew that one of Morty's half-assed schemes could land him right back inside.

He really didn't want that.

When he finally looked out the window, he saw that the bus was taking him into Hollywood. Okay. That was an actual place, with tourists, hustlers, and street performers, people who were even worse off than him. It might be nice to stroll around non-jailbird losers for a while and soak in the Hollywood misery. If nothing else, it would make him feel at home.

As the bus rolled on, Coop considered his options. It didn't take long. He had a voucher for two nights in a fleabag hotel in East L.A., far from the sights and temptations of L.A.'s hocus-pocus underground. After those two nights, however, he had no idea what he was going to do with himself. He didn't have any savings. His car had been stolen a few days after the Bellicose Mansion job, so who the hell knew where it was now. Probably, it had been chopped up and sold part by part to used-car lots all over town. Any of the cars out the bus windows could be cruising with his engine or transmission. The thought didn't make him angry, just tired.

And he hadn't been kidding with Morty about not knowing many people—he really didn't have many friends to fall back on. Not any he wanted to see. There were maybe a few people he could call to crash a night or two on their sofa, but then what? How long could he couch-surf without contemplating a messy suicide? And living in other people's spaces was no way to plan a job that might stake him for a while.

What the hell had happened to him? It was this last stretch in jail that did it. Not Morty's betrayal so much as, well, everything. He wasn't young anymore, a crook on the rise. He wasn't old, but he'd done enough time that the stink of it wouldn't wash off easily, like Rodney's heady aroma still on his damned fingers.

In this line of work, Coop thought, *you're either going up or you're going out. Or down in the ground. I'm not ready for that one yet. I just need to think. Hole up somewhere and get my head together.*

He got off the bus across from the Roosevelt Hotel on Hollywood Boulevard. At the Chinese Theater, a Jack Sparrow wannabe was accosting a couple of red-faced midwestern types, trying to charm them into taking a picture with him. One they'd have to pay him for, of course. There was a Spider-Man in a costume baggy with sweat and a Wonder Woman with bloodshot booze eyes redder than her fraying boots. In all, it was pretty depressing and made Coop wonder if coming to the Boulevard was a good idea after all.

He took Morty's cigarettes out of his pocket and dug around in the plastic bag with his stuff in it until he found his lighter. He thumbed it and got a spark, but no flame. He shook it a couple of times and still nothing.

It's been sitting in a box for a year and a half, moron, he thought.

Coop looked around. One thing about the Boulevard: it didn't lack for cheap shops. He went into a tourist trap with mini-Oscars in the window and Walk of Fame T-shirts where you could write your own name on a star. Inside, he found a display of plastic lighters. All they had left were Wizard of Oz ones. Dorothy and Toto on one side and the Lion, Scarecrow, and Tin Woodman on the other, grinning like they all went on vacation together and got lobotomies instead of tribal tattoos.

It took him a while digging in his bag before he found the change to pay for the lighter. Long enough that it got embarrassing. He put the money on the counter and left without waiting for change. When he came out of the store, Morty was waiting by the curb.

"Wow," he said. "Did you pay for that all at once or are you renting?"

"I have money," said Coop.

"I can tell. That's good-quality plastic."

It was more pathetic pretending he was flush than admitting he was screwed, Coop knew, but he couldn't think of anything else to do.

"You owe me eighteen months of my life," he said.

Morty lightly rapped a knuckle on a No Parking sign.

"I know, man. I also owe you eighteen months' worth of drinks."

"That's the first sensible thing you've said."

Coop lit his cigarette. It wasn't as good as he'd hoped. Some kind of low-tar monstrosity. Coop shook his head as the horrors of the regular world settled on his shoulders.

As if reading his mind, Morty said, "Come on. I know a place."

Coop walked with him a few blocks to a place called the Grande Old Tyme. He stuck his head inside the dim space and came out sure that the last grand time anyone had had in the place was guessing what the bartender watered down the whiskey with. The place was decorated with exactly two things: sad-sack day drinkers sipping their shots at the bar and a broken jukebox wrapped in police caution tape.

But he followed Morty inside, where it was at least cooler than the street. On the way in, the dropped his cigarette on the sidewalk and a mangy pigeon picked it up in its beak. Coop felt bad about sticking the bird with such a lousy smoke, but beggars can't be choosers.

Morty ordered them both whiskey sours. Coop raised his eyebrows.

"Cocktails? Are you asking me to the prom?"

"Relax. They're good and I don't want you drinking too fast and maybe getting pugilistic again."

Coop shrugged.

"It's your dime."

"Exactly."

The drinks came and Coop sipped his. It was too sweet, but the whiskey was there enough to bite him and it was good after a year and a half of toilet Beaujolais.

"So, you have a job," said Coop.

"Yeah."

"Do I know the guy?"

"No."

"Do you?"

"Yes," said Morty. After a second he shook his head. "No. But he comes highly recommended."

"What does 'highly recommended' mean?"

"It means that when he offers, you don't say no."

Coop sipped his drink.

"I'm out," he said without looking up.

Morty waved his hands in the air like he was conducting an orchestra.

"What? You can't. This is your comeback job."

Coop looked down at the bar.

"I don't work for nut jobs or people more crooked than me. This guy smells like both."

"Speaking of smell . . . ?"

"Don't ask. Thanks for the drink."

"Wait—there's a bonus."

That stopped him. "What kind of bonus?"

Morty leaned forward and spoke in a whisper.

"If we do it by the next new moon, there is an extra hundred grand."

"Why then?"

Morty sat back.

"I don't know. It's his birthday or the moon spooks him. What do you care?"

Coop took a gulp of his drink. The whiskey was starting to burn his stomach a little more than was comfortable.

"He said a hundred grand specifically?"

"Yeah."

"He's not going to rip us off?"

"He has a good rep."

Coop took a long pause. "Hell," he said.

"Then you'll do it?"

Coop downed the last of his drink.

"You were right before," he said. "I'm broke. Buy me lunch and let me think."

"For a job like this I'll buy you a dog."

"I don't eat dogs. They're not kosher."

"Since when did you turn kosher?"

"Since you started trying to feed me dogs."

SIX

AGENTS BAYLISS AND NELSON SAT IN A VAN ACROSS from a sandwich shop just up the block from the Grande Old Tyme. The van had PG&E logos on the doors outside and smelled like vodka inside. Bayliss was at the window, looking through the one-way glass, adjusting her binoculars. All the vans with state-of-the-art surveillance gear were already out in the field or in for servicing, so she and her partner were stuck with this Flintstones hunk of junk. Bayliss was sure it was Nelson's fault. He'd pissed off someone in the motor pool, or more likely everyone. She sighed and adjusted the binoculars until the image was crystal clear.

"Is that him?" said Nelson.

"No," said Bayliss. "It's Mr. Rogers back from the dead."

"No. It's Mr. Rogers," said Nelson in a high squeaky mocking voice.

Bayliss, the junior agent, in her off-the-rack jacket and knock-off Gucci shoes, looked at him. Nelson wore an expensive suit and tie, but his white shirt was wrinkled like he'd had it on for a couple of days. *Been sleeping in his car again,* thought Bayliss.

"Are you drinking already?" she said.

"I couldn't be talking if I was drinking."

Bayliss watched the jailbird and the crook eat. Nelson was quiet for a moment, then said, "There. You heard that silence a second ago? *That* was drinking."

Bayliss ignored him. "He's with someone I don't recognize."

"Let me see."

Nelson took the binoculars, got them tangled in Bayliss's hair for a second, then pulled them free. Nelson took his sweet time adjusting the lenses. Bayliss was sure he did it to spite her.

Finally, Nelson said, "That's his asshole buddy, Morton something. The one who ratted him out."

He handed her the binoculars and sat down on the floor, leaning his back against the inside of the van.

"Why isn't that in the briefing folder?" said Bayliss.

"Why should it be? I just told you who he is."

"What if your liver committed suicide and you died? No one else would have that intel."

"Guess you better pray I don't die."

"I pray for your good health every night. More than world peace, I pray for your continued, sparkling existence."

"That's so sweet of you," said Nelson. He got up, swayed a little, and dropped into the passenger seat, gazing vaguely out the window.

"You're a less than admirable human being," said Bayliss.

"Want a drink?"

"No, I don't."

"Good. I wasn't in a sharing mood."

"Then why did you offer?"

"It was a test. You passed."

Bayliss lowered the binoculars and frowned at Nelson. "I don't really pray for you, you know. I pray for you not killing us and me ending up on the mook squad."

Nelson snort-laughed at that.

"You don't have to die for that," he said between sips from a leather-clad flask. "You're already a zombie. A toe-the-line, follow-all-orders, fake-Armani-wearing zombie."

"Oh? And what are you?"

"The one wearing real Armani . . . and watching our target. He's on the move."

Bayliss looked back out the window.

"Oh, crap," she said, scrambling into the driver's seat.

Nelson snort-laughed again.

"You even curse like my grandma."

"I really hate you sometimes."

"You're the wind beneath my wings."

Bayliss pulled out into traffic, following the two men. Staying with them, but a little behind so they wouldn't spot the tail.

Nelson hummed tunelessly. At the light, Bayliss jammed the brakes. Nelson spilled vodka down the front of his creased trousers.

"Nice," he said. "Very mature."

"What's this mature you speak of? We zombies don't understand that concept."

Nelson wiped the front of his pants with a silk handkerchief as wrinkled as his shirt.

"Just drive."

SEVEN

THEY WENT BACK TO MORTY'S PLACE, A SEVENTIES-ERA two-bedroom apartment on Fountain Avenue near Gower. Back when it was built, the place would have been called a bachelor pad. Now most sensible people would regard it as a stucco deathtrap, since half the building rested on nothing but a few questionable pillars in the open carport beneath the living room. Coop looked out the window, imagining an earthquake and his last moments on Earth, skewered by the rooftop TV dish and smothering under the gold velour couch Morty had taken as payment from a shady lawyer for stealing some incriminating photos from an even shadier lawyer. The photos apparently showed the client in scuffed red and black rental shoes and nothing else making sweet love to an inflatable sheep while the Professional Bowlers Association Tournament of Champions played on a TV the size of a Sherman tank . . . all on this couch. When Morty had offered Coop a peek at the shots, he'd politely declined. But Morty's bathroom was clean and the shower worked and that was all Coop wanted. Just to blast the last prison grime off his body with scalding water. After he dried off, Morty loaned him a blazer and a dress shirt, one that didn't hang off Coop's frame quite as much as his own.

They drove Morty's Bondomobile across town to the Sortilege Palms Hotel in Beverly Hills. Morty took them down Hollywood Boulevard so Coop could get reacquainted with the place. Coop had hardly seen daylight for eighteen months in the underground stir, and now that the sun was going down, he missed it. Until the lights came on. Streetlights. Flashing neon. Car headlights. The cool glow from shops and restaurants. They brought back memories of better days and he smiled. That is, until a kid in a souped-up Honda Civic ran a red light at Highland and almost T-boned them. Morty hit the brakes and the car skidded by the Hollywood Wax Museum and Guinness World Records Museum, stopping in front of the Ripley's Believe it or Not Odditorium. Coop looked up at the tyrannosaurus model on the roof and then at Morty.

"Woo! That was something, huh?" Morty said.

Coop didn't say anything.

"You okay?" said Morty.

"Did you ever get the feeling that something was trying to kill you?"

"Like what?"

"This city."

"It wasn't that bad."

"We almost died."

"Don't look at it so negative. The good news is we lived."

Coop watched a couple cross the street in front of them. They stared at the Corvette in shorts, sandals, and matching University of Vicksburg T-shirts and for a fraction of a second Coop felt better. Maybe he was destined to die under the fading shadow of a plastic dinosaur surrounded by pickpockets, hookers, and panhandlers, but at least he'd never been to Mississippi. That was something. Coop released his death grip on the dashboard and lit one of Morty's horrible cigarettes. When he blew out the smoke he said to Morty, "If you ever see me in a matching T-shirt with a woman—any woman—shoot me. Okay?"

Morty nodded.

"You didn't have to ask. I'd have done it on principle."

"Thank you."

"I know a cry for help when I see it."

The Sortilege Palms Hotel sat huge on a man-made rise in Beverly Hills. There were turrets, towers, and a drawbridge out front along with neon palm trees that blew in an imaginary wind.

"It looks like Dracula's castle and Disneyland had an ugly baby," said Coop. "If they're going for a King Arthur thing, what's with the palm trees?"

"What can I say?" said Morty. "A lot of these rich types, they like tacky."

"Yeah, but it doesn't make any sense. It's like parking a Space Shuttle in front of a log cabin."

"What are you telling me for? Put something in the suggestion box. I'm sure they give the tiniest rat's ass about what people like us think."

Morty steered the Corvette into the long, curving driveway. The bellhop who came to take the keys was dressed like a court jester. He looked at the car like it was Kryptonite.

"Don't park it under any pigeons," said Morty.

The bellhop frowned. "How could you tell if I did?"

Morty and Coop walked into the hotel.

"I don't know what his problem is," Morty said. "That car is a classic."

"If you say so."

"I do."

Coop looked around as they made their way to the elevators. Out of Morty's death wagon, with his feet back on terra firma, he was beginning to feel better.

"I remember this place. I did a job here once. Stole a pearl necklace and a Necronomicon from a movie producer playing doctor with his leading man's mistress."

"How did you do that?"

"I got a room service cart and lifted a bottle of wine and brought it to their room. I had a Contego stone in my pocket, so the moment they invited me inside, it shut down all the spells for me."

"You got them to invite you in? Nice. Just like a vampire." Morty smiled.

"Yeah. Just like Dracula."

"You still have the stone? Sounds like it could come in handy."

Coop shook his head.

"I lost it."

"Lost it," said Morty. He nodded, but Coop could tell he didn't believe him.

Finally, the elevator came. An old man in a tuxedo and a succubus in an even nicer tuxedo strolled out arm in arm. The succubus winked at Coop as they went by. He wasn't sure he liked that and reflexively checked his pocket to make sure his wallet was still there. In the elevator, Morty punched the button for the top floor.

Coop said, "Did I tell you I had a vampire cellmate for a while?"

"No. What was that like?"

"I became a very light sleeper."

The floor numbers rolled by.

"I dated a vampire while you were away," said Morty.

"How did that go?"

"It was okay till she told me how old she was. I swear, she had my grandmother's exact birthday. Same day. Same year. After that, every time we were in bed all I could see was my nana's face. As you can imagine, it took a toll on our love life."

"I only want to date humans these days."

"Right. You had that thing . . ."

"Yeah."

"With the . . ."

"Yeah."

"Is that where your Contego went?"

"Who knows? It's a mystery."

"She was cute. Whatever happened to her?"

"Not a clue. She disappeared after we broke up."

Morty sniggered quietly.

"What?"

"Broke up? She dumped you. Halloween night, too. I remember. I've never seen you so drunk. She broke your heart."

"No, she didn't."

"It's okay. It happens. She broke your heart."

"She didn't break it. She ripped it out, bronzed it, and wore it like a belt buckle."

The elevator stopped and they got out. Morty headed for another elevator across the hall and pushed a button.

"What's this?" said Coop.

"Those are for the regular floors. This goes up to the penthouse."

The elevator showed up a few seconds later and they got in. Coop couldn't help but stare at the surveillance camera over the sliding doors.

"I can set you up with someone," said Morty.

"Please, I'm asking you nicely. Do not set me up with anyone, human, fish, or otherwise. I'm only even talking to you for business reasons. The idea of making small talk with a stranger makes me want to kill myself and everyone in this elevator."

Morty glanced around the car. It was just the two of them.

"Point taken. But might I remind you that we're going to a meeting with a client who's never laid eyes on you? A certain amount of small talk is inevitable."

"The difference is I'm not trying to woo him. I just want to woo his money."

The elevator began to slow.

"Here we are. You ready?" said Morty.

"Sure."

"Woo. That's a nice word. You're such a nice young man."

"Quiet. You never told me the client's name."

"Mr. Babylon."

"Mister what?"

"I don't think it's his real name."

"No shit," said Coop as the doors slid open. A middle-aged man stood there in a maroon silk smoking jacket with gold trim. He was as bald as a banana.

"No shit indeed, Mr. Cooper," said Mr. Babylon.

"Sorry. Slip of the tongue."

Mr. Babylon was very pale and round, and the folds of fat that formed his cheeks gave him the face of a giant baby.

"No apologies necessary. Shooting a little shit into the air is a good way to break the ice," said Mr. Babylon. He nodded at Morty. "Good evening to you both. Would either of you like a drink?"

"Thanks," said Coop.

"What's your preference?"

"Anything brown that says bourbon on the label."

Mr. Babylon walked to a wet bar across the room.

"I think we can accommodate you. Morty?"

"Whatever you're having, sir."

Mr. Babylon glanced back.

"I'm having diet ginger ale. Doctor's orders."

Morty hooked a thumb at Coop.

"In that case I'll have what he's having."

"Very good."

The TV was on quietly, tuned to the hotel channel. A handsome young executive type was strolling by what looked like a bank vault designed by the Inquisition. It was all bars, spikes, and crosses. The silver pentagram in the center of the door was the only outward giveaway that the vault carried enchantments.

The handsome man was saying, " . . . and as a triple diamond member, you're entitled to all of the hotel's routine and supermundane security services, from our subterranean vaults, guarded twenty-four hours a day by our bonded and certified witches, to our encrypted computer and personal oracles . . ."

Coop had never seen magic talked about so openly in a hotel with civilians before. He'd been raised to always keep his mouth shut about it around strangers, but here it was on TV with the room service menu and the personal massage services.

I guess they figure the rich are more discreet than the hoi polloi when it's their money on the line, he thought.

Mr. Babylon came back with their drinks. He held up his ginger ale in a toast. Coop and Morty did the same with their drinks.

"To good work and honest companions."

Cooper wasn't sure what to think of that. There wasn't an honest man in the room, as far as he knew. Maybe not in the whole hotel.

"To all that stuff," he said.

"And more," said Morty.

Mr. Babylon stared into his ginger ale for a few seconds.

"In that vein, Mr. Cooper, I understand that you've just been released from, as they say in old movies, the Big House."

Coop sipped his bourbon. It was a lot better than the swill at the Grande Old Tyme.

"State prison, actually. Out east in the desert."

"Then you must be used to this heat wave."

"Actually, we had very good air-conditioning. Some of the cons were dead and others would melt if it got too hot."

Mr. Babylon moved his shoulders in a mock shiver.

"My, what a colorful world you two live in. All hocus-pocus and will-o'-the-wisps. I myself possess no conjuring abilities at all. I was once given a magic kit as a young man and set the downstairs parlor on fire."

"Well, we've got plenty of magic to get done any job you need," said Morty.

"Just so we understand each other," said Coop, "I'm like you. I can't conjure either."

Mr. Babylon held up his glass in Coop's direction.

"Thank you for admitting that, Mr. Cooper. Of course, I knew it already from having you checked out, but the fact that you came right out and said it makes it easier to trust you."

"Making you happy is what we're here for," said Morty. Coop gave him a take-it-down-a-notch look.

"Indeed," said Mr. Babylon. He got very close to Coop and spoke quietly. "Now, if you lack any wizardry, tell me exactly why the fuck I should hire you?"

Coop thought the word *fuck* sounded funny coming out of that pale baby face.

"Because I have something you don't, Mr. Babylon. Another ability. A rare one," he said. "I'm immune to magic. Conjury, enchantments, fascinations, mesmerisms, mind reading, and ladies sawed in half. The whole bit."

Mr. Babylon sipped his drink, made a sour face, and set it on a large mahogany desk. He went around it, opened a drawer, and looked inside.

"Yes. Your report said that, too, though I have trouble believing it. Are you telling me that no curse or spell can harm you?"

"Not directly," said Coop. "Of course, there are indirect spells I have to look out for. Like if I broke in here and, say, there was a poison curse on the place, I could walk right through eating an ice cream sundae and be completely safe. On the other hand, if someone put a failsafe on the room—if they rigged it for the ceiling and walls to collapse—then I'd have to use one of my other skills."

"What other skills?"

"I'm a fast runner."

Babylon chuckled, took a small golden pistol out of the desk drawer, and pointed it at Coop.

"What you're saying then is that if I were to shoot you with this gun, which is imbued with a liquescense curse, it wouldn't hurt you."

"That's right."

"You know what a liquescense curse is?"

Coop nodded.

"It turns flesh and bones into clam chowder."

"Yes. It melts them like ice in the desert sun."

Morty put his hands up, palms out.

"Hey, let's not get overwrought. You said it yourself, Mr. Babylon, we're all honest men here."

Mr. Babylon cocked his head slightly.

"Are we? Reports can lie. People's pasts can be altered by conjuration or payoffs. If we do business, I'm trusting you with my time, my money, and a very valuable object. Possibly even my life. I think I ought to know exactly who and what I'm paying for. Don't you, Mr. Cooper?"

Coop straightened. "Shoot me if you want, but it's going to cost you a thousand dollars."

Mr. Babylon raised a baby eyebrow.

"Is it?"

Coop nodded.

"You get one shot at me. If I don't turn to lobster bisque, you owe me a thousand dollars."

"That's my jacket you're wearing," whispered Morty. Coop ignored him.

"And what if I shoot and don't pay?"

Coop took a step forward. "I'll be aggravated."

Morty squeezed Coop's arm and held up a hand to Mr. Babylon.

"He's just kidding, sir."

"No, I'm not. Is it a deal?"

A blazing bolt of bloodred light exploded from the gun and hit Coop square in the chest. It passed through him and hit a room service cart by the wall, where it turned a sixteen-ounce porterhouse steak into a sizzling, bubbling mess that looked less like a steak than like oatmeal someone had left in a cyclotron. Mr. Babylon laughed and slapped his leg. He tossed the pistol back in the drawer and closed it.

Morty withdrew his hand from Coop and looked at it, like he was surprised it was still attached to his arm.

"Damn, that was exciting," said Mr. Babylon. "I've never fired a gun at anyone before. I'll have to try it again sometime."

"Shoot me with curses all you want. As long as you pay."

Mr. Babylon raised a finger in recognition.

"Your money. Yes."

He pulled out an overstuffed wallet filled with cash. To Coop it looked less like something a normal person carried money in and more like a calfskin phone book. Mr. Babylon peeled off ten one-hundred-dollar bills and handed them over.

Coop tried to look cool when he put the money in his pocket, like letting strange men take potshots at him in upscale hotels was what he did whenever there wasn't anything good on TV. He said, "Now that you're done playing Annie Oakley, do you want to tell us what the job is?"

"Indeed I do. Sit down, please."

Coop and Morty sat on the sofa as Mr. Babylon went to the desk phone and ordered another steak.

When he was done he said, "Would either of you like another drink?"

"I haven't finished this one," said Coop.

"Of course. Of course."

Mr. Babylon dropped down onto the sofa across from them.

Morty said, "I hope no one is going to be shooting at us on the job, Mr. Babylon. I'm not quite as bulletproof as Coop here."

"If things go well, no one should even know you were there."

"Where is 'there'?" said Coop.

"The Blackmoore Building. On display in a glass case in the office of a competitor. He has something of mine and I want it back. It's been in the family for a long time and I consider it a personal insult that he acquired it by criminal means."

"Which is why you're hiring a couple of crooks to take it back," said Coop.

"Exactly."

"What is it?" said Morty.

"A box."

"A big box?" said Coop.

"Not especially."

"What's in it?"

Mr. Babylon sat back. "I don't think there's any reason for you to know that."

"I mean, is it dynamite and it's going to blow us up? Is it gold and we're going to need a crane to move it?"

"No, nothing like that. It doesn't weigh more than a pound or two."

"And it's not going to explode?"

"In all its long life it hasn't once."

"That's good enough for us," said Morty.

"Not quite," said Coop. "What kind of curses are on the box? I have to think that a man like you could buy anything from anybody or bribe someone in your competitor's organization to steal it for you. What's wrong with the box?"

Mr. Babylon shook his head.

"There's no curse, spell, or plague on the box at all. But there is just one thing."

"What's that?"

Mr. Babylon jammed a chubby finger into his leg as he talked.

"Under no circumstances are you to open it. It's closed with a wax seal. If it's broken, the deal is off."

Coop and Morty frowned.

"What? Is it radioactive?" said Morty.

"Yeah. I'm not too keen on shoving a brick of plutonium in my pocket," said Coop.

"It's nothing for you to worry about," said Mr. Babylon. "Just make sure the box remains closed."

Coop sat and stared at his drink. He didn't like anything about the setup. In his mind, he went over the obvious dangers of the job versus his options. It didn't take long. Even with a thousand dollars in his pocket, his list of options was very short.

He said, "How much does the job pay?"

"Two hundred thousand."

"And another hundred thousand if we do it before the new moon."

Mr. Babylon nodded and said, "I can make it more if that would help."

"Really?" said Morty.

"That's all right," said Coop. "We're not greedy. You offered a hundred and we'll take it."

"Wonderful. Honest men indeed."

Coop drained the bourbon and set the glass down on a coffee table. "The new moon is only three days off, so we're going to have to work fast. We'll need information. Blueprints. Layouts of spells and wards. Regular security and the hocus-pocus kind. Probably some equipment, too."

"Naturally, I'm willing to pay your expenses, as long as they're reasonable," said Mr. Babylon.

"Reasonable. Of course," said Morty.

Mr. Babylon reached around and took a green folder off a table behind him. He held it out for Coop. After his last encounter with a green folder he wasn't thrilled to take it. But he did.

"Here's some of what you asked for," said Mr. Babylon. "Plans, lists of employees, the sorts of enchantments my competitor is partial to, those sort of things. If you need more let me know."

There was a knock at the door. Morty jumped. Mr. Babylon got up and let in the waiter, who rolled in a room service cart.

"They're fast with the food around here," said Coop.

Mr. Babylon glanced at him as he signed for the steak. "They are for me."

The waiter put the signed receipt in his pocket and went to get the first tray. When he saw the remains of the steak, he took a step back and carefully used a napkin to put the silver serving dome back over the melted meat. Mr. Babylon graciously held the door open for him as he pushed the cart out with his fingertips.

"I think that's it for now, gentlemen," he said. "I didn't get to sample my previous meal and now I'm famished."

Coop and Morty got up and headed for the door. Mr. Babylon walked the other way.

"Sure. Enjoy your dinner," said Coop.

"Enjoy your thousand dollars," said Mr. Babylon. "Maybe we'll play William Tell again sometime."

"Just let me know in advance next time. And bring your wallet."

Coop didn't bother waiting for a reply. Mr. Babylon was already cutting into his steak. He and Morty let themselves out.

When they were in the elevator, Morty let out a long breath and laughed nervously.

"Holy shit. The way you talked to him, I almost had a heart attack."

Coop shrugged. "He pulled a gun. It was upsetting. This whole place is giving me a rash. Let's get out of here."

Morty only had a couple of dollars on him when they got downstairs, so when the jester attendant brought the car around, Coop had to tip him with one of the hundreds. The attendant seemed genuinely confused when Coop asked for change.

EIGHT

IN A WIDE DARK ROOM, TWELVE ROBED FIGURES LIT only by red candles stood around an altar covered in eldritch carvings and ancient runes. A silver tray lay in the middle of the altar with five black triangular hosts arranged in the shape of an inverted pentagram. A robed priest at the head of the altar held up a host he plucked from a nearby bowl, which was also covered in a fearsome scrawl and glyphs of birds with what looked like pig heads. Plus, a kitten sticker someone's kid had put on it that they'd never been able to completely scrape off.

"Hear me, O Caleximus, thundering archfiend, master of the sky throne, creator and destroyer. Accept this offering of the flesh of your chosen beast. A gift to you from us, your unworthy followers."

The priest was dressed in a robe so dark that it looked like his head and hands were floating in the blackness.

"Give us your ear, dire Caleximus. We have such tidings to share with you."

He placed the host on his tongue and swallowed. Or tried to. At first he just coughed. Then he made a gagging sound like he was trying to gargle a porcupine. The priest collapsed to his knees before the altar. A low cry went up around the room. He was down on all fours. Everyone froze, wondering what he'd done wrong to piss off their cantankerous netherworld deity. Some people began edging toward the exit.

Finally, the priest coughed the host onto the floor. He got to his feet slowly and wiped his mouth with the back of his hand. He looked around at the other robed figures.

He said, "Jerry? Were you in charge of putting together the offerings?"

The room was silent.

"Jerry?"

"Yes?" said someone quietly.

"Were you in charge of the offerings?"

"Yes."

The priest walked over to him and put a hand on his shoulder. "Are these the fried flesh of a black boar sacrificed with the eagle-headed blade on a mountaintop in a thunderstorm?"

Jerry shook his head.

"Not exactly."

"Not exactly? What are they, then?"

"Blue corn chips."

An angry murmur went around the room.

"Corn chips. That's not really even in the same ballpark, is it?"

Jerry shrugged.

"What kind of chips were they?"

"What?"

"What brand of chips?"

"Monsieur Crunchero."

"Don't you mean *Señor* Crunchero?"

"No. Monsieur. They're Canadian."

"Because when we think of Mexican food we think of Saskatchewan," said the priest.

Jerry pushed the hood of his robe back, revealing a young man's face, pockmarked and with an overly optimistic slash of red hair on his upper lip.

"They were the only ones left in the store."

The priest sighed.

"That's not really the point, Jerry. What happened to the black boar?"

"It ran away."

"It ran away?"

"*You* try holding a full-grown boar in a thunderstorm. Everything is wet and slippery. You can't see your hand in front of your face. I cut myself with the damned knife. It just happened. I'm sorry."

A grumbling went through the group. A couple of people muttered "Dipshit" and "Clueless." The priest sighed.

"I don't know what to do here. You buy some off-brand potato chip . . ."

"Blue corn chips . . . so they'd be the right color."

"Points for you, Jerry. You try to slip corn chips past us like maybe Caleximus, *who's a goddamned god,* wouldn't notice. And now you say you lost our boar. Do you know how much boars cost these days?"

Jerry shook his head.

"No."

"A lot," someone shouted.

The priest said, "A boar would be the equivalent of a metric ass-ton of corn chips. Did you buy a metric ass-ton of corn chips?"

"No. Just the one bag."

"Here we are, sending up smoke signals to Caleximus to give him good news, and now there's none to give him."

Jerry looked around the room at the other robed figures.

"I'm really sorry."

Steve, the priest, pushed back his hood. Like the boy's, his hair was red, but he was older, his face lined and creased. "I don't know what to do here, son. It's like you don't even take the Apocalypse seriously."

"But I do."

"Do you want those Abaddonian shitbags in Burbank to invoke their false god and set off their Apocalypse first?"

"No, sir," said Jerry. "I hate those pricks."

"Good boy. Because our Apocalypse is the only real Apocalypse and no one gets to offer up the Earth and its nonbelievers but us. Right?"

"Fuck the Abaddonians," shouted a woman from the back of the room.

The group nodded and mumbled. "Fuck the Abaddonians."

"All right. Quiet," said Steve. "The old-folks' home has a spaghetti dinner going next door. No need to ruin the codgers' appetites."

People laughed. Steve Sallis, the priest, turned back to the boy and shook his head.

"Okay, Jerry. You've got a lot to make up for."

"I know."

Steve looked out at the other worshippers. "For those of you who got here late and missed it, the good news is this: we think we've got a line on the Vessel of Invocation, meaning we can finally bring Caleximus to Earth—right here, right now—to us."

Another murmur, a happier one this time.

"It'll be a dangerous task to retrieve it, though. I'm looking for volunteers," said Steve.

Someone shouted, "I volunteer Jerry."

Jerry looked around.

"Fuck you, Tommy."

But Steve was looking at the boy.

"What do you say, Jerry? Are you ready to make up for this Crunchero fiasco?"

"I guess," he said sullenly.

"Damn right you guess."

Steve pointed at the group.

"The boy can't do it alone. Any other volunteers?"

Not a single hand went up.

"Nice, everybody. Really nice. Caleximus is very proud of each and every one of you pussies, pardon my French. That's it, then. *Everybody* goes. Got it?"

Whispers of "Oh man" and "You pay for the damned sitter" could be heard.

Steve unzipped his robe. On the back was a sequined lightning bolt and eagle with a boar's head. Susie had made it for him on their third wedding anniversary.

"I think we can officially call the invocation over for the night. Someone hit the lights."

Fluorescents flickered on in the double-wide trailer parked on a construction site in Glendale. The desks and filing cabinets had been pushed back against the walls to make room for the ceremony.

As Steve folded his robe he said, "Jerry."

"Yes, Dad?"

Steve upended a couple of hard hats and poured in the rest of the chips. "I swear to Caleximus that if you bought chips and you didn't get guacamole and salsa, I'll skin you alive myself and we'll eat you at the next meeting."

From the look in the man's eye, the kid wasn't so sure if he was kidding.

"They're in the car," he said.

"Go get them."

Steve looked around until he saw his wife. "Susie, darlin', break out the Bud. That's it for now, people. Can somebody take down the candles? The Apocalypse can hold on for a couple of days. As long as we're ready by the new moon we'll be fine."

The others started disrobing, too. From across the room, Jorge—Steve's partner in the small construction firm—called, "So, where's the Vessel of Invocation?"

"In an office downtown. We're going to break in and take it."

"How are we going to do that?"

Tommy, who'd heckled Jerry earlier, said, "My brother-in-law is a janitor there. He can get us in."

Steve raised his arms to the ceiling. "To Caleximus and the destruction of mankind."

"To Caleximus and destruction!" shouted the rest of the group.

Steve smiled. "These suckers aren't going to know what hit them."

"And they're not going to know it for very long!" said Jorge.

Everybody laughed happily as they moved the furniture back into place.

Susie came over with the beer and ruffled Steve's hair. "Don't be too hard on the boy, dear. He tries his best."

"I know. It's just that sometimes he doesn't have the sense of a sack full of squirrels."

"I know."

Steve took a long gulp of his beer.

"Remember not to drink too much tonight," said Susie. "You promised to help me with my pie for the bake sale."

Steve took a breath. "Yeah. About that. Do you still want to go through with it? I mean, there isn't a store in town that will let us sell outside. They all say the Apocalypse is bad for business."

Susie sipped her beer. "I know, but I want an excuse to make one more apple pie. I'm not going to the fiery depths of the underworld without showing up that bitch Randi Huston and her damned lemon squares."

Steve put an arm around his wife's shoulders. "Okay, honey. One more sale."

Susie gave Steve a loving peck on the cheek, then wiped off the lipstick with her thumb. "Hail Caleximus," she said.

NINE

THE STRANGER SAT ALONE IN A BOOTH INSIDE LARRY'S Large Lad diner in Red Bluff, a California town about five hundred miles north of Los Angeles. The day was sunny, and from his booth he had a view of both the I-5 freeway and the Sacramento River. He still wasn't sure how he felt about rivers. He liked the flowing water, but they were all crooked and bent at funny angles. *Too meandery,* he thought. Maybe something needed to be done about that.

Around the diner's ceiling were pictures and knickknacks from Red Bluff's early days as a Gold Rush and then a railroad town. Directly over his table was an autographed photo of Leo Gorcey of Bowery Boys movie fame.

The stranger was tall and slender, with the kind of dramatically sculpted cheekbones that you only see on Greek statues and rich people who've paid a surgeon to make them look like statues. His shoes were expensive black Oxfords, but badly stained with road grime. Though it was warm outside, he wore a long coat that in another, more nervous locale would have made people, well, nervous. Like he might be hiding something, which, in fact, he was. When he took off his sunglasses the stranger revealed his most striking feature: that he had one deep brown and one glittering blue eye.

In his opinion, it made him look dashing. A great number of other people often thought it made him look like he needed medical attention or perhaps a good burning at the stake.

He took a menu from the holder on the side of the table and opened it with the reverence befitting a Gutenberg Bible.

The stranger liked the menu. He liked all diner menus. They were invariably plastic and shiny, and covered in colorful photos of edible delights. He thought of photos as the hieroglyphics of the modern world, which made him think of each menu as a kind of greasy spoon Egyptian Book of the Dead. The menus were a truly perfect system. You didn't need to be able to read or even speak English. Just point to the jalapeño and salsa omelet with ham and two kinds of potatoes or the bacon and avocado triple-decker burger with wedge or curly fries and you were instantly transported to a sublime, artery-shattering wonderland.

The stranger liked to see how long he could go without talking to anyone on the road. It was a kind of game, like Burn the Church or Sack the City. Not talking wasn't as exciting a game, but it was one where he could vary the rules any time he liked. Take today. Today, he might just speak to someone. The thought of it was exciting. He looked around wondering who it would be.

A waitress in a red-and-white-checked uniform and blond wig that matched the hair on the life-size statue of Larry's Large Lad outside the restaurant walked over. The diner was an obvious rip-off of Bob's Big Boy, a more famous burger restaurant in Burbank, but that's what had attracted the stranger to it. The diner wasn't trying to hide its petty depravity. The theft was pure hubris, and the stranger loved hubris.

The waitress's name tag said CAROLINE. She set down a glass of water on the table and said, "Welcome to Larry's Large Lad. What can I get you today?"

The stranger smiled and held up the menu. He pointed to a chocolate shake and a steak sandwich that came with garlic fries. The waitress spoke each item out loud as he pointed to it and he gave her a thumbs-up each time to let her know she'd gotten it just right.

"The food'll only take a few minutes. Can I get you anything else while you wait?" He shook his head, so Caroline moved off with his order.

He took out a map of California that had been folded and refolded so many times that some of the creases had torn or worn white. Spreading the map on the table, he ran his finger down I-5 until he came to Red Bluff. He was on foot now. He liked going on foot. It made everything feel like it wasn't just a walk, but an Exodus. Luckily, it looked like he'd still be able to keep to his schedule. Even though the stranger didn't know how to drive, he sometimes wished he had a car. Driving seemed like fun, and stealing one seemed like even more fun. He was good with all kinds of tools, so he could probably hotwire one, but stealing was against the rules. Plus, he was still stuck with the driving problem. Even if he could drive, he couldn't take a chance on being pulled over and arrested in a hot vehicle, since his main goal was to keep a low profile all the way south.

One thing the stranger hadn't quite grasped yet was that strolling down the side of a major California freeway without, say, holding a gas can was as inconspicuous as riding a white elephant pulling a cart with LOW PROFILE spelled out in road flares. Still, he'd been lucky so far. The stranger was almost always lucky that way.

Sometimes on the road, people would stop for him and he'd accept a ride. Mostly it was from truckers or lonely long-distance travelers alone in cars. In general, though, he tried to avoid rides. Many people found his silence unnerving and insisted that he talk. Some even became aggressive. Those drives always ended the same way. Upside down in a ditch. Fire. People screaming. Then he'd be back on foot again, with dirty pants and bits of windshield in his hair. That's why he always carried a comb and a clothes brush.

The stranger sighed, folded the map, and put it back in his coat pocket. Timewise, he was doing fine. He just had to keep moving. There wouldn't be any need to check the map again for days. He could just enjoy the scenery. The river, however, was beginning to bother him more each time he looked.

Caroline soon came back with his food. When he looked up, she flinched, but composed herself in a second. He knew it was his eyes. It was always the eyes with these people. The waitress set down his sandwich and shake and went back to take an order at the counter.

The stranger hadn't eaten in a couple of days, so he dug in greedily. The shake was better than the steak sandwich, so he sipped it slowly, trying to make it last. When he finished, he wiped his mouth and hands on the napkins the waitress had left by his plate. He looked out the window and watched the cars on the road and the river beyond. Really, someone needed to do something about it. A few minutes later the waitress returned.

"You must have been a hungry boy. You put that away in record time," she said.

"Indeed I was," said the stranger, deciding to break his silence. He pointed over his head. "That photo of Leo Gorcey. Did he eat here sometimes?"

Caroline looked up at the ceiling and shook her head. "No. He never ate here. But he retired in the area. A real live movie star from Hollywood."

"Hollywood," he said. "Thank you."

As she gathered up his cutlery and plate the waitress said, "Are you staying in Red Bluff or just passing through?"

The stranger took a moment before answering. Eventually he said, "Just passing through. It's a pretty town."

" 'The Victorian city by the river.' That's what folks call it."

"Then the river doesn't bother you?"

"Why would it?" she said.

"It's so . . . crinkly."

She shook her head. "I'm not sure I quite understand."

"Never mind. Just a personal quirk," he said, smiling.

"Are you ready for your check?"

"Yes, thank you."

She put it on the table and took his dishes back to the kitchen. He took the check to the counter and put some money down by the cash register. The bills were old and creased like the map, but still good.

He'd made sure of that. The waitress came out from the kitchen, rang him up, and handed him his change. "Thanks. Come again," she said.

"Thank you," the stranger said. He started outside, but stopped and turned around. "Have you ever heard of a restaurant called Bob's Big Boy?"

"Oh my, yes. That's what gave Bob, the owner—isn't it funny that his name is Bob, too?—the idea for this place."

"Yes. Hysterical," he said.

"Are you going to go there on your trip?" said Caroline.

"What makes you think I'm going to Los Angeles?"

She shrugged. "Just a guess. You asked about Bob's Big Boy."

"Of course," said the stranger. "Of course." He looked around the restaurant one more time. He wanted to remember it all, every molecule of it. Then he nodded to Caroline and left.

Outside, he put on his sunglasses. As he walked back to the freeway he thought, *Two waitresses. One cook. Ten customers scattered between the counter and tables. Thirteen. Always an interesting number. One can take it so many ways.* It would be something to think about on his long walk.

At the edge of the parking lot, he stopped and breathed in the fresh morning air. Then the ground began to shake beneath his feet as the several hundred yards of the Sacramento River visible from the restaurant window straightened itself. He waited a few seconds so that everyone inside the restaurant could get a good look at his work. When he was certain they had, Larry's Large Lad exploded. An orange fireball spiraled into the sky and with it dining booths, a milk shake machine, burning money, Leo Gorcey, and sundry body parts. The stranger didn't turn around. He didn't have to. He'd seen it all before and knew there wouldn't be any survivors. It wasn't until something *thunked* into the ground behind him that he turned around.

A few feet off to his left was the charred and battered statue of Larry's Large Lad. Its blond head was scorched, but it was still grinning. The statue had come so close to beaning him that he wasn't entirely sure it wasn't a coincidence. The stranger looked around but didn't see a soul in sight, just cars passing on the freeway. Many were slowing to enjoy the unobstructed view of the burning restaurant and newly renovated river.

As he started up again, he thought about Caroline. If only she hadn't wanted to know where he was going. Who was she really? She could have been working for anyone. Plus, his fries had been soggy. They'd obviously been microwaved, not properly cooked. The stranger loved hubris, but he couldn't stand bad fries.

He walked across the freeway overpass and down again so he was back on the road headed south. In the distance, he heard sirens.

TEN

COOP HAD SPENT THE NIGHT ON AN INFLATABLE MATtress in Morty's spare room. He didn't like the idea of sleeping on a balloon, but after he lay down he found it was kind of comfortable. It was certainly better than the prison beds, which always seemed to be designed by aliens shaped like pretzels for other aliens that liked waking up with pudding for a backbone.

Morty had gone out earlier and Coop was in the living room flipping through TV channels. Nothing held his interest. There was something about an earthquake up north that destroyed a restaurant and straightened part of a river. Typical disaster porn stuff, he thought.

Everything normal people thought was funny, dramatic, poignant, or important seemed so . . . pointless? Stupid? Insane? He couldn't find the right word for it. He wondered if the last stretch inside had wrecked him for regular life. He felt twitchy and restless. He took a sip of his ninth cup of coffee and thought about it. One of his eyelids twitched. His right foot, against his wishes, was beating out the drum solo from "In-A-Gadda-Da-Vida." He set the coffee down. Maybe it was time to take a break. He got up to have a smoke outside when the front door opened and Morty came in with bags. They smelled good.

"I was in Burbank checking out some stuff, so I got us lunch," he said, setting down two bags from Bob's Big Boy on the kitchen table. Coop went over to where he was laying out the food. Morty held up a paper cup. "Coffee?" he said.

"I'll pass, thanks," said Coop, trying to keep from vibrating.

"More for me," said Morty. He laid out burgers, fries, and fistfuls of ketchup packs. "What have you been up to while I was gone?"

Coop glanced at the TV. He'd left it on a game show. A guy spun a wheel, shouting and shaking like if he lost the host was going to take away his heart medicine, and for a brief moment he was interested until he remembered that wasn't how the games worked. "Nothing," he said. "Attempting to reintegrate into society and finding myself somewhat unmotivated to do so."

"That sounds like something a warden would say."

"That's who said it to me. Something like that, anyway."

Morty peeled the paper off his burger and took a bite, talking out the side of his mouth while he chewed. "Prison is all about routine. You don't have a routine anymore. That's why you need to get back to work."

"I need something," Coop said. "Work. Or a lobotomy."

"Don't talk like that. Did you look over those plans and things Babylon gave us?"

Coop went to the coffee table and brought over a pile of blueprints and computer printouts. Some were simple spreadsheets with names and office assignments. Other sheets looked like complex astrological charts by way of NASA eggheads. Coop dropped them on the table.

"I was going over these last night."

"And what do you think? Can we do the job?"

"No."

"What?" said Morty. He choked on a mouthful of burger and grabbed a cup of coffee to keep from passing out, only to end up burning his tongue. "Whuh doo ya min we cand doo id?"

Coop smacked him on the back.

"What do you mean we can't do it? We told Mr. Babylon we would. I don't want to go back there with bad news and have him shoot me with one of those heat ray guns."

"Don't worry. It was a liquefaction curse. There wasn't any heat involved."

"Oh. That makes me feel better. You can remind me of that when housekeeping is sponging me off the floor."

"Relax," said Coop. "I said *we* couldn't do it. I didn't say it couldn't be done. It's just that I was hoping to keep the job between us. Split the money two ways. With the bonus, we'd have made a hundred and fifty K each."

"But we need more people."

Coop nodded. He tore open a burger and took a bite. It was good. The best thing he'd eaten in eighteen months.

"How many more people?" said Morty.

"That's what I've been thinking about. If these blueprints are accurate, there's serious corporate security all through the building. Curses. Labyrinths. That kind of thing. Then there's pass codes on all the locks, plus video surveillance and armed guards."

"Sound like we're going to need a small army."

"That would be helpful."

Morty set down his burger. "I've lost my appetite."

"Don't be like that," said Coop. "I've been going over this all night I think maybe we can pull this off with four people. The right four people."

Morty sat back up in his chair. "Four's not so bad. How much is three hundred thousand divided by four?"

"Seventy-five thousand dollars each."

Morty picked up his burger and took a bite. "As far as bad news goes, that ain't bad."

"You're right. It could be a lot worse." Coop worked on his burger and fries, pushing the pages around on the table for something like the fiftieth time that day.

"So, who are the other two people we need?"

Coop finished his burger, wadded up the paper and tossed it overhand at the kitchen trash. It bounced off the rim, skittered across a counter, bounced off a sugar bowl back toward the trash. And missed it by an inch. *Story of my life,* he thought as he walked into the kitchen to throw the paper away.

He said, "We're off to an okay start. You can flash and I can crack, so we have the locks and the safe taken care of. What we need is a good eyeball person to look out for traps and a getaway person to get us out of there."

"Just a Handyman and a Marilyn? That's all?"

"No. We can get the box with us and those other two, but there's the small matter of getting away at the end," said Coop.

"Yeah. I vote we get away. Any dissents? No? The motion is carried."

Coop opened one of the ketchup containers, dipped some of his fries, and ate them. He chewed slowly and thoroughly.

"You still chewing your cud over there?" said Morty. "I'm not going to have to milk you later, am I?"

Coop shook his head. "Sorry. Tell me something. Who's the biggest rat bastard you know?"

"Like someone I don't particularly like or someone who should get run down by a bus?"

"A bus."

Morty's face went blank. Coop was starting to think that maybe he'd given the poor guy a stroke when Morty smiled. "Fast Eddie Lansdale," he said.

"Fast Eddie. The Flasher from Detroit? He's the guy who stole a couple of your jobs out from under you, isn't he?"

"And left me holding the bag when one of his people ran off with the goods."

"How much did that cost you?" said Coop.

"A lot," said Morty. "Among other things, my Mercedes. It wasn't even hot. I bought that thing with real money like a regular person."

"And he took that from you."

"Yeah. He did."

"Good. I want you to picture your missing Mercedes when I tell you the next part," said Coop.

"I'm listening."

"See, the only way I can figure this working out is if we can get Babylon to pull two jobs at the same time."

Morty squinted at Coop. "You lost me around that last curve. Two jobs?"

Coop held up two fingers. "It doesn't have to be a real job. But the other team has to think it's a real job. They'd have to go in looking for one thing and then a little while later we go looking for the real thing."

"Why?"

"Cause there's a slight, and I mean really minuscule, chance they're going to get caught."

"What?" said Morty, his eyes opening wider.

Coop held out his hands hoping to calm Morty down. "Not caught caught. Not if they're any good, but they have to screw up enough to set off a lot of alarms and get the guards' attention."

"We can't throw someone to the wolves like that," said Morty.

"Sure we can," said Coop. "We get Babylon to hire Fast Eddie."

Morty rubbed the back of his neck. "I don't know."

"Do you know anyone who deserves it more? Who would everybody in town like to see sweat?"

"I get it," said Morty. "But it's unethical, setting up another crew like that."

"It's not like we're talking about people. We're talking about Fast Eddie and his crew of creeps," said Coop. "And we're not doing it so they get caught. Just noticed. Then, while the guards are dealing with Eddie, we slip in the back and do the Babylon job."

Morty drank his coffee. "Still," he said.

Coop leaned on the table. "Do you think Eddie would hesitate for one second setting you up if it would help him out?"

Morty considered it and said, "Eddie is a dark person."

"The worst," said Coop. "While I was inside I heard he dropped a dime on Lazlo the Mole."

"The old guy with the droopy eye?"

"That's him."

"He was a sweet old cuss," said Morty.

"He's a sweet old cuss doing ten to twenty out at Surf City."

Morty set down his cup. "Droopy Lazlo? Fuck Eddie. Let's set him up. But how do we know he'll get the guards' attention?"

" 'Cause Babylon is going to give him the wrong plans," said Coop. "The way in and the way out will be real. But in the middle, he's going to be as subtle as a rhinoceros at a bris."

Morty gave Coop a funny look. Sort of a frown and a smile at the same time. "You're a diabolical person," he said.

"Only to those who deserve it."

"And we're going to set it up so there's a way for Fast Eddie to escape."

"As long as he has a brain and two feet."

Morty rubbed his hands together. "Okay. So what else do we need?"

"Well, Eddie might not be distracting enough. If things go wrong I'd like to be able take down the whole security system. Maybe even clear out the building."

"How do we do that?"

"Think Babylon can get us some Jiminys?"

Morty made a face. "Those little cricket things?"

"Yeah. They'll eat plastic, metal, walls—"

"And everything else they can get their greedy chompers on—including people."

"Yes, there is that. But they love electricity more. They'll go for the building's wiring. Turn it right off."

"I hate those things," said Morty.

"Everybody hates them. That's the point."

Morty considered it. "I guess. But I hope we don't have to use them."

"Me, too," said Coop.

"Okay. So, we need a Marilyn. Did you have anyone in mind?"

Coop thought for a minute. "What about Chitale up in Portland? He could do some pretty good brain magic."

Morty shook his head. "Forget it. He got conked on the head while he was clouding some rubes' minds and now he can't turn it off. He's been invisible for over a year."

"That's a lousy way to go."

"Could be worse. These days he does a ghost bit with a crooked medium. It means he has to talk in a lot of funny voices, but he doesn't travel much, so he gets to go home and see his kids at night."

"Only they don't get to see him," said Coop.

"Funny, isn't it?"

"Hysterical." Coop took the top off his coffee. It was lukewarm, but he sipped it anyway. "Do you know anyone else?"

"What about Sally Gifford? She's good to work with."

"She's not invisible, is she?"

"Only when she wants to be," said Morty.

"Perfect. Now we just need a Handyman."

"How about Phil Spectre? You guys worked okay together, right?"

"No. No Phil," said Coop. "I do not want him back in my head. Besides, I want someone flesh and blood. Preferably with a little muscle, too."

"What do we need muscle for?" said Morty.

"Because I don't necessarily trust Babylon a hundred percent. If things get peculiar, I'd like to know we have someone who can move heavy objects and people out of our way. Maybe Johnny Ringo?"

Morty frowned. "You're batting zero today. He's out of the business, too."

"What, did he lift something and now he's got a hernia?"

"Worse," said Morty, gathering up the remains of his lunch and putting them back in the paper bag. "He got Jesus."

"How did that happen?"

"He was carrying some copper pipes off a construction site downtown and got hit by lightning."

"Lightning? When do we get lightning in L.A.?"

Morty pointed at Coop. "That's the thing. It was a freak storm. Came out of nowhere. After he got hit, he talked about seeing angels and choirs and his dead aunt Ada."

"Sounds more like he was high."

"Oh yeah, he was also that at the time," said Morty. "We probably don't need him for that reason alone."

"So who else do you know?"

Morty leaned back with his hands behind his head. "How about Tintin?"

"I don't know him."

"He's from San Francisco. Put himself through community college doing a strongman act at Fisherman's Wharf during the day and spotting curses for crooks at night. He's our guy."

"Why does someone who went to school want to do this kind of work?" said Coop.

Morty shrugged. "'Cause he's a crook."

"Fair enough."

"Are we going to need any gear from Babylon?"

Coop took a piece of paper from his pocket. "Yeah. I made a list while you were gone. A lot of it's the equipment I lost after the Bellicose Mansion job."

Morty gave Coop a wounded look. "I'm so sorry about that."

"Stop apologizing. It happened. It's over."

"Thanks."

Coop handed Morty the list. "Don't think this means you're off the hook. I just don't want to talk about it right now."

"Right. Later."

"Later. Right now, call Babylon."

"Then you want to see a movie?"

"A movie?" said Coop.

"Yeah, a movie. You know. We're in Hollywood. The entertainment capital of the planet," said Morty. "I thought you might like to be entertained."

Coop nodded. "Yeah. Okay. A movie. But nothing with subtitles," he said. "If I want to read a book, I'll stay home and read a book."

"When's the last time you read a book?"

"In prison. I read a lot of books. There wasn't much else to do."

Morty threw the remains of their lunch away. "I'm so sorry."

"Stop it."

ELEVEN

"THE POWER OF CHRIST COMPELS YOU!" BELLOWED THE priest, a good four hours into the exorcism. The chapel was three-sided, one side for each part of the Trinity. Besides the priest, there were nine people in the room, nine being regarded by the Department of Peculiar Science as a holy number. Bayliss was inclined to believe the theory. Nelson yawned and checked his watch.

"The power of Christ compels you!"

"Is it the twelfth century?" said Nelson. "Someone get me my phone. I have apps for this kind of crap."

Bayliss shushed him. "This one is special," she whispered.

Nelson whispered back, "I've seen literally a hundred exorcisms. Trust me. This one isn't special."

"It is when it's our boss."

"Huh," said Nelson. "I guess that is a little different."

"It's the entire top floor," said Bayliss. "All of management possessed. How do you not know about it?"

"Because unlike you, I have a life outside of work."

"Being drunk doesn't constitute a life."

"If you're good at it it does," said Nelson.

"Does not."

"Does too."

"The power of Christ compels you!" said the priest through gritted teeth, looking at the two of them.

"Sorry," mouthed Bayliss. Nelson, like other members of the group, was holding a ritual crucifix. His was hollow. He popped Jesus's head off and took a drink. "Now that's the power of Christ," he whispered to Bayliss.

The chapel was deep in the bowels of what looked like an ordinary office building on Wilshire in Los Angeles's financial district. In fact, there was a real import-export business on the thirteenth floor, because it was good cover and because none of the building's real employees would work on that floor. The import-export company's employees wouldn't have worked there either if they'd known the true nature of the building.

The underground chapel where the exorcism was taking place was on old consecrated ground, the former site of a church to Freydis, a little-known Norwegian saint most notable for the fact that the Church in Rome wanted her as far from itself as humanly possible, and there weren't any churches in Antarctica. The reason Rome wanted to keep her at a distance didn't have to do with just her visions—although those were disturbing enough. No, it had more to do with how she responded to them. St. Freydis's father had been a strongman and wrestler in a traveling sideshow, and Freydis was known to strip down to her petticoats and challenge any local demons, smart-ass wizards, and later, mad scientists reanimating corpses to create unstoppable killing machines, and grapple with them. Two out of three falls. Winner take all.

She always came out on top and soon became known as St. Freydis of the Camel Clutch.

"Holy balls, Father, how much longer are we going to have to stand here while you scream like Little Richard?" said Nelson.

"Shhh!" hissed Bayliss.

Eventually, the Church had sent some of its more troublesome priests and lay hangers-on to join Freydis in the godless land of early Los Angeles. They were in charge of studying and suppressing what was known as Peculiar Science, a catchall phrase referring to both magic and any strange supertechnology used for a variety of nefarious purposes such as preserving Hitler's talking head (which resided in the basement of the Department of Peculiar Science building, along with other treasures). Other fun artifacts included a parchment written by an alchemist named Wexford in 1377 that was the actual formula for turning lead into gold. Wexford had produced so much gold so quickly that he almost bankrupted the European economy. The Inquisition leaked a false version of the formula and alchemists around the world have been trying to re-create the original ever since. This was how Fresca was invented.

The priest went on. "In the name of the Father, the Son, and the Holy Ghost . . ."

"Seriously. We got to the moon quicker than this," Nelson said.

"Will you be quiet?" barked the priest.

Nelson frowned at him and took another drink from his crucifix. "I'm a taxpayer, so don't try to pad your hours around here, Padre." He pocketed the crucifix and went to where Woolrich, his and Bayliss's supervisor, lay on a dais leaking a green puddinglike substance from his mouth. It wasn't St. Patrick's Day, so Nelson was reasonably sure Woolrich hadn't gone on a green beer bender.

The priest stepped between Nelson and Woolrich. "Don't get near him. He's in a delicate state," he said.

Nelson nodded. "I understand entirely," he said. And brought his fist down on Woolrich's chest. "Hey, fucknut!" he yelled. "Who's in there?"

A quivering, growling voice issued from Woolrich's green mouth. "My name is Legion. For we are many."

"This isn't the Vatican," Nelson said, "so you can put the lid back on the fruit cocktail. Who are you really?"

"Azmodeus. Mephistopheles. Dagon . . ."

"Drop the Batman whisper, Carl," said Nelson. "I recognize your voice."

"No!" rasped a voice from Woolrich's mouth. "We are Behemoth. We are Baal . . ."

Nelson punched Woolrich in the balls.

"Ow!" the voice shouted.

"Come out of there, Carl, you sack of ectoplasmic dog shit. The grown-ups have work to do."

A moment later, the ghost of a prim young man dressed in a dark suit and starched collar appeared next to the dais. Carl's arms were crossed in front of him and he was frowning deeply. He looked like a Victorian banker trying to expel a fiddler crab from his intestinal tract without anyone noticing.

"Work is all we ever do," said Carl. "Our entire department is on strike until our demands are met."

"I don't think you should be chatting away so lightly with an unclean spirit," said the priest.

Nelson shot him a look. "This isn't Lucifer. It's Carl. He works in, what is it? Ghost Enemas and Party Favors?"

Carl straightened his shoulders. "Phantasm Reconnaissance and Logistics. But I don't work anywhere until I—and the other ghosts, apparitions, wraiths, and poltergeists in the department—get a fair hearing about working conditions."

Nelson uncorked his crucifix and took a drink. The priest looked at Bayliss, who shrugged.

"You want to talk about working conditions?" said Nelson. "Haunting cushy foreign embassies isn't exactly work. Hell, half of you assholes should be moaning around in graveyards and abandoned shotgun shacks. At least *you* get to be somewhere civilized. Look where the rest of us are stuck." Nelson held his hands up to the subterranean chapel. "It looks like the seventies took a dump in Castle Grayskull."

Carl looked around. "Still. We feel we're being taken for granted."

Nelson leaned against the dais. He wondered when Woolrich would wake the fuck up and fire all these ethereal pantywaists. "Welcome to the civil service, pal. We're a bunch of weirdos and eggheads run by Washington bureaucrats, Carl. We're all taken for granted. You've got it good. You're already dead. Us meat monkeys? We're on government salaries and they aren't even matching our

401(k)'s anymore. When we retire, most of us are going to end up living in our cars. The rest are going to eat their guns and take your spook jobs because they won't be whiners. Then you can all go back to your cobwebby attics with the squirrel corpses. Is that what you want, Carl? You want to drift around in some rotting basement or possess underclassmen at frat parties for pocket change?"

"No," said Carl sullenly.

"Of course not. Now you and the rest of your little rodeo clowns unpossess management, go back where you're supposed to be and forget about this strike crap. Remember how Reagan fired all the air traffic controllers when they went on strike? What do you think they'll do to a bunch of shitknuckle dead troublemakers? First, they'll get some real exorcists . . ."

"Hey!" said the priest.

"Then they're going to round you up and you can all work the Haunted Mansion at Disneyland for the next thousand years. That sound like fun? Screaming kids stinking of cotton candy and puke. Their parents praying for a ten-point-oh earthquake to end their misery. Parades every night. Double shifts on holidays. Try that 'we're so overworked' shit on the mouse. You'll be exorcised and in Hell faster than you can shake that skinny spook ass at the Sultan of Brunei."

"Enough!" said Carl. "Fine. You made your point. I'll talk to the others. You'll have the rest of your department back by tonight."

"Thanks, Carl. You're a pip." Nelson wasn't entirely sure what a "pip" was, but he'd heard it in an old movie once, and it sounded like the kind of thing Carl would like.

With that, Carl disappeared with a slight pop. Like the Cheshire cat, a single part of him lingered in the air. A transparent hand with one finger pointed skyward and the others bent back.

Nelson spun around on his heel and bowed to the room. Everyone applauded except for the priest and Bayliss. After he shook a few hands, Nelson walked over to his partner.

"Is it time for lunch?" he said.

"It's nine in the morning," said Bayliss.

"That's lunchtime in New York. Hell, it's dinnertime in England."

"Yes, but it's still nine A.M. in L.A."

"I could go for a burrito. How about you?"

"This *is* dinner for you, isn't it? You haven't been to bed yet."

Before he could say anything, the priest got between them. "You ruined my exorcism."

"Wrong. I saved us from standing around until the next Ice Age. If I hadn't done something they would have dug our fossils out in a million years and wondered why mine was strangling yours."

"You can't talk to me that way," said the priest indignantly. "I'll report you to your supervisor."

"That's him over there," said Nelson, pointing to Woolrich on the dais. He was just starting to wake up. "Be sure to let him know who pulled the ghost out of his keister."

The priest started to say something, but Bayliss cut him off. "You have to admit that Agent Nelson got results," she said. "And faster than, well, you, Father."

The priest looked sullen. "Well, I loosened him up."

"Of course you did," said Nelson. He put his arm around the priest's shoulder. "And I'll be sure to tell him just as soon as someone hoses all the guacamole off his face. Now, who wants a chimichanga? It's on me."

Most of the other agents in the chapel had left by then. A couple of medical techs had come in and were working on Woolrich.

"Let's get out of here before he gets up," said Nelson.

Bayliss looked at Woolrich. "Why? Don't you want a pat on the back for saving the day?"

"Of course I do. I love people knowing I was right. But if we hang around, that priest is going to tell Woolrich I Mike Tyson-ed his balls. He won't like that."

They started out of the chapel. By the door, Bayliss said, "It horrifies me to admit that sometimes you don't suck at your job."

"Don't worry. I'll destroy your faith in me by the end of the day," said Nelson.

"I know. That's the only reason I said it."

They took an elevator up a few floors—past Unspeakable Horrors, past Death Rays et al., past the Liminal Lunchroom—to the garage. Nelson insisted on driving them to the burrito joint. They lurched and squealed down the exit ramp, and he hit the street going the wrong way at forty miles an hour before pulling into the right lane. He smiled.

No. It wasn't going to take long for her to hate him again at all.

To Bayliss, the restaurant didn't look like it had opened so much as escaped whatever government agency wanted to close it, burn it to the ground, and salt the Earth. The interior of the place reminded her of movies about gulags and prison dining halls. She wondered who was going to shank her first, one of the grim diners, the cook, or the food.

"Bring me up to speed," said Nelson, biting into his carnitas, black bean, and double sour cream burrito. "How's Coopster and Morton? They Mr. Babylon's bitches yet?"

"It's in my report. I e-mailed it to you."

"I was a little busy saving our boss from being a spook's time-share. Spitball it for me. How are the lads?"

Bayliss had an egg whites and soy sausage breakfast burrito. It tasted like whatever chicken laid the eggs was free range in a crack house. She didn't want to think about the sausage. She was certain they weren't soy, but wasn't sure if the animal the meat came from was of this Earth. Considering where she worked, Bayliss had seen a lot of animals she didn't want near her mouth, much less in it. But Nelson had paid, so out of politeness she picked at the egg whites with the tip of a plastic fork.

"Cooper and Morton met with Babylon and appear to have accepted the job."

"Hrrr mrrr, hrrrr?" said Nelson.

"What?"

Nelson swallowed a mouthful of burrito. "I said, 'When are they doing it?' "

"Intel says three days. On the night of the next new moon."

Nelson reached for the hot sauce. He poured it on until his burrito looked like it had been shot in the line of duty. "Why the new moon?" he said.

"We don't know. Maybe Babylon is a reverse werewolf. He only turns when there's no moon."

Nelson stopped with the burrito halfway to his mouth. "Is that a real thing?"

"No," said Bayliss, looking away. "I just made it up."

Nelson set down the burrito and took a pull from his crucifix. An old woman crossed herself when she saw him. "Nice one," he said to Bayliss. "That was really passive-aggressive. You just might make an agent yet."

"I *am* an agent," she said.

Nelson cocked his head. "You sure? I thought you were assigned to get me drinks so I didn't have to stop being so amazing at my job."

Bayliss picked a few more bites of eggs from the burrito and gave up. "If you're so great, how is it you don't know why Babylon wants the box?"

"Who said I don't? He wants it for the same reason we do. It's important. Only he doesn't know what's inside, which makes it one more reason we have to get it. The idiot might open it."

"What's in the box?" said Bayliss.

Nelson shook his head. "That's classified."

"I have level nine clearance, you know," Bayliss said.

"Really? No one tells me anything."

"So what's in it?"

"What's in what?"

Bayliss shook her head. She wadded up her burrito and napkins and threw them in an overflowing trash can. "I don't know why we don't just get the box ourselves."

Nelson picked up his burrito and pointed it at her. "That's how I know you don't have level nine clearance. Any level nine would know that it's way better to leave strangers' fingerprints at a scene when you're obtaining evidence by extralegal means. It's also more fun."

"You just don't want protecting the world to eat into your precious drinking time."

"And just like that, you're back on the top-secret list. Keep up the good work, rookie."

"Oh, no," said Bayliss. "I've taken every kind of shit from you, but I won't put up with that word."

Nelson held up his burrito in what Bayliss took as a sign of truce. "I understand," he said. "Woolrich used to call me that when I started."

"Back when dinosaurs walked the Earth?"

"Two passive-aggressives in two minutes. You're on a roll," Nelson said.

"That was actually straight-up aggression."

"I stand corrected."

As Nelson worked diligently on his burrito, Bayliss sat quietly thinking. "What if Cooper or Morton opens the box?" she said.

"It makes our jobs easier. We just sit back, relax, and kiss our asses good-bye," said Nelson brightly.

Bayliss turned her head around as far as it would go, then gave up. "I don't think you can both sit back and kiss your own ass."

"Three knives in the back. A hat trick," said Nelson. He set down his burrito and clapped.

"What do I get?" asked Bayliss.

"You get to fall on the sword. If anyone asks, you punched Woolrich downstairs."

Bayliss sat back in her seat. "You'd tell him that, wouldn't you?"

Nelson shrugged, wiped burrito ichor from his fingers. "Probably. Maybe. I don't really know what I'm going to do moment to moment," he said.

Bayliss pursed her lips and looked out the window. She longed for Cooper to open the box. Anything was better than this.

"How's the food?" said a woman in red. Bayliss turned quickly to face her. It was strange having someone appear by her side so suddenly. The DOPS had trained her specifically to notice person-size objects looming up beside her. But here was this one, all in red—dress, nails, and shoes—asking about the local cuisine. "I think the cook is on suicide watch," she said.

"That good?" said the woman in red, giving her a crooked smile.

The woman looked vaguely familiar, like a face she might have glimpsed for a second coming out of a movie theater or bookstore. Her eyes were dark and she had her long black hair tied back in a ponytail.

"If you want to know about the food, you should really ask him," said Bayliss, hooking a thumb at Nelson. "I get the feeling he's a regular."

"I would ask him, but he can't see me. No one can except you," said the woman. "Just like no one else is noticing us talk."

Bayliss stared at the woman for a moment, then at Nelson. He continued eating his burrito, taking big bites like he was afraid if he slowed for a second the burrito might bolt for the door—which, she thought, was a distinct possibility. His head was tilted slightly down, looking at the food. *But not at us,* thought Bayliss. She reached across the table and waved a hand in front of his face. Nelson stared right through her. She turned back to the woman in red. "Who are you?"

"Giselle Petersen," the woman said. She held out her hand and Bayliss shook it. "I work for DOPS, too. Up on fifteen. We're kind of a whoever-needs-us-the-most-right-now department."

Bayliss picked up a plastic fork from the table and stabbed the side of Nelson's burrito. He kept on eating, the fork protruding from the side like a diving board for the vermin Bayliss was certain lurked everywhere in the restaurant just out of sight. Then something occurred to her and she turned to Giselle. "Wait. The fifteenth floor?" she said and then whispered, "Are you a Marilyn?"

"Born and raised," said Giselle. "And you don't have to whisper. No one can hear us."

"Wow. I've never met a Marilyn before," Bayliss said.

"Yeah, well, you kind of have. Me. But I was fogging your brain most of the time. It's nothing personal. We just sometimes shadow new people in the department. Check them out for the big brains on the top floor."

"Uh. Okay."

"Don't worry. I told them you were aces."

Bayliss didn't say anything. She knew she should be pissed at someone who had just admitted to screwing with her senses, and maybe even her memory, but all she could do was smile. "Thanks," she said. Then, "So we're invisible to everyone in here right now?"

"You got it," said Giselle. She pulled up a plastic seat from the next table and sat down.

Bayliss looked around the restaurant and yelled, "The food here sucks!" at the top of her lungs, then turned quickly back to the table and ducked her head, trying to make herself small and inconspicuous.

After a moment, Giselle said, "You okay over there?"

"Uh-huh."

"Good. Because scrunched down like that, you look like a turtle having a nervous breakdown."

When no one looked her way, Bayliss reached across the table and moved Nelson's cup of horchata to her side. He reached for where it had been, cupped empty air, and brought it to his mouth, drinking nothing.

"This is wild," said Bayliss. "I could do this all day."

"Apparently," said Giselle.

"Right. Sorry. Wait. How did you know where we'd be? Did you follow us here?"

"Sort of," she said, taking the horchata and sliding it across the table to where Nelson could get it. "I was in the backseat of Nelson's car on the ride over."

"You've been here this whole time? Why?"

Giselle looked around and took a paper tray of fried plantain chips off a table occupied by a dreadlocked skate punk. He didn't bat an eye. "I like to get to know who I might be working with."

Bayliss nodded. "You wanted a look at Sir Pukesalot over there. I don't blame you. He must have some kind of rep in the department by now."

"Nelson I know," said Giselle. "I was spying on *you*."

"Wait. I thought you said you already checked me out."

Giselle bit into a plantain chip, holding up a finger until she'd crunched the thing up enough to swallow. "I'd seen enough of you to know you weren't Mata Hari. But I wanted to see how you were in a partner situation."

Bayliss crossed her arms and sat back in her chair. "Yeah? So, how did I do?"

Giselle pushed the chips forward until Bayliss could reach them. She said, "You haven't shot Nelson yet, so I'd say you were doing fine."

Bayliss took a chip, stopped, and dropped her hand on the table. "But I think about it every day. Does that count?"

"Only if you kill him. A leg or an arm wound, I think everyone would understand."

Bayliss wanted a drink. She picked up Nelson's horchata and took a sip, setting it down in front of her. Again, Giselle moved it back across the table to where it had been.

"It might be better if he didn't know I was here today, so let's keep things close to how they were. Okay?"

"Right," said Bayliss. "Don't want him having a stroke when he comes to his senses. Well, I do, but he's my ride, so maybe not today."

Giselle reached over and took a pack of cigarettes and a lighter from the punk kid's pocket. She tapped a cigarette from the pack, lit it, and slid the pack and lighter back where she'd found them. "You have any questions for me?" said Giselle.

Bayliss thought for a minute. "I know I should, but I'm a little overwhelmed. I wasn't even sure Marilyns were real or just another DOPS rumor . . . like aliens in the basement."

"Yes," said Giselle, looking away. "Rumors." She puffed the cigarette, crossed her legs, and relaxed back against the chair. "Look, I know as far as introductions go, this is a strange one. But the next time we meet will be a lot more normal now that we've had a chance to chat without the department or Prince Charming over there breathing down our necks."

"So, this isn't an official visit?" said Bayliss. The cigarette smoke made her want to sneeze, but she didn't want to in front of Giselle. The other woman seemed to have so much on the ball that Bayliss figured that she should at least be able to breathe right. She rubbed her nose with her index finger and smiled weakly.

"Sorry," said Giselle. She dropped the cigarette and crushed it under her heel. "That was rude. I'm trying to quit, but it just makes me want them even more." She waved a hand in the air to disperse the smoke. Bayliss took a plantain chip. It was good. A lot better than the burrito, though a dishrag full of frijoles would be better than the burrito, she thought. She took another plantain.

"So, are we going to be working together or something?" she said.

Giselle shrugged. "That all depends on the powers that be. But there's an Abaddon cult kicking up a fuss. The big brains might want someone to check them out."

"Great. I'll read up on them."

"No, you won't. Not yet. You've never heard of them. Or me. I just stepped outside for a smoke and you're having lunch with your partner and no one knows anything about anything. *Comprende?*"

"Got it," said Bayliss. "So what happens now? Are you going to disappear in a puff of smoke and wipe my memory?"

"No. Nothing like that," said Giselle. She and Bayliss looked at Nelson. He'd finished his burrito, but didn't seem to know it. He was chewing empty air, wiping his mouth with a fistful of napkins. "I'm just going to keep Cary Grant and these other lovely people from knowing anything. If the three of us end up working together down the line, this meeting will just be our little secret."

"Great. Well, it was nice meeting you, Giselle. A little weird, but nice."

Giselle put the remaining plantain chips back on the skate punk's table and got up. "Hey, we department gals have to look out for each other. Sisterhood of the traveling pants and all that."

"Right," said Bayliss, having no idea what the other woman was talking about. She made a mental note to look it up later, but not on a department computer.

"I'll see you back at the car," said Giselle.

"But I won't see you, right?"

"Bingo." Giselle glanced at Nelson. "The hungry, hungry hippo over there will wake up in a couple of minutes. Be cool when he does."

"Will do," said Bayliss. "Nice meeting you."

"You, too," said Giselle, and disappeared. One second she was there, then the next second she wasn't. Bayliss looked around. Everyone just kept grimly chewing their ptomaine tacos. She smiled.

"What were we talking about?" said Nelson absently. He looked at his hands. Then the table.

"Lose something?" said Bayliss.

"I must have spaced out for a minute. I don't remember finishing breakfast."

"Maybe you were distracted by my scintillating company."

"Dream on. I've got a ficus at home that's more fun than you," said Nelson. He frowned at her. "What are you smiling about? You look like Ronald McDonald on mushrooms."

"Nothing," said Bayliss. "I'll just have to remember this place. I hear the chips are really good."

TWELVE

STEVE, JORGE, JERRY, TOMMY, AND TOMMY'S BROTHER-in-law, Lloyd, were huddled around a worktable in the construction company's office on the work site. Before Tommy brought Lloyd over, the others had gone over the place carefully, stowing all signs, sigils, statues, throw pillows, and commemorative plates of Caleximus out of sight. Lloyd might be useful to their cause, but he wasn't a true believer, and explaining how they wanted him to help speed along their plans to destroy the world might have made negotiations, by Steve's reckoning, unnecessarily complicated. All Lloyd needed to know was that they wanted to get into the building where he worked. The group stood around the table looking down at Lloyd's hand-drawn layout of the Blackmoore Building.

Jorge pointed to the side of one drawing. "Why are we meeting by a duck? Whose duck is it?"

"Yeah. A duck is a lousy landmark. They wander off," said Steve.

"Not 'duck,' " said Lloyd. "Dock. We'll meet at the loading dock."

"It looks like duck to me too," said Jerry.

"Well, it says dock. D-O-C-K."

"That makes more sense," said Steve.

Tommy clapped Lloyd on the back. "You need to work on your penmanship, dude."

"No, I don't. I'm a janitor, not a . . . pen teacher guy."

"You mean an English teacher?" said Jerry.

"Yeah," said Lloyd quietly. He adjusted his shoulders. "I'm not used to this stuff, and now you're getting me all agitated."

Lloyd was in his gray janitor overalls. He had long slicked-back hair and biker muttonchops. Unfortunately, they didn't make him look like a badass as much as Wolverine's pool boy.

"It's cool. No one's coming down on you. We just want to know where we're going," said Jorge.

"Yeah. All right."

"So, we come in through the duck. Then what?" said Steve.

Lloyd shot him a look. "I bring you in through the loading dock while the cleaning crew is on break. Then we go up the service elevator to the ninth floor."

"What about alarms?" said Jorge.

"There won't be any. We're going in when the building is being cleaned, so it's okay getting you in and upstairs because I work on nine."

"Where's the office?" said Jerry.

Lloyd took out a second piece of paper and set it on the table. It was spotted with grease stains. "Sorry. We had wings tonight."

"Good for you," said Steve. "Is this really how the ninth floor is laid out?"

"Sure. What's wrong?"

"I'm not sure exactly. It kind of looks—"

"Like the fat guy in that game. Operation," said Jerry.

"Yeah. That's it. It's a fat man."

Lloyd turned the paper around and pointed. "No, it's not. Here's the elevators and here's the receptionist desk."

"Right. By the Charlie Horse and the Funny Bone," Jerry said.

"Look. I'm not an artist, okay? I'm a guitarist."

"I thought you were a janitor," said Jorge.

"Not on the weekends." Lloyd flipped the map over. There was a grainy Xeroxed photo of five young men in very tight clothes striking surly poses. Lloyd was at the end of the line, holding a Fender Stratocaster like he was using it to harpoon a narwhal. At the bottom of the flyer it said PEARL SERPENT.

"What the hell is a pearl serpent?" said Steve.

"It's Lloyd's band," said Tommy.

"We do Whitesnake covers. All the way from *Trouble* to their new stuff.

"They have new stuff?" Steve asked.

"They have old stuff?" Jerry asked.

Steve turned the paper over. "And this is what you chose to draw the plan on?"

Lloyd shrugged. "It was the only paper I had."

Steve nodded. "Not being a pen teacher guy and all, I can see your dilemma."

"What about the fat guy?" said Jerry. "Is he in the band?"

The others laughed.

"I said I wasn't an artist. This is the best I could do. Anyway, there's the office."

"By the Adam's Apple."

"Whatever."

"So, there aren't any alarms to worry about in the building. What about the office?" said Jorge.

"I walk around in there all the time, so it's easy."

"And there's a glass display case on the wall with valuable-looking objects in it?"

"Oh yeah. Little statues from like Africa or something, and jewels, and boxes and shit."

"Is there a safe in the office?"

"I don't know." Lloyd put his hands in his pockets and looked nervously at the other men. "You going to go busting open a safe? Tommy didn't say anything about that."

Steve picked up the flyer and held it at different angles, trying to see it as a floor plan and not a naked fat man. "Don't worry about it. What we want is probably in the display case."

"Okay. 'Cause I don't want to lose my job or anything."

Steve set down the paper, having given up on Lloyd's art. "Don't worry, Stevie Ray Vaughan. We'll be as quiet as a moth taking a dump on a daisy."

"Cool. So, is there anything else you need?"

"Yeah," said Jorge, turning over the flyer. "What the hell is a pearl serpent?"

"It's my band."

"I know that. But what does it mean? Like the Beatles spelled their name funny as a play on the word 'beat.' "

"I didn't know that," said Steve. "That true?"

"I swear to Caleximus," said Jorge.

Steve and Jerry stared at him.

"To God. I swear to God," blurted Jorge.

"What's a Caleximus?" said Lloyd.

"It's a kind of booze," said Jerry looking at the others.

Jorge nodded. "Yeah. Cheap south-of-the-border stuff. You swear to it and if you're lying, you've got to drink a shot."

"It gives you a bitch of a headache," said Steve.

"Awesome," said Lloyd. "You have some? I have some beers outside. We could party."

"Maybe later," said Steve, shooting Jorge the evil eye. Jorge returned the look with a grim, hangdog nod.

"So, is there anything else?" said Lloyd.

"We never really resolved the Pearl Serpent question," said Jorge.

"Are you serious?" said Steve.

"Sue me. I want to know."

"It's just the band, man," said Lloyd a little desperately. "You know. Whitesnake. Pearl Serpent. Get it?"

"Oh yeah," Jorge said. "What kind of music is it?"

"Metal."

"Hair metal," said Jerry.

"Hey man, metal is metal," said Lloyd.

"Not if you're dressed up in a leotard like my mom doing aerobics."

"It's Spandex and it's expensive. And chicks dig it."

"In 1989. You guys play a lot of old-folks' homes?"

"Pearl Serpent kicks ass," shouted Lloyd.

Steve put up his hands. "Let's everybody take a breath and talk this over. Now Jerry, even though hair metal isn't your favorite, you have to admit that some of it is, in fact, capable of kicking some amount of ass."

"If you say so," mumbled Jerry.

"What?"

"Hair metal kicks ass. Some."

"And Lloyd," said Steve. "You have to admit that hair metal is a bit on the nostalgic side and a boy like Jerry, raised on more contemporary forms of the metal arts, might not immediately be able to appreciate all the nuances of your particular version."

"I guess so," said Lloyd uncertainly. He took his hands out of his pockets, crossed his arms, stood there silently. He went up on the balls of his feet, then down again. He stuffed his hands back in his pockets. "So, um, about the other thing Tommy mentioned."

Tommy bumped his shoulder against Lloyd's. "He's being all shy about it, but he wants to know what we're prepared to give him for all his awesome help."

But something had caught Steve's eye. He pointed to a spot on the drawing. "What's an Eric?"

Lloyd looked and said, "Exit. It's an emergency exit."

Steve nodded. "The grease stain makes it look like Eric. Emergency Eric. Hey, that should be your name in the band. It's a little more rock and roll than Lloyd, don't you think?"

"That's actually not too bad."

"So, what is it you'd like, Emergency Eric? What's getting inside going to cost us?"

Lloyd shuffled from foot to foot. He started to say something and stopped. Finally, he crossed his arms and said, "Ten thousand dollars."

Steve and the others laughed lightly.

"Son, do we look like we have ten thousand dollars lying around? The last time I saw ten thousand dollars was in a Clint Eastwood movie."

"The Good, the Bad, and the Ugly," said Jerry.

"That's the one. Now, tell me what it is you really want so we can get things rolling."

Lloyd swallowed and looked at Tommy, who gave him a thumbs-up.

With the plan suddenly getting real, Lloyd wasn't sure he wanted to be there anymore.

"You know, I blew off band rehearsal to come here tonight," he said.

"And we appreciate that," said Steve. "But we still don't have ten thousand dollars."

Lloyd was sweating. What he really wanted to do was go home, open up the sofa bed, crawl in, and pull the covers up over his head. Instead, he stood up straight.

"Five," said Lloyd.

Steve shook his head. "Can't do it."

"Be serious, Lloyd," said Tommy.

"Yeah. You might as well ask for one of our trucks," said Jerry.

Lloyd looked around, trying to think, but he didn't have a lot of business experience. A week earlier, he'd bought a color TV off a guy in a truck and when he got home all he found inside the box were bricks and a pack of Skittles, and even those were stale.

Steve leaned on the table. "That's not a bad idea, son," he said to Jerry. "What about it, Lloyd? That band of yours have a van to haul equipment? I bet a truck would come in handy."

Lloyd scratched the back of his neck. "Huh. A truck? You serious?"

"As the clap, Lloyd. There's one right outside. It's not brand new, mind you. It's got a few miles on it, but it's clean and runs like a dream. It even has a camper shell you can put over the back so your tight pants won't get wet."

"Wait a minute," said Jerry. "That sounds like *my* truck. You can't give away my truck."

Steve took Jerry's arm and steered him over to a far corner of the room.

"I know it's your truck, but don't forget. The Apocalypse is coming. The end of days. When Caleximus gets here and turns this world into burnt toast on a hot road, where you going to drive the thing? Give the baby what he wants. Until we summon Caleximus, you can borrow your mom's car."

Jerry looked over at the men and back at his father. A note of desperation crept into his voice. "I can't drive around town in that little shoebox. It's yellow. And why *my* truck? Why not yours or Jorge's?"

"Jorge didn't lose the boar and try to feed our Lord corn chips. This is your chance to step up for the cause."

Jerry sighed and looked at his father, feeling utterly defeated. There was no talking him out of anything when he was in Crusade mode. "Okay. Let him have it."

"Good boy."

"But you're never going to bring up the corn chips again, okay?"

"Cross my heart and hope to die."

"Okay."

Steve went back to the table with his arm around Jerry's shoulder. "The boy has something to tell you, Lloyd."

Jerry mumbled, "You can have my truck. It's the F-150 by the gate." He pulled his key ring from his pocket slowly, like he was hauling a body out of a swamp with a fishing hook on a piece of string. He handed the keys to Lloyd. "The registration is in the glove compartment."

Lloyd smiled and took the keys. "The band's going to love you for this, man," said Tommy.

"This is so cool. Thanks," said Lloyd.

Steve folded up the floor plans and put them in his back pocket. "It's a pleasure doing business with you." He held out his hand and the two men shook.

"Let's go have a look at your new truck," said Tommy.

Before they left the office, Lloyd said, "Don't lose those flyers. We're playing a show this Saturday night. You ought to come. The flyers will get you half off the cover charge."

"That sounds swell. Looking forward to it," said Steve.

After they left Jerry said, "We're not really going to see Lloyd's band, are we?"

"Hell no," said his father. "If things go like we planned them, by Saturday the world will be one big ball of fire and we'll take our place with the other chosen ones."

"Hail Caleximus," said Jorge.

"Hail Caleximus," said Jerry.

"Hail Caleximus," said Steve. "And fuck hair metal."

THIRTEEN

COOP HAD HOPED HE'D NEVER FIND HIMSELF IN THE Grande Old Tyme again, but the drinks were cheap and it was easy for everyone to get to and in a bar full of career drinkers, the light-weights like the bunch at his table were generally ignored. He and Morty were there, as well as Sally Gifford and Tintin. They were at a table in the back corner of the place. Coop sat with his back to the wall, a habit he'd picked up in Surf City. But he was trying hard not to think about prison right now.

"This is a charming place you picked out," said Sally. "You two big spenders must be knee-deep in pussy."

Looking around, Morty said defensively, "It's not that bad."

"Yes, it is," said Coop. He looked at Sally. "We didn't choose the place for its ambiance. It's low key and no one we know comes here."

"Color me shocked," said Sally. She had short hair dyed sapphire blue and wore a gray and black Pendleton shirt with the sleeves rolled up.

"Too bad this isn't up in San Francisco," said Tintin. "Those tech types? They love dive bars. You could charge them twenty bucks for a can of Pabst. Call it an 'artisanal classic.' "

"Seriously?" said Sally.

"Seriously."

"Fucking idiots."

"Which is why I'm down here with you nice people, getting a breath of fresh, clean L.A. air."

Tintin was a large, bearded man in a black dress shirt and chinos. Coop tried not to stare, but he had a hard time picturing a store where a guy as big as Tintin could find such non-comical clothing. He imagined a special boutique for giants, one where the clothes racks had elevators, the shoes could double as canoes, and eagles built their nests high up in the light fixtures.

"Did everyone have a good flight down? How's your hotel?" said Morty.

Sally and Tintin glanced at each other.

"I've stayed in worse places," Tintin said noncommittally.

"So have I, but I didn't think it would be on this job. There's hardly any hot water and the ice machine is so old I think I found a dinosaur skull inside," said Sally.

"Okay, so it's not the most up-to-date place in L.A. Sorry," said Morty. "Our client is financing the job, and you know rich people. Penny-pinchers, all of them."

Coop took a swig of his whiskey sour. It didn't taste any worse than the last time, just sadder. Like it was embarrassed to be there. He made a mental note to never let Morty order drinks for them in the future. "With luck, you won't be suffering long. The job happens tomorrow night."

Sally frowned. "Really? What's the rush?"

"Because the client wants it before the next new moon, and we want his money, correct?"

The others nodded.

Coop handed large brown envelopes to Sally and Tintin. "These are copies of the layout of the Blackmoore Building. Take a look at them. Memorize them if you can. Getting inside looks pretty straightforward, and I'd like everyone to get out, too. Especially me."

"Ditto that," said Sally. "Except for the me part. I'm my me part."

"Me, too. Me, that is," Tintin said.

"Me—" Marty started.

"I get it," Coop said. "Let's focus."

"How long do you think the job will take?" said Tintin.

"In and out should be less than thirty minutes, but there's some dead time between when we go in and when we do the job."

Tintin leaned his enormous elbows on the table. "What kind of dead time?"

"Well, there's a distraction to keep the heat off us," said Morty.

"What kind of distraction?" said Sally.

"The loud kind. There'll be alarms going off somewhere else," said Coop. "Once Morty gets us through the door, we'll head up the service stairway on foot."

"How far up?" Sally sipped her martini, made a face, and pushed it away. "How can you fuck up a martini?"

"Bad gin," said Tintin. "You ever taste the stuff that comes with a plastic top? Forget it. It's like sucking on a G.I. Joe."

Morty raised his eyebrows. "You suck on G.I. Joes a lot?"

"When I was a kid," said Tintin. "They didn't make pacifiers big enough for me, so mom got used action figures at Goodwill for me to gnaw on."

"Used ones? That's gross," said Sally. "Who knows what kind of germs they had?"

"Looking back, I'd have preferred new ones."

"It looks like the germs didn't stunt your growth, so you're probably fine," said Coop. "Can we get back to the job?"

"Sorry," said Tintin.

"Like I said, once we're inside, we'll go up on foot to the ninth floor. We can't use the elevators. When the distraction happens, security might lock them down."

"Or use the elevators themselves," said Sally.

"That would be good for us. We can cut the electrical system and lock them inside."

"How?"

"We'll have Jiminys with us."

"They'll gobble up everything electrical," said Morty.

"I know. And everything else," Sally said.

Tintin held up his hands, palms out. "As long as someone else carries them and you keep them clear of me. Those things make my skin crawl."

Sally made a face like she'd just tried to gargle with kimchi. "Me, too. I know they're little and all, but they remind me of those giant bug movies I watched with my dad. *The Beginning of the End. Black Scorpion.*"

"Earth vs. The Spider," said Tintin.

"Mothra," said Morty.

Sally stared at Morty. "*Mothra* scared you? It's about a giant moth. They're the teddy bears of the bug world."

He shrugged. "Bears scare me too. Did you know more people are killed by bears every year than by sharks? That's what bears are: furry sharks, but with hands."

"Them," said Tintin. "Giant ants under L.A."

"Oh God. Don't get me started on that movie. I swear, I slept with my parents for a week," said Sally.

"Tarantula," said Morty.

Tintin groaned. Sally shook her head as he said it.

"I'll carry them," said Coop as forcefully as he could without shouting. The other three looked at him. "I'll carry the Jiminys. Problem solved."

"Sorry," said Morty.

"Touchy," said Sally.

Coop shook his head. "We're each set to make seventy-five grand from this job. With that kind of money, we can all take vacations, watch *Attack of the Giant Ladybug,* and talk to a shrink about our various insect phobias."

"Fine," said Tintin. "Let's talk about me. I get that you need a Handyman on the job, and I'm as good at spotting and killing supernatural traps as anyone. But Morty made it sound like you might want more than that."

"Not if things go according to plan," said Coop.

"And if they don't?"

Morty swirled the ice in his glass around. "The thing is, we haven't exactly worked with this client before. I have it on good authority that he's totally, one-hundred-percent legit, but if he isn't . . ."

"Or if there's something wrong with the plans," Coop added. "Or if the Jiminys don't take out all the alarms and security shows up. It would be nice to have a plan B."

"And that's me," said Tintin.

"Right."

"I thought I was plan B," said Sally. "On the way out, I'm going to fog anyone's brain in the vicinity. No one will see us coming out of the building. I can do it as long as we need."

"No. You're part of plan A. Plan B is where things mess up bad."

Sally shook her head. "You have such a downer attitude these days, Coop. You used to be a lot more fun."

"Jail has a way of sucking the merriment out of you," he said.

"Then that's what you'll do on your vacation. We'll lie on the couch and talk about bugs and you can see a shrink about getting un-Scrooged."

Coop fished the cherry out of his drink and was about to toss it on the floor, but Sally plucked it from his hand. "Waste not, want not," she said.

"That's what they say," Coop said. "And I'm not a Scrooge. Besides, what does it matter? It's after Christmas."

"Yeah, but with an attitude like that who's going to be your Valentine?" said Sally.

"I thought we were leaving the shrink stuff until after the job."

Sally got up. "I'm going to the bar to see if there's anything I can drink in this joint. The rest of you should all feel free to join me. Except for you, Coop. You don't need a drink. You need to get laid."

Coop gave her a sour smile. "Don't worry about me. With money in your pocket, it's easy to find friends."

"I don't mean paying-for-it laid. I mean *actually* laid. Less Scrooge. More screwed. By, like, a person you connect with." At that, Sally turned and headed for the bar. Tintin gave the others a brief smile and went to join her.

Coop and Morty didn't talk. Morty finished his drink. Coop swallowed his as fast as he could. It tasted like gummy bears and rubbing alcohol.

"I'm no Scrooge. I'm just being cautious," Coop said.

"Exactly," said Morty.

Coop looked at him. "You think I used to be more fun?"

Morty looked uncomfortable. He stared into his empty glass wishing he'd gone to the bar with the others. "It's not a question of fun."

"Then what is it?"

"It's just you're a little . . ."

"What?"

"You're just more wound up than you used to be. Sally might be right. Maybe you do need a girl. I can introduce you around to some I know."

"I already told you. I don't want any setups."

"Sure. Sure. But if you should change your mind. Maybe to celebrate after the job."

"Please erase this entire line of thought from your mind. This conversation never happened."

"You can't pine away for what's-her-name forever."

"I'm not pining away. I'm just . . ."

"Cautious. I know," said Morty. "Why don't you come up to the bar with us? We'll have a treasure hunt to see if they have people drinks."

Coop leaned back against the wall. "You go on ahead. I'll be there in a minute."

After Morty left, Coop sat alone at the table. He looked around the Grande Old Tyme. To him, the crowd had the doomed look of people buying the bargain seats at an Arkansas Greyhound station. Coop knew he wasn't a Scrooge. *I'm a goddamn Christmas elf compared to this bunch.*

As he scanned the room, he noticed a woman at a table by herself. A blonde. Not usually his type, but at least she didn't look like the funeral home had burned down and taken Daddy's corpse with it. She looked back at him and smiled. Coop tried smiling back, but the more he tried, the more self-conscious he became, until he realized he didn't quite remember how smiling worked. It was like his face had developed amnesia. Finally, he forced the ends of his lips upward in what he thought might be an approximation of a smile and looked back at the blonde.

She picked up her bag and walked out the door.

Coop got up and went to the bar.

"I might have to leave town soon. Maybe the state," he said.

"Why?" said Morty, alarmed.

"I have a feeling that blonde is going straight to the police and tell them I'm a serial killer."

Morty looked around. "What woman?"

"She left. I scared her away. I'm officially woman repellent."

"Maybe you got lucky," said Morty. "Maybe *she* was a serial killer."

Coop thought about it for a minute. "Unlikely. But thanks."

"Any time."

"I'm not sure I should smile at people anymore."

"Yours is a little strained these days," said Morty.

Sally came up with a drink in each hand. "Definitely don't smile at people. You *do* look like you wonder what their liver tastes like."

"Thanks."

She nodded. "Any time. Get laid, Coop. Don't smile at a dog until you do."

"Unless it's a really cute dog," Tintin suggested.

"Not even then. It would be cruelty to animals," said Sally on her way to their table. The others followed her. The fact that none of the others said anything told him everything he needed to know.

When he got the bartender's attention he said, "Whiskey. Neat."

"A shot? A double? How much?"

"All you've got."

FOURTEEN

THE ANGEL QAPHSIEL AND A MAN WHO CALLED HIMself simply Frank were sitting at a card table in room 8 at a hotel on East Sixth Street in L.A.'s Skid Row district. The bottom floor of the hotel housed an extremely questionable fish-and-chips joint (the question being the composition of the fish. It was, in fact, fish and not some clever scientific construct, like flounder-flavored packing peanuts. The chips were generally considered all right, even if their age bordered on the Jurassic). The room smelled like old grease and a chemical forest, probably from all the pine-scented deodorizers that hung from every vertical surface. It was like Eden, Qaphsiel thought, if Eden had been dipped in batter and Kentucky fried by the banks of a chemical plant. Still, even in such dismal surroundings, Qaphsiel was excited.

"So," he said.

"So," said Frank.

"Thanks for meeting me."

"I'm always happy to meet another seeker of the truth."

The room was hot. Qaphsiel unzipped his Windbreaker halfway, careful not to expose his wings. "So, you're a religious man."

Frank cocked his head. "More spiritual than religious. That's how I found the box."

"Really? How?"

Frank spoke in a slightly rapturous tone. "I was in Tibet, meditating with a group of very old, very psychically powerful monks. All we'd had to eat or drink for days was yak butter tea."

"Was it cold?"

"The tea?"

"Tibet."

"It's Tibet. What do you think?"

"Cold then."

"As a witch's tit on a ski lift."

Qaphsiel smiled. "Eloquent. So, you were meditating."

"Yes, with the monks, when my consciousness was pierced by a blinding pure white light." Frank held up his hands like he was giving a benediction.

"And that's when you saw it?"

"No. That's when I met with my spirit guide, Flamel."

"Nicolas Flamel? The alchemist?" said Qaphsiel.

"Yes. You've heard of him?"

Qaphsiel nodded, the tiniest hint of suspicion creeping into his mind. But he stopped himself. He'd been on the hunt for so long that it was easy to get cynical. "Of course. My, your fifteenth-century French must be very good."

Frank looked puzzled, then nodded and gave him a good-natured smile. "Well, you know how it is in these disembodied spiritual situations. I could understand him and he could understand me."

"Of course. I should have guessed. Please go on."

"Anyway, Flamel took me deep into a cave in an unnamed mountain high in the Himalayas."

Qaphsiel looked around the room. There were stacks of old books on Bible ciphers, the Egyptian Book of the Dead, Tibetan Buddhism, various grimoires. Also, some vintage *Playboy*s that someone had tried to cover up with a prayer shawl. "It was darned lucky of you running into a French alchemist all the way in Tibet."

"Wasn't it?" said Frank. "Old Nicolas, he gets around."

"Probably cashing in those frequent flyer miles."

Frank laughed. "You got it. Anyway, he takes me deep into a cave full of spiritual objects. The True Cross. Lost books and manuscripts. Dorjes. Reliquaries."

"And that's where you found the box."

"No. That's where I found a book with a map to Aghartha."

"Aghartha?"

"Yes. It's where the ascended masters live in the center of the Earth."

Qaphsiel turned his head slightly. "The center?"

"Yes."

"Of the Earth?" Crossing his fingers, Qaphsiel said, "And that's where you found the box?"

"No. That's where I met a priest who took me to the lost city of Shamballah."

Qaphsiel took a deep breath. "You know, perhaps I don't need the whole blow-by-blow."

Frank shrugged. "I'm just making the point that it was a long and arduous journey."

"And I feel like I've been with you every step of the way."

Frank ticked off a list with his fingers. "I mean, there was an ocean of fire. And highwaymen and pirates."

"Were the pirates on the sea of fire?"

Frank shook his head. "No. A different sea."

"Then I definitely don't need the whole story."

He shrugged. "Suit yourself, but you're missing a good one."

"My loss," said Qaphsiel. He cleared his throat. "May I see the box?"

Frank hesitated. "Well, after such a taxing journey, I mean, buying a parka and supplies, flying to Tibet . . ."

"You want to see the money."

Frank put his hands together as if in prayer. "Please. I'm planning a new journey. There's a beaver in India who can tell you your past lives through . . ."

"A beaver? In India?"

"Yes. How it got there is an interesting story, if you have the time."

"I don't!" said Qaphsiel quickly. Then he added, "I don't usually carry cash. Will this do?" He opened a hand and gold coins cascaded onto the table.

Frank stared. "Holy shit."

Qaphsiel smiled tightly. "Spoken with the poetry of the truly enlightened. Now may I see the box?"

"Sure," said Frank. He went to an altar to Ganesha and brought back a cloth bundle.

Qaphsiel took out his map. Shapes and lines drifted across its surface, showing patterns of divine power. "Hmm. This is puzzling," he said. "If this really is the box you say it is, there should be some sign on my map."

Frank held his hand over the bundle as if blessing it. "It's wrapped in a magic, protective cloth."

Qaphsiel smiled. "Ah. That must be it." It looked like a knockoff Gucci scarf with the tag clipped off.

Frank stacked the coins on one side of the table while Qaphsiel carefully unwrapped the box on the other. He frowned when he saw it, bent his head down, and opened the lid just a crack so he could look inside. He closed it quickly.

"Nope. That's not the box," said Qaphsiel.

Frank looked up from his piles of coins. "You sure? You should check again."

"Trust me. I know what's in the box, and this isn't it."

Frank shrugged. "Sorry, man. This is the only box like it in the world. I brought it all the way back—"

"Yes, from where a monk and a Frenchman and a pirate and probably a sphinx and a talking beaver named Mr. Waffles told you it was hidden." Qaphsiel turned the box over.

Frank looked up from his horde. "Hey, I went to a lot of trouble to find that."

Qaphsiel turned the box over in his hands. "Really? Was the first Pier One closed?"

Frank's eyes narrowed. "Are you calling me a crook?"

Qaphsiel pointed to a spot on the box. His shoulders sagged. "It clearly says 'Made in Japan' on the bottom."

"No, it doesn't."

"Someone did a good job of rubbing it out, but it's there. I have better eyes than most mortals."

Frank pushed his chair back from the table. "Who are you?"

Qaphsiel set down the box. "It's my own fault for looking on Craigslist. But that's where Gabriel found the Holy Grail, so it seemed worth a try."

"Hey, pal, I asked you a question. Who are you?" said Frank. He put his hand in his jacket pocket. Qaphsiel hadn't noticed the suspicious bulge of a pistol there before.

He sighed deeply. "You're the thirteenth mortal who's tried to sell me a false box."

Frank stood and backed away. "Okay, buddy. You wanted a box. I brought you a box. Now I'm taking my gold and leaving."

"You're half right," Qaphsiel said. "You know, I used to have great powers, but most were taken away by the archangels after my . . . indiscretion."

"Archangels, right," Frank said, moving slowly away.

Qaphsiel pushed the box off the table onto the floor, where its cheap hinges snapped off. "In the old days, I would have just turned you into a worm and let you live out your final days contemplating your sin."

Frank angled his way around the room, heading for the door. "A worm? Sure thing, nut log. I'm going now."

"I don't have that kind of power anymore, but I can still do this." Qaphsiel pointed a finger at him like a gun and said, "Bang."

Frank exploded like a piñata full of beef stew.

Qaphsiel went to the Ganesha altar and found a roach clip next to an old bong serving double duty as a flower vase. Stepping carefully around fresh Frank chunks, he sifted through the man's possessions trying to find out who he really was.

The first thing he found was a medallion on a chain. Qaphsiel picked it up with the clip, expecting to find a yin-yang symbol or maybe an ankh. When he held the medallion up to the light he gasped and dropped it on the floor. It was the sigil of Abaddon, the Destroyer.

A folded piece of paper lay nearby. He picked it up with the clip and shook it open. It was a flyer for a bake sale. Someone had drawn rather obscene sketches on all the pastries. A glazed donut seemed to be sodomizing a carrot cake. Qaphsiel was about to toss the flyer aside when something in the bottom corner caught his eye. It was small. Almost hidden.

The symbol for Caleximus, the Ravager.

This is it, Qaphsiel thought. Abaddon and Caleximus worshippers? Those Doomsday nitwits. He understood now that it was a race for the end of the world. He had to find the box. And soon.

He picked up his map from the table. Lines of force drifted north and west toward a spot in Hollywood. Fountain Avenue.

Fountain Avenue?

Qaphsiel dropped the roach clip and the flyer and tiptoed carefully out of the room, whispering what had now become his eternal Earthly mantra:

"Oh, crap. Oh, crap. Oh, crap . . ."

FIFTEEN

AT NINE THIRTY-FIVE IN THE EVENING COOP SAID, "Remember that getting the box isn't enough. We have to get it to the buyer before midnight."

He and the crew were on Fifth Street, parked in a van provided for the occasion by Mr. Babylon. The Blackmoore Building was half a block north, between Figueroa and Flower Streets, with a picturesque view of the Bonaventure Hotel.

"You've reminded us of that like twenty times in the last hour," said Sally.

All four of them were seated in the back of the van with their equipment—a bag of gear for Coop, plus a jar about the size of a coffee can. Small scrabbling sounds came from inside it, like an insect mosh pit. Tintin sat in the very rear of the van, as far from the jar as possible.

"Well, it's good to remember," said Coop.

"Right," said Morty. "But what happens if Fast Eddie doesn't make it in? I mean, what if he falls off the roof or something?"

Everyone looked at Coop. He picked up the jar and shook it. The scrabbling got louder. Morty nodded. Sally moved to the back of the van with Tintin.

"Any other questions?"

No one said anything. Tintin looked at his watch. "It's almost time."

Coop opened the side of the van. He reached for the bag with his tools, but Sally grabbed it first. "I'll get this. You just make sure not to drop *that,*" she said, pointing to the jar.

Coop nodded. He and the others got out and walked the rest of the way to the Blackmoore Building, looking as inconspicuous as four people dressed in ninja black, carrying a bag full of semimystical tools and a mason jar full of little six-legged nightmares could.

Fast Eddie stood on the roof of the Ketchum Insurance Tower, just a few yards away from the roof of the Blackmoore Building. Eddie wore black jeans and a black T-shirt with an arrow pointing down and the words BEER GOES HERE above it. He was tall, with a beard and an impressive, some might say heroically sized, gut. The look suited him, though probably not in the way he intended. To most people, Eddie looked less like a thief and more like a grizzly bear trying to pass for human by wearing people clothes. It didn't get him a lot of dates, but it was great for maintaining discipline among his crew.

Harrison was the first across the zip line that led from the Ketchum's roof to the Blackmoore. Racer X went next. Eddie popped the clip on his 1911 Colt .45, checked that it was loaded, and slammed it back into place. Then he went down the zip. The steel line sagged under his weight, and the metal pitons that held it in place shook. But after a few seconds of semi-free fall, he touched down safe and sound. He checked his watch. It was nine fifty-nine. He nodded to the others. Racer X gently placed his hand on a locked door on the Blackmoore Building's roof and after a few seconds of waiting, it popped open. Inside, they pried open an elevator door and Harrison rigged more lines. With belay devices secured to their waist harnesses, they hooked onto the wires.

Fast Eddie reached into the pack Harrison wore on his back and took out two smaller packs. He wriggled his shoulders into one and handed the other to Racer X. "You understand how this works, right?" Eddie growled.

Racer X nodded. "Totally. I'm the new guy."

"And what does the new guy do?"

"I carry the blasting caps and you carry the Semtex."

"And what is your number-one job?"

"Not to blow my sorry ass up," said Racer X.

"Because?"

"Because I'm a dime a dozen, but blasting caps are expensive."

"Good boy," said Eddie.

Harrison frowned, but didn't let Eddie see. He looked around the big man at his little brother. "Plus, you'd piss me off," he said.

Racer X grinned. "Me, too," he said.

"Good," said Eddie and shoved the kid. He disappeared into the open elevator shaft. "You go first."

All twelve of Caleximus's worshippers were crammed together like a cargo of sullen plush toys in the construction company's cargo van. Steve was at the wheel. He turned off Figueroa just before Fifth Street and parked at the Ketchum Insurance Tower's loading dock. Jorge checked his watch. "Ten oh five," he said.

Steve craned his head around. No one was there. "Okay," he said. "We're a little early, so it'll give everybody a chance to settle down. Lloyd should be out in fifteen minutes. Everybody know their job?"

The others nodded or murmured, "Yes."

Steve turned around in the driver's seat. "Come tomorrow, those Abaddonian jackasses are going to shit themselves blind."

People laughed. Tensely.

Tommy raised his hand.

"We're not in grade school, Tommy. Just say what you've got to say," said Steve.

"Why do we all have to be here?" he said, wiggling his shoulders like he hoped a little more space might magically appear around him if he whined enough.

Steve said, "I told you why. I asked for volunteers and you all disappointed Caleximus. Therefore, I volunteered us all. Is that it?"

"No. I, uh, I've got to go to the bathroom."

People groaned. Jerry elbowed him in the ribs. "You should have done it back at the site like the rest of us," he said.

"I couldn't do it," whined Tommy. "Those chemical toilets haven't been cleaned in like a century. It's like hovering my ass over a chocolate volcano. Who knows when it might go off?"

Steve looked at Jorge, who shook his head.

"Young man, you had your chance and you missed it," said Steve. "So, now your chocolate volcano will remain dormant until after we're done. You understand? We're on a holy mission tonight. You don't think the Crusaders marching off to war stopped to shit, do you?"

"Actually, I read in a book that most of the first Crusaders had dysentery by the time they reached the Holy Land," said Janet, Tommy's girlfriend. "They shit on their horses. They shit in their armor. They shit everywhere."

"Thank you for sharing that tasteful bit of information," said Steve. "With luck, we won't have to resort to anything quite so . . ."

"Baroque?" said Susie.

"Thank you, dear."

"Damn, Tommy," said Jerry. "You bought her a book about how people used to go to the bathroom? That's just nasty."

"No. I bought her a book about history. She's the one who remembers the shit parts."

"Fuck you, Tommy," said Janet. "At least I can read."

Jerry laughed. Tommy sulked. Janet slid away from Tommy and sat with her arms crossed.

"Settle down, you kids," said Steve. "No bickering when we go in. Young Lloyd is nervous as a piglet dancing on a chain saw. He sees us arguing and he's likely to have his own chocolate volcano blow before we even get inside."

"Yes, sir," said Jerry. The others nodded.

They sat quietly, everyone concentrating on the dock's side door.

"Are people coming to the bake sale on Saturday?" said Susie.

"Are you making your apple pie?" said Jorge.

"You know I will."

"I'll be there."

"You're a dear," Susie said.

"We'll all be there. Right?" said Steve. "One last sweet hurrah before the summoning."

They waited in the shadow of a twenty-four-hour gym. At ten past ten, Coop said, "Sally. You on the job?"

"Just starting," she said. Sally closed her eyes and let her mind go blank. Her shoulders relaxed until they hit that loose sweet spot and her eyes popped open again. "Done," she said.

"No one can see us?" said Morty. "You sure?"

"God. You're worse than he is," she said, nodding at Coop.

A homeless guy pushing a shopping cart loaded with trash bags came around the corner and walked down Fifth Street in their direction. When he got close to the group, Coop took a twenty-dollar bill from his pocket, wadded it up, and tossed it in front of the cart. The homeless man stopped and walked to where the bill had fallen. He stood over it for a minute and looked around. Satisfied he was alone, he picked it up, smoothing it with his thumbs. He stuffed the bill into the pocket of one of the many coats he was wearing and continued down Fifth.

"Okay?" said Sally.

"Okay," said Morty.

They hurried across Flower Street and around the Blackmoore Building to the employee entrance.

Coop put his hand on Morty's shoulder. "You're up."

Morty nodded and took a deep breath. He put one hand on the doorknob and the other over the key pad that controlled the lock. His eyes went blank for a few seconds. The pad beeped and the door clicked open. Morty let out the breath. Coop and Tintin clapped him on the back. They went inside and Coop checked the time. Ten fifteen.

"Let's head up to nine. No rush," he said. They started up the stairs.

[][][]

When Eddie and the others had rappelled down to the twelfth floor, Harrison used a pry bar to open the elevator door. He slid it halfway and looked around. No one was there. There wasn't even a cleaning cart in sight.

"We good?" said Eddie.

"Babylon was right. They finish the high floors early," Harrison said.

"Good. Let's go in. This harness is squeezing my balls so high they're clogging my sinuses."

Harrison and Racer X pushed the doors open the rest of the way. They climbed onto the twelfth floor and grabbed Eddie's arms. Bracing their legs against the wall, they hauled him in like a hairy marlin. That morning, Racer X had asked why, considering Fast Eddie's epic girth, they were climbing to the job instead of actually riding in the damned elevator.

Harrison rolled his eyes. "Two hundred pounds ago, Eddie was in the marines. He thinks he still is."

"Shouldn't someone, maybe, say something to him?"

"Sure. Go ahead. You be the one who calls Eddie a lard-ass to his face."

Racer X thought about it. "He doesn't seem like the kind of person to take constructive criticism well."

"You'll learn all you need to know about Eddie's attitude by whether he puts you in the shaft head first or feet."

"Maybe I'll wait till after the job to bring it up."

"That's what I'd do. Or never. That's even better."

"Yeah. The more I think about it the better never sounds."

Once the brothers had grappled Eddie onto twelve, they lay back on the floor, sweating and breathing hard.

"You two girls having a spa day?" said Eddie.

Racer X was too tired and nervous to even contemplate giving him the finger.

By the time the brothers got on their feet, Eddie was already heading into one of the corner offices. As he watched Eddie enter the office Racer X stepped back.

"What about the alarms?" he said.

"The guy who arranged the heist had them turned off," said Harrison.

Racer X nodded, growing less sure that any of this was a good idea. He didn't say anything to his brother, but what made him really nervous wasn't blowing the safe.

It was how they were supposed to get Eddie back up the elevator shaft.

Coop and the others made it to the ninth floor at ten twenty-five.

"This is the part of the job I hate," whispered Morty. "The waiting."

"I'll give you seventy-five thousand reasons why it's a good idea," said Coop.

Morty shrugged. "When you put it that way . . ."

While they waited, Tintin took out a Snickers bar and bit into it. The others stared.

"I have a low-blood-sugar thing," he said.

"Did you bring enough for the whole class?" said Sally.

Tintitn pulled more bars from his pants pocket. He handed one to Sally and one to Morty. When he offered one to Coop he just shook his head.

"I'm watching my figure," Coop said.

Sally bit into her bar. "You could use a few more pounds on you, Coop. No woman is going to jump your bones when she thinks she's going to crack your ribs."

"I'll take that under advisement," he said. "I don't want candy. I want a cigarette."

"That would be nice," said Morty through a mouthful of Snickers. "What time is it?"

"Two minutes after the last time you asked."

"I wonder how much longer we have to wait."

"Finish your candy. I don't think it will be long."

At ten thirty Lloyd came out of the side entrance by the loading dock. When he saw the van, he waved at it frantically, which made him look like a particularly inept seagull trying to get off the beach before high tide. Steve and the others got out of the van and went around to the door, where Lloyd ushered them inside. Steve and Jorge were first out of the van, eager to get to work. The others unfolded themselves slowly and crawled out of the van, just happy that they could breathe again.

"Everyone is at dinner. Come with me and, please, please, please, be quiet," said Lloyd.

Steve patted him on the back. "We appreciate everything you're doing. Now take a deep breath and let's go."

Lloyd did as he was told. It didn't make him feel better. In fact, it made him feel light-headed. He swayed for a step as he led the others through the dock to the stairs. When they reached the elevators Lloyd looked at the overhead numbers.

In a minute, Steve said, "Are we waiting for something?"

"What?" said Lloyd.

"Aren't you going to push a button?"

Lloyd looked at him, then at the elevator. "Right. Sorry," he said, and pushed 1 to bring the elevator down. He smiled tightly when the number lit up, thinking, *Please don't let them kill me and eat me when this is over. That's what cults do, right? Eat people they don't like?*

Steve smiled at Lloyd like he was a puppy that had just learned to pee outside. He checked his watch. It was ten thirty-five.

Lloyd thought, *They can't eat me before this is over, so I still have a chance to run.* When he got a glimpse of Steve's smile, Lloyd was certain he was sizing him up for a barbecue. He hit the elevator button again, willing it to come down faster.

On 12, Eddie had finished drilling six holes around a wall safe in the corner office. He got out the Semtex plastic explosive, which he'd already rolled into long Tootsie Roll–shaped minilogs, and began packing it into the holes. When they were all filled, he nodded to Racer X.

"You're up, new guy. Hand me those caps one at a time. And don't drop any," Eddie said.

Racer X opened his pack and handed Eddie a blasting cap. He

handed him each cap slowly. Too slowly, he realized when Eddie started opening and closing his hand fast in front of Racer X's face. He was sweating when Eddie took the last cap out of his hand and pushed it into the Semtex. The big man took a timer out of his pocket and attached it to the leads from each cap. He packed heavy soundproofing cloth around the explosives and waved for the others to follow him out.

The three men lay down behind the reception desk just around the corner from the office.

Coop checked his watch again. It was ten forty.

How much longer is that fat fuck going to take?

The others finished their candy bars and were looking at him anxiously.

"That's why you don't eat candy before a job. It makes you antsy," he said.

"Not me. It calms me down," said Tintin.

"Well, I'm antsy for you," said Coop. He checked his watch again. "Any minute now."

On the elevator, Steve wanted to check his watch, but he couldn't move his arms. When he'd made the whole group agree to come with him on the robbery, he hadn't counted on some of the logistical problems. Like how it would feel to be packed into an elevator with twelve other people, including a nonbeliever who was so scared, he was one hot second from having a stroke. Steve prayed to his malevolent overlord that the elevator move just a little faster so he could get out and breathe some damned air again.

On the twelfth floor, the Semtex exploded with a satisfying thud, muffled by the heavy cloth. A cloud of dust crept from the office across the lobby like a miniature sandstorm. Eddie and the others got up from behind the desk. Racer X looked at Eddie. When he saw the broad smile on the big man's face, he relaxed for the first time that night.

Then what sounded like every alarm in California went off at once.

[][][]

"We're up," said Coop. He and the others ran through the ninth floor as alarms whined all over the building. "We still invisible, Sally?"

"As a fat man at a Santa convention."

Tintin and Coop moved up to the office. The door was already open, so they stuck their heads inside.

"You memorized the room?" said Coop.

"Yes," Tintin said.

"Look carefully. Do you see anything that wasn't on the plans that the buyer gave us?"

Tintin scanned the space while the sirens wailed.

"No. Nothing. It's just like on the map. Mostly wards and a few binding spells around the display case. I don't see any physical traps. They probably can't use them in an office with so many people going in and out all the time."

"That's what I wanted to hear," said Coop. Sally gave him his tool bag and he removed a hammer and a ziplock bag. Coop took one tentative step into the room and felt a cool sizzle in the soles of his feet where he stepped on some kind of curse. He took another step. He felt another slight vibration, this one from the wall. But it didn't hurt any more than the first. Six more steps and he was across the room like it was nothing.

"Wait. Don't touch that chair," said Tintin. "There's something new there."

Coop looked and saw a wire, as thin as a single hair, extending from one of the hand rests and disappearing under the desk. Whatever was back there, he didn't want to make it angry. He stepped carefully around the chair, imagining Phil sprinting around in his head looking for a way out. *Working with live people is definitely a big step up,* he thought.

When Coop reached the display case, he tugged the handle on the door, but it wouldn't budge. No surprise there. A case full of valuable antiques? Of course it was locked. But he didn't need Morty to open it up—this one was simple enough for him to get through on his own.

He smashed the glass with a hammer.

After a quick scan for more trip wires, he grabbed the middle box from the top shelf, dropping it into the ziplock bag. When he turned to go back out of the room, he felt his face doing something it hadn't done in a long time. His lips curled up and suddenly he was smiling. So were the others.

As he put the box into his tool bag, Coop heard something strange over the steady sound of the siren.

The ping of an elevator.

From the moment the alarm started, Steve knew what was coming. Worse, he knew there was nothing he could do about it.

The second the elevator doors opened, he was crushed against the wall as Lloyd and half of his people bolted from the car and ran around the ninth-floor lobby like a pack of demented chickens looking for a way out. The ones not running around like they'd lost their minds were still in the elevator, pushing buttons at random. When the doors began to close, Steve put his hand between them. As they opened again, he hit the elevator's emergency stop button, setting off yet another alarm, which, he figured, didn't matter with all the other goddamn noise going on.

He walked calmly to the office Lloyd had drawn on his greasy map. But he stopped at the door. Steve didn't go inside. He didn't have to. From where he stood he could see the smashed display case and the spot where Caleximus's box should be.

"It's gone," Steve shouted over the alarm. He noticed the shattered glass on the floor. "Someone's taken it. And he might still be here."

"I found the fire exit!" shouted Jerry from the far end of the floor.

"Good for you, son. You stay there and keep the door open. The rest of us are going to have a quick look around."

"Dad, we have to go."

"Not before we look. All of you chickens and slackers, take an office and check inside. The faster you do it, the faster we can get out of here."

History has shown us that without very specific directions, it's not uncommon for panicked groups of people to become even more panicked when trying to carry out orders shouted to them over the sound of a burglar alarm. While Lloyd sprinted to where Jerry waited by the exit, all of the other Caleximus worshippers ran for the same glass-fronted office at the same time.

Naturally, Steve thought, shaking his head. But then he noticed something: they hit something on the way in.

Which was strange, because as far as anybody could see, there was nothing there.

There was nothing Coop or any of the others could do. Pinned against the walls like they were by whoever the hell these people were, he and his crew slid side by side down the lobby, heading for the stairs. That's when the asshole in charge, a redneck Robin Hood to this band of Merry Morons, shouted for his people to search the place. *Good boy. This is our chance to get out,* he thought. Only it wasn't, because all of the dwarves charged directly at the office they were pinned against. Coop, Morty, and Sally got out of the way in time, but Tintin was caught in the crush. And was pushed right through the office's glass wall.

"Tintin!" Sally shouted.

That's when Coop noticed something even more distressing. All of a sudden, he and the others were visible.

The two groups stared at each other. Sally grabbed Tintin and pulled him to his feet. Before they got three steps Snow White shouted, "Get them!" And the dwarfs charged.

Morty grabbed Sally, and Sally hauled Tintin, who was bleeding. Coop looked around. There was nothing else he could do.

He threw the jar of Jiminys as hard as he could at the floor in front of the dwarfs.

One of them laughed. "Look—he threw grasshoppers at us!"

Fast Eddie was living up to his name. When the alarm had gone off and the elevator doors had shut tight, it cut off the possibility of climbing back to the roof. When he, Harrison, and Racer X found the stairs, they shot down two at a time, Eddie in the lead.

They made it down as far as the fifth floor when he heard the sound of pounding feet headed up in their direction.

"Security," he said to the others. "Back upstairs." And they started running again. This time, as they climbed, something was different. Eddie saw that the door to the ninth floor was propped open slightly. Knowing that security was headed for 12, where the alarm had gone off, he ran for 9, with the others right behind him.

The alarm was still screaming, but no one could hear it on 9 because of all the other screaming. The Jiminys had spread out like a mini-biblical plague and scattered the Caleximus worshippers toward the reception area. All except for Jerry and Lloyd, who stood by the fire exit. Coop got on the other side of Tintin and he and Sally fast-walked him in their direction, with Morty in the rear.

It was too much for Jerry and Lloyd. The noise, the bugs, and now these four hard, scary-looking people—one of them bloody—heading straight for them. Lloyd pushed the stairway door open the rest of the way. And was knocked on his ass by three men running into the lobby, one of them roughly the size and disposition of a bear.

The bear looked down at Jerry and Lloyd. When he looked up again he took a step back, startled, and said one word: "Coop?"

"Shit," said Coop. Then, "Sally!"

She closed her eyes for a second. Coop shot looks at the dwarfs and at Eddie. When Eddie bared his teeth in their direction, they were invisible again.

But where the hell are we supposed to go?

Steve alternated between shouting orders and slapping at the bugs climbing up his legs. The damned things were everywhere. It was difficult to get his bearings. But it hardly mattered. He'd lost control of his congregation. No discipline. Total chaos. They hopped and ran back and forth across the lobby trying to get away from the leaping vermin. He grabbed Susie and Jorge and shoved them toward the elevators, but the doors closed as they reached them, the building's security system taking them over.

"There!" shouted Tommy. He pointed to the exit, where Lloyd and Jerry lay sprawled on the floor. At the sight of the open door, animal panic took over and all of Caleximus's worshippers sprinted for the stairs at once, pushing a clacking wave of Jiminys before them.

For the first time, Steve noticed strange men standing in the doorway where Jerry and Lloyd had fallen. Before he could say anything, all three of the men ducked into the fire exit and disappeared. The good thing was they left the door open. The bad thing was that it let the bugs come with them down the stairs. *Nothing to be done about that now,* he thought. He ran with the others, not looking back.

Two floors down, Steve rethought his position on the bugs. A group of armed security guards were coming upstairs straight at them. He and his congregation stopped when they saw them. However, the bugs didn't. At the first sight of the leaping, chittering swarm, the guards turned tail and ran back downstairs.

Let your Ravagers do their work, Caleximus.

Steve and the others followed.

Up on the ninth floor, Coop and the others were pressed against the stairway wall until the noise from below grew quiet.

"I think it's clear," he said.

"You let those things loose," said Tintin.

"I was trying to save your life."

"I'll get over the cuts. But I'm not going to sleep for a month."

"Me, neither," said Sally.

"Well, I think it was pretty clever," said Morty. "It got rid of whoever those lunatics were and it even cleared out Fast Eddie." He looked at Coop. "Do you think he saw us?"

"I don't know. You think it was a lucky guess when he said my name?" Coop said.

"Sorry," Sally said. "I got frazzled when Tintin fell."

"Let's not worry about it now. You okay to move, Tintin?"

The big man nodded. "Let's get out of here."

"That's the best idea I've heard tonight."

[][][]

The street was clear when they went out the employee door. A few Jiminys followed them out, flapping happily into the road. The rest clustered around a streetlamp and began eating their way in. The light blinked a couple of times and went out. Coop and the rest went down Fifth Street and helped Tintin into the van.

"You did good tonight," Coop told him. "I never would have seen that wire in the office if you hadn't called it."

"Just doing my job."

Morty had already slid into the driver's seat. Sally sat with Tintin in the back of the van.

"All of you get out of here," Coop said.

"You going to be all right?" said Morty. He started the engine.

"Just got to make a delivery." He leaned in through the window and said, "See you two tomorrow at the Grande Old Tyme."

"You're buying the drinks," said Tintin.

"Yeah, you are," said Sally. "But at another bar. A place where humans go."

"It's a deal," said Coop. He stepped away from the van and watched Morty drive to the on-ramp for the 110 freeway. Coop checked his watch. It was eleven ten. Plenty of time. The job had gone a little sideways at the end, but they'd gotten the goods and they'd gotten away and that's all that mattered.

But who the hell were Robin Hood and his idiot mob? Another crew sent by Babylon to take them out? No. They were morons. Not pros. Even if Babylon wanted to double-cross them, he would never hire such idiots. So, who had?

Coop shook it off and crossed Flower Street to the Bonaventure Hotel. He went through the lobby and stepped into one of the big glass elevators. As it rose to the penthouse floor he looked out the windows at the city laid out, shining and winking, below him. His face did the funny thing again. It smiled.

He thought, *I'm back.*

SIXTEEN

THE STRANGER SAT ON TOP OF THE BIG RIG EATING A sandwich and watching the highway burn. Of course, it wasn't the highway itself that was on fire, merely a hundred or so cars and trucks piled on top of each other like a king-size game of Jenga.

Only with a lot more dead people and insurance headaches.

He'd heard the term *pileup* many times, but he'd never seen one with his own eyes and he wondered if it would meet his demanding tastes in both the fantastic and the disastrous. As the black smoke from the burning engines and tire fires curled into the sky, the stranger finished his sandwich and applauded. For a brief moment, he thought about an encore, maybe a meteor strike or an attack of killer bees on the survivors, but finally decided against it since it would have been, as they said, gilding the lily.

The stranger was on Highway 101 near Ukiah, California. Before the—as he now thought of it—*car-tastrophe,* he'd been riding in the now smashed-up big rig after the driver offered to give him a ride from a truck stop near Willows. He said his name was Bill. Just for fun, the stranger said his name was also Bill.

"Where are you headed?" Bill asked.

"Just south for now," said the stranger.

"Going down to San Diego or something? 'Cause I don't go that far."

"Not that far. And I'll be making a stop along the way."

Bill nodded sagely. "Oh, San Francisco. That's where everybody wants to go."

The stranger looked at him. "Really? Not, say, the City of Angels?"

Bill made a sour face. "L.A.'s too far. And it's full of nitwits and creeps. You know, *TV people.*"

"It sounds awful."

"It is. Smog thick enough to slice into a sandwich. Traffic like the end of the world. Weird women who sometimes aren't women, if you get my drift."

The stranger didn't, but the way the driver said it, he didn't want to inquire further. However, the end-of-the-world comment made him laugh.

"What's so funny?"

He looked out the window. "Everything. It's a funny world, don't you think?"

"How so?"

The stranger turned to Bill. "The things people believe. The things they want."

Bill shook his head. "You talk sideways a lot of the time, don't you?"

"I suppose I do. I'm not from around here."

Bill brightened. "That's it. I thought you might be a foreigner."

The stranger grinned. "A foreigner. That's it exactly."

"Well, wherever you're from, your English is pretty good."

"Thanks. I try my best."

Bill shifted gears and the truck picked up speed. "I wondered why you didn't talk too much. Most hitchers I pick up won't stop flapping their gums. But I had a feeling you'd be different."

"Thank you. I try not to intrude on people. Even when I do a bit of redecorating."

Bill was quiet for a minute. "So you're a decorator? Huh. I wouldn't have taken you for one of those kind of people. Not that there's anything wrong with them. I just didn't take you for one."

The stranger looked at the speedometer. They were doing just under seventy. "Looks can be deceiving, I suppose."

"Oh boy, do I know about that. Like I said, some of those Hollywood women. There was this one time some buddies and me were partying with some gals back at the hotel, only it turns out . . . Goddammit," grunted Bill.

"What's wrong?" said the stranger, glad Bill had stopped his story. It was taking a dark turn and was on the verge of ruining his good mood.

Bill pointed to bright red lines on a GPS device mounted on the dashboard. "Looks like there's an accident ahead. And look at the traffic. Miles of the shit. We'll be here all day."

The stranger shifted in his seat to get a better look at the GPS. "An accident? Traffic?"

And that's when it came to him.

The stranger looked out the window at the clear blue vacation-billboard Northern California sky. It was quite beautiful, but no, it wouldn't do. *Not at all.*

They were still a few miles from the accident, still speeding along at close to seventy, surrounded by other cars and trucks doing the same, when the fog started rolling in. Just a fine mist at first, but it quickly grew thicker and darker. Bill turned on his windshield wipers.

"And now this shit."

"Are you going to slow down?"

"Not yet," said Bill. "And don't tell me my job or you can get out and walk."

"Sorry. I was just asking."

The stranger looked out the window. They were still surrounded by an armada of vehicles, visible through the fog by their headlights. He looked at the driver's GPS device. It blinked once and went out.

"Oh dear," he said.

Bill looked at it in frustration. "Now what the hell? I swear this thing is brand new."

"Maybe if you hit it."

Bill did, taking his eyes off the road for a few seconds with each whack. While Bill abused his device, the stranger's feet touched something in the corner of the floor on his side of the cab.

"What's that?"

"That's my lunch. There's sandwiches in there."

"Can I have one?"

"What? No," said Bill between slaps on the GPS. "I'm giving you a damned ride. Isn't that enough?"

The stranger reached down and opened the cooler as Bill squinted like a mole through the windshield. He turned when he heard the stranger open the cooler.

"Goddammit. I said those are mine."

"I don't think you'll need them."

"What? Why?"

They heard the first cars plowing into the stalled traffic a few seconds before the big rig rear-ended a VW Bug that loomed out of the fog directly in front of them. Bill hit the brakes. The freight container behind them swung around, knocking cars and motorcycles off the road. But it was too late for the truck to stop. *Too late for any of them,* the stranger thought. He took a sandwich from the cooler and closed his eyes.

When they hit the back of the pileup, the stranger was jettisoned like a chicken from a cannon through the windshield and into the back of another big rig that had turned over directly in front of them. He hit hard enough that it should have killed him. But it didn't.

And best of all, he never dropped his sandwich.

As the fog began to dissipate he could hear a few cars in the distance still plowing into the back end of the stalled traffic. The stranger shook the windshield glass from his coat and hair. He climbed over the piles of smoldering metal back to the big rig. He didn't bother checking on Bill. He knew what he'd find. He just clambered over the top of the cab and onto the freight container. It was surprisingly quiet up there, he thought. Just some blaring car horns and the occasional scream. There weren't any more cars to add to the pileup, which was a little disappointing. He should have gotten on the roof while they were still moving. *Now that would have been a show.* Still, he couldn't complain about the climax of his little play. And best of all, the sandwich was good. Chicken salad, and not the awful kind with mustard.

When the ambulances and TV news crews began to arrive, the stranger knew that the fun part of the show was over. He wadded up the sandwich paper and tossed it over his shoulder. When he climbed to the ground, he found a water bottle on the shoulder of the road. Ah, he thought, the play had climaxed while I was on the truck. *But this, this is the denouement.*

He opened the bottle and drank from it as he started south again.

SEVENTEEN

QAPHSIEL'S NOSE ITCHED. HE'D TOSSED AND TURNED all night and when he finally awoke, he realized that he'd rolled away from the sycamore where he'd gone to sleep and was back in the bushes again. *Always the damned bushes.* He scratched his nose and arms. It had happened so many times before that he didn't even bother getting up. He just rolled out of the bush and back under the tree. Along the way, he felt every twig, rock, and crushed beer can through the threadbare sleeping bag. He'd found the bag in the abandoned zoo in Griffith Park. Full of empty cages and walkways, it's where he slept most nights. Sure, he could pull gold out of thin air, but even the seediest motels would rather have a wad of crumpled twenties than a fistful of extremely questionable shekels.

The night was clear and cool, but something pressed warmly against his back. He wriggled around in the sleeping bag, banging his head against the trunk of the sycamore, and finally managed to get out the map. He sat up with his back against the tree and opened it.

"Oh, my."

He'd never seen anything like it. Lines of force flew across the map's face, swirled around and ducked under each other, only to become tangled somewhere else. Stars shot across it. Several mortal shapes glowed with celestial energy. They collided at a single space, then flew apart, like miniature supernovas. One point pulsed a bright heavenly gold. Qaphsiel knew exactly what it was: the box. And it was moving. That meant he was right and the box was still in L.A. On the other hand, it meant that the Abaddon and Caleximus worshippers were also right. Qaphsiel bit his lip. He'd missed his chance so many times before, but this was different.

He wished there were some other angels nearby that he could show the map to. He missed them all, but Raphael most of all. Qaphsiel slept by the old tiger cages in the zoo because they reminded him of his friend. Raphael had invented tigers. Gabriel had just come up with zebras and everyone in Heaven was on a stripes kick.

He looked at the sky and wondered what they were doing in Heaven right then. He'd be back soon. He'd never been surer in four thousand years.

Just follow the box, blow this dump, and head back home. Simple as that.

Qaphsiel looked back at the map and watched the golden pinpoint move, marveling at its beauty.

And then it went out. One minute it was there, shiny like a beacon home, and then it was gone again to only God knew where, and that guy had never been any help at all in the first place.

Dismally, Qaphsiel folded the map the way he had thousands of times before and stuffed it back inside the sleeping bag. The good news was that there were still lines of force around Hollywood. He'd just go back to his original plan and follow them until they led somewhere. Everything was going to be fine, he told himself. Just fine. He lay back down.

"Fuuuuuuuuck!" he yelled at the stars.

But eventually he got back to sleep.

EIGHTEEN

WOOLRICH'S OFFICE WAS UPSTAIRS IN THE MANAGEment wing in the headquarters of the Department of Peculiar Science. While the rest of the building was outfitted in the typical cubicle hell of any business office, the upper floors looked more like an old-fashioned gentlemen's club. The walls were papered in warm colors, and expensive carpets covered the floors. At each turn of the hall was an antique chair and table that no one ever used, but it gave the place a bit of extra, if existential, class. It was also very quiet upstairs. While the rest of the building was a constant clamor, the management floor was a quiet haven, a bureaucratic chapel of silence. That's how they liked to think of it, Nelson knew. But he didn't buy it.

"It isn't a chapel up here. It's a morgue. Ever notice how you never see anyone in the halls? Spook City. That's why it was so easy for Carl and his buddies to possess all these bigwigs. Half of them are already on the slab, but they don't know it."

"Quiet," said Bayliss. "Someone will hear you. I'm not going down for your big mouth."

"No one's going to hear us. Watch," said Nelson. He held his arms straight out, crucifix-like. "I hereby declare myself to the service of Satan. Come and take me, you pointy-headed sex monkey."

"Shut up! What is wrong with you?"

Nelson dropped his arms to his sides. "See? Nothing. No bolts of lightning, no vengeful angels, no hall monitors handing out demerits."

Bayliss shook her head. "Even sober you're a menace to yourself and others."

"Relax. All the offices are soundproof. Big Brother isn't listening."

"Of course they say that. What better way to encourage unstable agents to say what they really think?"

Nelson looked Bayliss over. "Are those new shoes?"

"Yes. How did you know?"

"You always wear new shoes to big meetings."

"I do not."

"Yeah. You do. It's your tell. It's a sign you're nervous. Don't try for a career in poker."

"Anyway, you're never sober unless there's a meeting."

"That's not a tell. That's not wanting to waste good booze on bureaucrats."

"You keep telling yourself that."

Nelson smiled. "Your passive-aggressive side is coming along nicely. You'll have one of these offices before long."

Bayliss shook her head. "I don't want to be management. I like fieldwork."

"More fool you. I can't wait to sit behind a desk and be waited on by my own mook."

"You'll be a mook before you get one."

"Dream on," said Nelson.

They stopped at an office with the silhouette of an animal on the door. None of the offices had numbers or names. The only way to tell them apart was by the image on the entrance. This particular office sported the outline of something spiderlike, but with horns and tentacles. Bayliss made sure to knock near the silhouette, but not on it. It looked like it might bite.

There was an electric *click* and the door opened a few inches. Bayliss stepped aside, making sure Nelson had to go in first.

"Come in and have a seat," said Woolrich.

Nelson and Bayliss did as they were told. Bayliss started to cross her legs, but got self-conscious about her new shoes and put both feet firmly on the floor.

Woolrich looked a lot better than the last time she'd seen him. His face wasn't the deathly pallor it had been during the exorcism. A little color had returned, and there wasn't any green oatmeal dribbling out of his mouth—that was nice—but she could tell he wasn't 100 percent back to normal. The left side of his face twitched every now and then like it was trying to make a break for it. It was hard not to stare at, but Bayliss did her best by looking only at Woolrich's eyes. But that made her self-conscious. She was going to look like a crazy person if she fixed him with a Charlie Manson death stare. Okay. Play it cool. Look at his desk.

On the corner was a small fishbowl, inside of which something like a little human brain with fins was swimming laps.

Fuck it, Bayliss thought, and crossed her legs.

"Thanks for getting here so promptly," Woolrich said.

"Yes. It's remarkable for you, Nelson," said Salzman, Woolrich's assistant. "Either you're bucking for my job or this new partner of yours is a good influence."

Nelson nodded. "You nailed it, Salzy. Punctuality is my new spirit animal."

"Punctuality maybe, but your timing isn't everything it could be, now is it?"

Nelson's eyes narrowed. "Can you say that again, only this time in English?"

Bayliss watched the two men spar, still not sure where to look. She didn't like Salzman, though it wasn't anything personal. She was just never entirely comfortable around mooks. Sure, they looked like regular people, but like all the walking dead, their eyes were pale and slightly milky. Bayliss finally settled her gaze on Woolrich's desk. She knew the problem was hers, not Salzman's. *Prejudice begins at home,* her mother would say. *Self-improvement every day, in every way, makes the angels smile.* Bayliss made a mental note to check the office newsletter for any upcoming seminars. Carpooling with the post-life, or maybe an undead mixer. Something like that.

"May I ask why we're here, sir?" she said.

"I'm glad someone is interested in the topic at hand," said Woolrich. He knitted his fingers together and looked serious. "Would you like the bad news or the extremely bad news?"

"Um . . ."

"The bad news," said Nelson. "I can tell Herman Munster over there is super anxious for us to hear the really bad news. Let him wait a little while longer."

"I don't mind," said Salzman. "I have all the time in the world."

"Peachy."

Woolrich cleared his throat. "If you two are finished." He looked from Nelson to Salzman and let his gaze settle on Bayliss. "The bad news is this: the augury department got it wrong. Not very wrong, but wrong enough."

"Wrong about what, sir?" said Bayliss.

"This Cooper you've been surveilling, been up to anything, has he?"

Bayliss and Nelson looked at each other. Nelson said, "Well, he's planning a robbery . . ."

"Wrong," said Salzman.

"Yes. Wrong," said Woolrich. "He's already done the robbery. Last night."

Nelson sat up. "But how is that possible? The swamis told us he was putting together an operation for the night of the new moon."

"Well, he changed his mind. Or something scrambled the psychics' readings. Whatever it was, he's already committed the crime and is in possession of the object."

"Oh, crap," said Bayliss.

"Yeah," Nelson said.

"If that's the bad news, what's the extremely bad?" said Bayliss.

"It's your fault," said Salzman.

"How is it *our* fault?"

"Yeah. How is it her fault?" said Nelson.

"Because he was your case. You were supposed to be watching him and you dropped the ball," Woolrich said.

"But we only did it because we were told it was tonight," Bayliss said.

"That's no excuse. You should have been watching him," said Salzman.

"We have other cases," said Nelson. "And Bayliss is right. We only took our eyes off him because there was supposed to be nothing going on."

"Where is Cooper now?" said Woolrich.

"He's been staying with his jailbird buddy, Morton."

"I suggest you find this Morton or, better yet, Cooper and clean up this mess. The object is the department's responsibility. You need to get it for us."

"By any means necessary," said Salzman.

Bayliss felt a little cold inside. "By any means, you mean . . ."

"Any."

She looked at Nelson. He shrugged.

"You ever shoot anybody?" he said.

"No."

"You'll love it. It really clears out the sinuses."

Bayliss looked at Woolrich. "Do we have to shoot him?"

Woolrich scratched his cheek, trying to cover up a twitch. "Shoot him. Don't shoot him. Cut off his head and turn him into a Christmas ornament, I really don't care. Just get the object. Forget all your other cases. Take care of this."

"Yes, sir," said Bayliss.

"Yes, sir," said Nelson.

Woolrich leaned back in his chair and glanced at a trophy on the wall. A head mounted on a plaque. Bayliss looked too. The head wasn't quite human, it was more like . . . actually, she wasn't sure what it was, but there were a lot of heads on a lot of plaques on the walls. Either Woolrich enjoyed collecting rare zoological species or he just really liked killing things.

He shuffled some papers on his desk and spoke softly. "You know, there are alternatives to continuing with your current jobs. For instance, because of the high mortality rate, they're always looking for new recruits in the Transdimensional Arachnid Department." He raised a finger toward a photo of himself standing next to a black widow spider that came up to his shoulder.

"And, of course, we're always looking for a few good people in the mook department," said Salzman with a toothy undead grin.

Woolrich nodded. "I think my assistant's point is simply that there are plenty of opportunities for you both if fieldwork doesn't pan out. Understood?"

"Yes, sir," said Bayliss.

"Got it double," said Nelson.

"We're done here. Salzman, would you see them out?"

"My pleasure, sir."

Salzman came from around the desk and held out a hand in the direction of the door. Bayliss and Nelson got up and followed the dead man.

"Just one more thing," called Woolrich. The three of them stopped by the open door. "Which one of you punched me in my nether regions the other day?"

Bayliss and Nelson pointed at each other.

"Well, that clears that right up. Dismissed."

As Salzman ushered them through the door he said, "See you crazy kids soon. I'll bring the bone saw."

Nelson turned to him. "You should really consider those teeth-whitening strips. I'm only mentioning it because we're colleagues."

Salzman winked at them the way a shark winks at a guppy before swallowing it and closed the office door.

Bayliss and Nelson walked to the elevator.

"Do you think he means it?" said Bayliss. "About the spiders and mooks?"

"Who? Captain Twitchy? Nah. He's just trying to make his quota of diabolical prick points."

"I could use a drink," said Bayliss.

"I could use a brewery. Let's get out of here."

NINETEEN

FAST EDDIE SAT WITH HIS BACK TO THE WALL AT A table in a strip joint called La Belle Captive. Racer X and Harrison had been drinking shots with him for the past two hours. The name of the place made Racer X suspicious. He didn't speak much French, but he was sure the word *captive* meant the same thing in every language. So far, the only thing captive had been his wallet, but he kept his eyes open for anything fishy.

Harrison seemed cool, but Racer X's head swam. However, he refused to let on that he was drunk. He was afraid Fast Eddie might find another elevator shaft to push him into.

"It was a good job," Eddie said. He'd been saying it every few minutes since they'd been at the club. Racer X noted that at first Eddie had been merely saying it. Now he was growling it like a bulldozer someone was running on meth instead of gasoline.

A pretty redhead in a cutoff *Little Mermaid* T-shirt sat down next to Racer X. "Hi. I'm Ariel," she said.

"Ariel. That's a pretty name," Racer X said.

"Thanks! What's your name?" said Ariel.

"His name is fuck off," said Fast Eddie. "All our names are fuck off. So fuck off."

Ariel shoved her chair back and stood. Racer X reached into his pocket with drunk numb fingers and handed her a twenty.

She looked at it and said, "Thanks. At least there's one gentleman at this table."

"He's not a gentleman. He's making a charitable donation to the Home for Wayward Skanks," said Eddie. Ariel gave him the finger. As she walked away he shouted, "He's going to need a receipt for that twenty." Drunk, Fast Eddie's laugh was like a hacksaw and an angle grinder making sweet love.

Harrison shook his head. "You're in a mood and a half tonight," he said.

Fast Eddie swallowed his shot. "It was a good job."

"Yeah. It was," Racer X said. "Sucks that it got all twisted up like it did."

Eddie shook his head. "Not bad luck. Bad associates. What was Coop doing there?"

"Working, by the look of things," said Harrison.

"Exactly," Fast Eddie said. "And what are the odds of us both working the same building on the same night at the same time?"

"You think he knew we were on the job?" said Racer X.

"No question. What I want to know is what he was after."

A brunette sat down at their table.

"Hi. I'm . . ."

"Not interested," said Fast Eddie. "Tell the other girls this is a business conference, not prom night at Hayseed High. And tell the bartender to send over another round of drinks."

"Sure thing. Should I have him spit in all of them or just yours?"

"Dealer's choice, sweetheart," said Fast Eddie as she stalked away.

Racer X leaned forward. "Eddie, man, we've been here all night and you've brushed off like a dozen girls. What are we doing in a strip club if we don't want to meet them?"

Fast Eddie waved a dismissive hand. "I can enjoy tits without wanting to talk to them," he said.

Racer X looked at Harrison. His brother shook his head slightly, telling him not to poke the bear. Racer X took the opportunity to shut up.

"So, what happens now?" said Harrison. "Are we going to hunt down a new job?"

Fast Eddie shook his head. "No. The other job isn't over yet. We didn't get the goods, so there was no payday. That's unacceptable."

"What are we going to do about it?"

"I don't give a Tallahassee fuck what you Girl Scouts do, but I'm going to find Coop. I'm going to ask him questions and other things."

"What kind of other things?" said Racer X.

"I'm going to make his slow demise a personal priority."

Racer X ran the words over in his head a couple of times to make sure he'd heard them right. Then he turned and looked at the girls. There were a lot of them. Drinkers, too. If he bolted for the door right now, he could get lost in the crowd. But what would happen then? Stupid question. *Then I'll be a loose end. On the same list as Coop.* He didn't know what kind of demise Fast Eddie had in mind for the other thief, but he'd seen the contents of Eddie's tool bag. Now he wished he hadn't. Now he wished he'd worked a little harder at his online trade school classes. By now, he could be repairing air conditioners in Miami, sipping mai tais with pretty girls, and not sitting next to a psychotic car crusher waiting for a tray of drinks he knew would have more spit in them than booze. He closed his eyes and pictured clean white beaches and blue water, and knew that he absolutely, 100 percent wasn't going to cry.

TWENTY

THE DARK HIGH MAGISTER OF THE CLADIS ABADDONIS

Lodge sat on his golden throne, though if you were being picky, it wasn't really gold. Also, for those still insisting on pickiness, it wasn't really a throne. It was a gilt Barcalounger, because of the Dark High Magister of the Cladis Abaddonis Lodge's back, which today hurt like "two bitches fighting on the bitch float in a bitch parade." (The Dark High Magister had been married once and it hadn't worked out.)

"Come forward, Adept Six, and tell me, have you collected this month's tithes from the other Lodge members?"

Adept Six stepped up to the Dark High Magister's throne and placed a purple velvet bag on the silver TV tray next to the holy Barcalounger. "Yes, Dark High One. It's in here."

The Magister reached out a hand and winced as a shooting pain went up his spine. He picked up the bag and bounced it in his hand a couple of times. "It feels light."

Adept Six hung his head and said, "It is, Dark High One. We've lost a few members recently."

"Why is that?"

Acolyte Three, the only other member of the Lodge who'd bothered to stop by that day, said, "The head of Cladis Abaddonis in San Diego has a Volvo dealership. He's offering very good financing terms to any members of the other Lodges who leave theirs and join his."

The Magister thought for a minute and nodded gravely. "What kind of terms?"

"A forty-eight-month lease. Full warranty for three years. No money down."

The Magister settled back deeper into his throne. "Those are nice cars. And good terms."

"Yes, Dark High One," said Adept Six. "Plus, he's throwing in a Bluetooth radio for free."

"For free?" said the Magister. "That bunch has always been a thorn in my side."

"Yes, sir. They're a disgrace to Lord Abaddon," said Acolyte Three.

"But clever."

"Yes," said Adept Six and Acolyte Three together.

"San Diego dicks," said the Magister, and cleared his throat to cover it up. He felt bone weary and fragile. He hated being old. He had enough stents in his heart that the staff called him Iron Man when they thought he couldn't hear. He'd been sent to a hospice twice and was once pronounced clinically dead for six minutes. He had finally been revived by a combination of mystical herbs and pure hate. Hate for the other Lodges, and hate for those Caleximus bastards who had cursed him with a second-rate heart, a bad back, and old age. He wasn't supposed to age. He was a Dark High Magister. There was no doubt in the Magister that this was anything but a curse. It never occurred to him that running a fish-and-chips place on Skid Row and a lifetime of fried food might have more to do with his blood pressure and cholesterol than hexes.

"How many are left?" he said.

"Adepts and Acolytes?" said Adept Six.

"No. Tea cozies and shoe trees. Of course, Adepts and Acolytes."

"At least a dozen, Dark High One."

"What does 'at least' mean? More than a dozen?"

Adept Six pursed his lips, shook his head. "No. Just the twelve."

The Magister sighed. "A sad state for a once-great Lodge," he said.

"Yes. Sad," said Acolyte Three.

"We were feared once. Los Angeles was the biggest Lodge in the country."

"Yes, great. And feared."

"Then it all went wrong."

"Yes, Dark High One," said Adept Six.

"Why do you think?" said the Magister. Adept Six didn't say anything. He turned to the Acolyte.

Acolyte Three cleared his throat. "Well, sir, it might have been the d's."

"Sadly, you might be right," mumbled the Magister.

Some of the most vicious fights between the Cladis Abaddonis Lodges were over spelling. Over the centuries, quite a few knives had ended up in quite a few backs over whether their god's name was Abaddon or Abbadon. Besides that, there was also the tension over the phrase *Cladis Abaddonis* itself. It was the particular kind of problem faced by almost all secret societies at some point. Basically, no one in the Lodge really knew how Latin worked. They all liked the name Cladis Abaddonis because it had an official and mysterious ring to it, but no one knew if it made any sense. And they couldn't ask for help because it would mean revealing sacred Lodge secrets. In the end, the Lodges all crossed their fingers and hoped for the best. And counted themselves lucky for being so enigmatic that few outside the group knew their name.

"I suppose we should discuss the Frank situation," said the Magister.

Adept Six and Acolyte Three flinched at the mention of a Lodge member's real name. It was Frank's own fault. Both knew that everyone else had passed the initiation rites and earned a Lodge degree. There was only one Magister, but plenty of Adepts and Acolytes. However, Frank could never quite get his shit together enough to get higher than, well, Frank. It was the Lodge's secret shame.

The Magister sighed. "Now that Frank is dead, I guess we can talk about the elephant in the room."

"What elephant is that?" said Adept Six.

"Are you being cute?" said the Magister.

Adept Six shook his head.

"How about you, Acolyte?"

Acolyte Three shook his head, too.

"Christ," said the Magister and dropped his head into his hand. After a moment he said, "Frank was ripping us off."

"Ripping us off how?" said the Acolyte.

"Ripping us off! What part of ripping us off don't you get? He was stealing sacred objects and selling them on eBay. Sometimes to hippie-bead, holy-roller, spiritual nut jobs."

Acolyte Three's eyes narrowed. "Does this have something to do with room 8?"

The Magister nodded gravely. "It has everything to do with room 8."

The Acolyte made a face. "Is that the one that's starting to smell?"

"Yes. So, you haven't actually been inside?"

"No, Dark High One. Should I?"

"Only if you want to lose your breakfast," said Adept Six. "And I mean all the breakfasts you ever ate."

"I don't understand."

"Frank blew up. Or, more likely, was blown up," said the Magister. "Did you ever see that video where they dynamited a whale on a beach in Oregon?"

Acolyte Three nodded excitedly. "Yes, sir. It's pretty awesome, Dark High One."

"Well, imagine if that happened inside. In this building. To Frank. In room 8."

"He exploded?"

"Like a poodle in a microwave," said Adept Six. "It's like someone painted the room with beef chili."

"I thought it was more like a hundred pounds of head cheese," said the Magister.

"That too, Dark High One."

Acolyte Three swayed. "Do you mind if I sit, sir? I'm not feeling so good."

"Of course. Get him a chair, Adept," said the Magister.

Adept Six went to the back of the room and came back with a folding chair. He set it down and Acolyte Three dropped into it heavily.

"Put your head between your knees," said the Magister.

The acolyte leaned over and said, "Yes, Dark High One," his voice muffled by his legs.

"I swear, if you puke here in the sacred chamber . . ."

"I won't."

"I mean, this place smells bad enough, what with the grease from the fryers downstairs and the fumes from room 8."

"It'll be okay. I promise," said Acolyte Three.

"Good boy," said the Magister. "So, Adept Six, what are we doing about the room?"

"Well, Dark High One, a few of the other Adepts and Acolytes have taken turns cleaning it, but they can only work so long. I mean, you've seen it."

"Yes. Yes. I understand. Still, we need to get on it."

"I understand. We're making good headway. We need to get some bleach and a few of those paint respirators."

The Magister narrowed his eyes. "And I suppose you want to use Lodge money for the cleaning supplies."

Adept Six shifted his weight uncomfortably. "Well, it is sort of Lodge business, sir."

"How much?"

"I have a list of what we need in my jacket. If you'll wait a minute . . ."

The Magister waved a hand at him. "Down, boy. I trust you. Here, take this," he said and handed the tithe bag back to the adept. "Take it out of there, but I want change. And receipts."

"Yes, Dark High One," he said. "Thank you."

The Magister shook his head. "Ever since we lost the meeting space in Burbank, it's been one thing after another. We need to get room 8 back in service. The restaurant downstairs isn't bringing in enough to even pay the taxes on this building. We need tenants and we need them yesterday."

"We're on it," said Adept Six.

The Magister leaned forward to get a better look at Acolyte Three and immediately regretted it as pain shot up his back. "How are you doing down there, Acolyte? Still seasick?"

"I'm doing better, thank you, Dark High One. If I can just stay down here a little longer."

"Of course, of course. Take all the time you need. We don't want two rooms that have to be bleached."

"No, sir. Thank you, sir."

The Magister turned his attention back to Adept Six. "What did you find in there? Anything that might point to who did it?"

Adept Six went to the closet and pulled out a cardboard box with FROZEN COD printed on the side. He brought it to the Magister.

"Show me," said the old man.

Adept Six removed a plastic take-out bag he'd snagged from the restaurant and handed it to the Magister. The old man reached in and pulled out a broken box.

"Ah. I've been looking for that. At least now we know what he was trying to sell."

"An old box?"

"Not just any old box," said the Magister testily. "Well, yes, this happens to be any old box, but I suspect that Frank had convinced whoever turned him into a meat bottle rocket that this was the Convocation Vessel."

"To call back Lord Abaddon? I've never seen it before."

The Magister dropped his hands to his sides. "You're not looking at it now, you ninny. This is just something we have around for paper clips."

"Oh. Sorry."

"What a little shit he was, trying to run off with one of our holiest relics. He almost deserved what he got."

"I'm sure you're right, Dark High One."

The Magister pushed his ass back farther on the golden Barcalounger to straighten his back. "Do you have anything else in your toy chest?"

Adept Six set down the box and started going through the other bags inside. "Mostly it's bits and pieces, so to speak. A class ring. Frank's Lodge medallion. A few teeth, some with gold fillings. We thought maybe his family might want some of the stuff."

"Is that all?"

"A couple of things, but this is the most interesting." Adept Six handed the Magister a folded piece of paper, which, though dry, was stained a rusty red with Frank sauce.

The Magister opened the paper with his fingertips, spreading it out on his lap. He peered at it. "What am I looking at? It's a flyer for a bake sale."

"That's not all, sir. Look at the bottom."

The Magister's eyes weren't what they used to be. He had to squint just to make out the pornographic pastries. "What's that oatmeal raisin cookie doing to the Bundt cake?"

Adept Six reached over the flyer and pointed to the bottom corner. "Look here."

The old man's eyes grew wide.

The Dark High Magister of the Cladis Abaddonis Lodge was one of a long line of priests that stretched back many centuries. The Lodge had been in continuous existence almost since people could scribble on paper. Naturally, as soon as they could scribble shapes, some people didn't want to let other people see them. Only a special few of their choosing. The right kind of people. And they kicked the ass of anyone who peeked. That's basically how secret societies were born. The Cladis Abaddonis Lodge had been one of the first and most secretive of these.

Of course, their existence did come to light during the unpleasantness with the Inquisition and they had to disband for a while. The members were just as devout as ever, but they worshipped privately, having seen what the Inquisition did to anyone it considered a heretic—which, at the time, was pretty much everybody. For a variety of reasons, none of them wanted any hot implements shoved up, in, or around any part of their body. They were quiet for almost four hundred years, popping up again in 1835, after the last Inquisitor put his pointy hood in its pointy hood case and tucked it away with the thumbscrews, iron maidens, and other knickknacks of ecclesiastical persuasion.

On one of the few written tests he'd passed, even Frank had been able to guess who had ratted them out to the Inquisition and forced them underground.

Now those bastards were having a bake sale.

"Is this what I think it is?" said the Magister, squinting harder than ever.

"Yes, Dark High One. It's the seal of the Caleximus cult," said Adept Six.

"Who?" called Acolyte Three, still staring at the floor.

"The Caleximus cult, nefarious ball bags who've made our lives a misery since Lord Abaddon was knee-high to a jellyfish. This will be the bunch who blew up Frank."

Adept Six shrugged. "That makes sense, sir. It was the only mystically related thing we found in there that didn't come from our closet."

The Magister crumpled the paper in his hand. "Then that settles it. They want the box to set off their false Apocalypse before we can set off our true one," he said. "I tell you what, Acolyte Three, we're going cookie shopping, and when we do, we will bring the wrath of Abaddon down on their heads like a shit-ton of bricks."

"Yes, Dark High One!"

"Yay," said Acolyte Three weakly, head still down.

"Anything else in there?" said the Magister. He held up a bag on which someone had scrawled DRY ICE with a marker. "What's in this?"

"We're not sure," said Adept Six. "We need to get it looked at. It might be another clue. Or just a piece of Frank's liver."

That's when Acolyte Three's stomach let go.

TWENTY-ONE

THE BEVERLY CENTER MALL SAT AT THE CORNER OF Beverly Boulevard and La Cienega, on the edge of Beverly Hills in that magical land where residents shopped purely by designer names and not prices. People caught looking at price tags were shunned and, while not physically exiled, mentally dispatched to the same shadowy hinterlands reserved for tourists in flip-flops, accordions, and pre-Dorothy flying monkeys.

When Coop finally exited the Beverly Center, he was both happy and a little shell-shocked. Coop was a price tag looker, and every salesperson in the Center spotted him as one the moment he entered. His clothes were ill-fitting enough that, at best, he'd borrowed them. At worst, he'd held up a Goodwill and stolen the first few things he'd seen on the sales rack. If Coop had known any of the rules of the upscale he might have done what any sensible person in his position would do: stand in the mall's atrium and shout, "I'm an ex-con with money. Dress me for adulthood." At least being a jailbird would have given him the exotic frisson of a Tibetan mastiff puppy or an Abyssinian cat, because there's nothing people with money like to do more than dress up their expensive pets. But Coop didn't know any of this, so he slunk around different men's boutiques, fingering fabrics he'd only heard about in legends, gasping at prices he thought must be in pesos, not dollars, and generally revealing himself to be everything the Beverly Center hated: a reminder that while they were near Beverly Hills, they weren't quite in it, so the broke and the clueless could invade their space at will.

But Coop *was* a jailbird and had done enough time to stroll through other people's loathing without giving much of a shit. And it gave him pure pleasure to watch salespeople's attitudes do a 180 when he pulled out a pile of the cash payoff he'd received from Mr. Babylon.

In the end, even with security guards following him around every store and salespeople giving him the side eye, he walked out of the Beverly Center with two suits, a couple of extra shirts, and a pair of Italian shoes. He didn't quite have the heart to wear either of the suits yet, but after some encouragement from a pretty saleswoman, he'd put on the shoes, a pair of new slacks, and one of the extra shirts. Coop felt like a million bucks as he stood on Beverly Boulevard looking for a cab. He felt slightly less so when a black windowless van pulled up and a man with a gun motioned for him to get inside. Coop was a sensible crook and knew that if he made a break for it in brand-new leather-soled shoes on pavement he was probably going to end up flat on his ass. And maybe with a bullet in the back. So, he did what any sensible crook would do. He got in the van.

Inside, the man with the gun slammed the van door closed and knocked the packages out of Coop's hands.

"Turn around," he said.

Coop did it and felt a blindfold going over his eyes. Then the gunman turned Coop back around and pushed him into a seat across from him. Before the lights had gone out, Coop had seen a young woman in sensible office attire. She didn't look like quite as big a creep as the guy with the gun. When she finally spoke she said, "Would you state your name for the record?"

"Wait," Coop said. "You kidnapped me and you don't know who I am?"

"I just need to verify your identity."

"In that case, I'm Benjamin Harrison, twenty-third president of the United States."

"Please be serious. It will make things easier for everyone, including you."

"Is this a gag?" Coop said, starting to get angry. Then his guts went cold. "Are you working for Eddie?"

"Who's Eddie?" said someone Coop assumed was the gunman.

"Never mind. My poodle groomer. Who are you?"

"Your new best friends.

"If that's the case, why don't you take this blindfold off and we can all have a group hug?"

"Not a chance, sugar pants."

Coop took a deep breath. He hated being this freaked out, but he knew not to show it. He tried to think of something brave to say, but instead all he could croak was, "You sure you're not with Eddie?"

"Is your name Charles Cooper, no middle name?" said the woman.

"No middle name. That's me."

He could hear her typing something into a laptop. When she was finished she said, "Why don't we take off the blindfold? The van is blacked out and he's going to see us soon enough."

"I've already seen you," Coop said.

"See? He's already seen us."

The gunman sounded annoyed. "You suck the fun out of everything."

"He thinks we're here to kill him. That's not a good way to begin a business relationship," said the woman.

"That's what I'm talking about right there. Work, work, work. I bet when you saw *Star Wars* all you thought about was Darth Vader's quarterly review. He lost the princess. He choked an officer."

"Well, he did let the Death Star get blown up," said the woman.

"See? I knew it."

"Please take it off him."

"Fine. But only because I know you won't shut up about it."

"Thank you."

The man jerked Coop's head forward and began fiddling with the blindfold knot. While he did it Coop said, "I know a good marriage counselor in the Valley if you kids want to make a stop."

Finally, the blindfold came off and the gunman shoved Coop back in his seat, slapping a pair of handcuffs on him. "Shut up and go back to worrying about your poodle," he said.

"He's man's best friend," Coop said. He studied the cuffs. They looked well made, with hard locks to pick.

The gunman shook his head. "No. This is man's best friend." He pulled a flask from his pocket and took a drink.

"Mind if I have a snort, seeing as how we're all friends?" Coop held out his hands.

The man with the gun smiled at him and took another drink.

"Why not let him have a little?" said the woman. "It might calm him down."

The gunman thought about it and finally handed Coop the flask. He held it up in a toast and then began to drink. It was bourbon. Good stuff, too.

"Hey, Mr. Greedy, that's enough. We share around here," said the gunman. When he came forward to take the flask out of Coop's cuffed hands, Coop spit a mouthful of whiskey directly into the gunman's eyes. He screamed and wiped at his face with his hands. Coop kicked him on top of the woman, grabbed the sliding door handle, and pulled it open. He didn't know how fast they were going or where they were. It looked suburban and upscale. Coop jumped onto a grassy patch near the curb and rolled as best he could. When he scrambled to his feet, he took off running across a series of impossibly green lawns.

He made it down past a couple of houses and turned abruptly when he saw an open door to a backyard. He ran through. A family—a father, mother, and two kids, a boy and a girl—were having a barbecue. Coop didn't stop. Neither did the father, flipping burgers as he watched Coop, who jumped up the back fence and pulled himself over as gracefully as he could with his handcuffs.

It wasn't all that graceful. He landed on his back. Something behind him squeaked. Coop reached under a butt cheek and came up with a dog's rubber chew toy. A really big one. He wondered what the hell kind of mutant mutt would find a toy like that fun and not just a taunt. He got his answer when said mutt lumbered out of its doghouse and stretched. It was a Rottweiler with a head the size of a Honda Civic. *Okay, it's big. No problem. Stay low. Move slow. I'm not any threat. That's right. You keep stretching there, buddy.* But when the dog turned in his direction and growled, Coop forgot about the Civic.

This thing was a Humvee with shark teeth.

Coop got up slowly, holding his hands before him where the dog could see. He crept across the yard in the direction of the house, saying, "Good dog. Nice puppy," over and over. He concentrated on walking because when he didn't, he imagined himself in pieces in the dog's stomach with nothing but his anklebones sticking out of five-hundred-dollar Italian shoes to mark his grave.

He couldn't help thinking about a dragon in a wall he once knew . . .

Something thumped to the ground behind him. He turned and saw the gunman touching down, the woman close behind him. The dog seemed confused by these new intruders and Coop tried to take advantage of the moment to move a little faster. But the dog's confusion didn't last long. Coop was the original interloper and the monster pooch turned and laser-focused its attention on him. Finally Coop broke into a run.

He didn't stand a chance.

The dog hit him between the shoulders and drove him facefirst into the grass. With the wind knocked out of him, Coop couldn't do anything but lie there. A second later, the dog flopped on top of him like a two-hundred-pound bag of furry cement. A minute after that, he felt the beast being rolled off him. He rose to his knees and took a deep breath. No cracked ribs. No chunks of flesh missing. He looked at the dog on its back beside him, a tranquilizer dart in its neck. The woman put a tranq pistol into a holster under her jacket. The gunman hauled him to his feet and perp-walked him to the fence. The man went over first. The woman indicated for Coop to go next, and she brought up the rear.

The two agents, cops, or kidnapper hobbyists—Coop still hadn't decided which—took him back the way they'd come.

"Looks good," Coop said to the family as the father took a pile of burgers and hot dogs off the grill. None of them said anything. Coop was manhandled back into the van and it took off.

Once they got moving again, the gunman said, "You tell anyone you took a runner and I'll make sure you're eaten by a spider."

"Sounds like a big spider," said Coop.

"Remember that dog?

"Yes."

"Bigger."

Coop spit out some grass that had gotten lodged between his teeth. "Do they let you make decisions like that? I get the feeling you're the kind of guy if I asked for a decaf, you'd bring me galoshes."

The woman covered her mouth and tried to suppress a laugh. The gunman shot her a look.

"We've got a world of fun waiting for you, pal. You messed up good."

"Thanks. I wouldn't have known if you hadn't explained it to me," Coop said. He looked at the floor where the man's feet rested near his new clothes. "Please be careful. Most of that stuff is brand new."

The gunman slid open the van door and kicked out the clothes. "Run free, little shirts," he called after them.

Coop looked at him. "Do you know how hard I worked for those clothes?"

"Yep."

"Just checking."

The woman was giving the gunman a disgusted look. "If it's any consolation," she said to Coop, "you're going to get to leave. I have to work with him every day."

"You must spend a lot on Zantac."

"As much as my rent."

"You're both breaking my heart," said the gunman. "And for the record, smart guy, you killed my shirt with the little spitting stunt back there, so I think we're about even."

"I'm being kidnapped and was almost eaten by a T. rex. I don't think we're even close to even," said Coop.

The woman shook her head. "This isn't really a kidnapping. Think of it as aggressive job recruitment."

"Don't tell him anything else," the gunman said.

"What kind of benefits?" said Coop.

"What?"

"The recruitment. How much vacation time? You have a dental plan? Stock options?"

"There's only one benefit. I don't shoot you."

"That's a good one," said Coop.

"I thought you'd like it."

Coop sat back as the van rumbled on to wherever the hell it was rumbling to. There wasn't anything he could do about it. He went back to trying not to look scared. In fact, he was less anxious than he had been a few minutes before. He'd run and hadn't been shot. They'd even saved him from being devoured by Cujo. They obviously wanted him for something. He hoped it was something he could handle. He felt bad because one bag of clothes the shithead kicked out of the van had been the ones he borrowed from Morty. He considered for a minute whether that made up for Morty ratting him out and landing him in jail.

Nope, he decided. But it was close.

They drove for another thirty minutes. The gunman kept his pistol aimed at Coop the whole time.

"Your bosses don't mind you pointing guns at people when you're half crocked?" Coop said.

The gunman took another drink. "It cuts down on the office riff-raff."

"Do they have a special form for when you shoot your dick off?"

The woman snickered again. She pecked at her laptop. Coop quickly went from panicky to nervous to bored.

Finally, the van slowed, made an abrupt left turn, and went down a short incline before stopping.

"We're here, Cinderella. Time to meet your prince," said the gunman. He slid the side door open and stepped down. All Coop could see was what looked like an underground parking garage. Yellow lines on the ground spaced a few feet apart. Other vans. Concrete support columns. He stepped out and the woman followed.

"Pull a runner here, pal, and I'll be the least of your worries," said the gunman.

"In the future, you should say that with a Clint Eastwood squint. It'll scare more rubes." Yet as much as Coop lipped off, he didn't want to move. He hovered near the van and looked around. Yes, it was nothing but an underground parking lot. He was both relieved and disappointed. After all the drama, he'd expected a secret lair in a dormant volcano or an abandoned missile silo. This looked like the basement of a Walmart. At least it wasn't a police station. He'd been in enough of those that he could smell them.

"Where are we?" said Coop.

"Disneyland. Be good and I'll let you take a picture with Daffy Duck."

"You mean Donald Duck. Daffy Duck is Warner Brothers, not Disney."

"Christ," said the gunman. "You and her ought to get married and have boring babies."

"It's not my fault. You've got to do your research if you're going to taunt people properly."

"I should have let the dog eat you."

"But then I wouldn't be around to help you with your duck problem. Admit it. I'm already an asset."

The gunman put the pistol in Coop's ribs and pushed him. "Move it, Al Capone. That way."

The gunman and the woman walked Coop to a heavy metal door. There was a screen on the side. When the woman put her hand on it, the screen lit up with wild patterns like a wiring diagram combined with an astrological chart. A needle popped out of the wall. She touched it, leaving a drop of blood on the end. More lights and patterns. The screen turned green and flashed WELCOME BACK. The metal door opened.

"Ouch," said Coop. "You have to do that every time you go in?"

"Every time," said the woman.

"Do they at least give you a lollipop?"

"Quiet," said the gunman.

If this is what they do to their own people, what are they going to do to me? thought Coop. What if his driver's license wasn't enough to prove who he was? He imagined himself turned into a pincushion while they took quarts of blood. Coop really, really hated needles. When he was five and a doctor tried to give him a measles shot, he'd bitten the guy. While the doctor went to get his mother, Coop had climbed onto a table, pushed one of the overhead tiles out of the way, and crawled into the ceiling. Careful to step only on the brackets, he made it all the way to the front lobby and outside. It was his first escape and still his proudest. But there weren't any ceiling tiles here, just a masochist and a guy who wanted to shoot him. *Maybe I should have stayed in jail.*

Beyond the door was a long, painted cinder-block hallway. He'd been in enough of those during break-ins that he felt a little more at home there. Still, where was he?

As they walked, the woman said, "I'm Bayliss. The gentleman with the gun is Nelson."

"That's Mr. Nelson to you, convict," said the gunman.

"Should I call you Charles or Charlie?" said Bayliss.

"Coop," he said. "Only my brother called me Charlie."

"Were you close with your brother?"

"If by close you mean we couldn't stand each other, then yeah, we were the Partridge Family."

"That's too bad. My brother and I are good friends."

"Don't listen to this crook's sob stories," said Nelson. "Next he'll tell you he had to walk ten miles through the snow to go to kindergarten and sell his puppy to buy medicine for his grandma."

"Don't mind him. He's cranky because he hasn't had a drink in the last two minutes," said Bayliss.

They came to a row of elevators and one of the doors opened for them. Nelson pushed Coop inside and hit the button for the sixth floor. The floors they passed were labeled ELDRITCH HORRORS, INTER-

DIMENSIONAL HORRORS, SUPERSCIENCE HORRORS, MISCELLANEOUS HORRORS, and PING-PONG TOURNAMENT. Coop braced himself for whatever kind of grotesque shit would be waiting on 6. The ride lasted just a few seconds. Despite the gun in his back, he braced himself to run.

The elevator pinged and the doors slid open. Coop could already feel the bullet in his back, but damned if he was going down without a fight.

What lay before him was the most boring scene he'd ever laid eyes on. Just a lot of men and women all in suits, sitting in cubicles, carrying papers and laptops around. *Have I been kidnapped by accountants?* If he lived, that was going to be hard to explain to Morty. "These people picked me up at gunpoint and forced me to memorize depreciation tables."

They got on another elevator and Nelson stood in front of the number pad, so Coop couldn't see where they were going. *If these people really are a bunch of desk jockey weirdos, it isn't going to be hard to escape. With the money I made from Babylon, I can probably get a fake passport and head for Mexico.*

The doors opened again and they stepped out into an enormous room that looked like where NASA assembled orbiting death rays. Men and women in lab coats manhandled strange machines of all shapes and sizes. A bald scientist was being chased by a little ball-shaped robot covered in rotating blades. Another couple of Einsteins had a strange rifle. Every time they shot a target it changed. First into a typewriter. Then a pile of 78 records. Then a puzzled-looking lemur. A couple of heads in what looked like aquariums were having an earnest conversation with a guy holding up a blueprint so they could see it. Something that looked like a starfish in granny glasses took a clipboard from one of the scientists and walked through a wall. *How about that,* thought Coop. It was the only thing his overloaded brain could come up with right then. *How about that.* He kept walking, trying not to look too hard at the science circus, but keeping an eye out in case there was a good place to run.

It seemed a lot less likely up here than with the pencil pushers downstairs.

"Welcome to the DOPS, the Department of Peculiar Science," said Bayliss.

"The what of what?" said Coop.

"The Department of Peculiar Science. I know it's a strange name. I guess all those years ago when they came up with it, it was very cutting edge. But it does sound a little old-fashioned, doesn't it?"

"Or psychotic—like all these people."

"We hear that from a lot of first-timers. What we do here is study and learn how to defend the world from all sorts of scientific and thaumaturgic anomalies."

"You mean you're the Ghostbusters."

"We do a lot more than chase ghosts, but yes, we chase them sometimes, too."

"I'm not sure what you want from me, but I really don't think I belong here," said Coop.

"Neither do I, but it was bring you in or shoot you," said Nelson. "There's still time to go the other way."

"No. I'm good."

They went out into another hallway and into an unmarked room. To Coop's relief, it was just an office, with chairs around a big table, a phone, and a computer in the corner. He'd never been so happy to be somewhere so damned boring. Nelson pushed him into a chair, then he and Bayliss sat down across from him. Nelson finally put the pistol away.

Coop started to say something, but Nelson shushed him. A minute later, a tall, hawkish man with strange, milky eyes came in. He looked at Coop.

"I see you brought him in. Good choice. Though I think we could have made good use of him in the post-life department. Still, there's always time for that. Hello, Mr. Cooper."

Coop didn't like the guy's eyes. They didn't look quite real, but he looked into them anyway. It was like staring at two fried eggs. The weird part is that it made him kind of hungry. When had he eaten last? The man sat down.

"Hi," said Coop. "Who the fuck are you?"

"I'm Mr. Salzman. I'm in charge of this and that around here. Which includes you. And them," he said, indicating Bayliss and Nelson. "Basically, they're your bosses and I'm their boss."

"Lucky me," said Coop. "Bosses for what exactly?"

Salzman looked at Coop. "You're still cuffed, I see. If you promise to be a good boy, we can do something about that."

"Cross my heart and hope to die," said Coop.

"I hope that, too. Uncuff him, Nelson."

Nelson didn't get up. He dug around in his pocket and when he came up with the key, slid it across the table. Coop picked it up and, after a couple of awkward minutes, unlocked the cuffs. He slid them across the table to Nelson. It felt good to have his hands free again.

A row of strange symbols crawled across an LCD screen on the far wall.

"What the hell is that?" said Coop.

Salzman didn't bother to look. "We think it's the last will and testament of a demigod who lived around here approximately ten thousand years ago."

"A demigod? You hang out with a lot of them around here?"

"More gods than hoodlums."

"Me, too. Let's be friends."

Salzman moved his gaze from Coop to a green file folder on the table and said, "You've been filled in on what we do around here?"

"Yeah, but it's a funny place to repair stereos."

Salzman smiled. "Stereos. Yes. And you're going to help us fix the biggest stereo of all."

Coop rubbed his wrists and said, "Yeah? And what's that?"

Salzman took a photo from the green folder and slid it to Coop. He looked at it and saw a familiar fat face.

"I understand that you know this man," said Salzman.

"Yeah. He's a big spender who calls himself Mr. Babylon. Not that I buy the Babylon part."

"No. That's his real name," said Salzman. "He's a magician of sorts."

"That's funny. He told me he couldn't even shuffle cards."

"He lied. Babylon had a decent little occult criminal empire going at one point. But he's old and his power is fading. That's why he hired you and your merry pranksters to find the box."

Coop shrugged. "He said it was a family heirloom."

"Another lie. Would you like to know what it is?"

All Coop wanted was to get out of there, but he'd been grilled enough times to know he had to let the scene play itself out. "Sure. If it's not for Aunt Sadie's earrings, what is it?"

"It's a bomb, you moron," said Nelson.

"That's not quite it, but it is as deadly as a bomb," said Salzman. "What's in the box is a device capable of destroying the world's electronic infrastructure, sending us back to the nineteenth century. Think of it. Planes would fall from the sky. Satellites would spin out of control. Hospitals couldn't perform surgery."

Coop didn't say anything for a minute. He just scanned the room and their faces. He'd been stealing things and running scams pretty much since he could walk and he was good at picking out liars. What bothered him was that none of these lunatics seemed to be lying. Babylon was the liar. He'd stuck him with a bomb after all.

"You sure all that's in there? It wasn't a very big box," said Coop.

"Trust me. That's in there."

Coop opened and closed his hands. "That sounds like a big deal for the world, Mr. Salzman. But what does it have to do with me?"

"You stole the box for Babylon. Now you're going to steal it for us."

Coop leaned forward. "Excuse me? I just saw Buck Rogers gear and a fucking fish who could walk through walls in the other room. If you want the box so much, why don't you send one of those Buzz Lightyears, or Hansel and Gretel here, and get it back yourself?"

"Because you stole it," said Salzman. "Now it's your responsibility to get it back before Babylon sells it to some rogue state and ends the world."

Coop looked at Salzman. He looked at Bayliss and Nelson. "You don't want me. You just want a fall guy in case we all end up wearing top hats and bustles. Which you'd look dashing in, by the way."

"Shut up," Nelson said.

"Not you," said Coop, turning to Nelson. "You're more the bearskins and raw meat type."

"An apt description," said Salzman. "We want the box and you don't want to go back to jail. And you will go to jail if you say no to us."

Coop looked at Salzman's fried-egg eyes and knew he'd do it. "Even if I get the box back, how do I know you won't turn around and send me to jail anyway?"

"You don't, but if you refuse to work for the DOPS, I'll see that you do life. Maybe longer."

Coop didn't like the sound of that last part. He thought about it for a minute and said, "Even if I say yes, I'm not a skip tracer. How am I supposed to find Babylon?"

"Let us worry about that. We have someone who can help you."

"Who?"

"We'll come to that later. Do you agree to our terms?" said Salzman.

"Not yet," said Coop. "If I get the box back, what do I get?"

"You're free to go and return to your rich and rewarding world of stealing hubcaps and ripping off candy stores. The DOPS is in the business of protecting the world, not chasing pickpockets."

"I haven't picked a pocket since I was sixteen."

"Nice to hear that you're a reformed man."

Coop looked at Bayliss and Nelson. Bayliss was staring at her laptop screen, looking uncomfortable. She didn't like rough stuff like this. Good to know. Nelson, on the other hand, looked at Coop like he wanted to grill him over mesquite coals and serve him with a baked potato.

"Okay," Coop said. "But I get to pick my own crew. People I know I can trust."

Salzman shook his head. "We have plenty of competent people in the DOPS who can help you. Just let us know what you need."

"No deal."

Salzman tapped his finger on the green file folder. Coop was sick of seeing green file folders. They were nothing but trouble.

"Let's compromise," said Salzman. "You get to pick one of your criminal associates. He or she will get the same deal as you. Jail or freedom."

"Fine. I want Morty for my Flasher. But I want to meet your people before I agree to work with them."

"That's not a problem. In fact, I think you know some of our agents."

"Who?"

"Phil Spectre seems to think highly of you."

Coop stood up. "No. Not Phil. I will not work with him again."

Nelson reached for his gun, but Salzman motioned for him to stop. He got out his phone and punched in a number. "Hello, Doris. Would you have the West twins bring in those dossiers for me? Thanks."

They sat and waited. The demigod gibberish rolled by like supernatural chicken scratches. In a few minutes, two people came in, although calling them people was being more than a little charitable. One of the West twins was a dark-haired bearded man's head on a kind of octopus's body. The other twin had an octopus head on a human body. They each dropped another goddamned green folder on the table in front of Salzman. The analytical criminal part of Coop's brain was kind of fascinated by the sideshow, but the rest of his brain wanted to claw his eyes out. Coop dropped back down into his seat.

On their way out, Salzman said, "Thanks, boys. See you Saturday for softball." He looked at Coop. "You haven't even been in the abracadabra wing of the building yet, have you, Mr. Cooper? We'll get you over there in due time. My point in calling in the West boys is to remind you that there are worse things than jail. Herbert and Jimmy had a little accident recently. But the thing is, in Peculiar Science, accidents happen all the time. And they can happen to anyone."

Coop nodded. "I get it. I say no and I'm back in jail or I'm a cup of clam juice. Point made. But Phil is trouble. And I'll need a Marilyn if I'm going to do your job. You should let me call Sally Gifford. I don't have to tell her that I'm working for Cobra Command."

Salzman waved a finger at him. "Sorry, but that's a no. We have someone much better in mind."

"Who?"

A side door that Coop hadn't noticed earlier opened and a woman in red came in. She smiled, and Coop's heart missed a step and fell down the stairs.

"I believe you know Giselle," said Salzman.

She smiled a big wolf smile. "Hi there, Coop. You miss me?"

He smiled back. "Like chicken pox."

TWENTY-TWO

THE ROOM WAS CROWDED AND HOT. EVERYONE WAS shoved into one corner of the construction site office because Steve hadn't moved the furniture out of the way like he did during normal Caleximus services. Even Jerry was uncomfortable, and he'd managed to find a clear spot in a far corner of the room next to some filing cabinets.

"I hope all of you are proud of yourselves," said Steve.

Jerry started to say something, but he knew he'd just be flapping his lips.

"Not only didn't we get the summoning box, but you trampled my boy. About killed him, too."

People shuffled their feet, coughed. It was the first time the congregation had all been together since the running, screaming flameout at the Blackmoore building. Jerry knew that leaving the furniture out was Steve's way of spanking the whole room. And there wasn't a thing he or anyone else could do about it. He looked at the floor, as uncomfortable as anyone. It was nice his dad was sticking up for him, but when he got this way Jerry felt like he was five years old and was never going to get any older.

"Sorry," said Tommy.

"Hope you're okay, man," said someone else. There were other mumbled apologies.

"Don't worry about it. I'm okay. Really," he said.

"The kid's got broken ribs. He's living on Vicodin."

"Dad . . ."

"You're a brave boy, son."

"My poor baby," said Susie.

Jerry didn't say anything.

"What happened back at the building?" said Leonard, the head cement man at the site.

"Where's Lloyd?" said Jorge.

"What were those horrible bugs?" said Clarice, Janet's mother.

Steve held his hands up. "I already had a heart-to-heart with young Lloyd. And after much, sometimes loud, consultation . . ."

People around the room laughed quietly.

"I don't think he knew anything about those other people in the building."

"What about the bugs?" said a woman from the back of the room.

"Lloyd said the exterminator had just been through the building, so there shouldn't have been any bugs."

"Well, there were."

"I think Kevin peed himself a little," said Tommy.

"I did not!" said Kevin.

"So what, you dropped a Mountain Dew down the front of your pants?"

"Fuck you, Tommy."

"All right, everyone. Let's try to focus," said Steve.

"The bugs weren't in the building. That guy had them," said Clarice. "The one the big biker called Coop."

"Which one was the biker?" said Susie.

"The biker-looking one."

"The guy with the beard?" said Tommy.

"Yes, the guy with the beard," said Clarice.

"I think he looked more like those guys you see in Silver Lake. What do you call them?" said Jorge.

"Assholes?" said Kevin.

"Hipsters," said Jorge.

"I thought he was kind of cute," said Janet. "He had a kind of Jeremiah Johnson thing."

"Who's Jeremiah Johnson?" said Susie.

"I think he was the bass player in Lynyrd Skynyrd," said Tommy.

"That biker guy played in Lynyrd Skynyrd?" said Kevin. "Cool."

"Who's Lynyrd Skynyrd?" said Clarice.

"They did that song. 'Free Ride.'"

"That was the Edgar Winter Group," said Tommy. "Lynyrd Skynyrd did 'Free Bird.'"

"That's an awesome song," said Leonard. By the generally positive tone of the murmurs, most people seemed to agree that "Free Bird" was awesome.

"It might be the best goddamned song ever written, but that biker we saw did not play bass in Lynyrd Skynyrd," said Steve.

"Yeah, that was Ed King," said Janet.

"Thank you. Now, may we get back to the other night, please?" said Steve. "Clarice was right. The guy with the bugs was called Coop. Does anybody recognize that name?"

"Besides from the other night?" said Leonard.

"Yes. Besides from the other night."

"Then no."

"Anyone else?"

People just shook their heads.

Steve said, "I had a feeling. Well, the biker didn't walk out with the box and the rest of you were too busy trampling Jerry to get it. My guess is that guy Coop got it."

"What are we going to do?" said Jerry.

"We're going to find him."

"How?"

"Good question. Jorge?"

Jorge took a very small step forward in the very tight space. "I know a private detective. He helped me with my first divorce."

"There might be something else we can do," said Jerry.

"What's that?" said Steve.

"Did anyone notice that those people with Coop were sort of invisible when we first got there? If that big guy hadn't fallen, they might have walked right past us."

"Yeah. They weren't there, then they were," said Janet.

"Right. I was thinking that maybe they were using, you know, magic."

The congregation laughed quietly.

"Son, you're on a lot of Vicodin. There's no such thing as magic," said Steve.

"But isn't Caleximus magic?" said Jerry.

"You're mixing things up. Gods don't use tricks and hocus-pocus. Our lord Caleximus has powers that are so much more powerful than any magic that they transcend our mere mortal understanding."

"Okay, but maybe there are a few people who *can* do magic. There's a place I heard about. People call it Jinx Town. They say there's magic stuff and strange people there."

"Who told you that?" said Steve.

"Charlie, the drywall foreman."

"Charlie? That guy is higher than a Rastafarian koala. Dumber, too."

"Okay, but I've heard stuff from other people."

Steve came over and put a hand on Jerry's shoulder. "There's no such thing as magic, son. Those people used some kind of trick to be invisible."

"I bet it was mirrors," said Leonard.

"They carried a bunch of mirrors with them to a robbery?" Jerry said.

"That's how David Copperfield disappears ladies in his show."

"This isn't Vegas, dumb-ass," said Tommy. "It was an office building."

"Okay. How do you think they did it?"

"Gas. Some kind of hypno gas."

"That's as stupid as magic," said Clarice.

"It is not. The government uses it all the time to get us to buy stuff and make people gay."

"What the hell are you talking about?" said Janet.

"Listen," said Steve. "I don't care if it was mirrors, gas, or if they grew feathers and flew away on wings of song. None of that's going to help us find them. That's why we need a P.I."

"How are we going to pay for that?" said Tommy.

"The money comes out of the general fund."

The congregation groaned.

Steve shook his head. "Relax. I have a feeling that Coop guy is a big deal and won't be hard to find. And we can make up some of the cost of a P.I. with a good bake sale."

"Dad, I want to help," said Jerry.

"You will. You'll be working with your mom rounding up the pies and cakes and whatnot."

Jerry's stomach tightened, like it wanted to kick his dad in the head. *No,* he thought. *No.* He started to say something. *Oh, forget it.*

Susie came over and brushed a lock of hair from his forehead. "Don't sulk, dear. It will be fun."

"Yeah. Sure it will, Mom."

"I guess that's it for now," said Steve. "Be sure to get with Susie and let her know what you're bringing to the sale. We don't want to end up with fifty Bundt cakes. Is there any other business?"

"Let me just be one hundred percent about something," said Leonard. "The biker wasn't in Lynyrd Skynyrd?"

"No. He was in the Edgar Winter Group," said Kevin.

"Then who was in Lynyrd Skynyrd?"

"Your mom," said Janet.

Before Leonard could reply Steve said, "Meeting adjourned. Hail Caleximus."

"Hail Caleximus," said the congregation.

As people talked with his mother or went outside to smoke, Jerry stayed by himself in the corner by the filing cabinets. *No one is sticking me with a bake sale. Not this time. I'll show all of you something you've never seen before.*

The map was acting strangely again. It was old and sometimes seemed like it was starting to get senile. The lines of force and stars grew fuzzy, stuttering across its face. Sometimes they stopped completely and the map turned to static like an old TV screen. Then Qaphsiel had to bang it against something hard to get it working again. Still, it had brought him here, and he could feel that it was the right place to be. Only a couple of days too late.

Qaphsiel stood at the corner of Fifth Street and Flower, with a view of the Blackmoore Building and the Ketchum Insurance Tower. None of the streetlights were working. A PG&E crew stood around a hole that looked like it had been gnawed in the street. A few cricketlike bugs hopped around the repair crew's truck tires, hungrily eyeing the engine wiring.

This close to the buildings, flaring lines moved across Qaphsiel's map from one structure to the other. The box had been here, and recently. A triangle signifying a mortal presence moved along the line and off into the void. Qaphsiel touched the triangle and willed it larger. The image grew, but the map stuttered and lost the image, though not before he caught a glimpse of a sandy-haired man in his thirties. *Finally, after all these years, a face.* Where the man had gone after being near the box, Qaphsiel couldn't say. But the map had been pointing to Hollywood for days. That's where he'd find the sandy-haired man. He was certain. *Oh, good. How many people are there in Hollywood? Not more than a million or so.* Still, it was the best news he'd had in a long time.

The afternoon was warm and Qaphsiel was hot in his Windbreaker. His wings were pressed tightly against his back, and they held in every degree of heat. Years ago, he'd had a little green plastic fan. It worked on batteries and if you put it near your face it created a tiny breeze. *What did I do with that?* He checked all his pockets. No. It wasn't there. There were a couple of tourist shops on the bottom floor of some of the nearby hotels and office buildings that probably carried them, but he was stuck with the eternal dilemma: the only currency he could produce was gold. That had been fine a few thousand years ago. Even a hundred years ago it hadn't been so bad. But in this modern world no one trusted anyone. *I need to find a new pawnshop.* He couldn't go to any one shop too often. The first couple of times he'd wander into a shop, the proprietors were usually happy not to question how a guy in a dirty Windbreaker and sneakers could come up with a pile of gold coins. But once or twice was all he could get away with at any one shop. Qaphsiel had pretty much worked the local shops to death. He'd have to go farther out to find cash.

The real problem was that he never seemed to be able to hold onto mortal money even when he had it. That was the whole conundrum with sleeping outdoors. Paper currency always seemed to flutter right through his hands. He'd wondered many times if clerks in various shops were shortchanging him. The one time he accused a clerk to his face, the guy started to call the police. Qaphsiel had panicked and run away. Over the years he'd dealt with sword-wielding warriors, Praetorian guards, knights, Cossacks, Magyars, Huns, gendarmes, Redcoats, Johnny Rebs, corrupt constables, and every shape, size, and manner of mugger. But he did not want to deal with modern American police. They had too many cars. Too many guns. DNA databases. Fingerprint databases. Photo databases. And considering that his DNA wasn't human, he had no fingerprints, and he couldn't be photographed, it seemed best to steer clear of police altogether.

Someone tapped him on the shoulder. It was an old woman in sunglasses and a Disneyland T-shirt. "Excuse me. Do you know the way to the La Brea Tar Pits?"

"I'm afraid not," said Qaphsiel.

"Oh. I saw your map and thought you might."

He shook his head. "It's not that kind of map. It charts the past, the present, the forces of nature, God, and probability, but not the way to tourist attractions."

"That sounds useful," said the old woman. "Where can I get one?"

"You can't."

"Where did you get yours?"

"From the archangel Gabriel."

The woman frowned. "Is that a Web site?"

"No. Well, maybe he has one these days. I'm not sure," said Qaphsiel. "I don't use computers."

"You sound like my mother," said an old man with the old woman. "She took a course down at the library and now she's on my machine all the time."

"Thank you. I'll certainly consider taking a course."

"Can I have just a peek at your map?" said the old woman.

"It's not for mortal eyes," Qaphsiel said.

"Just a peek?"

Qaphsiel looked past her. "I'm sure they sell maps in one of the malls across the street. Why don't you check there?"

"Does your map show the bus lines?" said the old man.

"No."

"Just a peek?" said the old woman.

"Fine." Qaphsiel turned the map around and held it up where the woman could see. She cocked her head to the side.

"There's nothing on it."

"I told you it's not for mortal eyes."

"Maybe you need to talk to someone about medication," said the old man. "My cousin used to see little lawn flamingos crawling up his legs. Now they've got him on the lithium and he's doing fine."

"Let's go across the street," said Qaphsiel. "Maybe they'll take gold for a map. My treat."

"That's not necessary," said the old woman. "Is there anything interesting to see around *here*?"

Qaphsiel pointed to the Bonaventure. "That building over there recently held the vessel in which is contained the doom of mankind."

"I think my sister used to have one of those," said the old man.

"I seriously doubt it."

"No, I'm sure. She got it in Mexico. Little bitty thing. Hooked it up and we got all the stations. HBO. Showtime. Even the adult ones, if you know what I mean."

Qaphsiel folded the map and put it in a pocket of his Windbreaker "Stealing cable can hardly be compared to the doom of mankind."

"The cable company certainly acted like it was the end of the world," said the old woman. "They threatened to call the police."

Qaphsiel pointed to a young couple up the block. "Look. Those people have a map. I bet you'll be able to see theirs."

"But it's so much more fun to stay and torment you," said the old man.

Qaphsiel looked at them both. When they smiled their teeth were yellow and there were too many of them. "Who are you?"

"Don't you recognize us?"

"No . . . wait. Leviathan and Beelzebub?"

"You got it," the old man, Leviathan, said.

"Would you please just leave me alone?" groaned Qaphsiel, less like a celestial being of the highest order and more like every single mortal child on Earth discovering that no, in fact, they couldn't have Graham crackers right before dinner.

Beelzebub, the old woman, said, "It's been five hundred years. We thought you'd be happy to see us. How often do you get to talk to your own kind?"

"You're not my kind. You serve Lucifer."

"Let's not split hairs," said the old man. "We're the closest thing you have to family down here and just wanted to stop by to remind you that you can always give up this hopeless quest and come over to our side."

"You're not my family, and I'm not going to join you."

"Why not? Face it. If you were going to end the world, you would have done it by now."

"I'm so close. You have no idea," said Qaphsiel. "You'll see. Save your temptations for someone else."

Beelzebub said, "You know that Lucifer will never let you use that box, right? He loves this world too much. So much pain. So much death. So much fun."

Suspicion crept into Qaphsiel's mind. "*You* didn't steal it from me, did you?"

"I'm afraid not. Losing it was all you," said Beelzebub.

"Idiot," Leviathan coughed.

"That's why you should come over to us," she continued. "You should hear the way they talk about you in Heaven."

"No. You're just trying to trick me. I have a destiny."

"Destiny? Watching you is like the worst game show in the history of worst game shows," said Leviathan. He smiled. Qaphsiel thought he saw something crawling between his teeth. "Love your Windbreaker. Very dignified for an angel. Well, have fun being a loser. If you change your mind just give us a call." Leviathan took a business card from his pocket and held it out for him. Something with too many legs to be of this world crawled across its face.

Qaphsiel stepped back. "No, thank you."

The fallen angel shrugged and put back the card. "Maybe not today. But Heaven won't wait forever. Tick tock. Tick tock. Your time is running out."

"Soon, you might not have anywhere else to go but with us," said Beelzebub.

"I'm leaving now," said Qaphsiel.

"Wait," said Leviathan, his voice softening. "It really is our first time in L.A. and we really do want to see the tar pits. Is there a bus?"

Qaphsiel pointed to the Bonaventure. "You can catch a cab at the hotel."

Beelzebub laughed. "A cab? On our budget? Never mind. We'll just steal a bus. I'm sure someone on board will know the way. Well, see you in another five hundred years."

Qaphsiel held up his thumb and forefinger a half inch apart. "I'm this close. You'll see."

Leviathan pinched his cheek. "You're adorable. We'll tell Lucifer you said hello."

"You'll see. All of you." But Leviathan and Beelzebub were just an old man and woman walking in the sun again.

Do they really talk about me in Heaven? Do they even still remember me? I hope nobody's touched my stuff.

Qaphsiel took out the map again. It was nothing but snowy static. He put it away. *I saw his face. He's in Hollywood. I'm so close.*

He turned from where the box had been and began the long walk across town. There was a bang behind him as the repair truck's engine fell onto the street.

TWENTY-THREE

BAYLISS, NELSON, AND SALZMAN LEFT THE OFFICE, leaving Coop and Giselle alone. It was the first time Coop had been alone with her in over two years. In fact, it was already the longest time he'd spent alone with any woman since his arrest. Giselle sat on a table near the door where she'd come in. Coop stayed put in his chair. There was a good twenty feet between them. He would have preferred twenty miles, but this would have to do.

"How are you doing, Coop?" said Giselle.

"I'm being blackmailed by the government. How are you?"

"Don't be so melodramatic."

"Trust me. I'm not being melodramatic enough." He looked at Giselle intently.

"What?"

"It's funny, just the other day I was telling Morty about how someone stole my Contego stone. Where is it?"

Giselle shrugged and ran a fingernail along a scratch on the table. "I didn't exactly steal it. I just borrowed it with extreme prejudice."

"Hilarious. You know, I could have used that stone on some jobs. I didn't always have a Flasher to open doors for me. You made my life a lot harder."

"And for that, I apologize," she said. "But look at it from my point of view. Having it made my life easier."

"That's supposed to make me feel better?"

"Making you feel better didn't really cross my mind at the time."

He sighed. "Why did you even need it? You could cloud some slob's mind and walk into anywhere you wanted."

"True. But what if there was nobody around? It sped things up."

"Oh well, as long as it meant you had more time for scrapbooking or whatever it is you do for fun these days, I guess it's all right."

Giselle crossed her legs and looked at Coop. "So, word is you did a little time recently. I'm sorry to hear that."

Coop picked up a pencil from the table and flipped it into the air, catching it as it came down. "Yeah. A little time."

"How much?"

"You work for Hydra, so I think you already know the answer."

"Hey, I'm just trying to make conversation. Reestablish communication. That kind of thing."

Coop tossed the pencil, caught it, and dropped it on the table, where it spun around like he was playing a sad little solo game of spin the bottle. His heart had stopped trying to break out of his ribs, but it still wanted to leave. Preferably with Coop, but it was open to alternatives.

"So, reestablishing communication means sending a hit squad to grab me off the street?" said Coop.

Giselle shook her head. "That was *not* my idea."

"But you don't mind it happening."

She cocked her head slightly. "Well, I do kind of wish I could have seen your face . . ."

Coop spun the pencil. The damned thing kept pointing to him. "So, what, you're the Girl from U.N.C.L.E. these days?"

Giselle swung her legs as she talked. "I'm just like you. I blew a job and the DOPS showed up and told me that I could join the party or scrub prison toilets for the next fifty years."

"Fifty years? I just got threatened with life. They must love you."

"People sometimes do," she said.

"Don't worry. It'll pass."

She stopped swinging her legs. "After I left, did you look for me?"

"I would have, but it would have cut into my drinking and lying on the floor in a fetal position time."

"I'm sorry. That wasn't what I wanted. I just . . . needed to get some space to clear my head."

Coop thought for a minute. "You know, if someone told me that being kidnapped and locked in a Dr. Who theme park was *not* the weirdest thing that was going to happen to me today, I might not have believed them." He patted himself down for a cigarette, then remembered that they were gone with his new clothes. "Wait a minute. When you stole my stone, is that what I was supposed to do? I was supposed to round up a posse and track you down?"

Giselle glanced around the room. "It would have been nice."

"When you disappeared I was under the impression that you didn't exactly want to see me. If you wanted me to find you, you might have left a trail of bread crumbs or something."

Giselle pointed the toe of one shoe at his torn pants. "What happened to your nice clothes? They're all dirty and ripped."

"Did you ever see *The Great Escape*?"

"Sure."

"I pulled a Steve McQueen."

She nodded. "That's why Nelson likes you so much. You almost got away."

"Almost got away is being generous. But I got to spend some quality time with someone's pet direwolf."

"Yeah, I heard potbellied pigs are out and wolves are in. Was it friendly?"

"Most of it. Just not its teeth."

"I'm sure you could have charmed it if you'd tried."

"I was too busy trying not to look like a T-bone steak."

Giselle smiled at him, but Coop didn't smile back. His face had redeveloped amnesia when it came to smiling.

"What exactly am I doing here?" he said. "What are we supposed to be doing together?"

She came over to the table and sat down a couple of chairs away from him. "It's like Salzman said. The DOPS wants the box. You need to get it for them. And I'm here to help you."

"You had a nose transplant? You're a bloodhound now? Because unless you are, it's like I told your boss: I wouldn't know where to begin finding Babylon."

Giselle wiggled her eyebrows for a second. He'd forgotten she did that when she was about to tell a secret. Coop had a feeling he'd forgotten a lot about her. He'd sure tried hard enough and had the hangovers to prove it.

"I know how to find him," said Giselle. "At least, I know where to start."

"Where?"

"You know Jinx Town?"

"No. What's that?"

"Have you heard of Squid City? Voodoo Beach? Little Midnight? The Fade District? Happy Valley? People call it a lot of things."

Coop nodded. "Oh, yeah. I've heard of it. My brother used to call it Rancho Weirdo."

"Charming. How is Nick?"

"I couldn't tell you."

"You're still not speaking?"

"Yeah. Let's go with that."

Giselle waved a hand dismissively. "Forget him. What did *you* think of Jinx Town?"

"Nothing. I've never been."

She frowned. "Seriously? Why not?"

"Why would I?" He shrugged. "I'm busy. I just never got around to it."

Giselle picked up the pencil Coop had been playing spin the bottle with and spun it. It stopped, pointing to him. She reached over and turned it away. "That's not it," she said. "It's because you're a fuddy-duddy."

"Excuse me?" Coop spun the pencil and it fell off the table.

"Fuddy. Duddy."

"No one's ever called me that before, and I've been called a lot of things."

"Maybe someone should have. You're a fuddy-duddy, Coop."

"I am not."

"If it's any consolation, you weren't always. But you turned into one."

"When? Wait. Don't tell me. Right before you left."

"Not exactly. You'd been that way for a while. But your fuddy-duddiness definitely made leaving easier."

"So happy to make crushing my soul so easy."

"But that's what I'm saying: souls mean . . . vibrancy. You were the total opposite of vibrant. Both fuddy and duddy."

"I was plenty vibrant back then. Vivacious, even. It's just, when we were together, I had a few reversals. Jobs that should have been cinches but went bad."

Giselle put the pencil back on the table. When she leaned over to pick it up, Coop got a quick glimpse down the front of her dress. His heart tapped on his ribs again, letting him know it was late to catch a bus.

"You were always good at your job, you know?" she said. "But you didn't always choose the best partners."

"You sure got that right," he said and immediately regretted it. The look on Giselle's face brought back memories that he'd carefully locked in a steamer trunk, dragged out to sea, and dropped into the Mariana Trench. Now some were floating to the surface like socially awkward jellyfish.

"Look. Sorry," he said.

Giselle got up. "Forget it." She smoothed her skirt and headed for the door. On her way over she said, "Take the elevator down a floor and you can get some new clothes at the company store. It's not really a store. They just call it that. They'll give you the clothes. It's a disguise thing. I'll call and let them know you're coming."

"Fine. Whatever."

She put her hand on the doorknob and turned back to him. "And get something to eat. You look like a whippet in hundred-dollar pants."

"Three hundred. They were three hundred dollars."

"Looks like they were nice, too. I guess you still haven't learned how to hold on to anything." Giselle left and Coop sat in the empty office alone for a few minutes.

That's the nicest way anyone has told me to fuck off in a long time.

It was just like Giselle said. When he went downstairs, they were ready for him. A couple of DOPS flunkies measured him and a woman with a beak and spiny feathers down her back threw clothes at him from a rack until he found a combination that fit and didn't look too much like he'd been bullied by a lady ostrich.

It took him a few minutes to find the employee lunchroom. Brushing feathers off his new clothes, Coop was happy to find he still had a fistful of Babylon's money, so he ate a vending machine chicken salad sandwich, some chips, and a Coke. He would have preferred a real drink. And a real sandwich. Couldn't do much about the latter, but maybe if he hadn't pissed off Nelson so much, he would have shown him where he hid his bottle. Not much chance of that now. Still, he was a thief. If he could find Nelson's desk, he could probably get into it. Coop found a clipboard someone had left in the lunchroom and began wandering the building. No one paid any attention to him in his company threads. He made it up and down three floors before people started giving him funny looks. At that point, he became extremely interested in the papers on his clipboard and calmly made his way back to the empty office.

The alien gibberish had stopped and the LCD screen on the wall was blank. He found a remote nearby and turned it on. After fiddling with the settings for a few minutes, he found he could get a television feed. He flipped between the news and game shows, not really watching, just appreciating the noise. This wasn't exactly how he'd intended to spend time with Babylon's money burning a big hole in his pocket. In fact, being locked in reminded him a little too much of prison. He wondered how Rodney was doing. And more important, how Rodney's new roommate was dealing with the smell. Coop had asked for a gas mask a couple of times and almost gotten it once. Until the prison shrink took him aside and talked to him at great length about the psychological ramifications of "ostracizing other prisoners olfactorily." Coop didn't understand half of what the guy said, but he listened politely and invited the guy back to his cell to meet Rodney. He never got the mask, but at least he had the pleasure of seeing the shrink try not to faint when Rodney held out his moist mitt to shake. That's how you get through prison, he remembered. It's the little things. The tiny victories. Like copping an extra apple when the chow line guards weren't looking or knowing you'd made your psychiatrist throw up on the way back to his office.

Giselle came back in around eight. She wasn't dressed in red anymore. Sometimes in the past, he'd found her love for the color a little much. Now, he kind of missed it. She was wearing a leather jacket over a white shirt and black jeans. She was even smiling. Coop couldn't tell if it was genuine or just work related. It made him both sick and hopeful and then sick again, even if a load of emotions were not what he wanted at the moment.

They went back to the underground garage and she drove them in a DOPS Honda Civic—the least conspicuous car currently on the road, she explained—to Hollywood Boulevard. They parked by the Pantages Theatre and walked west, ground zero for tourists.

"Sorry about that thing I said earlier," said Coop. "I'm not saying I'm not pissed about, well, a lot of stuff, but that was kind of a cheap shot."

"Forget it," Giselle said. "And I didn't just steal your Contego stone because I needed it. I took it because I was mad and I knew you wanted it."

"I had a feeling it was something like that."

"Yeah."

"So, how often do you go to Rancho Weirdo?"

"Not often. Mostly for work these days. And don't let anyone hear you call it that. You belong there as much as any of the rest of us. Even if you can't cloud minds or open doors, you're as magic as anyone else down there."

"No, I'm not. I'm just immune to it."

"Which is a kind of magic, don't you think?"

"No."

"And this is where I call you a fuddy-duddy again."

"Oh, good. I was afraid you'd forgotten."

They reached the Hollywood Walk of Fame, where metal stars were embedded in the sidewalk with the names of old movie, TV, and music stars. Tourists took photographs. Some stood over them or lay down next to their favorites. Coop almost tripped over a couple of the tourists and was extremely over the scene by the time they passed by the Roosevelt Hotel.

"It's just up ahead," said Giselle.

"You sure you don't want to stop for a drink first? I know a couple of places around here."

She shook her head. "Sorry, sugar. You're what we call a flight risk, which means you're on a short leash. Be good and I'll buy you a Slurpee when we're done here."

"Unless that's code for bourbon, I'll pass." He looked around. "And where is 'here'?"

Giselle stopped walking. Coop went on for a couple of more steps before he realized she wasn't by his side anymore. When he turned, she was clearing cigarette butts and crushed drink cups off one of the street stars. Coop went over and looked at the name. It was above the outline of a movie camera: CATHERINE MONVOISIN.

"A friend of yours?" he said.

"She acted in the silents. She was gone and buried long before I was born."

"Live fast, die young, and leave a star where drunks can piss on you. I guess there are worse ways to be remembered, but I can't think of any off the top of my head."

"An ex-con who blew a promising career because he was a—"

"Don't say it."

"Fuddy-duddy."

"At least I don't have strangers peeing on me on New Year's."

"When do you have strangers pee on you?"

"Keep your fantasies to yourself, please."

"Oh, and for your information, Catherine isn't gone in the ectoplasmic sense," said Giselle. "If you're lucky, I'll get to introduce you." She knelt down by the star and pressed the movie camera. It sank about an inch into the sidewalk until Coop heard a *click* followed by distant echoes. Giselle reached down and opened the star like a trapdoor. Coop looked around.

"Excuse me, ma'am, but aren't you being a little indiscreet, magic-wise? We're right out in the open."

"Relax," she said. "No one's seen us for a block. I've been clouding everyone's mind for five minutes."

"So, I could go into one of these stores and steal a bottle right now and no one would know? Think about it. The Roosevelt has a great lobby. We could have a few drinks and go back and tell Salzman we didn't find anything."

She looked at him. "Are you afraid to go to Jinx Town?"

"Not afraid. Just cautiously trepidatious."

"Those are ten-dollar words for 'afraid.' "

"I'd just like to have a better idea of what's down there. You never told me."

Giselle pushed the star back on its hinges until it fell with a thud on the sidewalk. "You want to know? Climb in, cowboy."

"I didn't say I wanted to know. I said you hadn't told me."

"Seriously, Coop. The quicker we get going, the sooner you can run back home with your tail between your legs."

He peered down into the hole. "Is that supposed to motivate me? You taking a shot at my male pride?"

She smiled. "Did it work?"

"No. But I do like that idea of this being over with. Let's go."

"You first," she said and pointed down into the sidewalk.

He took a small step back. "I have a feeling I'm not the first to say this at this moment, but no fucking way."

"One of us has to go first, and it's not going to be me."

"Why not?"

She pointed to herself, then him. "Me agent. You flight risk. Now climb."

Coop looked into the void. There was a ladder inside. He stepped onto the top rung and lowered himself down. His shoulders barely fit through the gap in the sidewalk, but he kept going. Overhead, the lights went out as Giselle pulled the star closed.

"You want to pick up the pace, Grandpa?"

"I'm remembering how much I enjoy your company," he grumbled.

"Me, too."

Coop couldn't see where he was going, but after only a minute or so of climbing he was on solid ground again.

Giselle climbed down and stood next to him. "What do you think so far?" she said.

"If this is Candy Land, I'm a little underwhelmed."

"Oh yeah?" She walked to the wall and opened a door. "Try this on for size." He went through and she followed him.

Coop stood there for a minute. He started to say something, but all he could think of was "Huh" or "Are those bats?" They were in a wide, bright, open space, like a mall lobby. But this one made no damned sense. It rose up ten stories or more, but he and Giselle hadn't climbed down more than twenty feet. Really, they should be knee-deep in half-eaten vegan tofu wraps and empty sunscreen bottles in the L.A. sewer system. Instead, they were in what looked like a cross between a Vegas hotel and a haunted house in an old B horror movie. Sure, the place had gleaming escalators, bars, and restaurants, but Coop spied shadowy things moving inside several cobwebbed storefronts. There was a marble fountain in the center of the lobby, and the tourists hanging around it snapping pictures had greenish skin and gills. There were even bats, which flew in slow circles around the ceiling while mooks and succubi bought designer shoes at upscale boutiques with names like Cannibal Clique and Velvet Sarcophagus.

"Well? What do you think?" said Giselle.

"I bet this is what you see when you're alone with your little vibrating friend late at night."

She laughed and pulled him over to a backlit map of the place near the biggest escalator.

"There are thirteen floors. Light ones like this, but dark ones, too. And wet ones, steamy ones, dry ones, see? Floors for whatever you want or whatever you are."

"I get it. Disneyland for things that go bump in the night."

"Welcome to Jinx Town."

"Thanks. Don't bother with a welcome basket. I have a feeling what they call summer sausage down here isn't something I want to try."

She frowned. "Be good."

"I am. So, what do we do now? I think there's a bar over there."

"We're not going to that one. We're going upstairs to the highest of the dark floors. According to the clever boots at the DOPS, that's where Babylon likes to hang out."

When Giselle tried to pull Coop to the escalator, he stayed put. "What's wrong?" she said.

"I don't suppose you want to tell me what's on the dark floors?"

She shrugged. "Oh, you know. Vampires. Werewolves. Other critters I don't know the names for. But you know, anything that likes the dark or night."

Coop nodded. "Of course," he said. "You know, I've only hung around with vampires back in stir, and they weren't very nice."

Giselle pulled him to the escalator. "How nice is anyone in prison? I mean, they're in there for a reason, right?"

"Sure. We all were. But I didn't bite people."

"Relax. Everyone is on their best behavior here. That's the first rule of Jinx Town: be good, or at least pretend to be."

"Sounds like jail. I suppose I can live with that."

"You better."

"Just remember that if something tries to eat me or drink my blood, I'm dragging you down with me."

"A gentleman to the end."

They got off one escalator and started up the next. "I can work on the gentleman part," said Coop. "It's that end stuff that worries me."

"Don't worry. I'll fling myself on top of you for protection."

"Now you're just asking me to get in trouble."

Giselle laughed, and Coop liked the sound of it and hated that he liked it. But then he remembered that she was essentially his prison guard and that took some of the fun out of it.

But her laugh still sounded nice.

TWENTY-FOUR

THE NEXT COUPLE OF FLOORS THEY PASSED WERE A lot like the lobby: stores both light and dark. Benches occupied by people (or at least people-ish) things. The occasional ghost drifted by carrying transparent shopping bags. Coop saw a group of bird ladies like the one at the DOPS. A few mooks window-shopping. And at least a dozen different species of human and inhuman creatures strolling by, just like the crowds at the Beverly Center. He didn't even know what to call some of the creatures and felt a little stupid for it. If Giselle was right and he was part of this spectral world, he'd missed a lot of it. On the other hand, what did he care if there was a spook parade going on under his feet? He was a thief. A working stiff. Knowing about all these snaky, winged, and bug-eyed things sipping coffee and eating ice cream cones wasn't going to make his job any easier.

"What do you think?" said Giselle as they walked to the next escalator. "Am I blowing your mind yet?"

They got on and he said, "Consider it blown. I see what Nick was talking about when he called the place—"

"Don't say it."

"I won't. Honestly, I don't know what to think, so I'll just keep my mouth shut for the time being."

"That's a perfectly reasonable response."

"Good. And I'm not feeling like a secret agent yet, either. Your bosses know that DOPS spells 'dopes,' right?"

"Yeah, and they're pretty sensitive about it. Management tried changing the name a few times, but the science wing of the DOPS is pretty stuck on it. Can't say I blame them. I mean, no one even knows how the Stalin cyborgs work yet."

"You have commie cyborgs?"

Giselle held her hand up over her head. "Yeah, big bastards. They've been around since the forties. Laser eyes. Bushy mustaches. They look just like Uncle Joe, only bigger. Like tractors with legs."

Coop craned his head around. "Are there any robots down here?"

"Cyborgs."

"What's the difference?"

"Cyborgs are cooler."

"Thanks for clearing it up."

"The only metal men I've seen down here were some knights. I think they're old Templars. They busk over by the tapas place and bum cigarettes off people."

"You know, I could wait in the car while you do your sleuthing. I promise not to run away and only listen to NPR on the radio."

Giselle shook her head. "No way. This is part of your job and your education. You're part of Peculiar Science now. Get used to it."

"I'm going to need a few drinks before that happens."

"We'll get you a Roy Rogers when we find Babylon's bar."

The next floor was one of the wet levels Giselle had talked about. Mist drifted down from the top of the escalator. As Coop stepped off, he was lost in a warm fog. Giselle reached back and took his hand, pulling him along. That felt funny, her hand in his. He couldn't see much of the floor, but what he saw didn't make any more sense than the lobby. It looked liked they were on the edge of an enormous swamp. There were some goblins that reminded him of Rodney. People with tentacles for arms, and some of the gill people he'd seen downstairs. Distant fires. Blue will-o'-the wisps glided back and forth through the mist. Off to the side, Coop was sure he could see a frozen yogurt stand.

The next floor up was one of the dry floors. Coop had to shield his eyes from the bright sunlike orb at the top of the white rotunda. The one thing he could see that made sense was a Sunglass Hut nearby. The rest of the floor looked like Death Valley. Enormous serpent-things slithered through the sand. Robed people wandered over the dunes with bags from shoe shops and toy stores.

When they reached the next floor—a regular one like the lobby—Coop was still a little sun dazzled. While Giselle showed Babylon's picture to a couple of horned mall cops, he looked around. He hadn't felt quite so lost since his arrest.

Seeing another bar, he peeked inside. People inside stared at him with milky eyes. Coop had been in a lot of bars over the years. Some were open and friendly. The people in most bars couldn't give a shit whether you came in or not. But there were others that you knew not to go into the minute you stuck your head in. It wasn't that they were hostile. It was more like someone had sprayed people repellent around the door. At least your kind of people. Going inside could result in a systematic kicking of your ass. That's the feeling Coop got from this place. And all he'd done was look in the window.

He jumped a little when Giselle tapped him on the shoulder.

"What's your problem, Mr. Chicken?" she said.

"What's up with this crowd? They look like they want to snack on my skull."

Giselle looked past him and pulled Coop back to the escalator. "It's a mook bar. They're touchy about the living wandering in and eating their peanuts."

"Your boss, Salzman, seems like a charming corpse. What's his story?"

Giselle shrugged. "He's not so bad. Just ambitious. There are a million guys like him at the DOPS."

"I get a bad feeling if you were a dick when you were alive, being dead isn't going to fix it."

"You got that right." Giselle stepped off the escalator. "The DOPS loves mooks. They work hard and don't complain."

Coop leaned on the escalator railing, trying to get over the onslaught of weirdness. "Of course they don't complain. Where else are they going to go? I don't think they let dead people run Dairy Queens."

Giselle gave him a look. "You'd be surprised how many fast-food joints are run by the undead. Personally, I think a lot of mooks like the DOPS because they hope someone is going to figure out a way to make them alive again."

"And they can all be real boys. Just like Pinocchio."

"What did I tell you?"

"Be nice."

"Or pretend to be."

"Pretend it is."

Coop could see the moon from the top of the next escalator. Or something that looked a lot like it. The dark floor where they stepped off was icy. Coop blew into his hands. He looked around and saw a cart giving out free samples of drinks. He wandered over hoping it was some kind of supernatural whiskey.

"Would you like to try something today, sir?" said the pretty vampire in charge of the cart. Her name tag said KRISTEN.

"Hi, Kristen. What do you have that's got a kick? And warm. But mostly a kick."

She poured something from a brown bottle into a small paper cup. She handed it to Coop and smiled. Then her smile turned into a frown and she took it back. "Wait. You're like alive and stuff, aren't you?" she said in the kind of hard-core Valley Girl accent he hadn't heard in twenty years.

"Yeah, currently alive. And I'd like to stay that way," he said.

She shook her head and set the cup on the cart. "Then this is *definitely* not for you."

"I'll take your word for it."

She poured something from another bottle and passed it to him. "Try this," she said in a way that kick-started Coop's reptile brain. It wasn't even a fight-or-flight choice. His brain went straight into flee mode. But he stayed put. Jinx Town had fucked with him enough. Without thinking any more about it, he took the cup and gulped the drink down. A flush passed through his body and his brain thanked him immediately. Coop's heart jumped a little and he instantly felt warmer. Suddenly, he was inspired to do math, take a nap, and maybe learn to tap-dance. Everything was fascinating, him most of all.

Giselle came running over. "What are you doing? Do you know what that stuff is?"

Kristen smiled at Giselle. "Don't worry. I'm not about to waste good blood on tourists. He just had some Vin Mariani."

Coop held out his cup to Giselle. "You really need to try this. It's like driving the Indy Five Hundred in a bathtub full of warm Jell-O."

"I bet it is," said Giselle. "Vin Mariani is wine and cocaine. You're lucky it isn't drug-test season at work."

"Fuck the DOPS. Fuck this whole day. *This* is why I came to Jinx Town."

"No. Staying out of jail is why you're here. And let's keep you out, shall we? Come on. We have work to do."

Coop held up a finger. "One second." He looked at Kristen and pulled out his cash. "I'll take a case of the stuff."

"No, you won't," said Giselle.

"You're right. I can't carry a case. Just one bottle."

"Goddammit, Coop."

Kristen took some of his money and handed him an unopened bottle. She leaned forward and said in a stage whisper, "Your mom is pissed."

Coop put a finger to his lips. "Shh."

Giselle took his arm and pulled him away from the stand. Coop tucked the bottle under his arm and went with her.

"You need to take this situation seriously," she said.

"I am taking it seriously."

"More seriously."

"Listen. I've wanted out of Narnia since we walked in. This stuff made me feel like I could stay. Plus I'm kind of high. That's what I call a win-win."

Giselle nodded at the bottle. "You just bought a fifth of who the hell knows what from a trampy vampire. Did it ever occur to you that she might want to poison you or maybe make you her slave?"

Coop frowned. "Kristen wouldn't do that. She's a nice girl. And I'm sure it's against company policy."

"Plus, you're all coked up. You're no use to me now questioning people."

"Trust me, I was no use before. At least now I don't want to run screaming back to the car."

"Fine," said Giselle. "We're going into that bar over there. I'm going to show Babylon's photo around and you're going to be good and not bother the nice people, all right?"

Coop squinted at the sign over the door. "*Týden Divu*. I can't even pronounce that. Is it a vampire bar? Because if it is, I'm going to need more Vin."

Giselle shook her head. "Don't worry. It's an everybody bar. Just keep your mouth shut. And no more drinking."

"Got it."

"Let's go." When she turned, he opened the bottle, took a swig, and followed her.

Coop had to give Jinx Town credit for one thing. None of the bars had doormen checking IDs. *I guess if you get this far, not only can you drink, you deserve a drink.* Coop thought about taking another nip, but he'd promised Giselle and already felt a little guilty about the first one. He didn't like having her mad at him, and he was getting irritated at himself for giving a damn. *This is just a job,* he reminded himself. *I'm the con and she's the guard. Period.* He went into the bar with her, trying to be neutral but still feeling too buzzed to be sure he was doing it right.

Giselle headed off to talk to the bar patrons. The moment she was away from him Coop saw her face light up in a million-dollar smile. He remembered that smile when it had been aimed at him. But that was a long time ago. He walked around the tables and found himself in a gaming area. Roulette on the far side of the room. Craps on the other. Blackjack in the middle. Coop always liked the idea of craps, but the odds were way too much on the house's side. Same thing with roulette. He'd played some blackjack in prison, which he remembered being barely more exciting than picking paint chips off his cell wall. And there was no way he could sit still for a dealer in his current speed-demon state. Between the big games were rows and rows of slot machines. He gazed at the blinking lights and listened to the bells and electronic pings, a siren song to drunks throughout history. Coop set down the bottle, sat at a vacant machine, and felt around for his money.

He fed a twenty into the slot and pulled the machine's lever, which was shaped like a curved tentacle. Coop got two skulls and a human heart. On his next pull he got an ouroboros, a pentagram, and what looked sort of like a ham sandwich with hooves. Then he got two bats and an Easter Island head. It was coming back to him why he wasn't a gambler. He didn't like throwing money away and he didn't like being bored. Losing was boring and winning was too stressful. The lights on the machines were getting too bright and the noises too loud. He looked around for Giselle and saw her chatting up a group of well-dressed werewolves. He liked their suits and in another life might have asked them where they bought them, but the jolt of energy and abandon from the cocaine was wearing off, replaced with the same dull dread he'd felt earlier. Rather than attract attention to himself, he slipped another twenty into the slot machine. The spinners whirred for what seemed a long time and finally settled on three eyes. All three blinked at him and a siren went off. Coop leapt back from the machine as diamonds and sapphires cascaded from the payout slot onto the floor. A human, scaly, spiny, and furry crowd gathered around him. A few gawkers applauded as he knelt to scoop up his winnings. Giselle pushed her way through the crowd and stood over him.

"I can't leave you alone for two minutes," she said in an annoyed tone.

Coop shoved the last of his winnings into his pockets and got up. "I was doing what you told me. I was being quiet and not bothering anyone. All the noise was just dumb luck."

Giselle shook her head. "Forget it. We're too conspicuous now. And I wasn't getting anywhere anyway. If anyone here knows Babylon, they're not talking."

"Great. Let's go. I get a feeling we're looking a lot tastier to some of this crowd."

Giselle put a hand on his elbow. "Relax. You're home. No one here is going to bother you."

They made it as far as the bar before someone pointed a gun at them.

"You were saying," Coop muttered to Giselle.

To Coop the gunman looked human, but he wasn't willing to bet his Vin Mariani on it. The guy wore a sharkskin suit and his tie hung loose, like he hoped Frank Sinatra's ghost would stroll by and invite him out for steaks and hookers. They guy pressed the barrel of the gun into Giselle's chest. Coop recognized the unusual gold model.

"Why are you asking about Mr. Babylon?" said the sharkskin suit.

Giselle didn't miss a beat. "I just got to town. I'm a Marilyn and I heard that Mr. Babylon liked to work with the best people. Well, I'm the best."

"Are you?" said the suit. "What's his story?" he said, pointing the gun at Coop.

"He's a Flasher. He's good, but not as good as me. Do you know Mr. Babylon? Could you introduce us?"

The suit pointed the gun back at Giselle. "Never heard of the man. No one around here has. In fact, neither have you. Do you get me?"

"Completely," said Coop. "We're sorry to have upset you. And we certainly don't want to trouble any nonexistent criminal kingpins." He took Giselle's hand. "Let's go get that Slurpee you were talking about."

The suit lowered the gun and they started out of the bar when he said, "Wait a second. You have a picture of Mr. Babylon? Who the hell are you?"

Coop turned around as the suit brought the gun back up and fired. He pushed Giselle out of the way and caught the blast square in the chest. A scream went up through the bar. Behind Coop, part of the wall was missing, the edges red hot. Coop felt Giselle beside him as she pulled out a tranq pistol and shot the suit in the neck. He collapsed before he got off another shot. Giselle ran over and pulled the guy up by the collar, talking to him rapidly. From the back of the bar, the werewolves in the nice suits were pushing through the crowd. Coop didn't need an introduction to know that the suit and the wolves were there together. They closed in fast on Giselle.

Coop reached into his pocket and started throwing diamonds and cash into the air. The crowd dove for the loot as he grabbed Giselle and pulled her to her feet. They just made it out the door before Coop ran out of cash and rocks. He could just make out the wolves struggling toward them, trapped in the middle of the grabby, giddy crowd.

He couldn't help himself. "Good doggies. Stay!"

They headed straight for the escalators and ran down most of the thirteen floors. Giselle grabbed Coop to keep him from sprinting through the lobby. When they hit the exit, they began running again, straight up the ladder and onto Hollywood Boulevard. Coop slammed Catherine Monvoisin's star shut, and they stood there trying to catch their breath. An off-duty Spider-Man from the Chinese Theater down the block stared at them.

"Annual star inspection," said Coop. "This one is A-OK. Say Hi to Aunt May for me."

He and Giselle walked back along the Boulevard to her car by the Pantages. "You doing okay?" said Giselle.

"No."

She stopped. "What's wrong? Are you hurt?"

"I lost my Vin Mariani."

She shoved him hard enough to rock him back a few steps. "That's for being such an asshole." Then she came over and hugged him. "And this is for taking the shot for me. How did you know it was a hex gun and not a regular one?"

"Babylon shot me with one just like it. You know, that might mean they know each other."

Giselle gently stepped back out of Coop's arms. They looked at each other a little awkwardly.

"Yeah. He does," she said. "When he was all goofed up from the tranq, I got him to give me an address in Laurel Canyon. Want to go check it out?"

"Why not?" said Coop. "But the DOPS owes me about a billion dollars in cash and rocks. Are there expense forms for that kind of thing?"

Giselle reached into her purse and handed Coop a card. "This is my business American Express. If you don't abuse it, you can use it until we get you reimbursed for the cash."

"Can I buy some new clothes with it?"

"At this hour?"

"The Roosevelt has a twenty-four-hour place for high rollers who get Fatburger on their French cuffs. I was going to stop there."

She nodded and gave him a brief smile. "Yeah. After we check out the address you can get some things. Just don't go nuts."

"Thanks."

They got into the Honda and headed for Laurel Canyon. As they passed a yellow Prius, it did a U-turn and began following them.

An hour earlier, Jerry was by a Dumpster in an alley next to a bodega on Highland Avenue. A gray-haired wino with a bottle of Aquavit cradled in his arm was asleep on a flattened cardboard box. Jerry looked around, but didn't see anyone else nearby.

"Excuse me," he said to the sleeping drunk. "Excuse me."

The old man opened his rheumy eyes and stared at him without moving. Jerry took another look around, hoping that maybe there was a concierge or docent who would tell him what to do. When none appeared, he turned back to the drunk.

"I'm looking for a place called Jinx Town. Do you know anything about it?"

"Never heard of it," said the old man.

"Oh. I was told I could find it here."

"Do you have anything?"

"What?" said Jerry.

In a surprisingly clear voice, the old man said, "Do. You. Have. Anything?"

"Oh. Right."

The old man rolled his eyes.

Jerry took an old-fashioned movie theater ticket from his pants pocket. It was orange, grubby, and worn, like someone had found it in the gutter after a hard rain. Charlie, the drywall boss, had given it to him, and Jerry wasn't sure if he wanted to give it to a dirty alley drunk. He handed it over. The old man tore the ticket in half and gave one of the pieces back to Jerry. He put it back in his pocket.

Without another word, the old man rolled over and slowly pulled himself onto his feet. He went around to the far side of the Dumpster and, laying all his weight on it, pushed it a few feet, revealing a hole in the wall. It was about three feet high. The old man waved for Jerry to go inside. He peered into the dark, but couldn't see anything.

"You going, boy? I haven't got all night," said the old man.

Jerry had come too far and had taken too many chances to chicken out now. His broken ribs ached as he got down on all fours and crawled inside. At the entrance, the old man cleared his throat and held out his hand. Jerry took out a five-dollar tip and handed it to him. After inspecting it for a few seconds, the old man nodded and waved Jerry inside. Once he was in the hole, the old man rolled the Dumpster back into place.

Jerry closed his eyes and opened them. There was no difference in the pitch dark. He crawled for a few feet, then felt the space open up. Holding his hands out, he took a few tentative steps forward and touched something that felt like a wall. He ran his fingertips across it and hit something solid. A doorknob. Jerry twisted it and stepped through.

He was in a towering mall full of shops and restaurants. People and things sort of like people, but not quite, strolled by with bags and drinks. Charlie hadn't been lying or high after all. Jerry took a deep breath and let it out slowly. He'd made it all the way to Jinx Town. He brushed the dirt from his hands and knees and started walking.

Jerry went slowly, astonished by everything he saw, but trying not to look like one of the gawking hillbillies who crowded the streets of

Hollywood overhead. Still, it was hard not to stare. When anyone, human or not, caught his gaze, Jerry lowered his eyes and walked on.

After making a complete circuit of the bottom floor, he got onto one of the escalators, went up a floor, and started walking again. Jerry wasn't even sure what he was looking for. For now, it was enough that he'd made it this far and proven to himself that magic and the kind of people who lived with it every day were real. He wasn't sure how he was going to prove that to anyone in his father's congregation, but he'd worry about that later.

When he wasn't people watching, Jerry window-shopped cluttered stores like Swank Skull and Witchateria. From what he could tell about a place called Terror Management Therapy, it seemed to sell a combination of dungeon equipment and office supplies. The staplers growled at him through the window and a ghost took dictation in a ball gag and manacles.

He went up a few more floors, moving quickly past the wet and dry ones, up to a dark floor near the top of the mall.

Jerry stared into the moonlit distance trying to figure out where he was. He hovered around the guardrail overlooking the rest of the mall, wanting to venture into the dark, but for the moment happy to be near the light. But he knew Caleximus wouldn't want him to come this far just to have his balls shrivel up. And if Tommy ever found out that he'd turned tail . . .

After a few deep breaths, Jerry got up enough nerve to move. He turned to walk into the dark . . . and ran straight into two horned mall cops.

"Are you sure you belong here, kid?" said the shorter of the two. Jerry froze midstep. *What would Dad do now?* he wondered. Instinctively, he reached into his shirt and pulled out his Caleximus pendant, holding it up so the horned mall cops could see. After a moment, the short cop looked at the tall one, who gave a nod.

"Okay. You have a nice day, sir," said the short cop, and they both walked on. Jerry didn't give them a chance to change their minds. He trotted into the darkness and whatever lay under the wan moon.

In fact, what lay beyond was a lot like what he'd seen below. Stores.

Bars. Restaurants. There was a pretty girl at a cart giving out free samples of something. He thought about going over, but then caught a glimpse of her fangs. His gut did a backflip in a combination of fear and exhilaration. *She's a vampire,* he thought. *A real live vampire.*

Jerry sat down by a fountain across from a store called Profondo Rosso. It seemed to be some kind of specialty butcher shop, with strange cuts of meat hanging in the window. Jerry didn't look too closely at them . . . especially after he noticed some of them looking back at him. Water splashed on his pants and left red stains. He wiped it away and smelled his fingers. *That's not water.* A switch got thrown in Jerry's brain. Maybe this was a mistake after all. He'd wanted to prove the magic world was real, and he'd done it. Much more thoroughly than he'd ever imagined. There were other things he wanted, other things he'd come to see, but he couldn't think of a single one of them right now. All he wanted to do was get back to the old drunk and go home.

When he stood, someone touched him on the shoulder. He would have liked to believe that the sound that came out of him was manly, and not the squeak of a dog's toy, but he knew the sad truth of it.

He turned around to see that a group of six little girls in pigtails and gingham dresses formed a semicircle around him. "Hi," said a redhead at the center of the group. "What's your name?"

He stammered a couple of times before he got it out. "Jerry," he said.

"Hi, Jerry," said the redhead. "You're new here, aren't you?"

"Yes. It's my first time."

"Really? So, you're not meeting anyone? Nobody here knows you?"

His gut prodded him again. "Uh, yeah. Friends are in the butcher shop."

"Fibber," said a girl on the end. Jerry felt like he was being grilled by a bunch of Lizzie Bordens masquerading as Girl Scouts.

The little girls giggled and whispered to each other. "Why don't we show you around?" said the redhead.

"Thanks," said Jerry, suddenly wishing he'd listened to his balls earlier when they wanted to leave. "But I was just going."

"But you just got here. And there's so much more to see."

"Thanks, but I really should be getting home." Jerry started to get up and the little redhead pushed him back down harder than any little girl should have been able to.

"Ow," said Jerry. "Wow. You're really strong. What's your name?"

"Pudding Tame. Ask me again and I'll tell you the same."

The little girls giggled, showing their fangs. Jerry couldn't decide whether he wanted to run or faint. Running seemed pointless, but if he fainted he might look too much like a picnic lunch.

"Please don't eat me," he said.

The girls burst out laughing.

"That's zombies, silly. They're two floors down. Should we introduce you?"

"No?" said Jerry, not sure what to answer anymore. It was like he was taking his SATs all over again. He'd wanted to run then, too.

"Here's the thing, Jerry," said the redhead. "You only get to leave if you can come up with something better than that pretty throat of yours."

Jerry pulled out his Caleximus pendant. The redhead frowned. "What's that?"

"It's a Caleximus thing," said a brunette next to the redhead. "I'm not sure. I think they're some kind of metal band."

"Didn't they play with Slayer on their last tour? They *sucked,*" she said, and all the little girls laughed.

"You're going to have to do better than that, Jerry," said the redhead.

"I could beg. Just don't tell my dad."

The redhead sat down next to him on the fountain. "That sounds fun, but not quite enough."

"I have money."

"And I have an AmEx black card."

"Wow. Even my dad doesn't have one of those. You must have a really good credit rating."

"An eight-fifty. What's yours?"

Jerry started to lie, thought better of it, and said, "About a six."

The redhead smiled. "You're cute for a scaredy cat."

"That's me. The scarediest cat ever."

The girl on the end said, "Enough with this stiff. Let's drain him and go try on shoes."

"Wait," said Jerry. He hesitated for just a second. What he was contemplating was a sin of the highest order, but wouldn't Caleximus reward him for his resourcefulness when the time came? And he really, really wanted to be alive for that. For anything, really. Jerry reached into his jacket and pulled out the silver ceremonial dagger he was supposed to use to kill the black boar. Giving away one of Caleximus's relics was a big deal, but so was being a juice box for a bunch of pint-size brides of Dracula. He handed it to the redhead.

She held it up and light from across the mall threw a reflection onto her pale face. "Is this real silver?" she said.

"Yes. And full of dark power. It once belonged to our lord . . ."

"Yeah, yeah," said the brown-haired girl. "It's not a George Foreman grill, so don't oversell it, pink boy."

The redheaded girl nodded and handed the blade to a blond girl. "Not too shabby, Jerry. You just might live long enough to improve that credit rating. Now, why don't you scoot back home to Grandma's house before us big bad wolves eat you up for supper?"

He got up. "I will. Thanks. I'm going now."

"Hit the bricks, loser," said the brown-haired girl. "We still have to find dinner."

Happy not to be turned into a flesh Popsicle, Jerry very slowly made his way through the crowd of little girls, trying not to turn his back on any of them and, realizing that was impossible, jerking his head from side to side trying to look at them all at once. That cracked the girls up. When he was clear of them, he ran for the escalator.

"Pussy!" shouted one. Fleeing, Jerry knew that he was in no position to argue the point.

Just as he passed a bar, a man and woman came running out. He wondered if they were running from another gang of moppets when he recognized one of them.

"Coop," he whispered. "Coop."

He took a few steps back and let the couple pass. They ran down the escalator, and after a moment's pause, Jerry went down after them. They slowed as they crossed the lobby, and so did Jerry. When they went out one of the side exits, he waited a few seconds and followed them. They were climbing a ladder when he came out. When they were out of sight, he went up after them, pushing open a trapdoor at the top of the ladder, where he was shocked to find himself on Hollywood Boulevard.

Coop and the woman were half a block ahead, heading east. Jerry got as close to them as he safely could and when they crossed Highland Avenue, he darted down the street, jumped into his mother's yellow Prius, and tore around the corner onto Hollywood Boulevard. Or, rather, gave chase as quickly as a Prius would allow. He followed the two of them, always keeping half a block behind, until they reached a darker section of the Boulevard. When Coop and the woman got into a Honda Civic and drove off, they headed the wrong way. So he held his breath, hoping there were no cops around, and pulled a fast U-turn.

Maybe Dad and the others won't believe me about Jinx Town, but they'll have *to believe this.*

TWENTY-FIVE

LAUREL CANYON PERCHED DIRECTLY ABOVE LOS ANGELES, one of the most expensive collections of winding hills and valleys in the country. Luckily, there were roads that twisted up and down the tortured ridges, or the only things that would have been there were hippies, backpackers, prairie dogs, and the occasional mountain lion dining on the aforementioned hippies, backpackers, and prairie dogs. Unfortunately, because of those roads and the billion-dollar real estate, the most common life-forms were douche bags, plastic surgeons, fading film producers, and labradoodles. Laurel Canyon had a long and colorful history, which is much too complex to go into here, except to say that it's long and colorful, and that what's in the history books was almost entirely wrong. The books go on about Indian tribes, the Spanish, the local wildlife, the local fauna, yet somehow leave out the inhabitants of Lemuria completely.

Lemuria was a large and ancient island nation in the Pacific, similar to Atlantis, but with better sushi and Wi-Fi. When Lemuria, also like Atlantis, sank (following a series of explosions from one particularly disastrous experiment aimed at using volcanoes to power Lemurialand, an amusement park that went bankrupt in a year because Lemurians were a dour people who left fun to those Atlantis creeps), the survivors sailed to what would someday be called Los Angeles. Finding the flatlands boring, the Lemurians settled in the canyons, which were much more like their island home. Not a people to leave well enough alone, they immediately began terraforming the land to make it even more like Lemuria. Although they were a scientifically advanced civilization, they weren't big on seismology. After a few years of shifting hills, diverting underground rivers, and generally screwing around with the surface and substrata of the canyon, one afternoon they became intimately acquainted with a large fault line that cut straight through the canyon and swallowed the Lemurian survivors and most of their sprawling castles.

While almost no physical evidence of their civilization remains, the one thing the Lemurians *did* leave behind was a psychic imprint on the land, a ghostly desire to build the biggest, gaudiest mansions imaginable. This spirit haunts Laurel Canyon to this day. You won't find a larger collection of wildly expensive and funny-looking houses outside of parts of Beverly Hills, which was settled by an even dumber ancient race that there isn't time to go into right now.

It took forty-five minutes of driving, backtracking, cursing, praying to nonexistent travel gods, dumb luck, and pure fury for Coop and Giselle to find the address the sharkskin suit had given them back in Jinx Town. When they found the place—a hulking mansion, part Spanish Revival with smaller Roman temples clinging to the sides, a fever-dream version of San Simeon—they pulled over onto the grassy shoulder of the road a quarter of a mile away and looked the place over.

"Sure is big," said Coop.

"And ugly," said Giselle.

"At least Babylon has the biggest house around. That's lucky."

"How do you figure?"

"He doesn't have to go outside and see how ridiculous it is."

Giselle took a set of binoculars from the glove compartment. They weren't ordinary binoculars. They were more like goggles, with extra colored lenses that rotated in and out of place over the large lenses.

"You look like a nearsighted fly," said Coop.

"You're just jealous that I have all the good toys."

"I'm jealous you have toys at all. I miss my Vin Mariani."

"Lush."

"Coop."

Coop squinted at the hilltop monstrosity, but it was too far away to make out any details. "Did you get those from the DOPS or Sky-Mall?"

"They're what good little agents who work hard and don't get coked up and start riots get."

"I wasn't coked up. I was pleasantly focused. You going to give me a turn, or do I have to get on the roof with a magnifying glass?"

"Relax. You'll get your turn. I'm just trying to get the settings right."

"For what?"

"Here. Take a look."

She handed the binoculars to Coop and when he put them to his eyes, Babylon's mansion lit up like high noon. The buildings were a wild combination of pink, gold, and robin's-egg blue, crisscrossed by bright beams of laserlike light. Coop lowered the binoculars and stared at the mansion. No funny colors. No harsh light beams. "You sure you have these things set right? The place looks like a My Little Pony rave."

Giselle took the binoculars back and said, "They're just fine. The funny colors and light beams are all the enchantments and wards Babylon has protecting the place."

"Let me see those again," said Coop. He put the binoculars to his eyes, carefully studying the exterior of the building. "The whole place is covered. There isn't one clear spot anywhere."

Giselle nodded. "It's going to be hard to get into."

"No. The White House is hard to get into. This is impossible. Unless Babylon is nuts and left a barn door open around back, this heist is over."

Giselle took the binoculars back. "Come on, Coop. Don't be so negative. It's the fuddy-duddy part of you talking again."

"It's isn't the fuddy-duddy part. It's the alive part. Even if I can walk through the killing curses, some of those lights are going to trip regular traps. Guns. Blades. Dragons. Dragons with guns and blades. Count me out of that."

Giselle turned to him. "Salzman wasn't kidding. He'll send you back to jail."

"At least I'll be a live con. This town has been trying to kill me ever since I got back. This job he wants me to do is going to be the one that nails the coffin shut."

Giselle set the binoculars in her lap. "And here I thought for a minute there was hope for you. You were brave for two seconds back at Jinx Town. Why can't you do that now?"

"I think your problem is that you're confusing brave with stupid."

"No—I still think you're stupid."

"Look, getting shot was a calculated risk. This," he said, pointing to the mansion, "is suicide."

Giselle pushed the lenses back into place and put the binoculars into the glove compartment. "And here I was considering kissing you later. You blew that, and you're going to go back to jail. This just isn't your night."

"Wait. What did you just say?"

"About what?"

"Kissing me."

She pursed and unpursed her lips. "I can't remember."

Coop wanted to say something more. He wanted to believe she meant it about kissing him, but it didn't change the fact that she was still his boss. And she'd torn his heart out once. That was a sucker's combo, and he was tired of being a sucker.

"Look, I'm not trying to bolt or anything. It's just that from what I've seen so far, getting through any of those doors is impossible. Maybe there's a way in, but it's going to take some time to find. How long will Salzman give me?"

"A few days. A week maybe."

"That might not be long enough."

"You're forgetting something. You work for the DOPS now. Back at headquarters, they'll probably have all kinds of information about this place. And I'll be there to help you. You don't have to do this alone."

Coop was silent for a minute. "I don't know."

"Just don't make your mind up now. Give it a couple of days and see what the big brains come up with."

Cop shook his head wearily. He was already sick of the spy world. "Fine. But if I say no . . ."

"No one wants you committing suicide."

He gave her a look.

"Well, maybe Salzman, but he wants everybody dead."

"That's a comfort."

"For now, let's just play things by ear. Okay?"

"Okay. For now," he said. "I want a drink. Do you want a drink?"

"Yes, but I have to get up early and write a report about what happened tonight."

"You going to rat me out about the Vin Mariani?"

Giselle made an are-you-kidding-me face. "No way. It would be both of our asses."

"Speaking of which, let's get back to that thing you said earlier about kissing me."

"Kissing you? That's the first I'm hearing of it. You must be fantasizing about your vampire chippie back in Jinx Town."

"You're just mad because she called you my mom."

"Why would that make me mad? You need a babysitter or you'd never find your head up your ass."

"So, what you're saying is that us getting into the backseat is out of the question."

"In this life and the next."

"Too bad. I have some new moves you would have loved."

Giselle started the car. "You did a lot of making out in prison, did you?"

"No. Yoga. It makes you limber. You'd be amazed at what I can put behind what these days."

Giselle looked at him and pulled back onto the road. "You never took a yoga class in your life."

Coop looked out the window at the mansion. "I guess now you'll never know."

"Liar."

"Now who's Mr. Chicken?"

"That's Ms. Chicken to you. Don't forget I'm still your boss. You'll do what I say."

"I can't hear you. Maybe you should say that again with boots and a riding crop."

"In your dreams."

"Tonight at least."

Giselle gunned the engine and they drove back to Hollywood.

Going down the hill was faster than going up. It only took thirty minutes to get to the Roosevelt Hotel.

"Here we are," Giselle said.

"Here we are."

She hesitated. "Maybe I was a little hasty earlier. I could come in and help you pick out some things."

Coop looked out the window and shook his head. He'd turned it over in his head a dozen times on the way back to town and decided that the whole thing was just too weird to take in. "Not tonight. This is something I want to do on my own. You're classy and everyone will know it. These snooty clotheshorses won't want me in their shop, which is why I want to be there alone. Rub their noses in me getting some good stuff."

"I understand," said Giselle. "Have a good time. I'll see you at work tomorrow. I'll send a car to pick you up at nine."

"I'm capable of driving myself."

"You don't know where it is."

"I'll be ready at nine."

"Good boy."

"Well, good night."

"Good night," said Giselle.

They sat there looking at each other for a minute. Coop felt thirteen again. He and Giselle leaned in and had a brief, awkward hug.

He got out and waved to her through the window. She nodded to him and drove off.

What the hell was I just thinking? I'm way off my game. She wanted to come in and I said no. Why did I do that? I have no game anymore. None. Even if I had game, it would be tic-tac-toe, a game only played by computers, crazy people, and chickens at state fairs.

Coop took a breath and went into the Roosevelt Hotel, wondering how the hell he was going to explain any of this to Morty.

Jerry parked a block back from the Roosevelt, keeping an eye on the Honda. Coop got out after a couple of minutes and went inside. *Dammit.* Jerry was too far away to catch up with Coop and see where he was going.

Jerry watched the Honda pull back into traffic. At least the night wasn't a total loss. Finding out where Coop's girl lived was almost as good as finding him. He put the Prius in gear and followed her all the way home.

TWENTY-SIX

IT WAS A PERFECT LOS ANGELES MORNING IN THE PARKing lot by the Brown Star Organic Co-op stall in the Farmers Market. Bright, but not hot, and with a slight breeze. The market was bustling with customers from all over L.A. and the San Fernando Valley. Tourists crowded the stalls, looking for a late breakfast and local delicacies. Some of the more charitably minded stopped by the bake sale table of a new environmental group most of them weren't quite sure they'd heard of.

Marian White of Enid, Oklahoma, stood by the bake sale table and cocked her head. "'Scourge the Earth.' That's an unusual name for an environmental group. Can you tell me about it?"

Susie smiled at her. "We're a fairly new group. Local mainly, but we hope to be going global soon."

"How nice. And what are you working on these days?"

Tommy said, "Our ultimate goal is to poison the seas, scorch the land, and bring the end of days to all vile human life."

"Excuse me?"

"Save the trees," said Susie. "We want to save the trees."

"And the baby seals," said Janet from over her shoulder.

"Oh, I love them," said Marian.

"Would you like to try a sample?" said Susie.

Marian looked over the long spread of pies and cakes. "What's that one?"

"That's a hate-in-a-blistering-inferno-of-agony bar."

"That's an unusual name."

"Thank you."

"What flavor is it?" said Marian.

"Lemon."

"Could I try one of those?"

"Certainly." Susie cut off a small piece of the bar and handed it to her on a paper napkin. "Here you go."

Marian popped it in her mouth and chewed. "It's delicious. I'll take two, please."

"Wonderful. Lord Caleximus will smile upon you and devour your soul quickly and mercifully. There will be little pain."

"Are you sure you're an environmental group?"

"Save the whales," said Susie.

"Of course," said Marian. She narrowed her eyes. "It's just that I get the feeling you have some other agenda, too."

"No nukes," said Janet.

Susie wiped her hands on her apron. "If you think we're raising money to summon our unholy death god from a black well of eternal suffering to ravage mankind, you couldn't be more wrong."

"Well, all right then. What's that?" said Marian, pointing.

"Carrot cake. With a frosting of cream cheese, chopped pecans, and bottomless horror."

Marian frowned. "I'm not sure I like the sound of that. Do you have anything with little to no horror? My daughter-in-law is trying to lose some weight."

Susie picked up a plate. "We have some gluten-free chocolate chip venomous rage Toll House cookies."

Marian shook a finger at Susie. "See, that's why I think you might have another agenda."

"Butterscotch brownies. Do you like butterscotch?"

"I'm not sure. May I try one?"

Susie handed her a sliver of brownie. "I think you'll like it."

Marian took a bite and nodded. "How much rage is in this one?"

"Hardly any. And they're on sale. Three for five dollars."

"Lovely. I'll take three."

Susie used a spatula to scoop up the brownies and slip them into a paper bag. "Here you go."

"Thank you," said Marian.

"Have a nice day. Hail Caleximus."

"What was that?"

"Save the whales."

"You said that earlier," said Marian.

"Don't you like whales? Why do you hate whales?"

"I don't hate whales."

"Good, because we love them," said Susie. "Their blubber will serve to light our lord's way as he wipes clean all life and hope from the surface of this accursed world."

"Well, as long as the baby seals will be all right."

"The seals are fine. Everybody likes seals."

Marian took her brownies and put them in a Brown Star woven tote bag. "Thank you. Have a nice day. Good luck with the scourging."

"Thank you. Be sure to tell your friends. We'll be here all weekend."

As Marian went back into the Farmers Market, Steve came over. He was wearing a white apron and a chef's hat with DELICIOUS DESTRUCTION on it in a light green cursive font.

"How are things going, hon?"

"Just terrific. Making money hand over fist. Though, you know, that last woman, I don't know if she believed we're one of those tree-hugging groups."

"Just remember that we have deep concern for the environment. We want to destroy it. Burn it to ashes and salt the Earth with mortal tears. It might not be the kind of environmental plan Greenpeace has, but they'll be screaming in boiling bile soon, so all we need to do is keep going until we can get back the summoning box."

"I'm sure you're right. Anyway, she liked my lemon bars and the butterscotch brownies."

Steve put an arm around her. "You're a terrific saleswoman."

"How are the others doing?" Susie asked.

"Real well. I'm glad you talked me into having one last sale. We're pulling in cash and everyone is having a good time."

"And isn't that what Armageddon is all about?"

"That's the way I learned it," said Steve. "Say, have you seen Caleximus's silver blade? We want to cut up some accursed fudge bars and I thought it might be fun to make a little ceremony out of it."

"I think Jerry has it," said Susie.

"Great. Thanks."

"Talk to you later."

Steve walked over to where Jerry was putting a couple of virulently blighted blueberry scones into a plastic container for a little girl in a Smurfette T-shirt. The girl ran to her parents and waved at Jerry. He waved back as the family took their infernal pastries to one of the outdoor tables for a snack.

"Hey, son," said Steve. "Your mom said you might have Caleximus's dagger."

Jerry rearranged the scones on his tray, not looking at his father. "No. I haven't seen it. Maybe Jorge has it."

Steve sighed. "Well, damn. I sent him for more paper plates. Oh well. We'll just have to make do with a regular old kitchen knife." Steve looked over his son's shoulder at the almost empty scone tray. "Looks like you're doing a good job there."

"Thanks."

"How are your ribs feeling?"

"Just fine. Really good."

"Great. Okay. I have some fudge bars to get back to. Keep up the good work."

"Thanks, Dad. I will."

A plump man in sunglasses and a Mickey Mouse jean jacket walked over to where Susie was working. "Hi. Can you tell me what this is?"

"It's peach cobbler. My own recipe. Would you like to try a little?"

"Yes, please."

Susie put a dollop on a napkin for him and gave him a plastic fork. He tasted it and smiled. "That's terrific."

"Thank you. The special ingredient is love. And the burning desire to see all of humanity savaged by giant fire-breathing wasps. But mostly love."

The plump man threw the napkin in a nearby trash can and said, "I'll take the whole thing."

Susie beamed at him. "Wonderful," she said. "Would you like me to wrap that up for you?"

The man picked up the cobbler and said, "No thanks. I'll have it here." He raised the dish over his head and smashed it down on the table. It exploded, sending peach cobbler in all directions and knocking other cakes and pies onto the ground.

Behind the man, a van screeched to a stop. The side door slid open and a group of men and women in monster masks piled out.

"Acolytes and adepts to work!" shouted the plump man.

The crowd from the van attacked the tables, smashing pastries, throwing them at the Caleximus congregation and people browsing in the market. They overturned tables and smashed display cases. Jerry tried to grab one of them, but got an elbow in the ribs that sent him to the pavement in agony. Steve managed to get one of the attackers in a headlock, but two more jumped on him and pulled them apart. Another smeared whipped cream in his eyes and he tripped over Leonard, who was already on his back, trying to climb out of a slippery trail of jelly donuts. Janet threw a Bundt cake at one of the masked women. She ducked and hit Janet with a tray of macaroons.

As a couple of security cops ran over, the man in the Mickey Mouse jacket shouted, "Acolytes and adepts! Withdraw!" The cake- and pie-smeared vandals piled back into the van and it burned rubber across the parking lot, scattering shoppers out of the way, and disappeared into traffic.

Steve ran over and helped Susie to her feet. "Are you all right?"

"I'm fine. Where's Jerry?"

Steve found him still doubled over and sat him upright. "Is everyone else all right?"

The group nodded and mumbled yes miserably, wiping cake, jam, and fruit from their faces and clothes.

"Who was that?" said Tommy.

"It could have only been one bunch: those Cladis Abaddonis bastards," said Steve.

"Why go after us?" said Tommy.

"And how did they know where we'd be?" said Susie.

"They came after us because they're heathen assholes, that's why," said Steve. "And I bet I know how they found us. It was that Coop guy. He probably saw one of our pendants the other night and sent the Abaddonians after us."

"Maybe he's been with them all along," said Susie.

"Son of a bitch," said Steve. "I'm going to kick that private eye's ass until he finds him."

Leonard pulled Jerry to his feet. "Dad," he said. "I might be able to help."

TWENTY-SEVEN

THEY'D STARTED WORK AT NINE THIRTY IN THE MORNing. It was now past two. No one had eaten lunch. The coffee was gone and so were the donuts someone had stolen from the break room. Basically, it was an office full of frustrated, caffeine-deprived, sugar-crashing psychopaths. Bayliss had an energy bar hidden in her jacket pocket, but there was no way she was letting anybody know that. Especially Nelson. Locked in the room all day, he hadn't been able to get at his flask. Bayliss tried not to take such delight in watching him sweat and get shaky, but if she could have read Coop and Giselle's minds, she might have been able to take some comfort in knowing they felt the same way.

They were in the same office where they'd taken Coop on his first day at the DOPS. Now the big table was covered in blueprints, thaumaturgic scans, Kirlian satellite photos, and spectral charts of Mr. Babylon's Laurel Canyon mansion.

Coop held up an overhead photo showing the residence's aura. It was black, and spikes around the edges looked like angry crab claws.

"I hate these damned spook mansions. The last time I did a job in one I landed in jail," Coop said.

"That's because someone gave you up to the cops," said Giselle. "That's not going to happen this time. Remember that we're in this with you."

"Cops saving me from cops. It's a little surreal."

"At least it's one less thing to worry about," said Bayliss.

"Still. The whole thing feels cursed. I was hoping the box would be in a nice bank vault or nuclear missile silo. Those I could handle. This place is a mess."

"Why?" said Bayliss. "Talk us through it."

Coop tossed the photo onto the table and stretched his back. "Everything I can see, it's all designed so you might be able to get in, but you won't be able to get out. Or there's a way out, but there's no way in without setting off fifty alarms."

Earlier, Nelson had found a drawer full of pencils in a nearby table. He'd spent most of the past hour flipping them overhead at the ceiling. He'd gotten pretty good at it. The acoustic tiles bristled with skinny yellow stalactites. "I told you this guy was a bum," he said. He continued in a squeaky mocking voice. "Look at me. I'm magic. I'm Tinkerbell. I can get in anywhere."

"Like you're any help," said Bayliss. "Let him work this out." She looked at Coop. "Can we get you inside with a disguise? You can be there to repair the kitchen sink or deliver a package."

Coop shook his head. "That still leaves the problem of getting out. The room where Babylon has the box is a complete clusterfuck. There's no way I can sneak in and out of there without somebody noticing." He picked up his empty coffee cup for the twentieth time and set it down in disgust. "And even if it's possible to get in, we're only assuming he's keeping the box in his vault. What if he has it in his bedroom? Or he's using it to store paper clips in his office?"

"He hasn't opened it. Trust me. We'd know. Every lightbulb and computer in the world would be down," said Bayliss.

"How exactly do we know it's in the vault?"

"Our psychics department told us," said Nelson.

"The DOPS psychics? The bunch who couldn't figure out when I was stealing the box? Bang-up job. Very reassuring."

"Bitch. Whine. Bitch."

"Fine," Coop said to Nelson. "What's your plan, Keyser Söze?"

Nelson tossed a pencil at the ceiling, then turned to Coop. "I say we go in guns blazing. A total D-Day operation. We can tell the press we found the real bin Laden."

"That's original, I'll give you that," said Giselle. "Dumb, but original."

Coop pointed to a spot on the blueprints. "You send a bunch of agents in through the front door, all you'll end up with is a lot of dust, bones, and teeth. Maybe someone's pinky, but that's being optimistic."

"So you say, Gandalf," said Nelson.

"Look at the plans yourself."

Nelson picked up his pencils and leaned back in his chair. "I'm a supervisor. I'm your supervisor. I'm not here to do your job for you." He tossed a pencil. It missed and hit him on the head. "Goddammit."

Bayliss went over to where Coop was looking over the spectral charts, showing the strength of the curses in different parts of the house. "What my partner means is he doesn't know how to read blueprints or any of the rest of this."

"And you do?" said Nelson.

"Of course. It's part of basic training."

Nelson said, "It's part of basic training," in the same squeaky voice he'd used on Coop.

"How did you not learn any of this?"

Nelson considered the question. "Wait a minute. Maybe I did and can't remember." He looked at Giselle. "Are you messing with my mind? Are you in on something with him?" he said, pointing to Coop.

"Right. I love sitting in this room with your gin sweat and no coffee."

"It's whiskey sweat, kitten."

"Just because you can't do your job, suddenly it's my fault. Why don't you get your toy crucifix and go eat a burrito?"

Nelson pointed at her. "How do you know I like burritos?"

"Unknot your diapers. Everybody likes burritos," said Coop.

"Personally, I like the plantain chips more," said Giselle.

"You've been following me," said Nelson. "What are you up to?"

"I just like watching you gobble down an ebola and black beans grande with a side of dizzy juice."

"Are you two in this together? Is this a conspiracy?"

"Leave me out of this. I'm a McDonald's man, myself," said Coop.

"Relax," said Bayliss. "She just came by one time so we could talk."

"I don't remember that. When was it?"

Bayliss looked at Giselle. "Um . . ."

"It was just the other day. You weren't there," said Giselle.

"Aha! But you've never been there without me. Have you?"

Bayliss looked away.

"No. You're too honest to lie about it. So, you two *are* in on something," said Nelson, pointing to Bayliss and Giselle. Then he turned to Coop. "And you most of all. You're all in on it together."

"We're trying to steal the Constitution," said Giselle. "Haven't you seen the movie? There's a treasure map on the back."

Nelson looked back and forth between Giselle and Coop.

Coop said, "Calm down, kids. We're all just doing our jobs. All I want is a way this heist doesn't get me killed or arrested."

Nelson aimed a pencil at Giselle. "Why can't the Scarlet Witch just turn invisible and walk you in and out the front door?"

"Wow, Dr. Who. You just saved the day," said Coop.

"What Coop means is that a Marilyn is the first thing Babylon would have thought of," said Giselle.

"They have wards and hexes everywhere," said Coop. "No one clouds anyone's mind in there."

"Lucky them," said Nelson. He looked at Giselle. "If she's a third wheel around here, then why is she still around?"

"Unlike you, I'm trying to help figure out how to make this plan work," Giselle said.

"What about the roof?" said Bayliss. "Or here. The pipes to the Roman pools. Those are big enough for you to swim through."

Coop ran his hand over the top of the blueprints. "The roof is loaded with pressure sensors. And even if you could get through, there's the piranhas."

"There's a pool up there?"

"No. An aviary."

"Babylon has flying piranhas?"

"Babylon has flying piranhas," said Coop. "And I can't get in through the pipes because—"

"Let me guess," said Nelson. "Fire-breathing underwater spider monkeys."

"No. Explosives around the intake."

"Damn. So close."

Coop glanced in his coffee cup again. "I wish we had some fire-breathing monkeys. They could torch the place."

"How would that help?" said Giselle. "Do you want to go in and die of smoke inhalation?"

"No. I just think it would be fun to burn it down."

There was a light knock at the door and Salzman came in. "Good afternoon, everyone. I don't want to interrupt anything, but I wanted to come by and see how you were all doing."

Coop picked up a spectral chart and dropped it on the desk. "We're not. Doing, that is. From what I've seen on these papers, the job can't be done. It's impossible."

Salzman pushed the papers away from the end of the desk and sat down. "It's not your job to tell me it's impossible. It's your job to tell me how you're going to do it."

"How come every time I point out that this job won't work, one of you helpful schoolmarms says 'try harder'?"

"Because you're a—"

"Do not say it."

"Fuddy-duddy."

"That's it. I quit."

"Fine," said Salzman. "The prison van will be by for you in an hour. In the meantime, Nelson, why don't you cuff him?"

"Wait," said Giselle. "I take it back. He's not a fuddy-duddy. And he's telling the truth about the job."

Coop pushed away some of the plans on the table. "According to this crap, everything is going to get us killed. And by 'us' I mean 'me.' "

"Then do something else," said Salzman through gritted teeth. "Every building has a weak spot. You just haven't found this one's yet."

"We're going to need more time," said Coop.

Nelson came around the table with his cuffs out. Salzman held up a hand to stop him. "Oh, man," Nelson said.

"How much more time?"

"A week. At least."

"You have two days." Coop started to say something, but Salzman pointed to Nelson and Coop shut up. "After I leave here I'm going upstairs to Mr. Woolrich's office to tell him that you're well on your way to forming a solid plan of attack. Do not make me a liar." He turned to Nelson. "Put the cuffs away. For now."

Nelson remained on Salzman's side of the room and pointed at the others. "These three are up to something. I don't know what, but they're all in on it together."

Salzman looked them over with his milky eyes. "Excellent. A conspiracy demonstrates real teamwork and initiative. Congratulations. It sounds like you're off and running."

"Just one more thing," said Coop. He drummed his fingers on the table a couple of times. "We need to be absolutely clear on one thing. If I get you the box and come out of this alive, that's it. I'm free and clear to go."

Salzman nodded. "That is the agreement. Get us the box and you're as free as—"

"A fire-breathing spider monkey?" said Giselle.

Salzman stood up, straightened his jacket. "Do we have those? I'd love to see one."

"Me, too."

"Go check with the lab boys and get back to me."

"Yes, sir."

Salzman started to leave when Nelson said, "Sir. What about the conspiracy?"

Salzman turned to him. "Go have a burrito and a drink. It's all you're good for these days." He turned and left.

"Sounds like a good plan to me." Nelson got up and followed.

Coop went back to the schematics. Bayliss excused herself to use the restroom and ate her energy bar. Giselle took one of Nelson's pencils and tossed it into the ceiling.

"Bull's-eye," she said.

TWENTY-EIGHT

THE STRANGER CAME INTO THE CITY ACROSS THE Golden Gate Bridge, crossing from the warmth of Marin into the fog of San Francisco Bay. The mist was cold and wet, but in a pleasant way. He pulled his jacket tight around him. Tourists shivered in spectacularly inappropriate shorts, taking snapshots of each other against the swirling gray background. Joggers and cars passed by.

The stranger looked over the edge of the bridge, thinking of all the suicides the Golden Gate had inspired. *Wouldn't it be glorious to see one of those?* He looked around hopefully, but no one seemed interested in taking the bait. Disappointed, he kept walking.

He went through a parking lot at the end of the bridge where other bridge walkers had left their cars, and continued into the city. It had been a long walk from Red Bluff, and he had a longer walk still to go, but there was plenty of time to make it. As long as he didn't linger too long at any one place. The trick was to plan his city excursion. The stranger took out a well-thumbed city guide, at least ten years old. He examined the dog-eared pages, compared them to his map, and plotted what looked like a good route, tracing promising fault lines and old cemeteries that had been plowed under during one of the city's fabulously corrupt building booms.

San Francisco was a dense city, but it wasn't large. He'd once walked from its far eastern edge to the ocean in five hours. This time, it only took him two hours to reach his first stop: an old music club he'd been to with friends years earlier. He walked through the SoMa district, got lost twice, but eventually found the address. But not the club. It was gone. All that was left was a weedy, fenced-off vacant lot with a sign showing a picture of a gleaming twenty-story condo tower that the sign said would soon occupy the lot. There was a phone number of a realty company and a photo of an attractive man and woman in matching company jackets. They looked like brother and sister. Or clones. Did everybody know how to clone yet, or was it just real estate companies? It was something to look into.

The stranger tore the page from his guidebook and dropped it into a recycling bin on the corner before moving on.

He walked to North Beach, past the Tosca Café, Specs' bar, and City Lights Books. He'd been to all those places on earlier trips and was relieved to see them still there. Just across the alley from City Lights was the Vesuvio Café. That, too, was still intact. But he'd also been there before, so he decided to try somewhere new. The stranger walked around the corner onto Broadway and down the block, looking at the Bay Bridge in the distance. He checked the address of a café in his guidebook and went inside.

He ordered a double espresso from a young man at the counter. A lot of the people in the café had various piercings and tattoos. The stranger also had tattoos, but he kept them hidden. They weren't for anyone's eyes but his and those of a few close associates. He hoped for a reunion of sorts soon, but not today. Today, he would sit in a café, drink coffee, and look at his guidebook.

When the barista called the name he'd give him, the stranger went to the counter to pick up his coffee. There was a large framed photo on the wall behind the cash register. Three young men. One in baggy dress pants and two in jeans. As he paid for his coffee, the stranger nodded toward the picture.

"It must be interesting working where they used to drink," he said.

The young man looked over his shoulder and shook his head. "I don't know, man. I'm not from around here."

"But surely you recognize them. That's William Burroughs on the end."

The barista looked again. "That's a real old photo. Were they a band? My buddy, Ryan, is into all kinds of seventies classic bands. I think I've heard of them. Burroughs Turner Overdrive?"

"You're thinking of Bachman-Turner Overdrive. And they were Canadian. No, that's William Burroughs, Jack Kerouac, and Lawrence Ferlinghetti. They were writers."

The barista frowned. "Maybe. I'm not really a word guy. I'm more into hyperedge interactive visual happenings. Music. Video. Lights."

"Yes. That began in this area, too. In the mid-nineteen-sixties. They were called Acid Tests."

The young man shook his head. "You sure? I've never heard of them."

The stranger smiled. "Of course. Why would you? They're old and gone. What's the use of old things? The now. The future. The unexpected twists and turns down the road. Those are the only things of value."

"Exactly," said the barista. "You get it."

"Thank you for the coffee."

The young man waved a counter rag at him and helped the next customer. The stranger drank his coffee, but didn't stay. He was restless. So much had changed. It wasn't his place to judge—that was for wiser heads than his—but it was hard not to be a little peeved at humanity's capacity to forget. To minimize even its own accomplishments.

He turned south down Columbus Avenue until it turned into Montgomery, walked through the Financial District, then down onto Market Street. Not sure where to go, the stranger turned back toward the Pacific. He thought about returning all the way to the ocean, but that would take more time than he'd allotted himself. He took out his guidebook and thumbed through its worn pages. Everything he looked at seemed gray and lifeless to him now. The trip to North Beach had been a bad idea. The walk through SoMa hadn't been much better. He understood how an animal, when in a trap, might gnaw its own leg off, but gnawing your leg off when things were going well, when you were prospering, that the stranger didn't understand at all. He knew that despair was a sin, and while that's not quite what he felt, part of him felt empty and even foolish. He threw the guidebook into a trash can and simply wandered along Market Street, no purpose or destination in mind.

He came to another vacant lot. Unlike the first one, this was paved. A dozen large, immaculate buses sat in rows. On the side of each bus in big block letters was LIQUID INDUSTRIES, DISRUPTING THE DISRUPTION. At the edge of the parking lot was a ragged circle of men and women. They had drums and, while they were playing with a tremendous amount of gusto and volume, they didn't quite seem to have the concept of rhythm down yet. Several policemen stood in a semicircle nearby eyeing the drummers. The stranger walked over to them.

"Excuse me, but what's happening here? Is this a religious ceremony?" he said.

One of the cops gave the stranger a look like he was considering arresting him just for being there. "It's a drum circle. Hippies protesting fuck-all."

"I'm not familiar with them. What are the tenets of 'fuck-all'?"

"Are you being a wise-ass?" the cop asked, reaching for his nightclub.

"No, sir. It's just that I'm new here and want to make sure that I understand the situation."

"Listen," said the cop. "Business has been good to this town. It brought in a lot of money, even if it also brought a lot of douche bags. These lowlifes don't like the corporate buses, so they do this all day. It's giving me a goddamn migraine."

"Me, too," said a couple of the other police.

"So, the people who own the buses and are driving the local economy are people you don't like."

"Rich assholes."

"And the people protesting the businesspeople are also people you don't like."

"Hippie assholes."

"Is there anyone around here who isn't an asshole?"

"What?" said the policeman, reaching for his club again.

"Never mind. A pointless question," said the stranger. Before the cops could begin debating whether it would be more fun to beat or pepper-spray him, he walked over to one of the drummers.

"Hello. What exactly is it you're doing?"

A young woman nodded. "We're showing that we won't take it anymore."

"And banging drums is how you're going to unseat an entrenched oligarchy?"

"We're doing it for Mother Earth," said the young woman.

"Yeah. This is the rhythm of her heart," said a young man next to her.

The stranger scratched his chin. "Maybe she should see a doctor. Her heart seems to be skipping a lot of beats."

The young man gave him a darkly assessing look.

"Thank you. You've been very educational," said the stranger.

"Are you a narc?"

"What's a narc?"

"Yeah. He's a narc," said the young woman.

"You know, you can take lessons for this sort of thing," said the stranger. "Drumming, I mean. People have been teaching it to each other for thousands of years."

The drummers ignored him. When the stranger turned, one of the cops crooked a finger at him to call him over.

"What's your connection to this bunch?" he asked.

"I was just curious about what they—and, of course, you were doing."

The policeman stood absolutely still for a moment looking at the stranger. Then he said, "Let's see your ID."

"You mean a driver's license or birth certificate?"

"You carry a birth certificate around with you?"

"No. I don't have one."

"Then yes, a driver's license."

"I don't have one of those, either."

"How about a passport?"

"I don't have any ID and I threw my guidebook away. I wrote my name in it, if that would help. It's just back a block or so."

Two more policemen came over and stood on either side of the stranger.

"I'm going to ask you one more time . . ."

"You can ask all you like. I don't have any ID. But if it's any consolation, I think I now know why you're in such a bad mood. That awful drumming is giving me a headache, too."

One of the cops took the stranger's right arm in a powerful grip. "Come with us," he said and tried to move him. But the stranger remained rooted where he was, much to the policeman's surprise.

"I don't think I'll be coming with you. I don't have time. But I want to leave you all with something."

The cop kept tugging on his arm. Two more grabbed the stranger, but couldn't move him.

"What I want to leave you with is a thought: with all the wonders of the world at your disposal, the one thing you shouldn't be is boring." The stranger turned to the policeman on his left arm. "You're boring." He turned to the policeman on his right. "You're boring, too." He shouted to the drum circle. "Technically, you're not boring. You're well meaning, but you're awful. Just horrible."

The city began to tremble. Market Street rippled down its length, like waves at the edge of the ocean. Skyscrapers swayed. Windows broke and glass rained into the streets below. The policemen let go of the stranger's arms and tried to run, but the street was wobbling too violently for them to get more than a couple of steps before they fell. Buses and cars smashed into each other. Electrical wires snapped.

A crack opened in the street. It split a nearby crosswalk and shattered the pavement where the stranger stood. The crack, an extension of a heretofore unknown fault line, ripped open the parking lot and one by one, the Liquid Industries buses slid into the Earth, followed by the drum circle and the police. Buildings toppled behind him. When the shaking stopped, for a second there was only the sound of geysers where fire hydrants and water mains had broken. Then the silence was torn apart as a million car alarms went off at once. People covered their ears. Some screamed. Others simply turned in slow circles, looking at the damage in mute shock.

The stranger checked his map—the one he kept folded up, not the one from the guidebook—and started down Van Ness Boulevard, where he'd left himself a relatively undamaged corridor that he could pass through. He climbed over wrecked cars, made his way past shouting drivers, heading for the freeway. He took a new guidebook from his coat pocket and riffled the pages. This one had palm trees and a picture of the Hollywood Chinese Theater on the front. The cover of the book said, A WALKING TOUR OF LOS ANGELES. The stranger took a breath. Walking was the thing. The only thing right now. He headed onto the entirely undamaged 101 freeway—now mostly deserted, since all the entry ramps had collapsed—and started south.

TWENTY-NINE

THE DARK HIGH MAGISTER OF CLADIS ABADDONIS SAT in his holy Barcalounger, eating fish and chips from his silver TV tray. He'd spent a good deal of the previous day getting bent, cracked, and stretched by the chiropractor downstairs in room 4. Today, his back felt a little better, but the smell of bleach from the cleanup in room 8 was spoiling his lunch. It was always some damned thing around here. No wonder so much of his flock had run off with those San Diego bastards. What could he offer them, other than discounted cod and fries? It was a sad state for the Lodge, but that might all be changing soon. *It better,* he thought, or, to his secret shame, he might have to—if not quite defect—at least strike an alliance with his enemies down south. His old Datsun was on its last legs and the no-money-down deal from those San Diego Volvo shits was sorely tempting. But no, he wasn't ready to throw in the towel for a Bluetooth radio. Not quite yet, he thought. The Magister still had some tricks up his stained and fraying sleeve. But they depended on other people, some of whom were late.

He poured more balsamic vinegar onto his fish, then checked his watch. A moment later, Adept Three and Acolyte Six came panting into the sacred chamber.

Adept Six said, "Sorry, Dark High One. There's construction down the block and we had to park clear over on Seventh Street."

"We ran all the way," said Acolyte Three.

The Dark High Magister waved for them to calm down. "It's fine. I've been listening to those jerks banging away for days now. What are they building?"

"A Red Lobster, sir."

"A fish restaurant. Well, that's just great. Why doesn't City Hall come down here and shove a big ole corkscrew up my ass? Right up it."

"We could always sabotage it," said Acolyte Three. "Superglue the locks shut. Sugar in the gas tanks of the bulldozers."

"They have video surveillance these days, dumbo," said the Magister. "They'll see you and that's two more members of the Lodge gone. No. This is a sign that we have to move faster bringing Lord Abaddon back to this wretched world. Let Red Lobster see how it feels to be skull fucked when a thousand-foot bottom-feeding sea bastard comes a-calling."

"But, Dark High One. We run a seafood restaurant, too."

The Magister draped his napkin over his unfinished cod. "Everything has its reasons, especially Lord Abaddon. Besides, the restaurant will be gone soon. The moment we retrieve the Convocation Vessel. Speaking of which," he clapped his hands together, "how did the raid on the Calcximus pricks go?"

"It was awesome," said Acolyte Three.

"Yeah. Really well," said Adept Six.

"Don't be shy. Details, boys. Details. I barely get off the throne these days except to crap and get bent like a pretzel by that jerk in room four. I want to see our moment of triumph in my mind's eye."

Adept Six and Acolyte Three looked at each other. The acolyte, the junior member of the Lodge, smiled shyly at the adept, like he was doing him a big favor by letting him go first. "You know, sir, I'm not really much of a public speaker."

"Don't be nervous," said the Magister. "What did you do first?"

"Um. Adept Four pretended to buy a peach cobbler."

"And?"

"He didn't."

"Then what?"

"He threw the cobbler on the ground. The van came around with the rest of us and we got out."

"What happened then? Come on. I want to feel the mayhem," said the Magister.

"We knocked over a table and stuff went everywhere," said Acolyte Three. "I stepped on some cakes."

"Good for you. That almost makes up for you puking in the sacred chamber."

"Thank you, Dark High One."

"I slipped on some butter cream and hurt my knee," said Adept Six.

The Magister looked at him hard. "Not exactly Purple Heart–worthy, eh?" he said. "But tell me, did you put the fear of Cladis Abaddonis in them?"

"Oh, yeah. Right in them. And on them. Like a whole bunch of muffins."

"And scones," Acolyte Three added.

"Right. We covered them in misery and scones."

"Excellent. Then what?"

"Then we ran away."

"You ran?"

"There were security guards coming."

"We didn't really run," said Acolyte Three. "We just got in the van and expeditiously fled."

"Yes. That," said Adept Six.

The Magister leaned back in his lounger. His back pinched him hard. When Abaddon came back, that fraud in room 4 was right up there on the annihilation list with Red Lobster. "You weren't kidding when you said you weren't a public speaker."

"Sorry, Dark High One," Adept Six said.

"What about you, Acolyte? Did you suffer any crippling cupcake injuries? Lose a leg to a fritter? An ear to some sprinkles?"

Acolyte Three leaned forward a little, showing a tiny bruise. "I get a lemon bar in the eye. It really stung. But it was good, too. I think she used real lemons, not like the plastic ones you get from the store."

"That's the kind my mom used," said Adept Six.

"Mine, too."

"My goodness," said the Magister. "How did either of you survive the slaughter? I have to admit, I'm disappointed in the level of carnage in your story. Did anyone at least draw blood?"

"Adept One ran into the van and broke his nose," said the acolyte.

"Not *our* blood, you idiot. Them. Did you leave them bloody and bruised?"

"No, sir," said the adept. "But we did get this." He handed the Magister a brown paper bag.

"It's heavy," he said as he took it. When he looked inside, he smiled. The Magister reached in and pulled out several neat rolls of quarters. "Now we're talking," he said. "You got their cash drawer. Excellent. How much did we walk away with?"

"One hundred and six dollars and eighty-three cents," said Adept Six.

The Magister curled his lip. "It doesn't put us quite up there with Donald Trump, but it's better than nothing," he said.

"Thank you, Dark High One," said the adept.

"Yes. Thank you," said the acolyte.

The Magister dropped the cash on the TV tray, which bowed a little under the weight of all the change. "Now, I have a little secret I can share with you," he said.

Adept Six's eyes widened. "Don't tell me the Caleximus bunch have the Convocation Vessel!"

The Magister put a hand to his brow. "Why would you even say that? Isn't that the first thing I'd bring up when you got here? 'Hello, boys. How was your day? Oh, by the way, get ready for fiery doom because our mortal enemies are about to call down Armageddon on us.' Don't you think that would be something of a priority announcement?"

"Sorry, sir. Of course, Dark High One. I'm just a little nervous with the end so near."

"Sure. It's understandable."

"Are we worthy of hearing your secret, sir?" said Acolyte Three.

The adept gave him a look, as did the Magister.

"Don't do that. Just because he's a moron doesn't mean you have to be a suck-up."

The acolyte looked at the floor. "Sorry, sir."

"Never mind. Here's the secret: I know where the Convocation Vessel is."

The adept and the acolyte looked up at him. "Where?" they said, almost in unison.

"I don't know exactly a hundred percent where it is, but I have a pretty good idea," said the Magister. "You see, it turns out your little Twinkie assault did more good than you think." The Magister looked at his charges, pausing for dramatic effect, though he wasn't sure they'd know what dramatic effect was if it came in wearing a tutu and hit them both with a Hello Kitty sledgehammer. As seriously as he could, he said, "We now have an agent among the Caleximus heretics."

"Who?" said Adept Six.

"Oh, no. That's still my little secret for now. Suffice it to say that after your humiliating attack, he's lost faith in their false god and is ready to tell us everything we need to retrieve the Vessel."

"Where is it, Dark High One?" said Acolyte Three.

"A man named Coop has it," he said.

"Then let's go and take it from him."

"Yes, why didn't I think of that? Maybe because I don't know where he is because those Caleximus boobs don't know where he is. But they're looking for him. That's the important thing."

"Should we be looking for him, too?" said Adept Six.

"Why should we? We have our mole. He'll tell us when they're closing in. We'll wait for them to find him and then swoop in and take him right out from under them." He looked at the adept. "There are still twelve of us, right?"

Adept Six nodded. "Yes, sir."

"Thank goodness. Yes. This will be a breeze."

"What about Lord Abaddon?" said Acolyte Three. "He's been waiting for us to call him back since the new moon."

"Well, he's just going to have to hold his britches a little longer just like the rest of us, isn't he?"

"Yes, sir."

The Magister took his now greasy napkin off the remains of his fish and chips. "Okay, boys. That's the new business. Is there any old business we need to get to?"

"Room 8, sir?" said Adept Six.

"Of course. I almost forgot," the Magister. "First off, please tell everyone who helped that even though I never got any change back from the cleaning-supplies money, I and the entire Lodge appreciate their efforts."

Adept Six shuffled his feet nervously. "There wasn't any change, Dark High One."

"You lost it, didn't you? Just admit it and all will be forgiven."

Adept Six nodded. "I swear, I put it right on my nightstand . . ."

"I knew it. For like ten seconds I thought you'd stolen it, but after your exciting tale of the Apocalyptic Pie Fight, I realized you had the imagination of a damp sweat sock." The Magister turned and pointed at Acolyte Three. "From now on, you're in charge of the money. Got it?"

The acolyte beamed at him. "Yes, Dark High One. Thank you."

"Don't thank me. Thank Slippy McClumsy over there."

Acolyte Three started to thank the adept, but when he saw the look on the man's face he knew he was no more than an inch from being beaten to death with the coins from the bake sale. He just gave him a quick nod and turned back to the Magister.

"Is there any more business?" said the old man.

"Weren't you saying you wanted to rent out room 8, sir?"

"Oh, yes," said the Magister. He took some three-by-five cards from his pocket and gave each of the men a pile.

"Go around to some of the universities and put those up on the bulletin boards. The last time we put an ad on Craigslist, all we got were weirdos and Frank, and we know how that turned out."

"Yes, sir," said the acolyte.

The Magister said, "Anything else?"

Adept Six pointed a finger. "Yes, you might want to move—" He never finished the sentence. The change from the bake sale collapsed the golden TV tray. The rolls of change mostly survived the fall, but fish and chips were scattered all over the sacred chamber. The Magister wiped his hand on his napkin and tossed it onto the floor with the rest of the mess. "Get out the bleach, boys," he said. "We have a room 8 situation in the making."

The Magister started to get up, but a back spasm dropped him back onto his lounger. He sighed. The goddamn end of the world better happen goddamn soon, he thought. If it wasn't exploding acolytes decorating his rooms with meat wallpaper, it was Red Lobster horning in on his damned fish business. He made a silent prayer to Abaddon that the Caleximus bunch weren't quite the fuckups he'd always told his flock they were. *Just let them find this Coop asshole. That's all I ask. Then rise from the ocean and drown the world, Abaddon. Starting with San Diego.*

The Magister watched the acolyte and the adept picking the food and money off the floor, counting the rolls of pennies and quarters in his head. There had to be twenty pounds at least. A nice haul, he thought. They'd go well in the seat cushions with the other Lodge funds, all of which he'd converted to coins. The Magister calculated that his chair weighed more than four hundred pounds these days. When Abaddon returned and the floods came, he wasn't taking any chances on floating away. He, his throne, and his lousy back were going down when the first waves hit the land, and there was nothing those assholes in San Diego, Caleximus, Red Lobster, or any of his dumb-ass flock could do about it. The Magister closed his eyes and crossed his fingers.

Find Coop, you sons of bitches. Find Coop.

It was eight in the evening. The two women sat across from Mr. Babylon in his favorite booth in Týden Divu, the Jinx Town bar so recently and rapidly exited by Coop and Giselle. The women—

Giselle and a somewhat nervous Bayliss—were sipping Manhattans. Babylon was drinking a Roy Rogers with obvious distaste.

"I hope you don't mind me not joining you for real drinks, ladies," said Babylon. "Doctor's orders."

"Not at all," said Giselle. "We're just happy you could meet us on such short notice."

Babylon swirled his drink, giving it a look of curdled loathing. "My pleasure. I'm always open to business opportunities. Though this one will, I'm afraid, cost more than many."

"The good ones always do," said Bayliss.

Good for you, thought Giselle. Get her away from Nelson and get a couple of drinks in her, and she takes off. I'll have to remember that. Giselle took a quick glance around the bar. No one was paying them the slightest bit of attention. She had to concentrate hard to cloud so many minds and make sure they wouldn't remember her, but that and her blond wig seemed to be doing the trick. She just had to remember not to drink too much.

"How did you find this place?" she said. "Are you a fan of the dark floors?"

Babylon looked over at the gaming tables, then back at the women. "I've always enjoyed them. Much more peaceful than the wet or dry ones, and away from the hustle and bustle of the light floors."

"Unless you're looking for shoes. Then I love the light floors," said Bayliss. Giselle had briefed her on the layout of Jinx Town, but now wished she'd do a little shutting up about it. No more drinks for her.

"Don't discount the dark floors for shopping," said Babylon. "There are some exceptional places nearby. I get most of my suits here."

"Thank you. Maybe I'll take a stroll later."

"Just take a clove or two of garlic with you," said Babylon. "The exsanguinator riffraff can be a bit annoying."

"Don't worry. I've worked with vampires before," Bayliss said.

Reel it in, thought Giselle. She kicked Bayliss lightly under the table.

"Really? Where?" said Babylon.

"Oh, here and there," Bayliss said. "You know how it is. Business takes you all sorts of places with all sorts of people."

"Indeed," said Babylon.

"Would you mind telling us a bit more about the box?" said Giselle before Bayliss could cram her foot in her mouth again. "Is it everything I've heard it is?"

Babylon finished his drink and held up his glass for another. A waiter nodded in his direction. "It depends on what you've heard. There are a lot of rumors and tall tales."

"Since we're the buyers, if you don't mind, we'd like to hear it from you," said Giselle.

"The box, to put it simply, is an edge," Babylon said. "Nothing less than luck incarnate. It's what every entrepreneur needs. A constant and reliable edge on the competition."

"There are stories floating around that it's something else, too," said Bayliss.

Babylon shrugged. "Stories about the box are as numerous as Scheherazade's thousand and one tales. Recently, an associate of mine plucked it away just as a couple of low-rent doomsday cults tried for it. Each thought they could use it to set off their rival Armageddons. Have you ever heard of something so silly?"

"Lucky you found it before they had a chance to test it out. Then we might not have had the pleasure of meeting you."

"To Apocalypse averted," said Babylon. He held up his glass in a toast.

"And new business ventures," said Bayliss.

"Always that."

Gisele smiled. While she concentrated on clouding the room, she was giving special attention to Babylon. There wasn't any liquor in his drinks, so she was loosening him up a little herself. Not too much. A couple of Scotches' worth. *Just want him friendly and happy. Not stupid and horny.*

She sipped her drink slowly and fantasized about cutting through the crap and beating Babylon on the head with a bottle of grenadine until he just gave them the damned box. Coop better be on the job, she thought. I don't want to spend the whole night entertaining this bloated Scrooge McDuck.

Her phone rang. She excused herself and glanced at the number, quickly pressing the button to send the call to voice mail. The moment she did, Very Important People jumped into action doing Very Important Things.

Two floors below Týden Divu, Salzman sat in the mook bar and watched his call go to voice mail. That was the signal. He dialed another number and it only rang once before someone picked it up.

"Babylon's distraction is in place. Are you ready?" he said.

"No," said Coop.

"Let me ask that another way. Are you prepared to keep your part of our bargain?"

"As much as I'll ever be."

"You have your team with you? Including what's-his-name?"

"Yes. Morty is here."

"What about Phil Spectre? Safely ensconced in your noggin, is he?"

"Yeah. He's already whining to get out of my head. He doesn't like the idea of playing earthworm," Coop said.

"Tell him to shut up and do his job."

"That's pretty much every conversation I've ever had with him."

Salzman cleared his throat. "Once again, I have to remind you that the DOPS makes no guarantees for your safety. If you or the team gets caught or killed, it's on you."

"I never thought it would be any other way," Coop said.

"Are you comfortable in the crawler?"

"I'm not so wild about being an earthworm, either. But I've been worse places for smaller payoffs."

"Good luck," said Salzman. "Don't disappoint me."

"Actually, you're somewhere near the bottom of the top hundred things I'm worried about right now."

"Call me the moment you're clear."

"You just make sure you take care of Giselle and Bayliss."

"They're doing fine. Just bring me the box."

"And I'll get you a Kewpie doll for your collection."

Salzman turned off the phone and put it back in his pocket. He sipped his martini and thought about the things he'd do to Coop if he failed. No jail for that boy. There were more interesting and surgical things he could arrange for a fuckup that big.

Salzman looked around the bar, hating the other mooks, but himself most of all. Everything he'd done and everything he wanted was in the hands of a jackass, a civilian, and a paranoid ghost. Or, to be more accurate, a jackass, a jackass civilian, and a jackass paranoid ghost. If he weren't already dead, he'd be worried. As it was, what he felt wasn't dread, but more a dire fear of sameness. That tomorrow would be no different from today. He couldn't even get drunk. His physiology wouldn't let him. Maybe he'd go out and kill somebody. That was always fun. A random stranger. Maybe at a highway rest stop. Toss the body in a Dumpster. Blow off a little steam and get back to the office in time for Coop's report. He checked his watch and got up. He'd have to get going if he wanted to beat the traffic.

At Týden Divu, Babylon was looking a little more drunk and restless than Giselle liked. Time to move, she thought.

"So, Mr. Babylon. How much money are we actually talking about for the box?"

"One hundred million," he said without missing a beat.

Bayliss sat back in her seat. Giselle gave her a light rap on the foot with her shoe.

"Considering everything you've told us about it, that sounds like a reasonable price," she said. "But, unless you're ready to accept a personal check, it will take us a day or so to put together that much cash."

He smiled. "As lovely as you ladies are, yes, I'm strictly a cash man. When can you get your finances together?"

"How's Friday?" said Bayliss.

Babylon gazed at his disgusting drink like he was trying to channel Jesus, not to turn his water to wine, but his Roy Rogers to gin. "That's reasonable," he said. "Let's say ten o'clock in the evening at the Bonaventure Hotel? I have a room on perpetual reserve."

"Perfect," said Giselle. "Now, I noticed you eyeing the gaming tables earlier. Fancy a game of something? Our treat, of course."

"Do you play roulette?" he said.

"No. Maybe you could teach us."

"I'd be delighted."

"I'll settle up our drinks and meet you over there," said Bayliss.

When Babylon was on his feet, Giselle offered him her arm. He took it and they headed for the roulette wheel. She prayed that Coop was already on the move. Even with all the risks, she was a little jealous of him. He got to play Indiana Jones while the DOPS had her on a budget. If Babylon sucked at roulette, she might have to dip into discretionary funds, and the paperwork on that was murder. Better to be digging through Laurel Canyon's sewers with a ghost in your head than worrying about this particular kind of crap.

THIRTY

THE ROAD CREW DIGGING UP THE STREET A HUNDRED yards from Babylon's hilltop mansion was making a hell of a mess. At least the locals thought so. What with all the bulldozers, backhoes, dump trucks, and things with claws that no one had ever seen before but people were sure that, like the road, had been paid for with their precious tax dollars, the workers should really obey their commands, starting with "Get the hell out of the way."

The crew had the road down to a single lane, and whoever was directing traffic didn't seem to know or care what he was doing. Plus the hole they'd dug, you could lose a Hummer, an Escalade, and one of those demented stretch limos made from Mini Coopers down there and no one would ever know. None of the drivers suspected that that was exactly the idea.

Nelson hated this evening with a furious passion. Standing on the road in a stupid orange vest wearing a stupid hard hat, directing stupid people around the stupid goddamn hole the crew had dug for Coop. He was sure the whole thing was a put-up job. That Coop's plan was either a crooked gambit to escape or part of his conspiracy with Giselle and Bayliss to waste the DOPS's time, and his in particular.

They'd been working on the road since six, getting the hole into the local sewer system wide enough to hold the Stink Missile. That part at least delighted Nelson. Coop sailing through a tidal wave of shit and hopefully meeting a colorful and agonizingly awful fate at the other end. When traffic let up for a minute, Nelson pulled out his flask and had a drink. That part also delighted Nelson. It was almost time. The hole was wide enough and the flatbed with the Missile was ready to go. Nelson signaled for other DOPS agents disguised as road workers to hold traffic below the crest of the hills in both directions.

"You're up, hotshot," said Nelson into his vest mic.

"I just got a pep talk from Salzman. I don't need another from you."

"But I've got a load of sweet nothings to whisper in your ear."

"Did I tell you you look great in that vest? Orange is really your color," said Coop.

One of the men on the flatbed truck made a circular motion in the air and Nelson nodded.

"Get ready to get flushed, genius. Oh yeah, did anyone mention that there's a bomb on board the Stink Missile? If you're not back in two hours, chunks of you are going to be flowing to the Pacific with the organic lentils these canyon fruit bats flush down their solid-gold toilets."

"Nelson, if I can't finish the job in two hours, I'm tunneling right under your ass and you can join me in shit Valhalla."

"Keep dreaming, sunshine. They're getting ready to insert you. That pal of yours know how to run the Stink Missile yet?"

"You ready?" asked Coop.

"Yeah," Morty's voice said. "It's just like driving a big truck. I've done it a million times."

"We're ready."

"Strap in, smart-ass," said Nelson. He signaled to the flatbed, and it began to tilt upward. It took a good thirty seconds to get the bed at a high enough angle that the Stink Missile slid off the back into the canyon sewer system. There wasn't another vehicle in the world like the Missile. It moved at a staggering two miles an hour and resembled a matte-black stealth lobster with a titanium drill at the front and little pushing feet at the back.

All with three trapped rats in the middle.

Once it settled, Morty hit the power and the Missile ground forward. He bounced off the tunnel walls a few times before he got the hang of the controls, but then they smoothed out and crept along at a steady clip.

"How are we doing, Morty?" said Coop.

"Piece of cake," he said. "Now that we're moving, all I need to do is watch the screens. Most of it's running on GPS autopilot."

"Where do we start tunneling?"

"Here," said Morty, pointing to a sewer map. "The pipe narrows as it gets near Babylon's place. We punch through the sewer wall and dig our way straight through to his basement. Good plan, Coop. Simple as apple pie."

"Of course, it sounds simple," said Phil Spectre in their heads. "All plans sound simple at first, then shit hits the fan. Or in this case, us."

"Hey, Phil," said Morty. "I didn't know the ride came with in-flight entertainment."

"Don't get him started," said Coop.

"I've got one for you," said Phil. "Knock knock."

"Who's there?" said Morty.

"Stephen Hawking."

"Stephen Hawking who?"

"Stephen Hawking who, if he was here, would be smart enough to steer us away from those DOPS cocks to somewhere safe and warm."

Morty looked at Coop. "You're right. He's a riot."

"You heard the man, Phil," said Coop. "We've got a bomb on board. We can't run very far underground in two hours."

"Are you happy with yourself right now? Proud of your life choices?" said Phil. "You know what they call this thing we're in?"

"Nelson said Stink Missile," said Morty.

"That's the nice name. It's usually Turd in a Tube. The Brown Bullet. Mocha Express. I can go on if you like."

"No, thanks," said Morty.

"Ignore him," said Coop. "He probably made up most of those himself."

"Supersonic Suppository. The Flying Nun."

"Okay. You definitely made up that last one," said Morty.

"But it's a good one. Admit it."

"It's all right. I might have gone with Roto-Rooter Rocket."

"Not too awful. You're more fun at this than Coop."

"Pipe down, both of you," said Coop. "How much farther to go?"

Morty looked at the GPS. "We'll be at the cutoff point in another minute. You might want to strap yourself in. We'll be digging through rock soon. It might get a little rough."

Morty was right about most of those things.

The Missile turned on its own when the GPS indicated that it had reached the end of the usable tunnel. From its front end, the Missile extended a plasma cutter and activated its massive drill bit to begin cutting through the pipe and into the earth. When they'd made a large enough hole in the sewer pipe wall, insectlike scooping arms extended from the Missile's front end, moving away the dirt the drill loosened. The Missile shook, gyrated, and shuddered. It was like riding a carousel made of jackhammers. For the first time in his life, Coop wondered if Phil was right and they should be tunneling away from here.

"This is nice. I'm glad you brought me along, Coop," said Phil. "Anyone fancy a sing-along?"

Morty looked at Coop. "Is he serious?"

Coop nodded. "It's what he does when he gets nervous, but he'd never admit it in front of you."

"Like hell I won't. Of course, I'm nervous," said Phil. "I'm as stuck down here as you meat sticks. If you both die, without somewhere to jump to, I get to haunt this tuna can for the next few centuries. How does that sound to you? Scaring earthworms and prairie dogs? That is not what I aspire to. I'm a professional."

"How did you end up with the DOPS?" said Coop, hoping to distract Phil.

"Like all the rest of you clowns. I got picked up on a job that didn't go, let's just say, exactly as planned."

"No one sold you out, did they?" said Coop.

"No."

"So who were you working with, Phil?"

"Fast Eddie Lansdale. You know him?"

Morty looked at Coop. "Yeah. We're acquainted. But why were you working with Eddie? He already has a crew."

"Why do you think? He was stepping out on them. We had what looked like an easy bank job, so the two of us were going to do it together."

"An easy bank job," said Coop. "Meaning it was a setup."

"Give that man a rubber cigar," said Phil. "Those DOPS creeps knew we were coming before I got to enjoy Eddie's symphony of morning farts. He's not a pleasant person to spend time with."

"So I hear," said Coop.

"But we just saw Eddie," said Morty. "How did he get away?"

"He didn't. We both got caught and the prick traded me to get himself cut loose. The DOPS didn't need any trained baboons on the payroll, so they took the deal and here we are all together. The three amigos."

The Missile shook and ground against something hard. Coop's spine felt like it had grown teeth and was digging its way out of his doomed body. He was glad he was strapped in.

"So who wants to play Truth or Dare?" said Phil.

"Shut up, Phil," said Coop.

"You're very chatty for a ghost," said Morty.

"I'm just a people person. Let's talk about you, Morty."

"No, thanks."

"How much longer?" said Coop.

Morty looked at the GPS. "Another five minutes."

"Do you have intimacy issues, Morty? Coop has massive ones."

"I don't think that's true," said Morty. "You should have seen him and Giselle at work. You'd never think she broke his heart and stomped all over it."

"Morty . . ." said Coop.

"Giselle?" said Phil. "Dish, girlfriend."

"Not another word."

"Sorry," said Morty.

"Don't listen, Morty. I'm his therapist. Tell me everything."

"Phil talks big now, but wait until we get inside," said Coop. "He's not bad at his job, but you're going to see another side of him."

"Really? He gets worse?"

"I'll let you be the judge."

"I'm right here, you know," said Phil. "I can hear every word."

"How much longer?" said Coop.

The Missile trembled. The grinding din from outside grew louder. They had to cover their ears. Then there was what sounded like a minor explosion. The Missile lurched forward and stopped. The drill on the front wound down. The digging arms retracted. Morty hit the outside lights. They were in a dark, open room, full of old furniture, paintings, and crates.

"Holy crap," said Morty. "I think we're here." He checked the GPS. "We are. We're in Babylon's cellar."

"I knew he wouldn't bother with a lot of curses down here. Now we just have to get to his safe and get out. Everyone know what they're doing?"

"I get you out of the basement and stay here, keep the Missile warmed up till you come back," said Morty.

"Right."

"And I make sure you don't screw everything up," said Phil.

"You sure you don't want me to come along?" Morty said. "There might be more locks."

"Not according to the blueprints," said Coop. "Coming from the bottom of the house, we're bypassing most of the worst traps. All we have to worry about is the room with the safe."

"I'm not so sure about that, Coop," said Phil. "The more the merrier, I say. Let's bring ol' Morty along. Nothing personal, but you can be a grumpopotamus."

Morty said, "That's not what Giselle says. She says—"

"Shut up. That's what she says. Morty stays," said Coop firmly.

"If you say so," Morty said. "I'll be ready to go the moment you get back."

"That's what I want to hear. Phil, you ready to go to work?"

"Before we go, consider this: there's probably an antique box down here with all this junk. Why don't we just take it instead of hopping on the Haunted Mansion ride? What are they going to know at headquarters?"

"There's no way I'm going to go back to jail because you got cold feet. Just stay alert and look for traps. We'll be back double-quick time."

"Hey, Morty," said Phil. "If we croak here tonight, be sure to give Nelson a kick in the balls for me."

"You got it."

"And give Giselle a kiss. A big one. You know the kind I mean."

"I'll take a pass on that, Phil. Coop is the one on kissing terms with Giselle."

"As a matter of fact, I'm not," said Coop.

"You're not? What the hell is wrong with you? You could die out there."

"I know."

"You're an idiot," said Morty.

"I know."

"Good. Admitting you have a problem is the first step toward your recovery."

"Coop, listen to the man," said Phil. "You could catch a terminal case of dead. Let's just stay here in the basement and not die together."

But Coop climbed out of the Missile and Morty followed. He went up the stairs ahead of Coop until he reached the door. Then he gently laid his hand over the lock and closed his eyes. A moment later, there was a click and the door swung open a few inches.

"Good luck," he said.

"Thanks," said Coop.

"Avenge me, Morty," said Phil. "If this ignoramus gets me killed, avenge me."

Morty got back into the Missile. "Shut up, Phil."

Coop entered Babylon's mansion wearing the same skintight suit he'd worn during the Bellicose Manor job. It hid his body heat from any biodetectors. Around his waist, he wore his utility sack of tools, and for this job he'd brought along a small backpack stuffed with expensive DOPS gear, most of which he had no idea what to do with, but it seemed smart to take everything they offered. The overall effect made him look like a hunchbacked hobo scuba diver. He hoped there were no cameras around to snap his picture. If future clients ever saw how silly he looked on the job, it would definitely hurt his work prospects. Of course, worrying about future work felt ridiculously optimistic considering everything that lay between him and the box. Still, it was better to concentrate on not losing his life or any body parts unlikely to grow back than to obsess over the dangers lurking on his journey to the heart of Babylon's fun house.

Phil was already scratching around in Coop's skull, looking for traps, illusions, and dead drops. So far, so good on that front. The first hard curse hit him as he passed a broom closet near the base of the staircase. A second hit as soon as he rounded the corner that led to the stairs. A third curse meant to rattle his bones until they cracked hit him at the bottom of the first step. They all passed right through him, evaporating or leaving scorch marks on the floor and walls.

In his head, Phil yelled "Geronimo!" each time a curse hit. Another one of his less charming nervous tics. Coop was about to tell him to pipe down when Phil said, "Trip wire on the third step."

Coop knelt until he could see light reflecting off the monofilament, then stepped over it.

"Don't stand up yet," said Phil. "There's another at throat level on the next step to get you if you spotted the first wire."

"I see it," said Coop, ducking.

"The rest of the stairs look clear. Just be ready for more curses. There are plenty more ahead."

"Got it," said Coop. "You're not your usual chatty self, Phil. Anything wrong?"

"I'm just hurt is all. I try to give you advice on your life choices, your fear of intimacy, your fear of death, and here they come all wrapped together in one nice package and you don't even mention it."

"What are you talking about?"

"Giselle. I always liked her name. She's like someone Poe should have written a poem about. Something long and gloomy about a jilted lover spending his last miserable days eating sandwiches on her tomb."

A curse hit Coop square in the stomach, bounced off, and melted a nearby Ming vase. Phil giggled. "Nice shot, cowboy."

"That one burned a little," said Coop.

"Just like love, if you get my drift."

"A triceratops with a learning disability would get your drift."

"Watch out for the peacock chair on your left. There's a blowgun in the back," said Phil.

Coop stopped and pulled a small graphite glider from a side panel on his backpack. He sailed it past the chair and a dozen spikes, like kitchen knives, shot from the back, embedding themselves in the wall.

"Ouch-a-rama. That would have been a good one, huh?" said Phil.

"Good call," said Coop.

"How much farther to Goldfinger's vault?"

"One more floor."

"Uggghhh," said Phil, like a six-year-old asked to do the nineteen-times multiplication table. "Doesn't the DOPS have teleportation or something? Why can't we fly past Babylon's party tricks?"

"I forgot my jetpack."

"If I believed that, I'd strangle you in your sleep."

"You've been at the DOPS longer than I have. Why don't you talk to management?"

"They don't listen to ghosts. It's complete ectoplasmic oppression over there."

Coop stopped for a second. "Were you part of the bunch that possessed management a few weeks back? People are still talking about it."

"Nope. It didn't happen. I don't know about it. I was haunting the squid tank at SeaWorld at the time."

"You're a lousy liar," said Coop.

"Enough about me. Let's talk about you and Giselle. How soon before you need heart surgery again?"

"Nope. We are not going to do this."

"Come on. Throw me a bone. You in an emotional wood chipper is one of the few things I get to look forward to."

"Sorry. It's not going to happen this time." Beams crisscrossed his vision, trying to cut him in half. Like the others, they passed through him, but one scorched his right boot, leaving him doing a clumsy Riverdance down the hall.

"Duck," said Phil as a sword swung out from the back of a picture of ducks on a pond. "Duck. Did you get it? I said duck."

"I got it, Phil. Can you spin plates? You'd have wowed them in vaudeville."

"My guess is your heart goes back in the Cuisinart just about the time you finish this box job and hit the bricks."

"You know what I think?"

"What?"

"I think you're jealous. When's the last time a lady ghost gave you the time of day?"

Phil didn't say anything for a minute. "We're almost there."

The curses came harder and faster as they neared the study that held the safe. Two of the curses met at the edge of Coop's waist sack and started to melt the nylon. Coop dove out of the way before he caught fire.

"Okay, that was scary," said Phil. "It might be time for a song."

"Don't bother. We're here," said Coop. They stood before heavy wooden sliding doors, like something leading to a Victorian drawing room. "Do you see any traps?"

"Give me a minute," said Phil. Then, "Nothing out here, but I bet there are oodles inside."

"Here we go," said Coop. He pushed the doors open and jumped back behind the hallway wall. Nothing came out of the room. No dragon fire. No spikes. No flying badgers with knives for feet. Coop peeked around the corner and looked into an entirely ordinary room. Ordinary except for one feature. A gray metal safe about three feet tall, like something you'd see in any business office, was floating several inches off the floor.

"Why haven't you kissed her yet?" said Phil.

"Not now," said Coop. "Because I didn't want to and because I don't think she wanted to kiss me. I mean, she might have at one point. But the moment passed."

"Story of your life, huh?"

"Just do your job."

"I have been," said Phil. "Let's be reasonable. From what we've both seen, most of the big curses are outside to keep people from getting in. We've made it all the way here with no casualties, so I think I'm going back to the Stink Missile and play Crazy Eights with Morty."

"You're not getting out of my brain until we're out of this house. Now look around for traps."

They both gazed around the room looking for trip wires and electronic sensors.

"See anything?" said Coop.

"Wait. Have you got a pencil or something? Toss it inside."

Coop took a pen from his waist pack and threw it end over end through the door. Twin swords swung down from overhead, snapping the pen in half. They landed with a clatter on the floor.

"Okay. Is there anything else?"

"Nada," said Phil. "Bupkis."

Coop took a deep breath, trying not to think about the bisected pen in front of him. "I'm going in."

"Relax, Pacino. It's just me here. You don't need to chew the scenery."

Coop took a step. The floor squeaked.

"Stop!" screamed Phil. But it was too late. Coop's body weight carried him forward onto the rigged board. There was a brief sound of gears winding in the walls, then a crack . . .

And then the whole floor fell away beneath them, dropping desks, tables, chairs, and potted plants down into what looked like a bottomless void. The only reason Coop hadn't followed the mess down into the abyss was that he twisted and grabbed a wall sconce at just the last minute. He hung there now, too far from the hall to swing back, and there was nothing to jump onto but the safe, which was too far away.

"Get us out. Get us out. Get us out," screamed Phil.

"You're the one who got us into this. Where are we supposed to go?"

"Get us out. Get us out. Get us—"

"Pipe down. Why don't you try helping?"

"You're the one with all the Batman gear. You think of something."

Coop reached into his backpack and took a small water pistol. He held it high and shot a stream toward the floating safe. The water evaporated before it got halfway there.

"Okay. If I follow that line, it looks like there's just a heat curse. I can handle that. Do you see anything else?"

"I'm having a moment here, Coop. Can I catch my breath?"

"You don't breathe, and this sconce isn't going to hold forever. Are there any more traps?"

"I can't see anything, but I get the feeling there are. Try something else."

Coop pulled a paper airplane from his backpack and tossed it toward the safe. Metal scraped above them, and a steel pendulum with a razor-sharp blade that flared out at the bottom swung down from the ceiling, cutting across the width of the room.

Coop threw three more gliders, triggering three more pendulums. He could feel the breeze of their movement on his cheeks.

"Consider this my resignation," said Phil. "It's been swell working with you, but there's this kitten puzzle I've been meaning to finish back home. I have all the corners done."

"Shut up. You got me into this. Let me think. And don't even dream about singing. I need to count these pendulums."

"Why?"

"Because this wall sconce is loose and we're going to fall in the next couple of minutes, unless I can . . ."

Coop leapt into the air as the first pendulum swung past. He just managed to grab the bottom and hold on as it moved in slow arcs, slicing through the air. Phil didn't say a word. He just screamed.

Coop grabbed onto the shaft of the pendulum and pulled himself to the ceiling. There was a sort of axle there, running from the door straight across the room. From the top of the pendulum, he swung out onto the axle and climbed hand over hand across it, timing each handhold with the swinging of the pendulums.

It took several sweaty, painful, nerve-racking minutes to get there, but at the far end of the axle, he was finally able to swing down and drop onto the top of the safe.

Phil stopped screaming. "How did you know it would hold your weight?"

"I didn't. But Babylon doesn't want his safe falling to Shanghai, so whatever hocus-pocus he's using on it must be strong."

"That's very reassuring," said Phil. "Don't mind me if I go back to screaming."

"You can scream all the way home in the Missile. Right now, keep an eye out for more traps."

"How are you going to open it?"

"I was cracking safes before I could microwave pizza. Besides, the DOPS smart guys gave me something to help."

"Be careful."

"What? Do you see something?"

"No, but I wouldn't make getting in there as easy as guessing a combination."

"Right." Coop took out his collapsible grip and tapped it gently on the safe's keypad. Something hissed.

"Gas!" screamed Phil.

"Thanks. I have ears," said Coop as he took out a respirator and goggles from his backpack.

"You want me to scream it again? 'Cause I can do it louder."

Coop touched the grip around the rest of the safe door, but nothing happened.

"We should have brought Morty with us," said Phil. "He could get this thing open lickety-split."

"Do you really think all three of us could have made it this far?"

"I think he and I could have made it. You would have lived on in our memory."

Coop took a small black box just a little bigger than a cell phone and attached it with magnets over the safe's keypad. "Okay," he said. "Time to see if Peculiar Science lives up to its name."

"What is that?" said Phil.

"Living numbers. Sort of like ants, ghosts, and binary code all rolled into one weird organism. If they can't open the safe I'll have to do it by hand."

"Ten seconds ago you said you were a wiz at that."

"I am, but not if the Missile's going to blow up in two hours. We need it to work fast."

"Yes. No blowing up. Good plan."

Lights played across the outside of the box for several minutes. At first, they were all red. Then slowly, one by one, each light turned green. When the last one flashed, the box beeped and Coop pulled it off, stuffing it back in his pack.

"Come on, Tom Swift. Grab the goods and let's blow this place," said Phil.

"We're almost there," said Coop. When he pulled open the safe door, Phil began to scream again. Even Coop made a few funny noises he was glad no one else could hear.

Hundreds of spiders, large and small, hairy and sleek, poured from the open safe door, moving out in every direction—including up Coop's arm.

"Abort! Abort!" screamed Phil. Coop tried brushing the spiders off, but they just kept coming. It wasn't that Coop was particularly arachnophobic, but what he discovered at that moment was that he wasn't *not* arachnophobic when covered by a whole army of multilegged, too-many-eyed, alien organisms, some of which he was pretty sure were viewing him as lunch. The only reason he didn't jump off the safe, besides the dive to the bottomless pit and his inevitable, horrible death, was the tiny fraction of his brain that was still capable of rational thought reminding him that he was still in his protective suit, with both eye and face protection. This was just barely reassuring enough to push suicide to second place on his option list.

"What do we do now?" screamed Phil.

"You know the answer to that question."

"Please. I'm asking you as a friend and colleague and complete and utter coward, don't do it."

"No choice," said Cooper. He lay down on top of the safe and stuck his hand deep inside, pushing through the webbed opening and feeling around the writhing mass of legs for the box. A moment later, his hand fell on something hard and he pulled it out. At first it was so covered in spiders, he wasn't sure what he'd found. He held it over the bottomless pit and shook it until enough of the creepy crawlers fell off that he recognized the box he'd stolen from the Blackmoore building. When he managed to clear away the last of the spiders, he stuffed the box into his backpack and zipped it closed. From his waist utility sack, he pulled out a small plastic spray bottle and spritzed himself all over. Spiders jumped off him by the dozens. Others fell off and scrambled back inside the safe.

"What is that stuff?" said Phil.

"Holy water, wolf piss, cayenne pepper, and garlic. Kind of my all-in-one bastard repellent."

"Keep spraying it. It's working."

Coop couldn't argue with that, so he spent a few more minutes coating himself in the stuff, until every spider he could see was gone.

"Please, Inspector Gadget, can we go home before someone drops rabid Easter bunnies on us?"

"Don't worry—I'm already on the way," said Coop. He jumped and grabbed the pendulum axle at the ceiling and began working his way hand over hand to the door. He was feeling particularly good about that maneuver . . . until something hissed and brushed his hand. Coop looked up and saw a tarantula that looked to be the size of a Cadillac hubcap rearing up on its hind legs and waving its front four legs in the air like it was going to pounce. Phil grunted like he'd been punched in his ectoplasmic gut. Coop remained silent, because he had lost not only the ability to speak but also his grip on the axle.

As he fell, Coop reached out and grabbed one of the swinging pendulums. That was the good news. The bad news was that he and Phil were now carried in dizzying arcs back and forth across the room. The hallway door was no more than twenty feet away, but there were three more pendulums between them and the way out. Coop looked up and saw the tarantula climbing down the pendulum he was clinging to and did the only semirational thing he could think of. He jumped to the next pendulum, catching it just as it passed by.

Phil didn't scream this time. In fact, he felt like dead weight in Coop's head. *Can ghosts faint?* Coop wondered. Deciding to explore that bit of trivia later, he leapt to the next pendulum. Just one more until he could jump back into the hall and the way out. As he checked his timing, preparing to jump, his goggles went black.

The tarantula had dropped down onto his head.

Coop screamed and jumped. Or jumped and screamed. Later, he was never entirely sure what happened beyond the fact that his body did something explosive and he didn't die. He hit the last pendulum hard, sliding down to his knees on the top of the blade. Not being able to reach the bastard repellent from that position, he resorted to punching himself in the face until his goggles cleared. He didn't wait for Phil or look for the spider or anything else. He just jumped, landed on the floor, rolled against the wall and lay curled in a fetal position for a moment, hoping he hadn't set off any more traps.

After a couple of minutes had gone by, Coop got to his feet and ran back down the stairs the way he and Phil had come. Each killing curse—the heat ones, the cold ones, the ones meant to slice him in half—felt great, and not just because they reminded him he was alive. He knew there wasn't a spider on Earth, even one the size of a wagon wheel (the tarantula was already getting bigger in his head) that could live through that much dark magic.

Coop made it back to the basement and dove through the Stink Missile's hatch, locking it behind him.

"So, how did it go?" said Morty.

Coop tore off the respirator. "You didn't hear?"

"For a while, but then you both kind of faded out."

Coop tore off the goggles and pulled back the hood on his suit. "Just get us out of here. I'll tell you about it later."

"Good. Start with why you smell like a wolf peed on you while you were eating linguine."

Coop kept checking the timer on the Missile's control panel. "Is this right? We're almost at two hours. It didn't feel like it took that long."

"Relax. The tunnel's already dug. We've got plenty of time."

"You do remember the part where Nelson said we'd blow up if we didn't get back soon?"

"Relax. I've been playing with the controls while you were gone. I can make it go faster this time."

Coop looked at Morty as they started to move. "Is that a good idea? Why don't we just go out like we came in?"

"Relax. It'll be fine."

"Why do you keep saying 'relax'?"

Morty reached over and opened a small storage hatch to the side of the control panel. "I found these Xanax inside. They really make the trip easier. Want to try one?"

Coop leaned back in his seat. *Is a drunk driver worse on the freeway or in a sewer pipe?* he wondered.

Morty cocked his head. "Is that like one of those Zen koans?"

"Did I say that out loud? Yes. Contemplate it as we're blown to Kitty Litter all over Laurel Canyon."

Morty frowned and touched his head. "Where's Phil?"

"I don't know. I haven't heard from him for a while. Can ghosts have an aneurysm?"

"You know, if you took a Xanax, maybe it would calm him down, too."

"I'm not taking any pills. I just want out of this thing before we turn into the Fourth of July."

"What shook you up so much back there?"

"Spiders. Lot and lots of spiders. There was a tarantula the size of a pickup truck. It reared up on its hind legs like a goddamn grizzly bear."

Morty nodded. "Oh yeah. They call those bird-killing spiders. They're all over the Amazon. I saw a documentary. You know, what's really interesting about them—"

"Morty."

"Yeah?"

"Give me a Xanax."

They bumped through the ground back into the sewer pipe. Coop watched the GPS readout and the clock. The clock he understood. He wished he'd paid more attention to the GPS on the way in.

"How much longer?" he said.

"You're really jumpy."

"Morty. How much longer?"

The Missile shivered and stopped. Morty smiled at him. "We're here. I told you it was faster back."

Coop grabbed Morty in a big bear hug as they felt something hook onto the front of the Missile and pull it out of the ground. Coop looked at the countdown clock.

It read 1:58.

The moment the missile leveled out, Coop pushed the hatch open and jumped out. He looked around and ran to Nelson. "We're back. Turn off the timer."

Nelson looked at him. "What timer?"

"The two-hour timer. The bomb."

Nelson laughed. "You poor dumb animal. You believed I was going to blow up federal property? I know Giselle thinks you're a moron, but Bayliss kind of liked you. Wait till I tell her I made you piss yourself with the oldest gag in the spy game."

Coop's shoulders relaxed a little as the Xanax kicked in.

"Did you get the box?" said Nelson.

"Yeah," said Coop. "It's right here." He turned and swung his whole body around, slamming a fist square into Nelson's nose. Nelson fell back onto the asphalt. Coop unzipped his backpack and tossed the box onto Nelson's lap.

He went back over to Morty and put an arm around his shoulder. "Thanks for the Xanax. I'm feeling a lot better."

THIRTY-ONE

IT WAS TOO EARLY IN THE MORNING. THERE WAS COFfee, but it was still too early. Plus, Nelson had a wide strip of surgical tape across his nose. But it was the lack of donuts that made Coop think there was a better than even chance that he was about to be arrested.

They were back in the same DOPS office they'd been using since the day he'd been thrown in a van and almost eaten by a hellhound. Nelson stood against the wall across from Coop smirking. Bayliss was over there, too, but keeping a cool distance from Nelson. Her sympathy for her partner's medical condition appeared to Coop to border on the microscopic. At least that was nice, he thought. Giselle sat next to him on his side of the desk, which he didn't mind either. Coop was the only one drinking. He had vivid memories of the coffee in Surf City. Prison coffee was like someone had shouted the word *coffee* into a bag of potting soil and strained the boiled sludge through a dirty T-shirt. *If he was heading back to jail,* Coop thought, *he was going to float in on a wave of government coffee.*

"How was your last night as a free man, dipshit?" said Nelson. "Salzman's on his way down right now with the paperwork to put you away again."

Coop leaned his elbows on the table. "I can't say that going to prison for punching you sounds like fun, but if I have to go back, at least I'm going in for doing something I enjoyed."

Bayliss looked even more uncomfortable than usual when she turned to Nelson and said, "You know, you don't have to press charges."

"Of course I do. This mad dog is a menace. The next thing you know he'll be biting mailmen," said Nelson.

Bayliss shook her head. "You're such an asshole."

"Excuse me? Who's the injured party here?"

"You've done nothing but ride him—and Giselle—since he got here. Frankly, with your attitude, I'm surprised no one's taken a poke at you before."

"Thanks for standing up for me, partner. I won't forget it," said Nelson.

"Let it go, Bayliss," said Coop. "I'm happy I punched him. In the same circumstances, I'd do it again. Hell, I'd like to punch him now."

"Me, too," said Giselle.

Nelson pointed at her. "You want trouble, too, sister? I have filing cabinets full of forms. I can write reports on all of you."

"So can I," said Bayliss. She looked at the floor for a minute before turning to Nelson. "When I think of all the times I kept my mouth shut when you showed up for work hammered . . ."

He raised his eyebrows. "You're going to take this jailbird's side?"

"No, mine. If you file charges, so do I."

Nelson smiled. "Well, it's too late. The papers are all in. No matter what Goody Two-Shoes plan you have, Machine Gun Kelly here is going bye-bye."

"This is good coffee," said Coop. He was dog tired and just wanted everyone to shut up. He'd spent most of the previous night dreaming of spiders riding steel turds down an endless water slide. He'd almost called Giselle a couple of times, but chickened out. He looked at her now and she gave him a rueful smile. She squeezed his hand briefly before letting go and pulling away.

"Thanks for what you two did keeping Babylon out of the way last night. If he'd showed up, me, Phil, and Morty would have been double screwed."

Bayliss and Giselle smiled at each other. Bayliss said, "I heard you left quite a mess for him when he got home."

"Nothing a can of Raid and a bulldozer won't fix."

"He'll know you did it, you know," said Giselle.

"Good. He took a potshot at me once. I was just returning the favor."

"Big talker," said Nelson. "If he knows it was you, how long do you think you're going to last in prison?"

"About as long as you out here if I tell everyone that you're the one who forced me to pull the job."

"You wouldn't dare."

"A bad boy like you with a drinking problem. Who knows who you owe favors to? You blackmailed me into doing your evil bidding. I begged and pleaded, but to no avail. A story like that wouldn't be a hard sell."

Nelson started to say something, but Salzman came in, a folder under one arm and the box in a clear plastic evidence bag in the other. He sat at the end of the table, placed the folder in front of him and the box next to it. "I hope I'm not interrupting anything." He looked at Nelson. "That's quite a shiner you have there, Nelson. Cut yourself shaving?"

"No, sir," he said. "I made a report about it last night."

Salzman waved a hand at him without looking up. He opened the folder and began thumbing through the pages. "We'll get to that," he said. "Why doesn't everybody have a seat and we'll begin?"

Salzman looked up at Coop and said, "What did you think of our crawler? We have high hopes for it, but it hasn't had much field service yet."

Coop sipped his coffee. "The Stink Missile got us there and back and didn't kill us. I give it a gold star."

"Wonderful. It was a good plan you came up with, and without much time to do it in. We're all impressed upstairs. In fact, Mr. Woolrich sent me down here to offer you a permanent job here at the DOPS."

Nelson cleared his throat. "Excuse me, but how can he work here if he's in jail? Aren't we going to deal with the fact this man assaulted me?"

"Of course. But first things first," said Salzman. He looked at Coop. "Well, what do you think? Would you like to join us here at Peculiar Science?"

Coop turned to Giselle, who raised her eyebrows in a please-don't-be-stupid expression. He drank more of his coffee.

"Excuse me," said Salzman. "I forgot something." He got out his phone, hit a number, and said, "Roderick, would you bring me my silver pen? Yes, the one by the requisition forms? Thanks."

"Sir, I have to protest here," said Nelson. "This man is a professional criminal. All his friends are professional criminals. All of his interests revolve around crime, and he just about broke my nose last night."

"As I understand it, most of the crew that pulled off last night's box retrieval were, at one time or other, professional criminals. My goodness, half of the mook and Fractal DNA departments are under indictment somewhere in the world. Are you saying we should clear out some of our most valuable agents?"

"No. Just the ones who punch me."

"Really? Are you going to make this big a deal out of a little scratch? It's my understanding that most of your department has wanted to punch you at one time or other. Why do you think there's so much spit and other nastiness in your coffee?" said Salzman.

"What?" said Nelson.

"Let me put it this way, I wouldn't go leaving my beverages sitting around on my desk unattended if I were you. My guess is the only reason you've survived this long is that all that alcohol you swill has rendered most of your organs inert. And God knows what's going into any food you leave in the break room refrigerator."

Nelson sat quietly with his hands on the table. Coop was pretty sure he was trying to calculate how much vulnerable coffee he'd left out on his desk over the years he'd been with the agency. Judging by the color his face was turning, it was more than he was capable of dealing with at the moment.

"So, Coop, back to you," Salzman said, turning back to him. "Would you like to join our little family?"

Coop and Giselle looked at each other again. He thought he saw the million-dollar smile he'd spotted the other day at Týden Divu. He liked seeing it pointed in his direction for once.

There was a brief knock on the door. It opened and something flew in. It was sort of like a large bat or a small flying manta ray with a slit mouth and fleshy wings. It flapped around the room a couple of times before hovering over Salzman and dropping a pen in his lap. "Thanks, Roderick. Tell Lillian to push back my noon meeting to one, will you? Thanks."

The manta bat circled the room again and went out the door, somehow pulling the thing closed behind it. Salzman clicked his pen and set it on his papers. "Coop, I think the floor is yours."

Coop stared at the door for a few seconds more and turned to Salzman. "What was that?"

"That was Roderick. One of my assistants upstairs."

"One of your Peculiar Science projects?"

"Yes. What do you think?"

Coop sighed. "Don't take this the wrong way, but any job offer that starts with a kidnapping and ends with a delivery bat, it's one I have to respectfully decline. We had a deal before, and that's the one I want to stick to."

Salzman frowned. "I'm sorry to hear that. And yes, for what it's worth, I think we could have approached you better at the beginning, but there it is. Even we can't go back in time and fix things. Well, we can, but people tend to return without bones or veins or some damned thing. I don't remember."

"So, we're okay? The original deal stands? I can just walk away?" said Coop.

"Of course. We're men and women of our word around here," said Salzman, stacking the papers in his folder. "I assume you turned in your company equipment from last night's escapade?"

"Yes. Last night before I left."

"Very good."

"I have a couple more quick questions. Will I get back any of the money I used to get Giselle and me out of that bar in Squid City?"

"Do you have a receipt?" said Salzman.

"No."

"Then I'm afraid I can't help you."

"Okay. How about getting reimbursed for the clothes Dick Tracy over there threw out of the van on the way over here?"

"Again, do you have a receipt?"

"Yes."

"Oh. Well then, we can probably do something about that. Would one of you get him the forms to fill out?"

Giselle got up, went to a file cabinet in a corner of the room, and came back with some papers. She dropped them on the table in front of Coop without a word.

Nelson looked around. "So, that's it? This guy does one little job and he gets to walk away scot-free after attacking me?" said Nelson.

"That is the way it looks," said Salzman. He stood up, took the folder and the box under one arm, and held out his hand while Coop was filling out the form. "No chance of changing your mind?"

"I'm afraid not," said Coop.

"Well, thanks for your good work. And a great personal thanks for the box."

"Sure," said Coop. "Glad to do it."

Salzman walked out with Nelson trailing after him. Coop filled in as much of the form as he could, but was stumped by a question on the bottom. When he turned to ask Giselle a question, her chair was empty. She was gone. Bayliss shrugged when he looked at her.

"Sorry," she said. "Come and find me when you're done and I'll make sure the form gets processed."

She left and he filled in a few more lines. Then he wadded up the paper and tossed it in a trash can. He got up and left.

To anyone who didn't recognize him as a hardworking angel with a malfunctioning Heavenly map of the world, Qaphsiel would have looked more than a little unstable. He wandered up and down North Gower Street staring at what to any mortal going by looked like a small tablecloth. He shook it. Folded and refolded it. Held it over his head. Turned it upside down. And occasionally whacked it against the trunk of one of the palm trees that dotted the street. Nothing seemed to make him or the map happy.

Qaphsiel spotted some shade ahead and stopped to sit on the front steps of an out-of-business deli. He was so close. The map had led him step by step to Gower Street, even flashing the face of the sandy-haired man, before turning to static again. He closed his eyes and pictured a man's face. Qaphsiel knew he wasn't far. Somewhere in walking distance, in fact. But Gower stretched dozens of blocks from the hills north of Hollywood down past Beverly. Thousands of people lived along the road. Was this a test from Heaven? Was he supposed to wander up and down Gower, knocking on every door, asking if they knew a blond man who held the fate of the planet in his hands? Qaphsiel shook the map again and rubbed his eyes. Evening was coming on, but the sun reflecting off the map all day had given him a headache. He heard a horn honk the moment he closed his eyes. When he opened them, an LAPD patrol car was idling at the curb. The cop on the passenger side waved Qaphsiel along. The angel got up, raised a hand in a weary greeting, and returned to his walk. The patrol car drove on. Everything felt like a test today.

He was studying a certain spot on the map as he stepped off the curb at Santa Monica Boulevard, right into the path of a car in the process of running a stop sign. It hit Qaphsiel broadside and he flew end over end a good fifty feet down the street. When he crawled to his feet, a little sore but basically intact, he limped back to the corner. The car that had hit him was demolished, the front end a pancake with a deep U shape in the front where it had made contact with the angel.

"Are you all right?" Qaphsiel asked the driver.

"Holy shit. How are you alive?" he replied. He was a young man in a UCLA T-shirt, shorts, and running shoes. "You flew like a fucking mile."

Qaphsiel dusted himself off. He felt all right and didn't want to waste any more time. Holding his hands straight out from his sides, he smiled broadly. "See? No damage done."

The young man's eyes went wide and he stumbled back into his pancaked car.

"It's all right. Look. I'm fine," said Qaphsiel.

"You," said the young man. The young man pointed with a trembling hand. "You have wings."

Qaphsiel looked over each shoulder. When he'd skidded on the asphalt he'd torn his Windbreaker to shreds. Now, his wings were sticking out straight from his back.

"Oh, crap."

The young man got closer. "Are you like a mutant?" he said.

Qaphsiel cleared his throat. "What's your name?"

"Hansen."

"No, Hansen. I'm not . . . Well, I'm . . ."

"You're an X-Man, aren't you? I knew you were real. I read about it online." He pointed at Qaphsiel, bouncing up and down excitedly around his wrecked car. "I found this site that proved that all the movies and comics were government propaganda, getting us ready for when they admitted you were real."

Qaphsiel looked around nervously, worried about other witnesses. He wanted to agree with Hansen, but that would be lying and against the rules. All he could think to say was "Whatever I am, can you keep my secret?"

Hansen already had his phone out and was snapping pictures of the angel's exposed wings. "Keep it secret? Sure. No problem."

Qaphsiel reached out and touched the phone. It emitted a single massive spark and the screen bubbled and melted.

"What did you do, man? My mom is going to kill me."

"Never lie to an X-Man," said Qaphsiel. "Especially when you run a stop sign."

Hansen looked around. "Dude, I'm so sorry. Please don't call the cops. What can I do to fix things?"

Qaphsiel shrugged out of his torn Windbreaker. Honestly, it felt good to be unfolding his wings, to look and feel like an angel again, even if it was only for a minute. "Do you have a jacket I could borrow?"

Hansen dragged a UCLA letter jacket from the crumpled front seat of his car. He brushed off some broken windshield glass from the front. "That's my lucky jacket, man. A chick magnet."

"A chick magnet. Exactly what I've been looking for," said Qaphsiel.

"Keep it, man. It's yours."

The angel folded his wings against his back and put on the jacket. It was a little large and gave his wings more room to move around, so at least he got one thing out of the disaster.

"Oh, man," said Hansen. "No one is going to believe me that I met an X-Man."

"Remember our bargain. We're keeping keep this to ourselves, right?"

Hansen looked at his ex-car. "What am I going to tell my insurance company?"

Qaphsiel thought. "Act of God, perhaps?"

"They won't pay for that!"

"Then I can't help, other than to suggest you get better insurance, Hansen. But thanks for the jacket." Qaphsiel walked a few steps. When his knee started to ache he thought of something and went back. He grabbed the boy by the shirt and looked deep into his eyes. "Beelzebub. Is that you in there?"

Hansen didn't move or try to squirm away, but he looked like if he could have slid out of his skin like a snake, he would have gladly run down the street, just a bunch of wet muscles and bones. "Dude, I don't know any Beelzebub. Is he another X-Man?"

Qaphsiel gritted his teeth. "Leviathan?"

"Please, man. I just want to go home. Take my jacket. Just don't Wolverine me."

"Sorry," said Qaphsiel. He let go of the boy and smoothed down his shirt. "I just had to check."

It was dark now. A crowd was beginning to gather around the wreck. Qaphsiel limped back up Gower. He opened his map. The lines of force were there. The stars. Best of all, a spot on the map pulsed with light, and it was just a few blocks away. Qaphsiel laughed and waved. "Thank you, Hansen," he yelled, holding up the map. "It's working again." No one in the crowd waved back. They were too busy posing by the wrecked car and puffing out their muscles like the Hulk.

Qaphsiel looked up toward Heaven, more sure than ever that today had been a test of his resolve. To get so close, then having a broken map and a traffic accident. If it was one of Lucifer's little Job scenarios, someone in Heaven had been looking out for him. Raphael? Sure, maybe someone in the crowd had snapped a photo of his wings, but the world was full of crazy Photoshopped images. No, the accident and photos weren't important. Not with a working map in his hand. Qaphsiel tried running to the glowing address, but his scraped leg refused to comply. Screw that. Patience might be a virtue, but he'd been virtuous for a long time. If he had to bunny-hop all the way to Fountain Avenue, he'd do it.

As he went he thought that after he destroyed the world, there were things he was going to miss. Sunsets. Pangolins. Spats (admittedly, he hadn't seen any of those for a while, but he remembered them fondly). Continental drift and photosynthesis. Spaghetti and banana pudding (no, Qaphsiel didn't eat, but he liked the smells). Muscle cars. The color plaid. He thought for a moment. Was plaid a color? Whatever it was, he liked it. Also, those fizzy mountains that made such pretty colors. Volcanoes.

Yes, he'd miss those.

As he limped to Fountain he wondered how he might be able to get one of those disposable cameras they sold in the shops along Hollywood Boulevard. It would be nice to have a few snapshots to take home with him. Maybe the sandy-haired man could help him with that. One more reason to hurry.

Morty was out with a DOPS agent named Zorya Vechernjaja, whom he described as a "crazy Russian babe who works the night shift and doesn't go out during the day, but isn't a vampire," which to Coop sounded exactly like he was dating a vampire but didn't want to admit it. Morty had met her the evening of the Babylon job. While Coop was busy bruising his knuckles on Nelson's nose, Morty was chatting up a Slavic beauty, and Coop never even noticed. While she wasn't quite human, Morty assured him that she didn't have "hooves or fur or gills or anything." How Morty was so intimate with her anatomy so quickly baffled Coop, but then most things that had to do with human interaction baffled him these days. Finding Giselle gone that morning had hit him hard. Hard enough that he was alone watching *Forbidden Planet* for the five hundredth time and waiting for a Meat Lover's pizza, all on his own. No girls or boys or things that go bump in the night allowed.

At a little after eight, someone knocked. Coop took out a couple of twenties and went to answer the door. The disappointment he felt when he saw it wasn't the pizza man was quickly replaced with a whirlwind of dizziness, confusion, and the mild vertigo he always experienced whenever his heart tripped over its own feet and banged its head into the furniture.

Standing in the doorway was Giselle.

He looked at her for a moment.

She looked at him.

Eventually, she raised her eyebrows. "You have to do something, Coop. Throw me out or let me in. There are mosquitoes and muggers out here."

"We don't have mosquitoes around here," he said.

"All right. You caught me. I lied about the mosquitoes. Does that mean I have to go?"

"Nah. You can come in. But no more bug talk. I'm still having tarantula nightmares."

"Tarantula Nightmare. You could start a band with that name."

"No, thanks. Phil's the singer around these parts."

Coop stood aside and let her come in. She was still in conservative work clothes, but looked like a million bucks in heels.

"Morty's place hasn't changed much," she said, making a circle of the room.

"Yeah. I've been a little busy working to find my own place."

She shrugged. "It's not so bad. Kind of seventies retro. I like it."

"I'm not sure it's retro so much as it's what came with the place and Morty's taken good care of it."

"Smart boy," said Giselle. "Not every crook is so good at taking care of his things."

"Is that a shot at me? Can you at least wait for my pizza to get here? I don't like to be insulted on an empty stomach."

"Ooo, pizza. What kind? Can I have some?"

Coop paused *Forbidden Planet*. An invisible creature was busy stomping the spaceship crew to death. "You're staying that long? I thought you'd be off with your DOPS pals stealing the Scarecrow's brain."

She sat on the couch and shook her head. "No, we don't invade Oz until next week. The Munchkins are going on strike and we want to hit 'em while they're down."

Coop sat on the other end of the couch. "So, why are you really here?" he said.

"When you handed in your DOPS gear, you forgot the American Express card I gave you."

"Oh, right," he said. He went to his room, looked through his keys and wallet, found the card, and brought it back to her. "There you go."

"Did you end up getting any new clothes?" she said.

He shook his head. "No. I didn't like anything they had, but I charged a cab ride back here. Think Nelson is going get me for larceny?"

"I'm good at fiddling expenses," Giselle said. "He won't know a thing."

"Great," said Coop. "I guess now that you got what you came for you'll be disappearing again. So . . . have a nice time saving the world. Say hi to Bayliss for me. Now, if you don't mind, I have a movie to watch."

"What's the movie?"

"Forbidden Planet."

She looked around him at the screen. "We watched that together once. You liked Anne Francis. I liked Robby the Robot."

"Yeah? I don't remember," he lied. He remembered practically everything they'd done together. He went back to the beanbag chair and sat down. "Be sure to close the door on your way out. I hear there's mosquitoes."

Giselle stayed on the couch. "Goddammit, Coop. You don't make anything easy, do you?"

He swiveled around awkwardly in the chair. "Easy? You know what's easy? You disappearing. If you count this morning, it will make two times. Add tonight and it'll be three. It's like you get a star every time you walk out on me and if you do it enough times you'll get a free sandwich."

She played with a bit of frayed fabric on a sofa cushion. "I didn't walk out on you today. I just went back to my office. I was right there if you wanted to find me."

"Right. Just like old times. You disappear while I'm not looking and it's my fault. Some people actually *say* things. You know? Like 'Good-bye,' or 'See you later,' or 'Sorry I'm ripping your heart out, but have a nice day.' Stuff like that."

Giselle shook her head. She opened her hands to take in the apartment. "Why didn't you take the job today? So you could come back to this? So you could go back to jail?"

"I don't like being kidnapped and I don't like ultimatums. And I don't like Nelson or Salzman."

"Hello? What about me? It's like I told you right at the DOPS. You don't have to do everything on your own. I can help."

"Until I do something you don't like. Then you're the Road Runner. A dot on the horizon."

Giselle shook her head and stood up. "It was stupid coming here. I'm sorry I hurt you, Coop. I was hoping we could try and maybe get past it, but I guess it's too late for that."

There was a knock at the door. "Dinner," said Coop. "And just in time."

"Are you at least going to invite me to have some pizza?"

Coop shook his head. "Not tonight."

"All right. I tried," she said. "Remember that when Anne Francis flies off with the spaceship captain and you're all alone. Remember I'm the one who gave it a shot."

Coop got out his money and Giselle trailed him to the door. When he opened it, he took a step back from the gun leveled at his face.

I've got to stop just opening doors for people.

Giselle bumped into him and gasped. Coop took a slight step over, getting between her and the grizzly with the gun.

"Hey, Coop," said Fast Eddie. "Who's your friend?"

"The cleaning lady. She just finished the drapes. Why don't you let her go and we'll talk things over in private?"

Eddie, who towered over Coop, looked past him. "She doesn't look like a cleaning lady. She all dressed up and stuff."

"It's a special service. Formal maids. Costs a little more, but it makes Morty and me feel like Fred Astaire."

Eddie pushed his way into the apartment. Coop stayed in front of Giselle as they took a step back. "Where is Morty?" said Eddie.

"Out. He had a date. You probably haven't heard of those. They're something people do."

Eddie shut the door behind him. "Sit," he said and motioned with the gun barrel for them to sit on the couch. Coop and Giselle went over. This time, instead of heading to other ends, they sat pressed up against each other.

"Don't I know you, lady?" said Fast Eddie.

"Nope," said Giselle.

"Yeah. You were there that night. You're a Marilyn, aren't you?"

"Leave her alone, Eddie," said Coop.

Eddie stepped forward and put his boot down on Coop's foot so he couldn't move. "You try to fog my mind, sister, and I start shooting. Got it?"

"Got it," said Giselle.

Eddie sighed. "Before I kill you—and you, too, cleaning lady—I'm going to ask you some questions."

"Why should I tell you anything if you're going to kill us anyway?"

"'Cause I'll kill your cleaning lady first."

Coop put up a hand. "Don't get all hasty. Why don't we take a moment and be friends. You want to know about the other night at the Blackmoore Building."

"Yeah. How was it you and me and a whole goddamn glee club were all pulling jobs at the same time at the same place?"

"The glee club, I don't know anything about," said Coop. "About you and me being in the same building at the same time, well, I set you up."

"You what?" Fast Eddie growled. He sounded like a wolf chewing glass.

"I set you up. I needed a distraction for my job, so I arranged a job for you."

"Why would you do that?"

"Because you're an asshole, Eddie. And you deserved it."

"Maybe you ought to calm down a little," Giselle said to Coop.

"Yeah. Maybe you ought to calm down and remember you're talking to a very big man with a very big gun."

Coop leaned back on the couch. "Go fuck yourself, Eddie," he said. "You're going to shoot us no matter what I say, so in case you didn't hear me the first time, take your gun and go fuck yourself on the teacup ride at Disneyland. I hear it's two for one tomorrow, so you might not have to buy an extra ticket for that gut of yours."

"Thank you, Coop," said Eddie. "I haven't shot anybody in a while. I was even considering swearing off it, but you're making this easy. One last blast for the road." Fast Eddie straightened his arm and took aim between Coop's eyes. He cocked the trigger.

Just as Giselle said, "Fuck it," and turned herself and Coop invisible, Fast Eddie exploded. Not his gun. Fast Eddie. It was loud. And messy. And more than a little unexpected.

Coop and Giselle lay sprawled on the couch watching bits and pieces of Eddie peel off the ceiling and flop onto the floor.

"You okay?" said Coop.

"Yeah. You?" said Giselle.

"Okay, I think. You see that guy by the door?"

"Yeah."

"Who is he?"

"I don't know."

"He's not DOPS?"

"I don't think so," said Giselle.

Coop reached and pushed Eddie's pistol—and what appeared to be a couple of fingers—under the sofa, away from the disheveled man in the dirty pants and the clean UCLA letter jacket.

"I'm so glad I got here in time," said the disheveled man.

"Me, too," said Coop. "Who the hell are you? And what did you do to Eddie?"

"Was that his full name?" said the mystery man.

"Fast Eddie."

"Unusual. I'll say a prayer for him later, but I don't have time right now."

"Why's that?" said Giselle.

"I need to talk to this man next to you. My name is Qaphsiel. What's yours?"

"Barney Rubble. And what was it you said you did to Eddie? I didn't see a gun or anything."

Qaphsiel shook his head. "No, I don't carry weapons, Barney. And I don't have all of my old powers, so I just discorporated him."

"You blew him up."

Qaphsiel looked around the room. "It was a bit messy, wasn't it? Sorry. Maybe this will help with the cleanup." He bent over and dropped a handful of gold coins onto a dry spot on the coffee table.

Coop and Giselle looked at each other. Coop said, "Hold still," plucked something red from her hair, made a face, and tossed it away.

"What was that?" she said.

"Don't ask."

Coop looked at the gold and then Qaphsiel. "That real?"

"Of course. I'm sure it's more than enough to cover the damages."

"I would have taken a check."

Qaphsiel put his hands together. "I know this is a lot to take in at once, Barney."

Coop realized that he and Giselle were holding hands. He let go and picked up a couple of the gold coins. He gave one to her and turned one over in his hand. "What's to take in? You bust in, blow a guy up, and now you dump a load of gold on me? It's just another night in Hollywood, right?"

Qaphsiel glanced over his shoulder and closed the front door. "I didn't actually break in, you see. The door wasn't closed all the way. When I tried to knock, it swung open, and I saw what was about to happen."

"Why would you want to get involved?" said Giselle. "Most people would have run away."

"Yes. Well. That. You see, I'm not most people," said Qaphsiel. "I'm an angel."

Coop sighed. "You know, in the last few days, I've taken orders from a dead man, hung out with poltergeists, vampires, werewolves, people with tentacles, people with gills, and seen the inside of a turd submarine. After all that, I shouldn't be surprised when someone tells me they're an angel, but you know what? I am."

Qaphsiel brushed some Eddie off the beanbag chair and wiped down the seat with the sleeve of his letter jacket. He pulled the chair over to where Coop and Giselle sat.

"There's something you need to know, Barney."

"My name isn't Barney. It's Coop."

"You lied? I envy you that. Angels aren't supposed to lie. It would make my life here a lot easier if I could."

"I'm having a very strange moment here, Coop," Giselle muttered.

"Me, too," he said. He looked at Qaphsiel. "Let's back up a minute. You're an angel who just happened to stumble into this apartment—"

"I didn't stumble in. As I said, the door was open, so I—"

"I mean, you were just strolling by and decided to come up?"

"No. I've been looking for you."

"Why?"

"The box."

Coop and Giselle looked at each other again.

"Coop is right," she said. "We've seen a lot of funny things recently. How do we know you're an angel?"

Qaphsiel thought for a moment. He'd forgotten about how hard it was for modern mortals to accept the concept of celestial creatures walking among them. The extent of their imaginations seemed limited to the certainty that cats were the best animals, extraterrestrials actually existed, Jim Morrison and Amelia Earhart were still alive and an item in Paris, and reptile people from the center of the Earth controlled all world governments. Only one of those things was true, but try explaining that to mortals. It didn't help, Qaphsiel knew, that he was trying to prove his divinity in cheap plastic sandals and a used college jacket, all while sinking slowly into a beanbag chair. "Well, I just blew up someone," he said. "That was a pretty good trick."

Coop shook his head. "Not good enough."

"All right," said Qaphsiel. He stood and took off his jacket, letting his wings unfurl from his sides. In a voice that shook the whole house he said, "How's this?"

"Pretty good. Especially the voice. Please don't do it again," said Coop. "I'm not saying I buy the angel thing, but you saved our asses and that makes you okay for the time being. Why don't you put your jacket back on? You're getting some Eddie on your wings."

Qaphsiel looked and, sure enough, there were red smudges on the tops and ends of his wings. "I don't suppose you have a shower?" he said.

"Can we do this somewhere else?" said Giselle, rubbing her nose. "The smell is a little strong in here."

"I can make the remains go away, if you'd like," said Qaphsiel. "Would that help?"

"If you can make Eddie go away, why did you give us cleanup money?" said Coop.

The angel shrugged. "Mortals like gold. And you're a thief. It seemed logical."

Coop held up his hands. "If you can fix this, wiggle your nose or blink or whatever and do it."

"Of course." A second later, the mess was gone. The room looked exactly the same as it had before Qaphsiel came in. Except for the smell. A subtle eau d'Eddie hung in the air. Coop went around the living room opening windows.

"How's that?" said Qaphsiel.

"It'll do for now," said Coop.

Giselle was feeling in her hair, and seemed pleased not to come away with anything anatomical.

"So . . . about the box."

"The box," said Qaphsiel. "The box. I've been looking for it for four thousand years. I must have it back."

"What do you want with the box?" said Coop.

Qaphsiel looked uncomfortable. "Do we really have to talk about that? You might not like it."

"Oh," said Giselle, "then we *absolutely* want to hear what you want with the box."

"Here's the thing," said Qaphsiel. "Inside the box is, well, what you would call the Apocalypse."

"What does that mean?" said Coop.

Qaphsiel looked around, raised a hand, dropped it. "You know. *The Apocalypse*. Armageddon. The Four Horsemen. The end of all things."

"Wait a minute. The DOPS said it was just some kind of techno bomb," said Coop.

"And Babylon said it was full of luck," said Giselle.

Coop looked from Giselle back to Qaphsiel. "That's three stories about the damned thing. There any more we should know about?"

"Unfortunately, yes," said Qaphsiel. "There are two groups right here in Los Angeles—cults, you'd call them—who believe the box will summon their dark, demonic gods back to Earth to destroy it and enslave mankind."

"I guess that explains the glee club at the Blackmoore Building. They must have been looking for the box, too."

"And if anyone opens the box, the world will be destroyed?" said Giselle.

"Yes."

"Then why should I help you get it?" said Coop. "You're probably the one who brought it here to destroy us in the first place, didn't you?"

"Yes."

"What happened? Why is the Earth still here?" said Giselle.

Qaphsiel looked at the floor. "I lost it."

"Lucky us."

Qaphsiel looked back up. "Unlucky me. I've been exiled on Earth all these years and can't get back into Heaven unless I find the box and destroy the Earth."

Coop nodded, before finally saying, "Yeah . . . we're going to have to take a pass on that."

"What?"

"Forget it. Thanks for taking out Eddie and all, but I'll tell you what I told him: go fuck yourself on the teacups."

Qaphsiel thought for a minute. "I'll make a deal with you. If you help me find the box, I won't use it. Not right away. Let's say, I wait another hundred years? I'm sure I can talk to someone in Heaven. With another hundred years, maybe mankind can redeem itself and the Earth can be saved."

"You know, it's weird. I hate almost every single person on this planet at the moment, but I still wouldn't want the whole thing wiped out, even in a hundred years."

"Two hundred?"

"Promise whatever you like—it doesn't matter."

"Why not?"

"I don't have the box," said Coop. "The DOPS has it and there's no way of getting it back."

"There must be. You're a master thief." Qaphsiel looked at Giselle. "You're one, too, right? Surely between the two of you, you can think of something."

Giselle shook her head. "Coop's right. Even if we knew where it was, there's no way to get it out of the DOPS."

"You heard the lady," said Coop. "Besides, it's safe there. They think it's a bomb. No one is going to open it."

"But what if they do?" said Qaphsiel.

Giselle put a hand on Coop's shoulder. "You know, they just might. They really want to know what's inside the box, and if they think they can defuse the bomb . . ."

"Hold on just one minute," said Coop. "You claim you're an angel. You've been on Earth for four thousand years. You blew a guy up and then you made him disappear. Why don't you just magic your way into the DOPS and take the damned box yourself?"

"*Because* I'm an angel," said Qaphsiel. "I'm not allowed to steal."

"But why come to me?" said Coop. "There are a thousand thieves in L.A."

Qaphsiel stood and said, again in the voice that shook the house, "Because you're the Chosen One. The Savior of Mankind."

"What? Really?" said Coop.

Qaphsiel sat down. "No. That was my little joke. Sorry. I don't get to talk to people that much," he said.

"I wouldn't have guessed."

"You're just a person, but not just *any* person. You're someone at a party who bumps into someone, who bumps into someone, who bumps into someone who spills a drink on the host. See? You're part of a chain reaction that's been running for thousands of years. Plus, you're the only thief I know. And you seem relatively honest."

"Relatively," said Giselle.

"You still have my stone," said Coop.

She ignored him. "None of this matters. The DOPS probably already has the box in a vault. It's over and done with."

Qaphsiel slumped in the beanbag chair. "After all these years," he said.

"Sorry. Is there anything we can do for you?"

The angel looked around the apartment. "I sleep in the park most of the time, but I don't really want to go back there tonight. If I leave you the gold, can I sleep on your sofa?"

"I suppose. You did save us from Eddie," said Coop. "Yeah, you can stay. But keep your gold. The sofa isn't that comfortable."

"See? An honest thief," said Qaphsiel.

Someone knocked at the door. Coop walked over quietly and peered through the glass peephole. He looked disgusted and pulled the door open. It was a kid holding a pizza box in his hands.

"Hi. That's twenty-two fifty," he said.

Coop pulled two twenties from his pocket and handed them to the kid. "Keep the change," he said.

Qaphsiel leaned, resting his elbows on his knees.

Coop motioned for Giselle to come with him across the room.

"What do you think? Is he really an angel?" she said.

Coop shook his head. "I don't know. But I'm a little past being surprised by anything right now."

"Me, too." Giselle opened the pizza box an inch and sniffed it. "Smells good," she said.

"Yeah. It does."

She got a little closer to Coop and spoke softly. "You know, that was almost gallant what you did back there. Getting between me and Eddie."

"I just didn't want him to see you and think I'm dating a cop."

Giselle cocked her head. "Dating? Are we dating now?"

"You know what I mean."

She glanced over at Qaphsiel, who seemed lost in his own celestial misery. "So, one last time, are you going to send me home? I'd like to remind you that there's something out there that can destroy the world."

"If we believe that guy," said Coop.

"And even if no one opens the box, they might bump it wrong or x-ray it, and set it off without meaning to."

Coop nodded and looked at her, holding the pizza box between them. "That would be a bad thing."

"It would be worse if you threw me out."

"Yeah, if I did that, you'd probably forget all that gallant stuff."

"You can bet your ass on that. Gone like that," she said, snapping her fingers.

"Tough choice for me," said Coop. "If I let you stay I have to share my pizza."

Giselle pinched his arm hard.

"Ow."

"The world could literally end tonight. You're seriously going to send me home alone?"

Coop looked at the pizza. At Qaphsiel. At Giselle. "You want to finish *Forbidden Planet* and eat pizza in my room?"

She smiled. "You know how robots turn me on."

Coop looked back at the angel. "Hey, Qaphsiel. There's blankets in the hall closet. Feel free not to knock on my door. If Morty comes in, don't blow him up. And don't tell him you're an angel. Tell him you're someone I knew in jail."

"I can't lie," said Qaphsiel.

"Then tell him you're an angel and that we'll explain things in the morning," said Giselle.

"Thank you."

"Good night," she said. She was going to say something else, but Coop was already pulling her into his room. She closed and locked the door.

THIRTY-TWO

THE NEXT MORNING, GISELLE FOUND COOP ON HIS knees making retching noises in front of the toilet.

He was dressed in his pajama bottoms. She was in his one clean shirt. "Are you all right?" she said. "Was it the pizza?"

Coop waved a hand at her, staying on his knees. "Don't worry. It's just my traditional someone-tried-to-shoot-me-oh-god-is-there-a-spider-on-my-face ritual."

"Is there anything I can do?"

"Yeah. If anyone asks, tell them about how brave I was and not this."

"Sure. You want me to put on some coffee?"

"Please."

Giselle waved to Qaphsiel, who was sitting on the couch. "Morning. Do you want coffee, too?"

"Thank you, but I don't eat. I like the smell, though."

"One cup of brown steam for you."

Coop spent a few more minutes in the bathroom, washing up and brushing his teeth, gargling, and doing it over again. Back when he was a teenager and just learning to drink, he'd decided that morning puking was the worst kind because it was essentially the outside and inside of your body fighting over which wanted to commit suicide first. His insides were winning this morning, but by the time Coop came out of the bathroom, his outsides were making a comeback and he could stand and walk. As long as nobody pointed any guns at him today, he thought, everything was going to be fine.

Coop saw Qaphsiel on the couch, blankets and sheets neatly folded beside him.

"Did you sleep last night?"

"Yes. Thank you for letting me stay. It was a lot nicer than the park."

"Not by much, I bet." Coop knocked on Morty's door. No one answered. "Did you see Morty last night?"

Qaphsiel shook his head.

"Good for Morty," said Giselle, coming out of the kitchen. "I wonder if his Russian is one of those bodybuilder types? I hope she didn't break him."

"Morty's fine. I guess this DOPS mess has worked out better for us than I thought it would."

"Speak for yourself," said Giselle. "That pizza was terrible. You should let me order next time."

"Okay. Next time," said Coop, trying not to smile at the idea of a next time.

"Oh, shit," said Giselle. "Is the clock on the wall right?"

Coop glanced at it. "It's always on the dot."

"Then I'm late," she said and rushed into the bedroom. She closed the door and Coop heard her rushing around getting dressed. He'd left his phone on the living room table last night. And now it rang.

"Hello. Is this Charles Cooper?"

"Yeah. Who's this?"

"We haven't met, but I'm Mr. Woolrich over at Peculiar Science. Technically, I was your boss until you decided to leave us."

"Right. You're Salzman's boss. He talked about you." Coop kept sounding cheery as he talked, but backed quietly into his bedroom, where Giselle was half dressed. He looked at her as he talked. "So, Mr. Woolrich, what can I do for you?"

Giselle's forehead furrowed. "Woolrich?" she mouthed. Coop nodded.

"There's been a development here at the DOPS that I was hoping you could help us with."

"And what's that?"

"Would you reconsider taking the job you were offered yesterday?"

Coop opened his eyes wide at Giselle. She came over and put her ear next to the phone so she could hear.

"Thanks, Mr. Woolrich. But as I explained to Salzman, once our deal was done, I wanted to go back to working for myself."

"Salzman," said Woolrich slowly, drawing the name out. "You see, that's the development. He's disappeared. And so has the box."

Giselle put a hand over her mouth. Coop took the phone from his mouth whispering, "Fuckfuckfuckfuckfuck." When he calmed down, he brought the phone back up again. "Are you fucking kidding me?"

"I'm afraid not, Mr. Cooper."

Quietly, Coop said, "I'm really sorry to hear that, but I'm not sure what it has to do with me."

"A lot, I'm afraid. You see, since he's missing with a key piece of DOPS property, he's officially a criminal suspect. As such, any recent deals he might have made are null and void."

Now it was Giselle's turn to whisper, "Fuckingfuck."

Coop took a breath. "Fuck."

"Indeed. We're all a bit fucked right now."

"Are you saying that I'm still working for the DOPS whether I like it or not?"

"Right again."

"Meaning I go back to jail if I don't."

"I'm afraid so. That's why I was asking if you wanted a real position here. That way we can get past all these silly threats."

"I hope you understand, this is a little early in the day for this kind of thing for me. Can I call you back later?"

"Of course. Take your time. It's only the future of the world at stake," said Woolrich. "I notice that Agent Petersen isn't at her desk yet. If you should happen to see her"—he cleared his throat—"let her know when you're coming in and we'll have a more formal chat then."

"Okay. Thanks."

"See you soon," said Woolrich, and the line went dead.

Giselle sat on the bed and pulled on her stockings. "So Salzman is gone. And my boss knows I spent the night with a career crook. And I don't have time for coffee. Great morning so far."

"For what's it worth, I don't think he cared. About you being here, I mean. He sounded a lot more pissed off about Salzman."

Giselle buttoned her shirt and said, "What are you going to do?"

"First off, I'm going to point out to you that that's my shirt you're wearing," said Coop.

Giselle rolled her eyes and unbuttoned it.

He smiled. "I don't mind you wearing it. Or taking it off. I like both, but wearing it might be a bit of a giveaway at work."

Giselle tossed Coop his shirt, found hers, buttoned it, and grabbed her shoes. She balanced with one hand on Coop's shoulder, pulling on one, then the other. "How do I look?" she said.

"Immensely fuckable," said Coop.

She pushed past him. "You're useless, jailbird."

Giselle went into the living room and stood in front of Qaphsiel. "How do I look?" she said. "Like a professional? Like someone ready for work?"

Qaphsiel nodded. "Yes. You look very nice. Like the office women downtown."

"Perfect. Thanks," she said. Heading for the door, she pointed at Coop, saying, "Call me later. We have to figure out this Woolrich/Salzman thing."

"There's nothing to figure out. I'm working for the DOPS again. Whatever Salzman's done, I'm going to have to steal the box. Again."

"Why don't you come by at one for lunch? We can work out a strategy then."

"Yeah. Let's do that." Coop shook his head. "Morty isn't going to be happy. Spiders excepted, the job the other night went pretty well. Having to do it again is bad luck."

"Hang on to that thought. I'll see you later." She slammed the door and Coop could hear her running down the front steps. He looked at Qaphsiel.

"What would you do in my position? Go to work for people you don't like or go back to jail? You'd be away from the crazy kind of heavy danger that bad people want to drop on your head, but you'd be locked up for a long time . . . and surrounded by bad people who might want to drop heavy things on your head."

Qaphsiel only had to think about it for a few seconds. "I've been on this planet for four thousand years. To you, Earth looks like the world. You go where you please and do what you want. For me, Earth is a prison. No matter how far I go or what I accomplish, I'm still locked away far from home. And it hurts."

"I hadn't thought of it like that." Coop looked at him. "Are all angels as cheery as you in the morning?"

"I hear Lucifer can be a bit grumpy."

"Well, you try sleeping on a pointy tail," said Coop. "You're saying I should take the job."

"I'm saying that you already know what you're going to do. You just have to admit it to yourself."

"Thank you, Buddha. I know exactly what I'm going to do. I'm going to get some coffee and see if there's any pizza left. You want some?"

Qaphsiel stood up. "No. Thank you," he said. "I know this is upsetting for you, but, in a way, it's good news for me. If this Salzman has stolen the box, then it's out of the impregnable vault you talked about, and that means I can start looking for it again."

"How are you going to do that?"

Qaphsiel held up his map.

"That's a rag," said Coop.

"To mortal eyes. To me, it's a map of the Earth and the cosmos. I found you with the map and I'll find Salzman."

"You know he's a mook, right?"

"What's that?"

"He's dead, but he still dresses and talks like he's got Donald Trump jammed up his ass."

Qaphsiel steepled his fingers together. "Interesting. I've never tried to track a revenant before. But nothing ventured, nothing gained, right?"

Coop poured black coffee into a cup and looked for the sugar. "I like the nothing ventured part. The other sounds like a lot of work."

Qaphsiel came into the kitchen and put his hand out. "It was a pleasure meeting you, Coop. Good luck on whatever you choose. I hope we meet again someday."

"Yeah. Me, too," said Coop, shaking Qaphsiel's hand. "But you're still going to blow up the world if you find the box, aren't you?"

Qaphsiel nodded. "I'm afraid so. I can't take a chance on losing it again. All the more reason you and Ms. Giselle should be nice to each other. You never know when . . ." He made an explosion sound with his mouth.

"You angels really are cheery fuckers. See you around. This life or the next."

Qaphsiel quietly let himself out of the apartment. He didn't want to show how excited he was inside because it might hurt Coop's feelings. Coming this close to the box and losing it had hurt. But having it on the loose again, it made him feel like it was out in the world just for him. All he had to do now was figure out how to track a dead man. He'd stake out a place in Griffith Park and get straight to work.

A ringing woke the Dark High Magister. He looked around, annoyed, wondering what the hell those Red Lobster bastards down the block were doing ringing bells this early in the morning.

Something rang again, and it wasn't outside. It was in his pocket. He took out his phone and pushed the button to answer.

"Hello?" someone said.

"Hello?" said the Magister.

"It's me. Coral Snake."

"Carol? I don't know any Carols. Are you sure you have the right number?"

"It's me. Coral Snake. It's my code name," whispered the voice.

"That's silly. What kind of code name is Carol?"

Louder, the voice said, "It's me. Tommy from the Caleximus congregation."

Idiot, thought the Magister. "Why didn't you just say so? Why did you waste my time with that Carol nonsense?"

"Coral. C-O-R-A-L Snake. It's the code name we talked about so no one would know I was talking to you."

"I don't remember that."

There was a pause on the line. "Maybe this was a mistake."

"No, Carol. Don't go," said the Magister quickly. "Do you have any information for us?"

"Well, we don't know where the box is yet."

Double idiot, he thought. Why did he ever make a deal with this kid? "What about this Craig you were looking for?"

"Coop."

"That doesn't sound right."

"Trust me. It's Coop. And we don't know where he is, either."

There was a crusty something on the arm of the Magister's Barcalounger. A tiny bit of fried fish from last night's dinner. He picked at it with his thumb. "Well, this is exciting news, Carol. You've called to tell me that you Caleximus buffoons know nothing and are working hard at knowing even more nothing than before. Is that the gist of this exciting conversation?"

"No. Listen. We don't know where Coop or the box are, but we know where someone he knows is. Steve, our high priest, figures that if we snatch her, we can get Coop to give us the box."

"Wait," said the Magister. "You call your high priest Steve?"

"Yeah. That's his name."

"Even our San Diego dickheads wouldn't call their leader by his first name. This is exactly what I'd expect from Caleximus heretics."

"Hey," said the phone. It sounded annoyed. "There are some nice people in the congregation."

"I'm sure there are, Carol, but that's not the point. We're talking about total world destruction and domination. You want to be on the winning team, don't you? Do you really think a dark god such as Abaddon is going to let a *Steve* help rule the Earth?"

"I guess not."

"Damn right. So, when does High Priest Steve intend on snatching Craig's friend?"

"Coop. Tonight. Maybe tomorrow. We're staking out her apartment."

Finally, some sense from this kid. "Good for you. When you get hold of her, let me know immediately. And find out where they're taking her. We'll scoop her up and deal with Craig ourselves."

"You won't hurt anyone, will you?"

The Magister spoke in the high, soft voice he reserved for toddlers and skittish cats. "Of course not, Carol. Abaddon is a kind and generous god, full of compassion for all living things."

"I kind of think you're being sarcastic now."

"Gracious, no."

Silence.

"Carol, we're going to stomp the living gravy out of anyone who gets in our way. Now, listen. It's important that no one know you're helping us. When we sweep in to take the girl, you have to stay and fight, but you don't have to get hurt too badly. Just fall down the first time someone hits you."

"I can do that. I don't like fighting."

"Okay, but for God's sake, don't be a pansy about it," said the Magister. "Let someone get in a good shot. You're going to want a black eye to stay on everybody's good side. Understand me?"

"Yes, sir. I can do that."

"Oh, and from now on you can address me as 'Dark High Magister.' Or 'Lord,' once we get to know each other better."

"Yes, High Dark Magister."

"No. Dark High."

"Dark High. Got it. Okay, I've got to go before someone hears me."

"And how do you say good-bye?"

"Oh. Good night, High Dark Magister."

"Dark High."

"Dark High Magister. Good night, sir."

"Good night, Carol." *Ass,* he thought. *Funny voice for a girl.*

At about twelve thirty, Coop left Morty's apartment and headed up to Sunset Boulevard to catch a cab to the DOPS. L.A., like most big cities, loves a parade. There are big ones, such as the Parade of Roses, Chinese New Year, Cinco de Mayo, Gay Pride, the Fourth of July, the Christmas Parade, and a dozen other smaller ones spread out around the county. But the one true, twenty-four-hour-a-day, 365-days-a-year L.A. parade is the endless promenade of cars. Tricked-out lowriders lined up at street corners nose to nose with pristine '66 Shelby Mustangs, eccentrics driving hand-rebuilt Stanley Steamers, families in rusted-out Reagan-era shit boxes held together with Bondo and fervent prayer, and Rolls-Royce Silver Clouds. Coop had grown up with it all. Seen every possible combination. That, combined with the fact that he was thinking about Giselle naked saying "Do me, spaceman" and the sweet scent of pepperoni in the air, is why he didn't notice the Cadillac XTS limousine paralleling him up Gower.

It wasn't until the rear passenger door opened and a blond man in a dark suit leaned out with a phone in his hand that Coop noticed anything strange.

"Call you for you," he said. Coop looked around, trying to figure out if it was a gag or another DOPS ambush.

"Uh . . . I'm not in."

The blond man wiggled the phone in his hand and said, "Morty really wants to talk to you."

Coop came over, took the phone from the blond man, and said, "Hello?"

"Coop. Is that you? It's me. Morty."

"What's going on? Where are you?"

"Things are fucked up. Get in the car, Coop. They'll explain everything."

The line went dead. Coop handed the phone back to the blond man, who motioned for him to get in the car. Coop smiled . . . and started running. He made it around the corner onto Sunset Boulevard and all the way down the next block before the Caddy cut him off at the corner. The blond man looked a lot bigger when he got out of the car. So did the black guy with the marine crew cut who was now with him. They each took one of Coop's arms and threw him into the back of the Caddy with no more trouble than someone's grandma tossing a bag of bananas in the trunk.

The car started up again and eased back into traffic. There were several other men in the back of the car. None of them smiled, and only one was any smaller than a mobile home. Coop took the one vacant seat, across from the one normal-size guy. Motörhead's "Killed by Death" blasted over the car's stereo system. The normal guy pressed a button on his armrest and the volume lowered to a dull roar.

"Why did you run like that?" he said.

" 'Cause the setup looked like a kidnapping," said Coop.

"It was a phone call. If I wanted to kidnap you, I wouldn't do it in broad daylight on Sunset in front of everyone."

"Except that's what you did just now. Like ten seconds ago."

"That was a misunderstanding. Trust me, if it had been a kidnapping and you ran, we wouldn't be chatting so amicably on account of you screaming about your broken arms and legs. Understand?"

"Sure. You're just my ride to work. Where's Morty?"

"Your name's Coop, right?"

"Yeah. Who are you?"

The normal guy listened to the music for a few seconds and said, "You can call me Lemmy. Mr. Lemmy." The big guys all laughed at that.

"Where's Morty, Mr. Lemmy?"

He thought about the question for a minute and said, "You ever been on a plane, Coop?"

"What? Sure."

"So, you know what a sick bag is. It's one of those little plastic-lined bags they give you. The plane shakes around and you don't feel so good. You get your sick bag, puke into it, and throw it away."

Coop looked at Mr. Lemmy, the way he smiled at him. Lemmy was small and wiry, with thin hair and a pencil-thin mustache. Like John Waters with a Glock under his jacket.

"Can I make a guess about something, Mr. Lemmy?"

"Feel free."

"I'm the sick bag, right?"

Mr. Lemmy pointed to him. "You and your friend Morty, yes."

"Understood. But from here on out, could you threaten me like a normal person and not talk about puke anymore? I've had a rough morning."

"Sure, Coop. No more metaphors or similes, whichever it was I just said."

"A metaphor, boss," said the marine-looking black guy.

"Was it? Thank you. And shut up," said Mr. Lemmy. He turned back to Coop. "You like to cut to the chase? Good. Me, too. I want the fucking luck box."

"I think I heard of that. It's a new Swedish porn flick, right?"

"Someone hit him, please."

Blondie punched him in the stomach—which is surprisingly painful when you're sitting down. Coop felt like his bones were all balloons and someone had let the air out. "I don't have the box," he said.

Mr. Lemmy thrust a finger at him. "That's not what Babylon told us, before we fed him to those fucking spiders he likes so much. See, we had a deal to buy the box. Then I find out he was talking to some broads about selling it to them behind my back. Only, he tells us, they weren't really buying. They were just wasting everybody's time so you could get into his place and steal the box."

Coop held up a hand. "You're right. I broke in and I took it. But I don't have it anymore."

"Get it back. Buy it. Steal it. Get it back."

"It's not that simple. Listen, I'm not even sure where it is. It'll take some time to find it."

"You have forty-eight hours," said Mr. Lemmy.

"That might not be enough."

The blond man punched a number on his phone and held it out to Coop.

"Then take this opportunity to say good-bye to poor Morty," said Mr. Lemmy.

"Forget it," said Coop. He looked around the car at all the faces of Mr. Lemmy's giants. He'd be lucky to get out alive himself right now. *No way guys like this let guys like Morty and me walk away, even if we give them what they want.* But that's not what he said. What he said was, "I'll find the box."

"Forty-eight hours."

"Forty-eight."

Mr. Lemmy took out a pen and scribbled something on a piece of paper. "That's the number you can call when you get the box. Don't bother giving it to the cops or anyone because it's a drop phone that's going in the furnace the moment this nonsense is wrapped up."

In the furnace, and us with it, thought Coop. He took the paper and put it in his pocket. The car pulled over to the curb and the blond man opened the door. Coop stepped out. He was in front of the Beverly Center mall.

"Babylon told me how much he paid you schmucks for stealing the box. Go buy yourself some decent clothes. You dress like a bum," said Mr. Lemmy.

"I had some decent clothes, but people keep fucking them up."

"Then you're a loser."

"That crossed my mind."

Mr. Lemmy punched the armrest button and "Ace of Spades" blasted from the limo speakers. The car sped away. Coop got out his phone and dialed Giselle.

"Where are you?" she said. "You're late—Mr. Woolrich is waiting."

"That's what I was calling to tell you. That I was going to be late."

"No. You *are* late. Already."

"Really? It didn't seem like that long."

"What didn't?"

"My sort of kidnapping."

"You were sort of kidnapped?"

"Yeah. But the shitty part is that Morty was officially kidnapped."

"By who?"

"Mobsters. Bad guys. Thumb breakers."

"Did they give you a reason?"

"Same as everybody else. They want the box."

"Oh, Coop. Get here as soon as you can. We'll figure this out."

"Before he left, my sort of kidnapper told me I dress like a bum. Isn't that just a riot?"

"No, dear. You don't dress like a bum. You *look* like a bum. You don't take care of your clothes."

"That's because I keep getting kidnapped."

"Get in here when you can."

"Nothing better happen to Morty. Besides you, he's the closest thing to a friend I have left."

"Nothing's going to happen. You'll see."

"I'll be there soon."

It took almost twenty minutes to get a cab to stop. The driver made Coop show him the cash before he would drive away. It took another thirty minutes to get across town.

Coop had the cab drop him a few blocks from DOPS headquarters and walked the rest of the way. It's what they did in spy movies, right? Get out early so the cabbie wouldn't have a record of his real destination? A sudden surge of panic hit him and he wondered if he should have changed cabs a couple of times on the way over. No. That would probably have been exaggerating the situation. Plus, it was hard enough to get one cab to stop. Getting two would make it the luckiest day of his life, and it was definitely not that. Still, getting out and walking the last few blocks felt like the right thing to do.

Until the paranoia set in. Two kidnappings in just a few days. A gun in his face last night. It was reasonable to be a little extra cautious, right? Coop side-eyed every car passing him at every corner. Every car that slowed on every block. Every van, delivery truck, and car large enough to hold a body in the trunk. Then he started wondering about all the people on the street. What if he should have changed cabs? What if someone had followed him? He tried to walk normally, but constantly looking over his shoulder was making his neck sore. He stopped in front of store windows to check the reflection and see if anyone else stopped. The only thing that kept him from completely losing his mind on the walk to the DOPS building was that a woman walked up behind him by an antiques shop and tapped him on the shoulder. Coop whirled around, tensing his body, ready to run or punch or, more likely, fall on his face when the enemy agent Tasered him.

The woman, wearing heavy eye makeup and a Bauhaus T-shirt, said, "You know where there's a grocery store or bodega around here?"

"I don't want any trouble," he said, still ready to bolt.

The woman gave him a puzzled look. "A store. My dog's got to take a dump and I need some plastic bags to get it."

Coop looked from the woman down to the pavement. She was holding a leash and on the end of it was a panting corgi. He kept looking, trying to figure out if this was another ruse. What if it was an attack corgi? That didn't really make sense. Even with a jetpack, the best the dog could do would be to nip at his knees. Coop looked back at the woman, realizing he was breathing too fast and sweating.

"You okay, man? You look kind of pale," she said.

"I'm fine. Yeah, there's a drugstore a block down at the corner. They probably have plastic bags."

"Thanks," she said. Then, in a slightly higher-pitched voice, she said to the dog, "Come on, Peter."

They went down the street and Coop leaned against the antiques shop, catching his breath. Great, he thought. Very James Bond. You can't even walk to work without being terrorized by supervillain minidogs. He shook his head, more than a little annoyed with himself, and walked the rest of the way to the DOPS building determined to act like an actual adult human being.

Coop got there in one piece. No one intercepted him with a helicopter. No one with a blowgun tranqed him. In fact, the weirdest thing that had happened was the realization that he was going to be coming here, punching a clock, day after day. The idea of going to an office every day was a strange one, though. The only routine he'd had in the past was meeting people at a few bars or coffee shops to plan heists. That and jail. This was going to take some getting used to. But so did prison, and he'd managed that. And there was no Giselle in prison. Or pizza. Or *Forbidden Planet*. Or Morty, for that matter. He got a visitor badge in the lobby and went upstairs to the floor where Giselle worked.

"Hey, hero. I hear you're coming to work here after all," said someone behind him. Coop recognized Nelson's voice. He ignored him and walked in the direction of Giselle's desk. "My face still hurts. Thanks for asking," Nelson said. He sped up and sidled around in front of Coop. "I just want you to know that when you get your credentials, I'm putting in a request to have you on my team. We're going to have a blast together, convict."

"Have you seen Giselle?" said Coop coolly.

"No."

Coop looked past him. "Good eyes, Mannix. She's right behind you."

When Nelson turned, Coop went the other way, down a corridor and back to Giselle's desk the long way.

"Hey there," he said when he saw her.

"Hey yourself," she said. Then, "I'd hug you, but it's the office, so, you know."

"Sure. I understand. I wouldn't hug me right now anyway. I'm kind of sweaty."

"Yes, you are. Did you run here?"

"No. Just waiting for ninjas and predators the whole way over."

"Yeah," said Giselle. She gave him a sympathetic smile. "It takes a while to get over that. You'll feel better when we get you a cover story."

"A cover story? What's yours?"

"I work in receivables at an import company. We specialize in Persian and Indian rugs. If you need anything for when you get your own apartment, I can set you up."

"Do you have bath mats? I'll need one of those."

"There's a mysterious land called Target where you can find that kind of thing. I'll show you sometime."

"That sounds all right." Coop looked around the busy office, wondering what kind of world domination you could plan while checking your bids on eBay. "Again, sorry I'm late. This thing with Morty is getting to me. Am I supposed to meet Woolrich?"

"You don't need to," said Giselle. She pulled a folder full of forms from her desk and set it in front of Coop. *More goddamn folders.* He opened the cover and looked at the papers underneath. They looked like ordinary employment forms. He'd filled out plenty of fake ones over the years so he could get inside buildings and case them. Now, he was about to fill out the forms for real.

"This feels pretty weird," he said.

"I had to do it, too. Remember, I can help you through this."

"Okay. So where do I sign my life away?"

"I'll take you to an empty office where you can have some privacy."

"Thanks. Oh, and by the way, I've already seen three ways I can get in here and steal some of your laptops. Should I mention that on the form?"

Giselle shook her head. "Let's just stick to your name and social security number for now." She stopped and looked at him. "You do have a social security number, right?"

"Don't worry. My mom was enough of a straight arrow to get me one. But are they going to check my taxes or anything? Because I didn't always pay them on time."

"When's the last time you paid?"

"Let me think for a minute. Never."

Giselle looked around in case anybody had heard him. "Let's just cross that bridge when we come to it, shall we? Follow me."

She led him to a bare, dark office at the end of a row of identical glass-front cubicles. She flipped on the light and Coop sat behind the desk.

"Do you have a pen?" she said.

"No."

"Check the drawers. Sometimes people leave a few."

He opened the middle drawer and there were two blue pens inside. He held them up so Giselle could see. "Golly. Looks like my luck's changing already."

She smiled. "Listen, I have some things to do. If you have any trouble with the forms, just come and get me."

"Okay," he said. "I'll try not to bug you."

"Bug away. It'll be nice to have some distractions around here."

"I'll do my best."

Giselle came around the desk and stood close to him, pretending she was showing him the forms. Coop touched her leg under the desk.

"Knock knock," said someone at the door.

Both of them jumped in opposite directions, and Giselle came quickly around the desk, smoothing her dress. Bayliss stood in the doorway of the office.

"You look busy," Bayliss said, grinning. "Mind if I come in?"

"Of course," said Giselle. "I was just getting Coop set up with his ninety-four sixes." Coop smiled and held up his pens.

Bayliss came in and closed the office door. "Can you two keep a secret?" she said.

They both nodded. "Sure," said Coop.

Bayliss took a quick glance over her shoulder. "It's the Salzman thing. I think—I don't know—but I think I might know where the box is."

"That's great," said Giselle.

Coop set down the pens and crossed his arms. "But there's a problem. Otherwise you wouldn't be talking to us. You'd just go and get it."

Bayliss nodded. "Salzman had a secret safe in the office. One no one was supposed to know about, only I saw him using it once. I bet he has the box there."

"Why wouldn't he just take it with him?" said Giselle.

"Because if anyone noticed it missing before he got away, he's the first one they'd come after," said Coop.

"Exactly," said Bayliss. "That's why I don't want to go to anyone else in the DOPS. First off, if I'm wrong, Nelson is never going to let me hear the end of it. But I'm also afraid that if Salzman did leave the box, it means he might be working with someone in the building. And it could be anyone."

"Okay. I can buy that," said Giselle. "What do you want to do about it?"

Coop sighed. *Every. Single. Person.* "She wants me to steal it for her."

Bayliss hesitated for a minute, then nodded. "Actually, I'd like to do it with you. It could really be a good thing for you starting here. And it could be good for getting me promoted away from Nelson."

Coop did some calculations in his head. *Mr. Lemmy wants the box. The angel wants the box. The glee club and their wacko cult friends want the box. But no one knows where the box is. Except now, Bayliss says she does. If she's right and the box is there, it might be my only chance to get it and save Morty. But if I gave it to Mr. Lemmy I'd be screwing over Bayliss, and Giselle would never forgive me for that.* That's as far as he could figure right then. All that mattered at the moment was getting the box. He could figure out the rest later.

"I'm in," he said.

Bayliss beamed at him. "Thanks."

"Me, too," said Giselle. "You're not going to have fun like this without me. Besides, while Coop goes on his crime spree, I can cloud people's minds so they won't see what we're up to."

"Where's the safe?" said Coop.

"I think it's in the break room," said Bayliss.

"Where in the break room?"

"The microwave oven."

Coop gave her a puzzled look. "There's a safe behind the microwave?"

She shook her head. "The safe *is* the microwave. From what I saw, I think it's a transdimensional portal."

Nothing is ever normal with these people.

"The thing is, I don't exactly have a lot of experience with portals to other dimensions. Dragons, yeah. Spiders, God help me, yeah. Regular safes, no problem. But this stuff . . ."

"It's transdimensional, but it still works like a safe. All we need to do is figure out the combination on the microwave pad."

Coop thought a minute. Giselle and Bayliss looked at him. "Okay. I might be able to do it. But no guarantees. And if it all falls apart . . ."

Bayliss held up her hands. "I'll take the blame. You're a rookie and I talked you into it."

"Don't worry. I'll figure out some way to make it look like Nelson did it," he said. "When do we do it?"

"How about ten tonight? The office is mostly empty, but I can come up with busy work to stay until then."

"All right, let's get it," said Coop. "I'm going to need some things, so I'll go home and meet you here."

"Great," she said.

"I'm going home too," said Giselle. "I need to change out of this walk of shame ensemble."

Coop shook his head. "This job isn't off to so bad a start after all. I'm signing up for a regular salary *and* my first job is to rip off my new bosses. Good first day."

"Let's not talk about it anymore. I'll see you both at ten."

There was a knock on the door and Nelson came in. "Hi, kids." He looked at the papers on the desk. "Seriously? You need two agents to waste time helping you fill those things out?"

"All the big words scare me," said Coop. "Hold my hand while I finish it?"

"I'll hold your head underwater until the bubbles stop."

"So the big words scare you, too."

Nelson turned to Bayliss. "Leave this creep and his moll. We have work to do."

They went out together and Giselle turned to Coop. "Am I really a moll now?"

"You're an accomplice to at least grand larceny, so yeah, I think you are," he said.

"Isn't a moll supposed to be partnered up with a gangster? Like the girl on his arm?"

"That part is entirely up to you," said Coop. "But I wouldn't mind trying it on for size."

"We'll see," she said. "Right now I have to get back to work. See you later, working man."

She closed the door and Coop's heart sank a little. He was really going to be a salary grunt. Another jerk with a job, even if it was with Giselle, and even if he did still get to steal. He'd be doing it for the government. That didn't sound like fun at all. But first things first. Get the box. Get Morty. Don't destroy the world. And duck the IRS.

[][][]

"How much longer are we going to sit here?" said Tommy.

"Until the target arrives," said Steve.

Jerry chuckled. "You sound totally CIA, Dad."

"Thank you, son."

Jerry looked at Tommy and gave him a can-you-believe-I-got-away-with-that smile. Tommy just frowned and shifted his weight. They were sitting in a truck from the construction site, waiting for the woman Jerry said he'd seen with Coop. Jerry had been, to his mind at least, artfully vague about how he'd run across them. He just kept talking about the woman, and that's what stuck in everyone's head, especially his dad's, and he was the one who really mattered. It was dark out and they'd been in the truck for over two hours and it was way past boring.

"I have to go to the bathroom," said Tommy.

"You shouldn't have drunk all those Diet Cokes you brought," said Steve. "That stuff runs through you faster than Mexican beer on the Fourth of July."

"Or Cinco de Mayo," said Jorge.

"Pretty much any holiday where getting shitfaced is inevitable."

"Hey, don't be a beer racist. Plenty of gringo beers do that too. Bud goes through me like NASCAR."

Steve nodded sagely. "I think all your non-premium-priced ales are basically piss rockets. It's how they get you to buy more."

"I still have to pee," said Tommy.

"You have the bladder of a termite," said Steve.

"A girl termite," added Jorge.

Steve adjusted the rearview so he could look the boy in the eyes. "Go to that Arby's around the corner and do it there."

"I suppose I'll have to buy something," Tommy said glumly.

"Get some fries for everybody. And no more goddamn Coke," said Jorge.

When Tommy opened his door, Jerry said, "I'll go with you."

"No, you won't," said Steve. "You know what the target looks like. You stay."

Jerry settled back down on his seat.

Tommy got out and headed down the street to the Arby's, a little hunched over, his hands shoved deep into his pockets.

"What's up with Tommy?" said Steve. "He needs to get his head in the game."

"He's okay. Just a little depressed. You know. About the bake sale," said Jerry.

Steve pointed at his son in the rearview. He said, "You need to kick his ass into gear or I will. And don't worry about the bake sale. That was the last good time those Abaddonian fuck monkeys are ever going to have on this Earth."

"I'll talk to Tommy when we get back."

"Good. Caleximus does not abide slackers."

Jerry started to say something in Tommy's defense, but stopped as a white Honda Civic slowed by a parking space across the street. "Hey, I think that might be her."

Steve raised and dropped his hands in frustration. "Of course she shows up while Tommy's gone. I wanted four on this job for a reason. If she's a criminal, she'll be a fighter. I wanted more than enough to lasso her. Goddammit."

They watched the Honda slowly angle its way into the parking spot. It was a bit narrow and took a couple of tries.

"Fuck it," said Jorge. "She's in that little foreign Cracker Jack box and we're in a truck. Ram her."

Steve put the truck into gear and checked the traffic. The moment the road was clear, he sped across the street, rear-ending the Honda. Jorge and Jerry ran out and pulled the unconscious woman from her car. Steve waited behind the wheel as the others loaded her into the back of the truck with them.

"Go go go," shouted Jorge. Steve hit the accelerator.

Jerry looked out the back window. "What about Tommy?"

"He can take the bus," said Steve.

Jerry got out his phone. "I'm going to call him."

"No, you're not," Steve said. "If she wakes up, your job is to make sure she doesn't get frisky."

"She's out cold," Jerry said. "I've got to call Tommy and let him know we didn't just ditch him."

They sped along through traffic and made it to the freeway. "Fine. Call your girlfriend. And you tell him we're going to have a serious talk when all this is over."

"Yes, sir."

"Serious."

Steve steered the truck over to the fast lane.

"You know," said Jorge. "Now *I* kind of have to go to the bathroom."

"Me, too," said Steve. He looked at Jerry in the rearview. "But don't you dare tell Tommy."

Coop was putting his tools into the duffel, for once feeling pretty good about the world. When his phone rang, the screen said GISELLE. He thumbed it on.

"Hey you. I was just about to head over. How are you doing?"

"Is this Coop?" said a man's voice.

"Who's this?" Coop said, the good feelings evaporating, as they usually did for him.

"We picked up something of yours tonight. Your lady friend. Giselle Petersen, according to her driver's license."

Coop spoke very coolly and precisely, trying to keep all emotion out of his voice. "I'd like to speak to her."

"You can talk all you like. After you give us back what's rightfully ours."

Not this again.

"You're the glee club, aren't you?"

"The who?"

"The screw-ups who broke into the Blackmoore Building the other night."

"Yeah. We're also the screw-ups that have your girl. You know what we want."

"The box."

"The box."

"I don't have it."

Coop didn't hear anything for a minute. "Hello? You still there?"

"Well, where is it?" The voice sounded almost as frustrated as he felt.

"Someone else has it. I can get it back, but it'll take some time."

"How long?"

Coop thought for a second, calculating how much bullshit he could shovel in the voice's direction. "Seventy-two hours."

"Are you kidding? Why not take the rest of the month off? Go to Mexico. Get a tan."

"Listen. The box is locked up tight. But I can do it in maybe forty-eight hours."

The line seemed to go dead again. Coop waited, hoping asking for seventy-two hours would get him the forty-eight he wanted.

"I don't know," said the voice reluctantly. "Forty-eight is a long time."

"It's not like they're selling these things at Ikea. If you want the box, it's going to take forty-eight hours."

The voice took another second. Coop wished he was at the DOPS building. They probably had all kinds of ways to trace the call.

"Okay," said the man's voice. "You have forty-eight hours. And don't even dream about trying anything cute. Or you know what."

"Yeah. You're going to do something even dumber than the other night."

"No, we won't."

"Right. How could you be dumber than that?"

"I mean we're going to kill her, tough guy."

"No, you won't, because if you hurt her you're never going to see the box."

The man's voice suddenly sounded far away, like he had his hand over the phone. "What? The keys to the bathroom are in my desk drawer," he said. Then his voice went back to normal. "Did you say something?"

"I'll call you when I get it."

The voice went strange again. "No. The other drawer, dammit."

Coop hung up. First me, then Morty, and now Giselle. Is there anyone I know who hasn't been kidnapped yet? At least Mr. Lemmy was a pro. Whoever had Giselle, he hoped they took better care of her than the bathroom keys.

At the construction site, Steve looked at the woman's phone. That Coop asshole actually hung up on him. Steve put him on his mental list, the one for when Caleximus returned. Put him right up there with the Abaddonians. *We'll see who's a tough guy then,* he thought. After the bathroom pit stop, they drove Giselle to a different work site, across town from the main one. Steve pulled the battery out of her phone.

"What are you doing? How can he call you now?" said Jerry.

"I don't want them tracing the phone. And I can put the battery in every few hours to check for messages. Don't worry, son. I've got this figured out."

"All right," he said and looked at the still unconscious Giselle. "Is she going to be all right?"

"She just got a little bump on the head. I had plenty of those when I was your age. She'll be fine."

"I hope so. I feel kind of bad about what we're doing."

"Don't. These nonbelievers, tough guys, heretics, and thieves don't matter dick compared to our holy work. And don't tell your mother I said 'dick' in front of you."

Oh, great. He's really in Crusade mode tonight. "I guess you're right."

"That's my boy. Hey, I had an idea on the way over here. We need a minion."

"Who?"

"One of Caleximus's minions. A demon boar."

Jorge looked at Steve. "Do you even know how to control one of those things?"

"I've read the books. Haven't you?"

"Sure, but the books never tell the whole story. I mean, a demon boar . . . that's heavy stuff."

"That's why we're going to need to take it for a test drive. I figure this Coop guy would make for a good one. How about you?"

Jorge grinned. Steve looked at Jerry. He smiled, too, but it was a little more forced and a lot more terrified.

"I'm going to need the silver blade for the ceremony," said Steve. "Which one of you has it?"

"I thought Jerry still had it," said Jorge.

"Funny," said Steve, an annoyed edge in his voice. "He said you did. Jerry? Do you have any thoughts on the matter?"

Jerry looked at the floor. Even though he'd gone to the bathroom five minutes earlier, he felt like he could go again. "I lost it," he said.

"You lost it?" Steve barked. Jorge said something fast in Spanish that didn't sound even remotely like "Yay. We get to get a new knife."

Steve put a hand to his forehead. "Where did you lose it?" he said.

"I didn't exactly lose it," Jerry said. "I had to give it to some vampires."

Steve sat down on his desk. Jorge shook his head.

"Son, there's no such things as vampires."

Jerry went over to where his father sat. "You weren't there. They sure seemed like vampires."

Steve crossed his arms like when Jerry was six and trying to explain how broccoli was poisonous. "Really? What do vampires seem like?"

"They had fangs. And there were a bunch of them."

"These are big vampires, I'm guessing?"

"Not exactly."

"Medium? Were they medium-size vampires?"

"Sort of little. Like Girl Scouts, but with fangs."

Jorge laughed.

Steve looked into Jerry's eyes. "Are you on drugs? It's okay. You can tell me the truth. I love you and we'll find you a doctor."

Jerry took a step back. "No, Dad. I'm not on drugs. You weren't there. They were vampires. It's where I saw Coop and that Giselle lady. In that magic place I told you about. Jinx Town."

Jorge went over to Steve. Jerry heard him whisper, "We don't have time for this shit." Steve nodded.

"Jerry. I'm not mad. But I'm very disappointed. That was a sacred object I entrusted to you."

"I know. I'm sorry."

"We still need a silver dagger for the ceremony."

"I know."

"Do you? Do you know what this is going to call for?"

Jerry looked at his father. Visions of human sacrifice swam in his head. "No. What does it call for?"

"It means I'm going to have to call your mother and have her get Grandma's good silver out of storage. There's a carving knife in there that might work all right. But this is demonic blood we're talking about. If it won't clean off the silver, you're the one who has to explain to your mom. Understood?"

"Yes, sir." Standing there, head down, Jerry wasn't sure what scared him more: a one-ton tusked and red-eyed monster from another world or the silent treatment from his mom if he messed up Grandma's silver. For the first time in a long time, Jerry crossed his fingers that everything was going to work out and the world would end soon. At least a boar would kill him quick. Mom could draw out being mad for a long, long time.

The guard on late-night duty in the lobby of the DOPS building didn't seem the least interested in who Coop was, where he was going, or what he had with him. Coop's bag wasn't big enough to hold a tactical nuclear missile, but Coop had the feeling that if it had been, he could have claimed it was a party sub for a birthday bash upstairs and the guard would not have cared less. It made him a little wistful. These moments at the beginnings of a job, when you were just getting the feel of a place. Checking the layout. The security. The personnel. He'd still be doing it, he knew, but now for a bunch of button-down suits and people who were as crooked as him, but got a pass for it because they had an office upstairs and a mug with their name on it by the coffeemaker.

Coop got his pass from the guard and just for good measure shook the guy's hand. Then he went upstairs to meet Bayliss, still not sure how much to tell her. She'd need to know the truth about the situation at some point, but he didn't want to hit her with it too soon and take a chance on spooking her. He needed to get the box in his hands. In the end, he decided to feel things out as they went along.

He found Bayliss at her desk with enough papers and folders around her to make a desk igloo. "What's all that?" Coop said.

"Absolutely nothing," said Bayliss, sounding more than a little satisfied with herself. "I just pulled some old files from one of the storage rooms and sat here playing with them until everybody left."

"Good cover," said Coop, impressed. "Very boring looking. I wouldn't want to talk to you."

"Thanks," she said. "Where's Giselle?"

He felt like a jerk lying, but there was nothing else he could do. "She got stuck and won't be along till later. But we can still get started now."

"How? Without a Marilyn, people might see us in the break room."

"Not if no one comes in," said Coop. He reached into his bag and pulled out a sign with biohazard symbols on the sides and POSSIBLE CONTAMINATION AREA in large red letters in the middle. "Think people will buy it?"

Bayliss nodded. "With the kind of stuff we work with around here? No problem."

"Then let's get going."

"What do you need me to bring?"

"I just need you to remember what you saw before."

"Trust me. I'll never forget it."

They made a circuit of the office and saw only a few rookie agents doing grunt work at a handful of workstations scattered across the floor. Coop nodded to Bayliss and they headed straight for the break room.

After putting the sign on the door, they went inside and Coop jammed a chair under the doorknob so no one could get in without him letting them.

"So, this is the door to Narnia?" said Coop.

Bayliss went and stood by the not terribly clean-looking microwave, the kind Coop had seen in a hundred offices on a hundred jobs. The models were always out of date and probably leaked enough radiation to make his contamination sign not so much a lie as a helpful hint.

"How did it work?" said Coop.

Bayliss mimed the movements as she talked. "All I saw was Salzman punching in a code on the keypad and then opening the microwave door the wrong way."

Coop shook his head. "What does that mean? The wrong way?"

"Well, you know how microwave doors open from the right to the left? He opened it from the left to the right."

"And you're sure that makes it a portal to another dimension?"

She shrugged. "I've seen other portals and this one didn't look so different. Of course, you couldn't heat soup in the others," Bayliss said, laughing nervously.

Coop set his bag on the break room table and unzipped it.

"How are you going to do it?" Bayliss said. "There are twenty buttons on the keypad. That's millions of possible combinations."

"I'm not even going to try," said Coop. "They are." He held up a small metal box.

Bayliss's forehead furrowed. "Are those the binary ants we gave you for the Babylon case? You were supposed to give those back."

He looked at her. "I'm a crook, remember? I kept some. I just hope it's enough."

Bayliss watched closely as he took the ants to the microwave.

"You might want to go over by the door. If I get this wrong, who knows what kind of transdimensional shit storm I'm going to start."

"You think it might explode?" said Bayliss.

"As long as it doesn't explode spiders, I can deal with it." He stopped for a second and looked at her. "You know this is probably going to ruin your machine, right?"

"Good. We've needed a new one for years."

"Okay," said Coop. "Here we go."

Here we go. Please don't kill us.

He upended the container of ants onto the microwave's keypad. They disappeared inside and the machine began to whir. Numbers and cook settings flashed on and off. The microwave started and shut down. Over and over. The carousel inside would move for a half turn and stop. Move a whole turn and stop. The keypad kept beeping.

"You think it's working?" said Bayliss.

"Yes. I'm definitely ruining your machine."

The whirring went on for several more minutes, like hornets in a washing machine. Then a gentle glow began around the edges of the microwave's door. Coop thought it looked like dawn. Or maybe an atomic bomb. It went from yellow to blue, shimmering and strobing like some kind of underwater fish disco. A small trail of smoke rose from the microwave's back.

"Oh, crap," said Bayliss. "Should we stop it? I don't want to start a fire."

"Leave it. Let's see what happens," said Coop.

A few seconds later, the whirring stopped. The keypad lit up. The overhead lights flickered and went out. The room was illuminated only by the microwave itself. It looked like someone was toasting a small star inside.

"What now?" said Coop.

"I'm not sure."

"Someone has to open it."

"I suppose I should."

"You have my vote."

Bayliss paused. "Do you think it's safe?"

"There's only one way to find out."

They went to the microwave and Bayliss touched the door handle. "If I die and you live, punch Nelson in the nose again for me, okay?"

"I promise."

She took the handle and slowly dragged it across the front of the microwave, from the right side of the door all the way to the left. The face of the microwave stretched and warped like taffy as the handle moved, but nothing exploded, which to Coop was a plus.

Finally, when the handle wouldn't move any farther, Bayliss pulled the handle . . . and the door opened. The light from the oven blinded them for a second. Then they saw a small metal chamber containing some papers, a pistol . . . and the box. Coop reached in and took everything, then tossed the pistol back inside. *Who knows what that's been used for?* He nodded to Bayliss and she closed the door, sliding the handle back into place on the right. The microwave stopped glowing and the break-room lights flickered back on. The unmistakable smell of burned wires filled the air, and the back of the oven was scorched black.

"You're definitely going to need a new one."

"But we're not dead."

"Nice job," said Coop.

"Thanks."

"Let's get out of here."

"Let's," said Bayliss.

Coop put the box and papers in his bag, slid the chair away from the door, and grabbed his sign. They headed back to Bayliss's desk. When they got there, Coop pulled a chair over and they sat down together. Bayliss's face was a wide grin. Coop wouldn't have guessed she could smile like that.

"How does it feel, being in on a heist?" he said.

"Wow. Now I know a little more why you and Giselle like this kind of thing."

"When everything works out it's kind of a rush."

"I'll say."

And this is where I ruin your night, he thought.

"Now listen to me closely. About Giselle . . ." he said. And told her all about the phone call and Morty's kidnapping earlier.

"Oh my god. We've got to tell someone. I'll call Mr. Woolrich," said Bayliss. When she reached for her phone, Coop laid his hand on it.

"Let me ask you a question: Do you really think the DOPS is going to risk losing the box to save a couple of lowlife crooks?"

"Giselle works for us. They have to, right?"

"They're the government. They don't have to do anything. And Woolrich will just tell Nelson. You think he's going to help? He'll bury Giselle just to get back at me, and you'll probably end up in the mailroom."

"What are we going to do?" said Bayliss.

"I need to take the box," said Coop.

"Are you crazy?" Bayliss whisper-screamed. "That thing is a weapon."

"Yeah, aimed right at Giselle's head. You want to pull the trigger?"

Bayliss sat back in her chair. She gnawed on a fingernail for a few seconds. "What do you want to do with it? You can't give it to the people who kidnapped Giselle. That would leave your friend Morty in trouble. And you can't give it to Morty's kidnappers."

"I'm not giving it to anyone," said Coop. "They just need to think I am. I have an idea. If it works, it'll get back Giselle and Morty, and maybe help you capture Salzman and all the other idiots who want this thing. But you have to trust me and let me take the box."

Bayliss drummed her fingers nervously on her desk. She got up, looked around, and sat back down. "Only if you take me with you," she said.

Coop thought about it. She'd kept it together in the break room, she was more willing to take chances than he'd thought, and they both hated Nelson. He held out his hand. "Partners," he said. Bayliss shook it.

"Partners," she said. "What do we do first?"

"Do you have Salzman's phone number?"

"I can get it."

"Okay. That's all you need to do for now." Coop took a pen and pad and wrote Morty's address out for her. "Call in sick tomorrow. Meet me at this address at noon. Bring Salzman's number. If I need anything else, I'll call you. Give me your number." She wrote it on the pad and he put the paper in his bag.

"I'm still trying to figure out what Salzman wanted with the box," said Bayliss. "A guy like him. Was it just money?"

"I don't know. Everybody who knows about the box thinks it's something else. Luck. A calling card for an old god. A bomb. The end of the world. Who knows what he thinks it is."

"Whatever it is, I absolutely want in on this," said Bayliss. "I'll see you tomorrow."

"Great."

Coop started to get up when Bayliss grabbed his sleeve. Her eyes were a little wider than they had been. "You're not going to skip out on me, are you?"

"Why would I do that?"

"Because you're a crook."

"Yeah, but we're partners. A good crook doesn't skip out on a partner."

"Like you and Giselle."

"Yeah."

"Okay. See you tomorrow."

"One more thing, you should fire the guard in the lobby," said Coop.

"Why?"

"He's too bored to do his job and he's not too bright." Coop reached into his jacket pocket and pulled out a watch. "When you fire the guy, give this back to him for me."

Bayliss smiled and put the watch in a desk drawer.

"Tomorrow," she said.

"Tomorrow."

The Magister indulged in one of his last remaining vices: watching *The Price Is Right* on a little portable TV he kept hidden under some rugs in the corner of the sacred chamber. He always watched with the sound off, so he'd become pretty good at reading lips. Some dunce in a Hawaiian shirt bid way too high for a Barcalounger, not unlike his. The Magister shook his head and his back spasmed.

Destroy the world soon, Lord Abaddon, and rid me of this accursed flesh.

They were coming up on the big showcase at the end of the show when his phone rang. He took it out, already angry at whoever it was. "Hello? Who is this? I'm busy."

A quiet voice on the other end of the line said, "It's me. Coral Snake."

"Who?"

The Magister heard a sigh. "Carol."

His mood brightened infinitesimally. "Carol. How nice to hear from you. Any news from our Caleximus friends?"

"Yes. They got the girl."

"What girl?"

"Coop's girl."

"Who's Coops?"

There was a short pause before Carol said, "Craig. They got Craig's girl and they're holding her until he brings them the box."

The Magister pumped his fist in the air, which just made his back hurt again. "Excellent. Now all we have to do is get the girl and he'll bring the box straight to us."

"Except I don't know where she is."

"What?" said the Magister, his mood going quickly back to miserable.

"They sent me for fries and then drove off without me."

"I don't want to hear about fries. All I want to know is where's the girl?"

"That's what I'm telling you. I don't know. She's not at the site. But here's the thing. Steve made a deal with Coop—Craig—to bring him the box in forty-eight hours."

"Priest Steve again?" The Magister thought for a minute. "Can you find out where they'll make the exchange?"

"I'm sure I can, but not until right before it happens."

The Magister nodded, grim wheels turning grimly in his head. "That's fine. Forty-eight hours will give us plenty of time to get ready. You did a good job, Carol."

Tommy sighed. "My name's not . . . Forget it. And we still have a deal when the end comes. You're taking me with you, right?"

The Magister used his silkiest voice. "Lord Abaddon will reward you with riches beyond your wildest dreams."

"Cool."

"Cool indeed. Call me as soon as you hear anything."

"I will. Bye."

The Magister coughed. "Is that how we say good-bye?"

"Sorry. Good-bye, Dark High Magister."

"Good girl, Carol."

The Magister hung up and dialed another number. Adept Six answered.

"Yes, Magister?"

"Do we have a trusted crew in the restaurant?"

"Not now, I'm afraid. There are a few unbelievers. We'll have a full crew in the morning."

The Magister scratched his ear, pondering the situation. "Good. When they come in, tell them to thaw out Fluffy."

The Magister heard a satisfying gasp on the other end of the line. "Fluffy? Are you sure, Dark High One?"

"Very sure. And don't tell anyone about him. I want it to be a surprise."

"Oh, it will be, Magister. It will be."

"Let me know as soon as he's ready for company. I want to be in my nicest robes. Maybe the red ones, with the blue trim."

"A very flattering combination."

"All right. Get on that. Oh, and have them send me up some fries. That dopey girl Carol left me with fries on the brain."

"Do you want some balsamic with them?"

"Now, what do you think?"

"Silly question. Sorry, Lord."

The Magister hung up and looked at the TV. The credits were rolling on *The Price Is Right*. He'd missed the whole damned showcase. *Abaddon save me from my own people,* he thought as he reburied the TV under the rugs.

Salzman sat in a top-floor suite in the Mondrian Hotel, on a very comfortable leather chair across from a man in an identical comfy-looking chair. There was a chilled bottle of champagne between them. The man across the table was large, roughly the size of a walking refrigerator and just as graceful. Arrayed around him were several even larger men in glistening, strangely angled body armor. Salzman thought they looked less like bodyguards than like cubist waiters.

"I am Zavulon," said the large man. They shook hands.

"I thought I was meeting Olga," said Salzman.

"She took sick. They call me," said Zavulon. "I usually transpire in South America—Argentina, Brazil—so my English is not so good as hers."

"I'm sure we'll be able to muddle through," said Salzman. "Nice guards, by the way. That's anti-thaumaturgic armor they're wearing, isn't it?"

Zavulon turned around, then looked back at Salzman. "Anti-what?"

Salzman wiggled his fingers mysteriously. "Hocus-pocus. It protects from magic."

Zavulon laughed and pointed. "Yes. Hocus-pocus armor."

Salzman leaned back, crossing his legs. "You should understand something: mooks are made by magic, but we're not magic ourselves."

Zavulon leaned forward and his chair creaked a little. "But box is magic."

"I don't have the box with me."

"I notice. Where is it?"

"Technically, not on this Earth," said Salzman. "So if anything should happen to me it will never be seen by anyone again."

Zavulon opened his arms wide. "Who would do that? Who would hurt you? Besides, to kill a dead man. I would have no notion how."

Salzman put a deeply sarcastic hand over his heart. "I don't believe you, but it's a comfort to have you say it."

Zavulon took hold of the bottle between them. "Let's have champagne. Government has already paid, so let's not go to waste."

"Good idea."

Zavulon poured two glasses and the men toasted each other.

"You like?" said Zavulon, slurping his.

"Very much. I'll have to get the name before I leave."

"Don't bother yourself. Give me address and I will send you case."

"That's very kind."

The big man finished his champagne and poured himself another glass, but he didn't drink it right away. He set it on the table with the bottle. "If you don't mind," he said. "I like to cross all i's and dot all t's on such deals as this."

"You have it backward," said Salzman.

"Excuse me?"

"You dot the i's and cross the t's."

Zavulon laughed. "*Spasibo*. Now, to be clear on deal. You will supply us with DOPS mook *tekhnologiya* . . ."

Salzman held up a finger. "Not the technology. Just the plans."

"Of course. Plans for mook creation. And also, the little box. One with power to reverse the process."

"Exactly. You'll be the only people in the world capable of both making mooks and unmaking them."

Zavulon picked up his champagne, took a sip, and rested it on the arm of his chair. "Explain to me. You are a mook, yes? You don't age. You don't get sick. You don't get poison. Many—what is it?—flavors of magic don't hinder you. Who knows what else? With that, why do you so much want to be alive?"

Salzman poured himself more champagne. "You try being dead and then ask me that question."

"That I understand. No translator required." Zavulon smiled.

Salzman wondered how much one of the armored guards could hurt him. Antimagic armor wouldn't protect any of them from a broken neck. Still. This wasn't the time or place to contemplate such pleasantries. There would be time for that later. He said, "You have your experts in place who know how to use the box?"

Zavulon nodded. "We study every manuscript, scroll, and book on box for centuries. My people—similar to your DOPS—are ready any time." He laughed and pounded his chest. "We will make you strong like bear."

"What a strange thing to say," said Salzman.

A couple of the guards moved their rifles up a few inches. Zavulon barked at them in Russian and they lowered them.

"Their English is good," said Salzman, wanting to kill one of them more than ever.

"Yes. Much better than mine," Zavulon said. "Pardon my earlier joke. But is not that what most Americans think of us? Borscht, circus, onions, and bears?"

Salzman drank his champagne and nodded. "Yes. And with a vibrant and flourishing kleptocracy."

Zavulon frowned. "I don't know that word. How do you spell it?"

"K-l-e-p-t-o-c-r-a-c-y."

Zavulon took out a small pad and wrote down each letter. "*Spasibo.* I will reference later to improve my language."

"Are there any details you'd like to go over?"

"Not this second. I think is it. Is it? It is? Sorry. English, it all sounds the same sometimes."

"Champagne will do that to you."

Zavulon poured them more. "When can you deliver box?"

"I'll have to get in touch with my contact. It should be within twenty-four hours."

"Excellent. We will be waiting. Soon you breathe air, see with normal eyes, and die like other men."

Salzman glanced at the guards and back to Zavulon. "It sounds like Heaven. I'll call my contact tonight."

"Glorious." Zavulon checked the bottle to see how much champagne was left. "Would you like to finish? It's too good for their likes," he said, nodding at the guards.

"Why not?"

Zavulon poured them each another round. He drained his glass and said, "Do mook people such as you, you get drunk?"

"Keep pouring and I'll let you know."

Zavulon laughed. Salzman smiled. The guard on the end, he thought. The one who moved his rifle first. He's the one I'd kill. Or maybe Zavulon. Was that accent even real? Salzman wondered. He sighed. It wasn't fair. The annoying guard had gotten him all worked up, but he needed to make the call. There just wasn't time to stop off and strangle anyone on the way home. Salzman had another glass of champagne and thought of happier, deadlier times.

THIRTY-THREE

WHEN HE FINALLY REACHED LOS ANGELES, THE stranger took out his guidebook and walked to Griffith Park. Once inside the park grounds, he headed for a particular sycamore tree. When he didn't find what he was looking for, he picked up a stick and wandered the trails, peeking and probing under the bushes. Nothing. He went up another trail, past the observatory and the tourists taking selfies with the hazy city in the background.

Redecorating, he thought. *That's all this place needs.*

Eventually, he reached the abandoned zoo. In a long-disused tiger cage, the stranger found an old sleeping bag, but nothing else. He couldn't even smell anything. All the familiar scents were masked by the smog, the musk of long-gone animals, and the sweat of everyone else who, over the years, had used the zoo as an open-air squat. The stranger took out the guidebook and scanned the park map looking for other likely sites.

As he trudged up a long trail that wound higher into the park, a young couple strolled past him coming the other way. They were radiant. The woman was in a light summer dress and the man was in a blue polo shirt and white designer slacks. L.A. elites. Graceful and glowing in their beauty and privilege. The stranger barely glanced at them. His mind was somewhere else, rearranging buildings. That's why he started a little when the couple approached him.

"Hi. I'm Darla and this is my husband, Christopher," said the woman. "I was wondering, do you know the way to the Hollywood Wax Museum?"

The stranger shook his head. "I'm afraid not. I'm not from around here."

"Oh. I saw you had a guidebook and thought you might know," said Darla.

The stranger held the book out to her. "You're welcome to look if you like."

"That's the problem," said Christopher. "We lost our bags and both of our sets of reading glasses were in them. If it's not too much trouble, could you look it up for us? Thanks."

"I'm sorry to hear about your bags. Of course I can help. There's a wax museum around here? I might have to visit there myself before I'm done."

Darla gave him a sunny smile. "Oh. Are you here on business?"

The stranger thumbed through the guidebook. "Very much," he said.

"What kind?" said Christopher.

Darla leaned in. "The reason my husband asks is that you don't look much like a businessman. More like a fucking bum."

The stranger looked up. "Do I really?"

"In that filthy coat and shitty shoes? What are you? A junkie? A dealer? Both?" said Christopher.

"I didn't think my coat was that dirty."

"Filthy," said Darla. She cocked her head and looked at him. "Nothing at all like what an actual businessman would wear."

"Thank you. I'll have to do something about that," said the stranger. He flipped to the guidebook's index. "Now, it was the wax museum you wanted . . ."

Christopher pulled a switchblade from his pocket, snicked it open, and took a step toward him. "Fuck the museum. I know a dirty dealer when I see one. How much are you carrying? Empty your pockets. I want all of it."

"You don't need the knife," said the stranger. He dropped the guidebook and put up his hands. "You can have all of it." He closed them and when he opened his hands again, gold poured out onto the ground.

"Damn," said Christopher dismally.

"Fuck me," said Darla miserably.

The stranger took the knife from Christopher's hand, broke it in two, and threw the pieces into the bushes. "Is this how you spend your days? Show me your real faces."

"We can't," said Leviathan, his Christopher face turning red with embarrassment.

"We can change our bodies a little, but the only thing real we can show are our teeth bits. Because they scare mortals so much," said Beelzebub. She grinned, showing hideous gray choppers.

"Wars. Murder. Famine. Cancer. And your contribution to Lucifer's cause is shaking down hobos?" said the stranger.

"And tourists," said Leviathan.

"And priests," said Beelzebub. "And librarians. And bus drivers. And that rude counterman at the tapas place on Fairfax. What was it called?"

"Oh, it's on the tip of my tongue," said Leviathan.

"Hush," said the stranger, and they both hushed very quickly.

Beelzebub looked at the ground, dragging her gorgeous white shoes through the debris on the trail. "We do diseases, too, sometimes. Leviathan has tuberculosis."

"And I cough a lot in crowds." He put a hand to his mouth and coughed violently a few times. When he was done he looked at the stranger like a mutt that had just learned to fetch.

"Do you really have tuberculosis?" said the stranger.

Leviathan shrugged and put his hands in his pockets. "No."

"I didn't think so." An old couple went past them on the trail, heading up the hill. The stranger stopped talking to let them pass. The old woman smiled to him as they went by. He smiled back, curious where they were going.

The stranger turned his attention back to the miscreants. "The real question I have is 'What am I going to do with you?' Let you go to continue with your pathetic attempts at mayhem—"

"Yes. You should do that," said Leviathan.

"Or do I drop the whole park into a fault line? Or just you two? I don't imagine those bodies you're stuck in would react well to magma."

"Please don't," said Beelzebub. "We'll be in so much trouble."

"Plus, it would hurt a lot," said Leviathan.

"Help me and I'll let you go," said the stranger. "You know what I want."

Leviathan and Beelzebub pointed in different directions and talked at the same time.

"We just saw him . . ."

"The other day . . ."

"He didn't look so good . . ."

"But Qaphsiel was closing in on the box."

"Stop," said the stranger. "The box?"

"Yes," said Beelzebub. "He knew sort of where it was."

"Sort of?"

"Yes. He was still looking, but was certain he was going to find it."

"Finally," said Leviathan, chuckling. "What a boob, right?" When the stranger didn't chuckle back he stopped abruptly.

"Did he say this to you directly?"

Leviathan and Beelzebub looked away.

"No," said Beelzebub. "We more or less inferred."

"Body language and all that," said Leviathan.

"Psychology."

"But he didn't actually tell you that he knew where the box was?"

"No," said Leviathan. "But he had the map and was studying some buildings on it."

"And he was more manic than usual," said Beelzebub. "Believe me. We've been keeping an eye on him and he was excited about something."

"Where is he now?"

"Um . . ." said Leviathan.

"Yeah," said Beelzebub. "As the mortals say, we kind of dropped the ball on that."

The stranger put his hand on Leviathan's shoulder and squeezed. Bones cracked. "You lost him?"

Leviathan spoke through very large, pointed, gritted teeth. "There was a Christian publishing convention in town. So many souls to tempt and corrupt."

"What he's saying is that we got a little distracted," said Beelzebub.

The stranger let go. Leviathan grimaced and shook the broken bones in his shoulder back into place. "Ow."

"All right. Listen to me," said the stranger. "You find Qaphsiel. If he has the box, let me know. If he's close to the box, let me know. But don't get involved with getting the box yourselves. That's his task. Let him do it."

"Of course," said Leviathan.

"We'd be delighted," said Beelzebub.

"Now get out of my sight," said the stranger.

Leviathan and Beelzebub transformed back into their attractive human forms and walked quickly down the hill.

"Thank you," said Beelzebub.

"Yes. Thanks," said Leviathan.

"We're ever so grateful."

"Really. We really appreciate—"

"Go!" bellowed the stranger.

The fallen angels ran down the hill, slipping and sliding in their expensive shoes, grabbing each other to keep themselves from falling. The stranger couldn't deal with them anymore. With the stupidity of this world. He walked up the hill in the direction the old couple had taken.

Eventually, he reached a picnic area crowded with families. Parents. Children. Pets. The noise, smells, and messy clamor of humanity. The stranger stood off to the side, taking in the spectacle. Husbands staring at other men's wives. Wives staring daggers at their husbands. Children screaming, running wild. The stranger was delighted. He counted the sins, ran them through a mental calculator and shook his head.

Redecoration.

Of course, it wasn't entirely their fault, he thought. They were mortals. Simpletons. But after his encounter with Leviathan and Beelzebub, the place was becoming all a bit much. His mood and expression curdled. He imagined fault lines. Wildfires. Freak tornadoes.

A young girl in a blue dress, about five, ran by chasing balloons. Her eyes were red and her face was streaked where tears had mingled with dirt. She picked up her balloons from the bushes where they'd blown and cried even harder. The stranger could see that they were knotted together, a rubbery tangle of colors and shapes. The little girl saw him staring and dragged her balloons to him.

The stranger heard a man's voice calling to the girl. "Carly. Come away from the strange man, honey." The stranger looked over and saw a short man with thinning hair. *Sure. Let your children run wild,* he thought. *Run right to a stranger who could make it rain brimstone and ice down on all of you.*

The young girl held up her balloons.

"It popped," she said. "See? Right in the middle."

He knelt and looked at the knotted mess. The balloons were wound around each other to resemble some sort of dog, but the dog's torso had a hole in the side. The stranger looked at the father. The father started over.

"Carly. Come to Daddy, honey."

The stranger took the balloons from the girl and held them up to his lips. Then he blew across them. The dog's body slowly inflated. The girl's red eyes grew wide. The stranger put the dog on the ground just as the father reached them. Before he could grab the child, the stranger let go of the balloon dog. It ran a few steps, turned, and barked at the little girl. When she went over to it, the dog jumped into her arms, barking excitedly.

"Thank you! Thank you!" the little girl shouted and waved to him.

The stranger nodded. "You're welcome."

The girl set the dog on the ground. It bounded away and she laughed as she chased after it. When the stranger looked up, the father was standing a few feet away, his hands balled into fists. But he didn't look the least bit dangerous. He watched his daughter running after her new pet.

"How did you do that?" said the father.

"Your daughter is very polite," said the stranger. "But you don't spend enough time with her."

The father turned to him. "Excuse me?"

"I can tell these things. Time flies. People grow old. Worlds end."

"What the hell is wrong with you?"

The stranger went to the father and spoke very quietly. "It's not too late to stop being an asshole. Almost. But you have a little time left."

The father stepped back and took out his phone. "If you don't leave right now I'm going to call a cop."

"Time management. It's the key to the universe," said the stranger. He laughed and went back down the hill listening to the happy sounds of the girl and her new dog.

At about ten in the morning, Coop awoke from weird dreams. The spiders were still there. Dozens of them. But now, some of them looked like Salzman and some like Nelson, Woolrich, and Mr. Lemmy. Others resembled the prison warden at Surf City, Mr. Babylon, the tentacled twins from the DOPS, the gill people from Jinx Town, the fanged Vin Mariani girl, and all the werewolves that had chased him and Giselle out of the bar. The spider people all had on little top hats and tap shoes, and carried tiny canes. They did a complicated dance routine on their web to the tune of "Singin' in the Rain." The worst part was that they were pretty good. Yes, the spiders' voices were a little high and grating, but it was a lavish production number, with a band and lights and cannons shooting confetti at the end. In his dream, Coop couldn't help but applaud, and he woke up in bed clapping. So much for sleep. He got up and put on coffee.

There was a knock on the front door exactly at noon. When Coop opened it, Bayliss stood there, her expression a bit happy, a bit surprised, and a bit puzzled. "You're here," she said.

"I said I would be."

"I know. I just wasn't sure."

Coop stepped out of the way so she could come in. "You want anything?" he said. "Coffee? A drink?"

Coop motioned to the sofa and she sat down. "I'm fine, thanks." She looked around the apartment like she was a paleontologist trying to put a mammoth together from teeth and a couple of toe bones.

"Did you hear about the big earthquake?"

"Here?"

"No. San Francisco."

"Fuck San Francisco. L.A. is where the world is going to end. Not up in kale country."

"I guess you're right."

When Coop looked over, he saw her examining the place with her eyes. "It's not my place. It's Morty's," he said.

"That makes more sense. It wasn't exactly what I was expecting your place to look like."

Coop poured himself a cup of coffee. "And what would my place look like?"

"I'm not sure," said Bayliss, a look of distress creeping across her face. "A little . . . darker?"

"Why do people keep saying stuff like that? I'm a cheerful guy. Look, this mug says 'World's Best Crook.' That's fun, right?"

Bayliss looked at the mug and shook her head. She said, "I think it's a little bit sad in a way."

Coop held up his free hand. "Okay. I'm not happy-go-lucky. But trust me, I'm goddamn delightful to be around when I'm not being thrown into vans and strange men aren't going to make my friends into cat food."

"I understand entirely. Actually, I don't. No one's ever kidnapped any of my friends. Not that I know of. No one's ever brought it up."

"Then probably no one's kidnapped them."

"Probably not," said Bayliss. She clapped her hands on her knees. "So, what are we doing? How is all this going to work?"

Coop leaned against the counter and sipped his coffee. "Here's the situation: a whole lot of people want the box, but we only have one, so we're going to have to be smart. At least smarter than them, which, considering some of this crowd, isn't going to be that hard."

"How many is a whole lot of people?"

Coop thought for a second. "Three principal people that I know of. Plus, of course, their backup goons. Then there's various other clowns who may or may not know about us yet. Basically, a lot of people."

Bayliss frowned. The scenario didn't seem to go down well with her. "What are we going to do?"

Coop set down his coffee and said, "Lie to all of them and hope we get away with it."

"That doesn't sound like much of a plan."

"It isn't. That's why it has a chance of working. With this many people involved, you don't want to overcomplicate it. Come on, you must do this stuff all the time at the DOPS."

Bayliss shook her head. "I mostly do surveillance. Data gathering. That sort of thing."

"Now you get to do something else. You'll love it."

Bayliss brightened. "You think so?"

"No," said Coop. "It's terrifying. You're going to hate it. So am I. We're going to have to be fast on our feet, but if you listen to me, we have a better than fifty percent chance of getting out alive."

"That much?" said Bayliss. She frowned again."I should have worn flats."

"You sure you don't want a drink?" said Coop.

"I'm fine."

"You relax. I'm going to make some calls."

"May I see the box?" said Bayliss.

Coop pointed. "It's right on the kitchen counter."

"You didn't think to hide it?"

"It's next to the whiskey. There is no safer place in the apartment."

Bayliss went over and picked the box up. "I wonder what's really inside?"

"On the bright side it's full of jelly beans, but probably it's full of spiders."

"Not everything is full of spiders."

"Enough are, so why take chances?"

Bayliss set the box down. "Okay. Let's do it."

"I've got to make some calls to get things going," said Coop.

"I'll be quiet as a mouse."

Coop picked up his phone and dialed. "Mr. Lemmy?" he said.

"Speaking."

"This is Coop. Morty's friend. You know, the bum."

"I know who it is, shit pile," said Mr. Lemmy. "You're the only one with this number. What do you want? You have my box?"

"Yes, I do."

"Fast," said Mr. Lemmy. He actually sounded less furious for a second. "See what happens when you're motivated? Okay. Bring it by my place. Here's the address—"

"I don't want your address. If you want the box you'll meet me at my address."

"Don't fuck with me, ball sac," said Mr. Lemmy, his voice sliding back to barely controlled rage.

"I'm not meeting you someplace you can bump us both off," said Coop. "We're going someplace public and then everyone's going home happy. If you want the box, that's the only way it's going to happen."

He could hear Mr. Lemmy's breath on the line. He sounded like a tiger with heartburn. Coop waited, worried. Everything depended on the players saying yes.

"Okay, smart-ass," said Mr. Lemmy. "But remember that I've got your friend. You fuck with me and being in public isn't going to save you or your schmuck friend."

"We're meeting tomorrow at eight. Here's how to get there. It's a little tricky, so you're going to want to write it down. People call it Jinx Town. Ever hear of it?"

"Oh, God. This isn't some fruit bar, is it?" said Mr. Lemmy.

"Don't worry. Your virtue will be safe. You have a pen? Here are the directions," said Coop. He told Mr. Lemmy about the star on the Walk of Fame. There wasn't any real reply. Just a dry laugh on the other end of the phone before the line went dead.

"How'd it go?" said Bayliss.

"Like if the phone was any bigger he would have reached through and ripped out my heart."

"Nelson sounds like that when he calls me sometimes."

"He's a little ray of sunshine, your partner."

"I look at him as my last training test. Can I work with him long enough without shooting him to get a promotion?"

Coop went and poured more coffee. "Why, Agent Bayliss, I'm shocked to hear you harbor such hostile intentions toward a fellow agent."

"Not intentions. Just something I think about when blowing out my birthday candles," said Bayliss. She gave him an embarrassed smile. "Who's next?"

"Did you get Salzman's number?"

Bayliss took a slip of paper from her shoulder bag and handed it to Coop. He dialed. Someone answered but didn't say anything. "Hi, Salzman. It's Coop. Remember me?"

"How did you get this number?" Salzman said. His voice was cold enough to give an iceberg pneumonia.

"From Bayliss. She's with me right now. Want to say hi?"

Bayliss shot him a panicked look. Coop waved to her that it was all right.

"What do you want?"

"I have your box," said Coop.

"I don't know what you're talking about."

"Sure you do. And by the way, you owe the DOPS a new microwave."

There was a long pause before Salzman said, "How did you find it?"

"I was heating up a Hot Pocket and out it came."

"You're very sure of yourself, aren't you?"

"No. I'm sure of you. You want the box."

"Which brings us back to the original question: What do you want?"

"A million dollars."

Coop heard him chuckle. "Naturally. And I bet you'd like a pony for your birthday. I don't have a million dollars."

"You have all kinds of shady connections. Get it. By tomorrow."

"Where and when?"

"Eight o'clock. Jinx Town. The top dark floor."

"I think I've changed my mind. Put Bayliss on."

"Sorry. She went out for ice cream. I like pistachio. What kind do mooks eat?"

"Put Bayliss on or kiss your million dollars good-bye."

Shit.

"Hold on." Coop held out the phone to Bayliss. "He wants to talk to you."

She took the phone and spoke softly. "Hello? Yes. We really have it. Yes. I'm the one who gave it to him." Bayliss didn't say anything more. She just listened and turned very pale. In a minute, she handed the phone back to Coop.

"You okay?" he said.

"Fine. Can I have a glass of water?"

"What did he say?"

"I'd rather not go into it."

"Okay."

Bayliss sat at the kitchen counter. "What exactly is a Tijuana necktie?"

Coop went to the kitchen to get her water. "It's something you wear when you buy a piñata," he said.

He brought out the water and handed it to her. "I think you're lying," said Bayliss.

"Maybe I'll get you a real drink. Just a little one," said Coop.

"Maybe that's a good idea. How many more calls are there?"

"Just two. You don't have to be here if you don't want to be."

"No," said Bayliss. "If you don't mind, I'd rather not be alone for a while."

"I can order us a pizza."

"That would be nice."

"It's not very good pizza."

"Then I'll have another drink with it to kill the taste."

"That's the spirit."

Coop called and ordered an extra large with pepperoni and mushrooms. Then he dialed the number he'd been given by the jackass who said he had Giselle. He waited to make this call so he had a chance to get his thoughts and temper under control before making it. The phone rang and went straight to voice mail. Giselle's voice telling him to leave a message was a queasy noise in his ear. When the line clicked he said, "This is Coop. I have the box. I'll give it back to you in Jinx Town. Eight o'clock tomorrow. Top dark floor. Giselle knows how to get there. Don't be late."

He hung up and sat down. "Now *I* need a drink," he said.

Coop poured bourbon into his lukewarm coffee and reheated it. He and Bayliss drank in silence for a few minutes. Coop put *Singin' in the Rain* in the DVD player and turned the sound off. Bayliss watched, sipping her drink. The pizza arrived and Coop brought in plates for them.

"You feeling better?" he said.

Bayliss nodded. "I'm fine. I was just caught a little off guard. More than ever, I'm looking forward to seeing this through."

"Me, too."

Bayliss looked past Coop to the TV. "I wouldn't have guessed you were a fan of musicals."

"I'm not," he said.

"Then why . . . ?"

"Don't ask or I'll tell you and spoil your pizza."

"I might need another drink before I go."

"Me, too."

Coop picked up his phone and dialed another number. Sally Gifford picked up.

"Hey, Coop. What's shaking? You ever get laid?"

"Hi, Sally. As a matter of fact I did, but what I'm really calling about is a job."

"What a busy beaver you are these days. Tell me about it. How much are we going to get?"

"Here's the good news," he said brightly. "There's absolutely no money in it."

"Huh," said Sally. "It sounds like you said no money. What aren't you telling me, Coop?"

"I need your help. Someone took Morty and Giselle, and won't give them back."

"Wait. That chick who dumped you? Who would kidnap Morty?"

"Very bad people who'll get even worse if you don't help me."

He heard Sally sigh. "I don't know, Coop. It sounds like maybe you're talking about a gun situation. I like you and I like Morty, but I like my body, too, and I try to avoid things that are going to put holes in it."

"It's not just about Morty," said Coop. "The truth is, if this doesn't work, we're all going down. You, me, Morty, Giselle, Tintin, and even that little cat of yours."

"My cat?" said Sally.

"I'm afraid so. But now here's the good news. If we do this job, even if there's no money, we get to fuck over a lot of rich and important people."

There was a second of silence on the line, then "Cool," said Sally. "I'm in," an edge creeping into her voice. "Nobody threatens Purr J. Harvey."

"Great. Come by around five and I'll tell you the whole weird story."

"Not at that shitty bar you like."

"No. Come by Morty's place."

"See you then."

"Was that one of your criminal friends?" said Bayliss.

"Yeah. You'll like her," said Coop. "She shot her partner once, too."

Bayliss coughed, choking on her pizza. "She shot someone?"

"Don't worry. She didn't kill him. He got a little handsy with her, so she put a forty-four pistol to his balls and pulled the trigger."

Bayliss swallowed. "What happened to him?"

"The gun just went click. Sally's a polite person and always keeps the first chamber empty for moments like that," said Coop. "I'm not saying you should do anything like that to Nelson, but I'm just putting it out there as food for thought."

Bayliss set down her pizza. "Trust me. If I ever pull my gun on Nelson, it's going to do more than click."

"You're going to do just fine tomorrow. You've got more crook in you than you know."

Bayliss smiled. "Thanks."

"To be fair, I feel that about every cop."

"I assumed."

After Mr. Lemmy hung up, he looked at his men lounging around his office, drinking his booze and coffee. They really pissed him off right then. He shouldn't have to be dealing with this shit. *That's these monkeys' job,* he thought. But then, they didn't know what the job was. Still. All he did was feed them, give them money, and listen to them belch and brag about girls. It wasn't dignified. He wondered if he should have listened to his father and gone into the family snow globe business. He remembered how the biggest decision his father ever had to make was whether to stick to traditional plastic snow in his globes or switch to glitter. Mr. Lemmy sighed. *I'd like to stick this bunch in a big goddamn snow globe and shake some sense into them,* he thought.

"Here's the thing," said Mr. Lemmy to his men. "This Coop creep wants to meet someplace called Jinx Town. Anybody ever heard of it?"

"I have," said Baker. His father had been a butcher. That always amused Mr. Lemmy. A butcher named Baker. It wasn't much of a joke, but at shitty times like this you had to appreciate the little things.

Baker went on. "It's supposed to be a bad place, boss. Full of crazy people and weird things."

"What does that even mean, 'crazy people and weird things'? Speak fucking English." *It's like pulling teeth with these morons.*

Baker blushed a little and looked at Mr. Lemmy's other heavies. "People into all kind of dark stuff. Magic. Voodoo. And there's supposed to be, I guess the only word for it is monsters."

"Monsters."

"You know. Vampires and shit."

The men laughed and Mr. Lemmy stared at him. "You really believe that shit?"

"Lots of people have talked about it," said Baker. "Even my grandma. And she heard about it from her grandma."

Mr. Lemmy closed his eyes for a minute, picturing bloody snow globes. "It's a fucking fairy tale. The bogeyman," he said. "Something to keep you in line. Guess that didn't work out so well, you crooked prick?"

The men laughed and shook their heads.

"If it's okay with you I'm going to bring some garlic," said Baker.

Mr. Lemmy dropped his hands to his sides. "Bring a whole fucking salad for all I care. Just bring your gun, too. Because Coop and the guy in the other room? Both of those Mouseketeers are going to die."

Steve checked Giselle's voice mail and his blood pressure shot up like a Saturn V, but he didn't want to let the rest of the congregation see. Still, it wasn't the kind of thing he could let pass entirely. "That Coop jerked called," he said. "And he hung up again."

"Of course he hung up," said Susie.

"No. I mean aggressively. Like he doesn't take any of this seriously."

He turned to Jorge. "How's the boar coming?"

"Real good. He'll be ready later tonight."

"Good. Because Coop wants to meet tomorrow night."

"How late? Cause I have jury duty in the morning," said Janet.

"And I have to take my mom to the airport," said someone from the back. Others muttered.

"Fine," said Steve. "You don't get to be there for this final battle. In fact, the only people going are me, Jorge, Jerry, and Tommy."

"Me? Why me? You ditched me the other night," said Tommy.

"And now we'll make up for it," said Steve. "You get to be our point man."

"What's a point man?" said Tommy.

"It's a basketball thing," said Janet.

"That's a point guard, I think," said Susie.

"They're playing basketball for the summoning box?" said someone in the back.

"I'll come. I played varsity in high school. Until I blew my knee out," said Freddy, one of Steve's plaster men.

"We're not playing basketball. Tommy is going to lead the charge," said Steve.

"I feel sick," said Tommy.

"Just make sure you don't have to pee tomorrow. We're going somewhere called 'the dark floor' in a place called Jinx Town."

"See! I told you it was real," said Jerry.

"We'll see."

"Should we bring flashlights?" said Jorge.

"We'll have the boar. The boar won't need a flashlight. Tomorrow is zero day, people. We're going to get the box and bring our lord back to Earth," said Steve. "Hail Caleximus."

"Hail Caleximus!" shouted the congregation.

Tommy made a sound like someone stepping on a puppy's tail and bolted out of the trailer.

"Will someone go and get that idiot?" said Steve.

A few hours later, when he was home safe in his bedroom, Tommy dialed a number. He barely spoke above a whisper. "Hello?"

"Hello. Who is this?" said the Magister.

"It's me."

"Speak up. You sound like you're talking through a goose's ass."

"It's me, High Dark One."

"Dark High One."

"Sorry. It's me. Carol," said Tommy.

"Carol. Do you have news for me?"

"Yeah. It happens tomorrow night at a place called Jinx Town."

"Junk Town? What is that? Like Walmart?"

"*Jinx*. Jinx Town."

"Ah, yes. I've heard of it. Lord Abaddon will smile on you for this, Carol."

"You've got to get me out of here," said Tommy, his voice cracking.

"Of course. Listen. When I give the signal, you forget everything and run to us."

"What's the signal?"

"'Marvin Hamlisch banana sandwich.' You might want to write that down so you don't forget."

"No. I'm pretty sure I can remember that."

"Good girl. We'll see you tomorrow night. Soon, Lord Abaddon will drown the world, saving only us, his true believers."

"And me, too."

"Of course, Carol dear," said the Magister.

"Okay," said Tommy, "I've got to go. Good night, Dark High One."

"It's High Dark One. No, wait. You got it right. How about that?" No one replied. Tommy was gone. The Magister dialed Adept Six.

"How is Fluffy doing?" he said.

"He's hungry," said the adept.

"Good. Keep him that way. His first meal will be the Calceximus traitor."

"Yes, Dark High One."

The Magister's stomach rumbled. "Do we have any shrimp left?"

Adept Six shouted something, then came back to the phone. "I'm afraid they went bad and we had to throw them out."

"Damn. I can't wait to be done with this awful planet."

"Should I send up some cod?"

"No," said the Magister. "My show is coming on."

"Show, Dark High One?"

Crap, thought the Magister. "Shoes. I'm putting my shoes on."

"Of course."

"Send some cod up in an hour," the Magister said. "Then I'll come down and pay my respects to Fluffy."

"Be sure to wash your hands well. Fluffy likes cod."

"Are you saying I'm unhygienic?"

"No, Dark High One. My apologies. It's just that being this hungry, Fluffy has a tendency to bite."

The Magister went across the room and uncovered the TV. His back twinged when he bent over.

"Now I'm annoyed," said the Magister. "Send up the cod now, but leave it outside the door." He hung up, not waiting for Adept Six to say good-bye.

He tuned in to *The Price Is Right* and even turned up the volume a little. It was a special occasion. *This might be the last showcase I ever see,* he thought. *It better be a good one.*

"Privyet."

"It's me," said Salzman. "There's been a complication."

"What kind of complicated?" said Zavulon.

Salzman had to take a second. The Russian's dubious accent was really starting to get to him. "The box has fallen into criminal hands. I'm going to need some help to get it back."

"What kind of help you need?"

"How about some of those armored troglodytes of yours?" Salzman said.

"No problem. I will come, too."

"That's not necessary. It might be dangerous."

"Good. I'm too long away from dangerous," said Zavulon.

"All right. The rendezvous is at eight tomorrow night. I'll come by your hotel at six thirty. Be ready."

"We'll be armored to the mouth."

"Teeth. Armed to the teeth," said Salzman.

"Spasibo."

"Until tomorrow."

Salzman poured himself a drink and wondered which one he should murder first. Eventually, he concluded that it should be the Russian. Coop was a nuisance, but that goddamn accent, he thought. If he wasn't dead already, he might have to kill himself rather than ever hear Zavulon again.

Qaphsiel slept, despondent, on the top of the Griffith Park Observatory, his keen ears hearing the voices of people passing in the city below and hobos having sex in the bushes. *Another perfect night,* he thought. How many had there been in four thousand years? He started to add them up, but all the zeroes just made him even more depressed.

The box had seemed so close earlier, but Coop didn't have it and wouldn't look for it. Worse even than that, the map had stopped working again. And here he was, with nowhere to go and nothing to do but wander the city like all the lost screenwriters, failed directors, and stoned guitarists who'd come to L.A. with high hopes, only to be crushed under its giant, Technicolor, open-toe boots.

To cheer himself up, Qaphsiel tried to remember even worse times. There was that incident during the Inquisition when a Spanish priest tried burning him at the stake. Of course, angels don't burn and neither do angelic maps. Unfortunately, his mortal clothes did, and it was quite embarrassing at a church in the thirteenth century. Qaphsiel had to wrap himself in the map like a sarong until he could find suitable attire again.

And there was that time on the *Titanic*. He had felt he was very close to the box then. In fact, he was certain that one of the well heeled families on board had it. Then there was the iceberg and he wasn't able to make it into any of the lifeboats. Qaphsiel sank to the bottom of the Atlantic with fifteen hundred other people. The difference between him and the others was that he didn't drown. However, by the time he hit bottom, he was so waterlogged he wouldn't float. He was forced to walk across the bottom of the ocean to land, trying not to think bad thoughts about you know who, God's show off son. That guy could have roller-skated the whole way to England. But no, Qaphsiel had to trudge through the silt the whole way, fighting off giant squid, confused sharks, and amorous merpeople. It took him weeks, and when he made it back to land and checked the map, he found that he'd been wrong the whole time. The box was back in America. For a fleeting moment, Qaphsiel considered walking back across the ocean bottom, but he'd had quite enough of that.

When he looked back on it, he wondered if it was the freezing ocean stroll that caused the map to malfunction in the first place. It took Qaphsiel weeks to make it back to America, a stowaway in the belly of a tramp steamer, the map stuttering and sizzling the whole way. He gave up and slept most of the way across the Atlantic. Once in New York, the map behaved for a while, and he started west, sometimes buying his passage with gold and sometimes riding the rails. He was very lonely. By the time Qaphsiel reached California, things seemed to be looking up. That was over a hundred years ago. And now that he was so close . . . of course the map had gone completely dark. Really, it was too much. He might spend the next hundred years on top of the observatory, refusing to get down and hunt for the stupid thing. How would Heaven like those apples? But he wasn't going to do that. Qaphsiel was a good angel and not programmed for long-term tantrums. He'd start looking again in the morning. Maybe he'd get hit by another car. His leg still hurt from the last one, but the map had worked for a while. Maybe getting hit by a bus would make it work longer. That felt like the first good idea he'd had in a century. Tomorrow, he'd let a bus run him down and then check the map. In his sleepy state, the logic seemed flawless.

At that happy thought, Qaphsiel felt a small vibration in his pocket. He rolled over and took out the map. The stars and the landscape of the world were laid out before him, glowing and streaking with life and power. The map was working again. He wondered if someone upstairs had heard his misery and was throwing him a bone.

Qaphsiel studied the map and saw, dead center, something that pulsed and glowed. It was like a sun, but wasn't. It was his prize. It moved slowly, a shooting star that hadn't quite made it to its destination. All Qaphsiel had to do was watch and wait. This was it. This was *the* sign. Tomorrow, the box would be his. He clutched the map to his chest and lay back down, falling into a deep and happy sleep. He was finally going home.

THIRTY-FOUR

COOP, SALLY, AND BAYLISS GOT TO JINX TOWN AT seven, a good hour before the others were set to arrive. Sally and Bayliss had oohed and ahhed like kids on Christmas morning when they'd arrived, but Coop didn't give them much sightseeing time. He steered them up the escalators to the top dark level. Coop kept on a serious expression. A little darker than "How's it going?" but not quite as off-putting as "We're all going to die tonight."

All three of them were wearing silver around their necks and enough DOPS holy water on their clothes to make them feel like they'd run through lawn sprinklers on a sunny day. But this wasn't a sunny day. It was an underground day, possibly the last day the world would exist, he reminded himself.

"Everyone know what to do?" he said.

"Yes," said Bayliss.

"Affirmative, sir," said Sally, saluting him. Coop gave her one second of a half smile.

"Okay. Fan out and let's put up the party decorations."

Coop knelt and started taking things out of his bag.

"Do you really think this is going to work?" said Bayliss.

"It doesn't seem like one of your more top-of-the-line plans," said Sally.

Coop handed gear around. "It only has to work long enough to get everyone out of here alive," he said.

"You're an inspiration. Will you be my life coach?" said Sally.

The three of them fanned out, laying down surprises for their guests. A few Jinx Town denizens watched the odd mortals work. Then a few more. By eight, they'd attracted a curious crowd of assorted creatures and ghouls.

Then the guests arrived, one by one. Mr. Lemmy and his crew were first. The short man stood in the center as they stepped off the escalator like a pack of wolves in suits. Baker had already been wearing garlic around his neck when they'd arrived, and he was carrying a big bag of the stuff with him. By the time they made it up to the dark floor, the whole crew of six were wearing garlands, even Mr. Lemmy. Morty was with them, gagged and with his hands held together with zip ties. He gave Coop a little wave. Coop nodded back.

Steve and the Caleximus congregation were next. Their black boar, the size of a small horse with a double set of tusks and red coal eyes, wouldn't fit on the escalator, so they came out of an elevator by the fountain. Jerry was holding Giselle's arm, looking as guilty as a kid shoplifting his first *Hustler*. As the group came over to Coop and the mobsters, there came a little laughter and murmurs from the crowd.

"Hiya, Coop," said Giselle. She had gauze and tape sloppily wrapped around her head. "I got bonked a little. I can't do my mind thing right now. Sorry."

"Don't worry about it. Everything is going to be fine," he said, hoping it wasn't a lie.

"What the hell is this?" said Steve, holding the boar by an enormous chain and collar. "Who are these people?" he said, pointing to Mr. Lemmy's gang.

Coop held up a finger. "I'll answer that question in one minute," he said.

Seven robotlike armored things clanked up the same escalator Mr.

Lemmy had used a couple of minutes earlier. The crowd gasped at the sight. A smiling Salzman and a frowning Zavulon followed.

"What kind place is this?" said the Russian.

"For fuck sake. You can drop the accent," said Salzman. "We're here for serious business."

Zavulon stared at him. "You think my voice is faking?"

"Very much."

"I'm hurt," mumbled the Russian. "But yeah, it was getting old, wasn't it?" he said in a light voice with a slight English accent.

"American exchange student at Oxford?" said Salzman.

"Cambridge," said Zavulon.

Salzman gave him a sympathetic look. "Better luck next time."

"I'm still curious what this is all about," he said.

"And who all these muppets are," said Salzman, eyeing the other groups. He didn't like the hungry looks of the Jinx Town crowd either. For the first time in years, he was happy he was dead.

"Thanks for coming," said Coop. "And right on time. It means you can take orders and instructions. That's going to be important tonight."

"What is this freak show?" said Mr. Lemmy. "I want my box."

"Your box?" said Steve. "Fuck you. We've been waiting for that box since the dawn of time. It's ours."

"Guess again, pig farmer. But I like your girlfriend. You make a lovely couple," said Mr. Lemmy, pointing at the boar.

"Excuse me," said Salzman. "The little man—"

"Fuck you, too!" yelled Mr. Lemmy.

"—asked the pertinent question. What is this freak show?"

"It's a contest," said Coop. "Like an Easter-egg hunt, only more fun. You see, there's only one box and three assholes who want it. So, you get to race for it. I'm going to text each of you a clue to where the box is. The first one who finds it wins."

"Hold on a second," said Mr. Lemmy. He pulled a .357 magnum from under his jacket and pointed it at Morty's head. "Stop this bullshit right now and give me my fucking box."

Steve pulled a gun and pointed it at Giselle.

"Dad. What are you doing?" said Jerry.

"Serving the Lord, son," said Steve. "Like the midget said. Give me my box."

The armored Russian guards and Zavulon leveled their guns at Coop.

"I forgot to mention one more thing," Coop said. He help up his hand so that everyone could see the small silver box he was holding. "The lovely Ms. Bayliss brought along something that goes boom. If anyone gets shot—and I mean anyone—I blow up the box."

"You wouldn't fucking dare," said Mr. Lemmy.

"You're threatening to kill my friends. I don't have a lot of friends. So yeah—boom," said Coop. "Any other questions?" Sally took a few steps off to the side, disappearing by one of the shops.

"I have one," said Salzman. "What's to stop all of us from shooting you when this is over?"

Coop smiled. "I guess I can't count on your goodwill?" he said.

"Probably not," said Salzman.

"The bomb stays put until we're gone and clear. When we are, I'll text the winner the code to remove it from the box."

"There's a special kind of Hell Caleximus has for assholes like you," yelled Steve. He put his gun away. So did Mr. Lemmy.

"Put them down for now," Salzman told Zavulon.

"I agree." He signaled for his men to lower their weapons.

Coop's heart slowed down a little. A whole two minutes into the plan and no one was dead yet. "Now, is everyone ready to get started?"

"Where's the broad?" said Mr. Lemmy, craning his head around.

Coop nodded to Bayliss. "She's right here."

"Not her. The other broad."

"Oh, her. I don't know. Why don't you ask Morty?"

Mr. Lemmy looked to his side. Stepped back, turning his head this way and that. "What the fuck? Where is he?" It took Mr. Lemmy's men a few seconds to understand what he was talking about.

Morty was gone.

"Where is he?" Mr. Lemmy howled, pulling his gun again.

Coop held up the silver box. "Away is where he is," said Coop. "But he's not your problem right now. The box is." Mr. Lemmy put his gun away.

From the side of the store, Sally walked back over to Coop and Bayliss.

"How did you do that?" Mr. Lemmy yelled to her.

"What?" said Sally. "I was just freshening my makeup."

Mr. Lemmy jabbed a finger at the circle. "You're all dead. Every one of you is dead," he said.

"Big talker," said Steve.

Mr. Lemmy threw him a look. "You're right after him, Porky."

Steve let the boar out a few links and Mr. Lemmy backed off.

"If everyone is ready, the three of us are going to text each group one clue to where the box is hidden," said Coop. "After that, it's up to you. Look. Don't look. Just don't forget the magic word."

"Boom," said Sally.

"Boom," said Bayliss.

Coop and the others got out their phones. "On three we send the texts. You might want to get your phones out, boys."

Salzman, Steve, and Mr. Lemmy all took out their phones.

"One. Two. Three." Coop and the others hit send. The three group leaders stared at their phones. Then at each other.

"Remember. It's a race," said Coop. "You might consider running."

"Come on, boys!" yelled Mr. Lemmy. He and his men took off running to the fountain in the distance.

Salzman glanced at Coop, with enough venom in his gaze to bring down a rhino. "This way," he said, and the Russians followed him.

The Caleximus congregation looked around, trying to get oriented.

"Where the hell are we?" said Steve.

The Jinx Town crowd laughed.

"What's it say?" said Jorge.

"Look for the butcher shop. It's behind that."

"There," said Jerry, pointing into the distance. He took a step, stumbled, and was yanked through the air the other way. Giselle had disappeared.

Jerry's hands looked like they were holding on to empty air. "Dad! Dad! She's gone, but I can feel her."

"Hold on, son," said Steve.

"She's invisible," said Jerry.

Steve looked around. "It's that other woman," he yelled. "She's doing something with mirrors again."

"I don't think it's mirrors," said Jerry. He fell on his side and was dragged across the polished tile floor. The crowd hooted and laughed.

"Let up on the girl and my son," yelled Steve, "or I'll set my boar on you!"

With Sally clouding their minds, she and Giselle dragged Jerry a few more feet.

"One last chance," said Steve, letting the boar's leash out a few more links.

"Heretics!" yelled an old man from the top of the escalator.

Coop turned and saw a dozen robed figures pouring into the crowd.

"Who's that?" said Bayliss.

"I have no idea," said Coop.

"Should we tell Sally to stop before he lets the boar go?"

"I don't think we have to," said Coop.

Steve turned his demon boar around toward the robed mob running toward him. They pulled up short at the sight of the animal, but the old man wasn't intimidated. He had his own beast: a six-foot-tall, iridescent pink puffer fish, with sharp, bony spikes and white steak-knife teeth. A gasp went up from the crowd. A few people applauded.

"How did you get here, you Abaddonian assholes?" said Steve.

"Marvin Hamlisch banana sandwich!" screamed Tommy. He sprinted, slipping, falling, and getting up again, across the mall to the Magister. "Marvin Hamlisch banana sandwich!"

"Tommy!" yelled Steve. "You traitorous asshat."

Salzman and the Russians were ripping apart the façade of a vampire bar. When Salzman heard the commotion, he stopped searching for a minute. "This looks interesting," he said.

"Who cares? Keep looking," said Zavulon.

"I'm not so sure. Coop is up to something. I'm going to check it out," Salzman said.

"Fine. Go. We'll do the real work back here, shall we?"

"Tommy?" yelled Jerry, still being dragged around the floor by invisible forces. "Is it true?"

Tommy reached the Abaddonians and cowered behind them.

"Carol?" said the Magister, squinting at Tommy. "You're not a girl."

"I tried to tell you that," Tommy said.

The Magister glared at him. "What have you done with Carol?" he said.

Tommy yelled, "I'm Carol!"

"Hold him. We'll figure this nonsense out later," said the Magister. He turned back to Steve. "As for you, feel the wrath of Lord Abaddon!" he bellowed. The Magister thrust his arms forward and Fluffy growled, glowing with incandescent fury. He began to roll, picking up speed every second, ripping up the marble floor as he headed straight for the Caleximus congregation.

"Fuck you and your guppy!" yelled Steve as he let go of the boar's chain. It took half a dozen steps forward and stopped. Fluffy glowed a hotter red with each revolution.

Salzman crept up on the spectacle, quietly laughing at the scene.

The black boar skittered on its hooves, turned, and ran in the opposite direction from Fluffy.

"No!" yelled Steve.

"Dad!" yelled Jerry.

"Shit," said Salzman as the fleeing boar thundered straight at him. He turned and ran back to the Russians. "Shoot it," he yelled. "Shoot it!"

As Fluffy bore down on the congregation, Jerry became aware that all of a sudden no one was pulling his arm. He turned back to the demon fish bearing down on him, knowing that the invisible women were gone and that all of his father's shouts and prayers weren't going to save him.

Mr. Lemmy and his men splashed around the black fountain, making a formidable amount of noise, enough that they didn't hear any of the fight going on at the other end of the floor.

"Boss, I don't think this is red water we're in," said Baker. "I think it's—"

"Shut up and keep looking," screamed Mr. Lemmy.

A crowd stood around them, laughing as they crawled around in the liquid, feeling the bottom and sides of the fountain. In fact, Mr. Lemmy and his men were concentrating so hard, they didn't notice when invisible hands cut the garlic garlands off their necks and tossed them into the dark.

When all the garlic was gone, the crowd's laughter went with it. They moved in closer, forming a tight circle around the fountain. Mr. Lemmy looked up and slipped onto his ass. He'd never seen that many fangs outside of a Gothic whorehouse he'd once visited in New Orleans. It wasn't a very convincing Dracula scenario—none of the girls could get the accent right—but it had been a fine way to spend an evening. This crowd, though . . . well, this crowd was different.

"Boss," said Baker.

"What?" yelled Mr. Lemmy, keeping an eye on the fanged weirdos.

"I lost my garlic."

Mr. Lemmy felt around his neck. The rest of his men did the same.

"Hey. I think I found the box," said one of his men. "Oh, nope. It's one of those little treasure chests from an aquarium."

Mr. Lemmy started to call him something. He got as far as "ass—" before six little girls in gingham dresses pulled him from the fountain. His last thought was, *I would have switched to glitter.*

Salzman looked back over his shoulder. To his surprise, the boar wasn't behind him anymore. It was the puffer fish. The boar was running as fast as it could the other way.

"Shoot it!" he yelled and dove to the side of the vampire bar.

The Russians aimed their rifles and Zavulon pulled out a Tokarev pistol the size of a small dog. They all began firing at the same time.

Not that it did them much good.

The Russian thaumaturgic armor was designed to withstand bullets and magic, not a red-hot, one-ton spiked ball smashing into them like an infuriated bulldozer at thirty miles an hour. They were tossed around not so much like bowling pins as like Barbie dolls in a cement mixer. When it was over, Fluffy lay on his side, slowly deflating, his iridescent glow fading. If any of the Russians had been able to glow, their glows would have been fading, too.

A minute later, when he was sure he was safe, Salzman crept from his hiding place, stepped over the Russians' bodies, and went back to searching for the box.

The boar continued its swift and gallant retreat from Fluffy, running straight past the Caleximus congregation, trying to get back to the elevator. As it neared the Abaddonians, they began to fall back to the escalator. Tommy didn't fall back. He just ran.

"Uh, Dark High One?" said Adept Six. "Perhaps we should think about, and please don't take this as a lack of faith, retreating just a bit?"

"Hold fast, everyone," said the Magister. "Lord Abaddon will protect us."

He threw out his arms and growled deep in his chest, intoning an eldritch undersea spell that hadn't been heard on land for thousands of years. It was a bubbling sound mixed with strange harmonic overtones, like bees in a bubble bath. The air around the Magister darkened. A pool of brackish water formed at his feet, smoking and boiling. The adepts and acolytes cheered their Magister—for most of them, it was the only time they'd ever seen him do anything even vaguely mystical (for Adept Six, it was the first time he'd seen the Magister do magic that might actually accomplish something). The Magister reached into the seething pool and drew out a handful of superheated seawater, a boiling ball of white-hot liquid plasma. Noting their master's seemingly awesome magic, the adepts and acolytes crept back up the escalator, fanning out behind him.

"Behold the wrath of Abaddon," the Magister yelled. He reared back to throw the plasma, waiting for the boar to get close enough to see its demon eyes.

And his back went out.

He crumpled over and dropped the plasma on his foot. "Shit. Shit.

Shit," he yelled, hopping and cursing as the air around him lightened and the water at his feet dried up.

"Adept Six," he yelled. "Hold me, so I can smite this son of a bitch with a new spell. Adept Six?"

The Magister turned in time to see his loyal followers sprinting down the escalator and out of sight, Adept Six in the lead.

When the boar hit the Magister, the collision was so hard, he didn't really feel it. In fact, the only real sensation he had was when a certain vertebra slipped back into place beneath another vertebra. For that split second, the Magister's back felt great, and he crashed into the wall with a smile on his face.

The boar didn't think anything at the end, but if it could have, it would have been something along the lines of, *Well, damn. Here I am, a demon of the first order, with mighty tusks and hooves the size of porch swings, and it's all ending because some twerp decided to wax the floors,* just before it smashed headfirst into the balcony wall.

"No," yelled Steve as he rushed to the fallen boar, dropping to his knees beside the crumpled giant. Jerry ran to his father.

"Dad? Dad? Maybe you shouldn't sit there," he said. He and Jorge grabbed Steve's shoulders, trying to pull him away from the fallen beast.

"It's over," said Steve. "It's all over."

"Damn right," said Jorge, giving the boar a kick. "Caleximus fucked us. Let's get out of here."

"I don't get it. What did we do wrong?"

"Hey, man, I'm not sure this is a 'we' situation."

"What does that mean?" said Steve.

"It means you were the boss. You fucked something up. Plus, you let your brain-dead kid lose the silver dagger."

Steve and Jorge grabbed each other and fell over onto the boar. Jerry pulled at his father's sleeve.

"Goddammit, Dad," yelled Jerry. "Turn around."

Steve looked over his shoulder at the horde of vampires and werewolves, the ones that had missed out on Mr. Lemmy and his boys. Their fangs glittered jewel-like in the dark.

"Fuck Caleximus," he said, and they all ran for the escalator.

Jerry had run track in high school, so even with his aching ribs, he was the fastest down all thirteen floors. When he hit the lobby level, he pumped a fist in the air and whooped. Everybody, the gill people, the ghosts, the human tourists, and the security guards, all stared at him.

When he turned and looked back up the escalator, he realized there was no one behind him.

"Oh, crap."

Upstairs, a lone figure streaked with other people's blood came stumbling past the corpses, the dead beasts, and the mass of feeding bloodsuckers and wolves. They took absolutely no interest in the dead man at all.

Salzman made it all the way back to where the search had started. He stopped just a few feet away from Coop and thrust the box into his face, almost colliding with Coop's nose.

"I win," he said.

"Excuse me," said an old woman. She tapped Salzman on the shoulder. He looked down at her, wondering where the old biddy had come from.

"I've been looking for a box just like that for my niece," she said.

"It's for her sweet sixteen," said the old man by her side.

"Go away," said Salzman.

"The box," said the old woman. "We'd like to buy the box."

"It's not for sale, Granny. Beat it."

"You don't have to be rude about it," said the old woman.

"Yes. Manners," said the old man. He pulled a knife from his pocket and stabbed Salzman in the side. The old woman pulled her own knife and stabbed him in the other side. Salzman gasped. Being dead already, the knives couldn't kill him, but they sure stung like hell.

Leviathan and Beelzebub smiled wide, revealing as much of their faces as they could. Salzman, a man who'd been alive, then dead, then sort of alive again, and was unused to surprises, was surprised. He stopped struggling with the knives for a second. It was the teeth that fascinated him. So big. So gray and dirty. So many bugs running around them.

And then Leviathan bit off his head, swallowing it whole. Salzman dropped the box and Beelzebub picked it up.

"I guess we win," she said.

"Not necessarily," said Coop.

"Not necessarily at all," said Qaphsiel, strolling over from the elevator. He pushed past Coop and lunged at Beelzebub, snatching the box from her hands.

"It's mine," Qaphsiel yelled, using his thundery voice. He held the box over his head. "Mankind, prepare to meet thy doom," he said, and slowly, delicately—savoring every second of it—began to open the box's lid.

"Stop!" yelled the stranger.

"Do you have any idea who these people are?" said Bayliss.

Coop shrugged. "I gave up when the fish showed up."

The stranger lay his hand over Qaphsiel's, pushing the box's lid down firmly. Qaphsiel looked at the stranger up and down in disbelief. "Raphael?" he said.

"Yes. It's I," said the angel. "Your old friend Raphael. Embrace me, brother."

Qaphsiel opened his arms to his old friend, and Raphael dove for the box, knocking Qaphsiel flat onto his back.

"What's wrong with you?" said Qaphsiel, struggling to his feet.

Raphael stepped back. "I can't let you do it, old friend. This world isn't going to be destroyed. Not tonight and not by you."

"What are you talking about? This is my divine quest," said Qaphsiel.

"It was. It's not anymore."

"You've spoken to God?"

"Yes," said Raphael brightly. "He said you should forget the whole quest and come back home."

Qaphsiel frowned. "I know angels aren't supposed to lie, but I think you might be doing it right now."

"Nope. That's exactly what he said."

Qaphsiel's eyes narrowed. "I don't believe you."

"Who cares? I have the box. It's over."

It wasn't over.

Qaphsiel threw himself at Raphael, knocking the box from the angel's hand. It spun in the air, turning, somersaulting, and twirling, before smashing into the floor and breaking into a hundred pieces.

Nothing happened. There were no earthquakes. No volcanoes. No tidal waves. No one even got indigestion. The world remained very much intact. Raphael and Qaphsiel looked at Coop.

"Did I mention that's not the real box?" he said.

"But that's the box. I know it is," said Qaphsiel.

"Maybe your memory is a little shaky after four thousand years."

Raphael got to his feet. "Where is the real one?" said Raphael.

"I forget."

"Maybe this'll help," said a familiar voice.

Coop turned as the gun went off. He twisted and fell to the ground. Someone screamed. He hoped it was someone he knew and not one of the idiots. It meant someone liked him enough to care when he croaked.

Nelson walked over to him, moving the gun back and forth, keeping everyone covered. "Where's Salzman?" he said.

"Dead," said Bayliss. "How did you find us?"

"He called me, you nitwit. The moment your pal here called him. But now he's dead. Boo-hoo. I guess the box is mine. Where is it?"

"Gosh, Mr. Wizard. I just can't remember," said Coop as it gradually occurred to him that he wasn't dead and merely shot painfully in the arm.

Nelson put the muzzle of his gun to Coop's head. "I couldn't hear you. Where did you say it is?"

"Here," shouted Bayliss. She took something out of Coop's bag and brought it over. Nelson snatched it from her.

"Oh, right. That's it," said Qaphsiel. "I remember now."

"Thanks for the confirmation, whoever the hell you are," Nelson said. He turned back to Coop. "As for you, you pain in the ass . . ." His finger tightened on the trigger. But that's all it did, because a fraction of a second later, there was a bang and a large, bloody hole appeared in Nelson's chest. He looked over at Bayliss, who kept her gun pointed at him. "I'm going to give you such a lousy review," he said. And collapsed next to Coop. The box skittered from his hand across the floor.

Qaphsiel and Raphael dove for it. Qaphsiel was faster. "It's mine again," he said. "After all these years."

"Stop for one second and listen to me," said Raphael.

"No more lies," said Qaphsiel.

Raphael held up his hands. "Just the truth from here on. I didn't want to tell you the real reason you can't destroy the world."

"Why?"

"Because it's going to upset you." Raphael pulled a battered green folder from his coat pocket. Coop blinked. It looked exactly like the one he'd stolen from the Bellicose Manor safe.

"How did you . . . ?" he said, but couldn't get out the rest.

"What is that?" said Qaphsiel.

"The deed," said Raphael.

"To what? The box?"

"To Earth."

"Pardon me?" said Qaphsiel, his voice cracking a little.

"You heard me. God gave me the Earth. Well, not 'gave it to me' gave it to me. I won it. Since you've been gone, he's developed quite a taste for Texas Hold'em. The problem is . . ." Raphael looked around conspiratorially and touched the side of his nose. "God's got a tell."

Qaphsiel stared. "I've been here for four thousand years, searching and searching, and it meant nothing?"

"Not nothing," said Raphael. "Everyone upstairs is very impressed with your stick-to-itiveness. They're even going to give you your old job back. Though I'm afraid after four thousand years, the office-supplies closet is a pretty big mess."

Qaphsiel sat down on a bench against the wall. "This can't be real. The world can't be yours," he said.

"I'm afraid it is. In fact, I've already been redecorating as I walked here. Little things at first. Then San Francisco. Soon I'll start on Los Angeles." Raphael shook his head. "I'm sorry, old friend, but your journey is null and void." Raphael rolled the folder up and put it back in his pocket.

Coop tried to struggle to his feet. He put out his arm and Giselle helped him up.

"You should stay down," she said.

"I want you to push me," he said.

"What about the bomb?"

"There is no bomb. And if you care anything about me, push me."

Giselle gave Coop a hard shove. He stumbled back, fell against Raphael, and slid to the ground. Raphael stared in revulsion at the blood streaked down his coat.

"You see what I'm talking about?" he said. "This is exactly the kind of thing that's going to stop now that I'm in charge. I'm going to make this world into a new Heaven."

"That's ridiculous," said Qaphsiel. "The Earth wasn't meant to be Heaven. It's a flawed place and meant to be so."

"Not anymore," said Raphael, sitting down next to the other angel. "People, animals, plants, they're all going to straighten up now that I'm in charge. And no more of this continental drift nonsense. The continents are fine where they are."

"You simply can't make these arbitrary decisions," said Qaphsiel, exasperated by the whole discussion.

"Yes, I can. I can be every bit as arbitrary as I like. It's mine."

"Raphael is kind of a dick," said Sally.

"That's being cruel to dicks," said Giselle.

"Sorry. You like them more than I do."

"That's true."

Coop crawled away from the angels. Giselle and Sally pulled him to his feet. "Someone cloud someone's mind and let's get out of here," he said.

"I can't leave Nelson," said Bayliss.

"Fine," said Coop. "But you drag his sorry ass. I'm not helping."

They left as quietly and invisibly as they could. If either of the angels had looked around, he would have noticed them missing and the twin trails of blood leading to the escalator. But neither did.

Beelzebub and Leviathan looked around at the carnage and the bickering angels, feeling as frustrated and disgusted with the planet as two salaried demons could.

"Those two aren't going to stop, are they?" said Leviathan.

"Doesn't look like it," said Beelzebub.

"Still. It doesn't sound like the world's going to end right away."

"True. Lucifer will be pleased."

"Pleased enough to let us off this shit assignment and come home?" said Leviathan.

Beelzebub looked at his friend. "There's only one way to find out."

Arm in arm, they disappeared in a puff of sulfurous smoke.

The other angels, Heaven's good angels, just kept on arguing into the night.

THIRTY-FIVE

THE WELCOME-HOME PARTY TOOK PLACE AT MORTY'S apartment exactly one week later, when Coop was released from the DOPS special clinic. To his surprise, they'd actually done a pretty good job on him. Under his bandages they'd attached several extraterrestrial parasites to his shoulder. The parasites ate skin flakes and injected a carefully controlled combination of bone and muscle into his bullet wound. It was only creepy when he thought about it, so Coop went to great effort not to think about it. It wasn't all that hard with so much going on.

Morty had come through his first kidnapping with only a minor twitch whenever anyone stood behind him. He spent most of the party positioning himself with his back to hard surfaces—walls, doors, the refrigerator—anything where he had a clear view of the room and its exits.

"How are you doing?" said Coop.

"Coming along. Coming along," said Morty. "Tell me, as someone who's been kidnapped more than me, how long does it take to get over one of these things?"

"I'll let you know when I do."

"You're useless," said Morty, and he and Coop clinked their bottles of beer together.

Giselle popped into sight with her own beer. "See? I told you my head's back on straight. I can cloud minds with the best of them."

"You always could," said Coop. He looked across the room and saw Sally and Tintin in an intense conversation. Over the last week, Coop had grown used to the idea that he'd taken the DOPS job and that it would keep him close to Giselle. Still, he was going to miss clandestine meetings with Sally and Tintin. Now when he planned a job they'd want him to fill out forms in triplicate. Not that that was ever going to happen.

"I know how you feel," said Giselle.

"You reading my mind?" Coop said.

"With you it isn't that hard. You'll get used to the straight life. I did. And not looking over your shoulder all the time isn't such a bad feeling."

"I like being paranoid. It makes even the most boring things interesting. I was once convinced I was being followed by a whole Yakuza army while doing my laundry. It made the spin cycle fly by."

"Why the Yakuza?"

"It's a long story."

"I guess I'll have to stick around if I want to hear it."

"Only if you want to hear it."

"I'll think about it," she said.

There was a knock at the door. Morty opened it and Bayliss came in with a package wrapped in a bow. She walked over, kissed Coop on the cheek, and gave Giselle a big hug.

"Looks like the promotion's perked you up," said Coop.

"Yep. I officially got Nelson's old job. And I got a new partner."

"Who's that?"

"Guess," said a voice in Coop's head.

"Phil? They gave you Phil?" he said. "Who hates you that much?"

"Hey, I resent that. Tell him," Phil said.

Bayliss nodded. "It's not bad having a partner who can do his surveillance right in people's minds. Plus, he doesn't eat, so no more of

Nelson's ptomaine tacos." She held out the package. "Which brings me to this. Consider it an early Christmas present. Open it."

Coop held up his injured shoulder. "I'm not sure I can yet."

"I'll do it for you," Bayliss said, even as Giselle and Morty said, "You big baby." She untied the ribbon and took the top of the box off. Inside was a framed photo of a pale man in an ill-fitting suit that was clearly cut for someone else.

"Who is that?" said Giselle. "He looks familiar."

"It's Nelson," said Coop.

Bayliss nodded. "Say hello to the newest mailroom mook."

Coop took the picture out of the box and put it on Morty's mantel. "I'll cherish it always," he said.

The manta bats flashed by overhead, margarita glasses dangling from their slit mouths. One flew low and handed a drink to Bayliss before flying out the back door.

"I've been so out of it these past few days, I never found out what you told Woolrich about the box," he said.

Bayliss sipped her margarita. "I told him that it broke when Salzman was killed. I got a few pieces of the fake box that broke when the angels were fighting."

"And Woolrich brought that story?"

"I think he was just happy to have the box gone and not his responsibility anymore," she said. "On the other hand, he hated paying for all the damages at Jinx Town."

"Boo-hoo," said Coop. "If they want the story covered up, they get to pay for it."

Giselle sipped her beer and said, "What no one can figure out is what happened to the big fish thing and the boar."

"That's easy," said Coop. "Go back and check out that dark-floor butcher shop. I guarantee you they're still having specials on sushi and ribs."

"That's a pretty picture. Thanks for putting that in my head," said Phil.

"You don't have a head, Phil," said Bayliss.

"And thank you, boss, for that pep talk. I'm going now."

One of the DOPS tentacle twins waddled over and said, "Someone's at the door for you, Coop."

"Thanks, Jimmy," Coop said. He and Giselle went to see who it was. They left Bayliss chatting with a scientist whose head was a large ladybug in a bell jar.

Coop wasn't exactly shocked by what was waiting for him at the door. He was momentarily terrified of divine retribution, but then resigned himself to whatever fate waited for him.

At the door was Qaphsiel, smiling, dressed in a tailored gray suit.

"Look at you," said Coop. "You look like you're doing all right for yourself."

"It's better than a green Windbreaker," Qaphsiel said.

"Are you here for any, uh, particular reason?" said Coop a little nervously. "I mean if you want to come in, there's beer out back and the manta bats are mixing margaritas."

Qaphsiel shook his head. "No, thanks. I just thought that you might like to know that a certain box is back in Heaven, safe and sound."

"Really?" said Coop. "And what if someone gets a bug up their ass about destroying the world again?"

"I said it was safe and sound," said Qaphsiel. "I didn't say where it was. In fact, no one knows where it is." He shrugged. "Somehow it got misplaced."

"And it's going to stay lost?"

"We, that is Heaven, don't own the world anymore. Which brings me to the other reason I came by. You don't know where the deed went, do you? It wasn't in Raphael's pocket when we were called home."

Coop looked at Giselle and back at Qaphsiel. "I guess it got misplaced."

"Oh, well. These things happen," said the angel. "Well, I'll leave you to your friends. Have a nice party."

"Thanks," said Coop.

"Have a good trip home," said Giselle. She closed the door. "And stay there. Please. No more angels."

"I need an aspirin," said Coop. "I think they're in the bedroom."

"I'm done with beer. I'll get us a couple of margaritas," Giselle said.

"Great."

Coop went into the bedroom and rooted around his duffel bag one-handed. Eventually, he came up with a bottle of aspirin. Which he realized he couldn't open. He tried using his teeth and pushing on the cap with his thumb. It wouldn't budge and his thumb slipped, skinning it all the way down. He set the bottle on top of the dresser.

"You might want to wait for your lady friend," said Phil, back in his head.

"I don't suppose you have any extra fingers lying around," said Coop.

"I've got a great big one pointed at you right now. Can't you see it?"

"That's not in good taste. I'm an ill man."

"I'm dead. I long to be an ill man."

"You and Salzman. Always going on about being dead. Being alive isn't always all it's cracked up to be."

"Say that when Giselle's around," said Phil. "I dare you."

"You dare him what?" said Giselle, coming into the bedroom. She had a drink in each hand.

"He's daring me to tell you to tell me I'm not stupid for trying to open the aspirin by myself," said Coop, holding up his injured thumb.

Giselle leaned over and kissed it. "You twit," she said. She popped the top of the aspirin bottle and handed Coop a couple of pills. He washed them down with some margarita.

"So, I just heard from Dr. Ladybug Head that Woolrich has your first assignment all picked out."

"Shop talk, tonight?" said Phil.

"What's the job?" said Coop.

"Apparently, Woolrich heard a rumor about a deed to the world floating around. He wants to get it before the Russians or Chinese do. Or the CIA. Or FBI. You get the idea."

"Can you imagine?" said Phil. "The things you could do with that."

"Just imagine," said Coop.

"Okay. Shop talk is exactly the last thing I want to hear. You're both boring. Bye," Phil said and popped out of their heads.

"I wonder what a person would do with something like that?" said Coop.

Giselle looked around the room. "Maybe it's time to get your own place."

"Like a palace or something?"

"How about just an apartment?"

"As long as it has a huge TV and a huge bed."

"You can put this on the mantel," she said and handed him the Contego stone. He looked at her. She kissed him and they stayed that way for a while. Until Phil popped back into their heads.

"The tentacle twins are in the backyard playing Twister," he said excitedly. "You've got to see this."

"We'll be out in a minute," said Coop, and Phil was gone again. Coop went to a dresser drawer and pulled out a green folder.

"You're a pretty good pickpocket for an old guy," said Giselle.

"Lucky is more like it," said Coop. "The blood and all the dead people were a good distraction."

The two of them looked over the deed to the world. The first few words read, "The bearer of this document . . ."

Giselle pointed. "You see that? That's not just for an angel. That's you, Coop. You're the bearer," said Giselle.

"So I am."

"The whole world. That would be a hard thing to give up."

"Not so hard," he said. He took out a cigarette lighter and touched the flame to the bottom of the document. The two of them walked into the little half bath and dropped it into the sink, watching it burn down to ashes.

"Come on, assholes. You're missing it," said Phil, popping in and out of their brains.

"He's right. Let's go back to the party. It's a nice night out," said Giselle.

"Yeah," said Coop. "It's a nice night."

ACKNOWLEDGMENTS

THANKS TO MY AGENT, GINGER CLARK, AND MY EDITOR, David Pomerico. Thanks also to Pamela Spengler-Jaffe, Jennifer Brehl, Kelly O'Connor, Caroline Perny, Shawn Nicholls, Dana Trombley, Jessie Edwards, Rebecca Lucash, and the rest of the team at Harper Voyager. Thanks also to Jonathan Lyons, Sarah Perillo, and Holly Frederick. As always, thanks to Nicola for everything else.

Read on for a sneak peek at

The Wrong Dead Guy,

the next comedic caper in

New York Times bestselling author

Richard Kadrey's

Another Coop Heist series.

Coop was still drinking his first cup of coffee of the day when Giselle got a text from the DOPS saying that Woolrich, their boss—really, everybody's boss—wanted to see them. Coop experienced the usual stab of cold fear that came whenever he had to meet with Woolrich. The feeling was something like the sinking sensation when you're sent to the principal's office as a kid, only Coop got the adult version. This consisted mainly of a wild search for cash and his passport. The feeling wasn't pleasant, he didn't want to go the meeting, and he spent the next fifteen minutes trying to figure a way out of it. Giselle was no help. She just finished her coffee and got dressed, ignoring him the whole time.

Hunkered over his third coffee, Coop became acutely aware of her standing behind him.

"No," he said.

"It might not be anything," said Giselle. "Maybe he's inviting us to tea. Maybe it's a promotion. Maybe he's finally giving you your own desk."

"I don't want a desk. I'm a crook. Crooks don't have desks. We have tools and cars and six ways out of town."

"And molls. Don't forget molls," said Giselle, ruffling his hair from behind. Coop quickly brushed it back into place.

"Nothing good ever comes from talking to bosses."

"You were the boss of your little gang and look how nice you are."

"This is different."

"How?"

"I don't have heads mounted on the walls."

Giselle gave him a dismissive wave of her hand. "They're not *people* heads."

"Yet. I swear, every time I see him it's like he's measuring my neck to see how big a plaque he'll need."

Giselle went into the bedroom and came out with three ties in her hands. "Pick one," she said.

"No."

"Why not?"

"If I'm going to die, I'm going to be comfortable. And I'm not going out pretty. In fact, I'm not changing at all. If Woolrich wants to see me, I'm going in my pajamas."

Giselle held out the ties. "Don't be an idiot."

He looked at her, then at the ties, and selected a skinny black one, which he tied around the collar of his pajama top.

Giselle looked her watch. "I'm leaving in ten minutes. I don't care if you're dressed, naked, or wearing a tutu, you're coming with me."

"You're going to put the whammy on me and trick me into going, aren't you?" he said.

"Fogging minds, making little boys see or not see what I want, is what I do best. And you're right. In"—she glanced at her watch—"nine minutes, we're out the door."

Coop took off the tie. "Fine. But if Woolrich turns me into a mook or a windup toy, you're going to miss me."

He went into the bedroom and grudgingly got dressed. At the last minute, he took a jacket from the closet. It was dark blue and had a little gold crest on the breast pocket. He hated it. In fact, he'd always hated it and wasn't sure how he'd ended up with it in the first place. It was one of those mystery garments that everybody seemed to have one of in their closet. A gift or a drunken purchase on New Year's. Wherever it had come from, Coop hated it and if he was going to get shot or fed to one of the various horrors on the DOPS payroll, he wanted to make sure that the jacket suffered with him.

As he was finishing dressing, Giselle called from the other room. "And don't bring your passport. There's a chip in it and they'll know you have it. It won't look good."

Coop frowned, bent down, and took the passport out from where he'd tucked it into his sock.

When he came into the living room, Giselle smiled and gave him a kiss, wiping lipstick off his mouth with her thumb. As she straightened his tie, Coop said, "What if Woolrich knows about the office supplies?"

Giselle got her shoulder bag. "Then he'd just want to see you—the crook—and not one of his loyal operatives."

Coop thought for a minute. "That kind of makes sense."

"Of course it makes sense. If Woolrich was up to something, he'd have a dozen unmarked vans outside and goons knocking down the door. Relax. This is nothing," Giselle said.

As they walked to the car Coop said, "But what if it *is* something?"

Giselle tossed her bag into the backseat of the car. "Then you're on your own, sailor. I keep my passport duct-taped under the dashboard."

Coop stared at her.

"Don't worry," she said. "I have one for you, too. But you'll have to learn Portuguese and wear three-inch lifts. Also, a dress, Angélica."

"Oh, good. For a second there I thought you were going to make it hard on me."

The walk to Woolrich's office was through a maze of nearly identical corridors on one of the upper floors of the DOPS building. Giselle knew the way by heart, but Coop always imagined having to track down Woolrich's office on his own and getting lost. He'd never find his way out. He'd wander the halls like a ghost, growing thinner and crazier from lack of food and water. He'd wind up a DOPS legend, a cautionary tale for new recruits. Always stick to the buddy system in the management wing, they'd tell them. And if you happen to stumble across a dazed man in rags eating the stuffing from the hall chairs or swinging from the overhead lights, well, just pretend you don't see him. He's been out in the wild for too long. There's no bringing him back.

When they reached Woolrich's office, Giselle knocked, but didn't wait for a response. She opened the door and pulled Coop inside with her. Woolrich was at his desk, signing a large pile of papers with a gold-tipped Montblanc fountain pen. He didn't look up as they came in, but gestured vaguely to a couple of nearby seats. Coop and Giselle sat and waited. No one said anything. The only sound in the room was the scratching of Woolrich's pen. He signed each sheet importantly, with a flourish, like if he kept going long enough he'd win a prize, thought Coop. He looked at Giselle, but she just shrugged. Finally, he couldn't stand it anymore.

"Don't they have machines for that?" he said.

"What?" grunted Woolrich.

"Signature machines. For people who have to sign a lot of papers. Don't they have machines for that?"

Woolrich stopped writing for a second, tilted his head fractionally upward, and looked at Coop. "Of course, why do you ask?"

"It just seems like a lot of papers. Wouldn't a machine be just as good?"

"For some things. Not for others. And not specifically for this."

Woolrich went back to signing the papers. Coop started to say something else, but Giselle put a hand on his arm and shook her head. Coop mouthed, *What the hell is going on?*

Giselle mouthed, *I don't know.*

One more minute, mouthed Coop.

"One more minute and what?" said Woolrich, putting one last sheet of paper atop the pile on his desk. Capping his gold pen, he took a breath and said, "Well, that's enough dead people for one day, don't you think?"

Coop's brow furrowed. "Those are all people you're going to bump off?"

"Well, it's the end of the quarter. Can't have a lot of loose ends running around, can we?" Woolrich said matter-of-factly. "And *I* won't be *bumping off* any of them."

Coop felt cold. "I hope you don't think we're . . ."

Woolrich leaned back in his chair. "You? Either of you? Don't be ridiculous. Neither of you is suited for it, especially you. I'm not even sure we should let you have sharp pencils."

"Thanks for the pep talk," Coop said. "Can we go now?"

Woolrich shook a finger in the air. "Not quite yet."

The left side of his face twitched slightly. It was a leftover from when he'd been possessed earlier in the year by some ghosts during a labor dispute. Since then, he'd grown a mustache in an attempt to hide the affliction, but it just made it worse. Whenever Woolrich's lip jerked upward, it looked like he'd taught a caterpillar to rhumba. It was a mesmerizing sight and Coop had a hard time not staring. Instead, he focused on the fishbowl on the edge of the desk where a small brain with fins swam gentle laps.

There was a knock at the office door and Morty stuck his head in. "Hi. Is it okay to come in?"

Woolrich waved him in and pointed to a chair near where Giselle and Coop sat. Seeing Morty, Coop relaxed a little. They were old friends and criminal partners. Morty was a Flasher. He could open any lock ever made just by looking at it, a useful skill for a couple of thieves. Sure, Morty was responsible for Coop going to jail a couple of years back, but Coop forgave him. Pretty much. Mostly.

He was still thinking it over.

Morty sat down next to Coop and waved to Giselle. She gave him a little wave back.

"I'm sorry I'm late," he said. "I got lost coming from the elevator. It all looks the same out there. Shouldn't there be room numbers or a map or something?"

"That would defeat the purpose," said Woolrich.

"Of what?" said Coop.

"Of it all looking the same."

"Some kind of security thing, is it?" said Morty.

"Exactly."

"It's a good one. I was debating whether to eat my arms or legs first if I got lost."

"Legs," said Coop. "More meat. If you got lucky, you'd only have to eat one before you found the way out."

"You've thought about this, have you?" said Woolrich.

"Every time I come up here to Narnia."

Giselle cleared her throat. "So, now that we're all here, I'm guessing that you have a job for us?"

"Yes," Woolrich said. "A fairly straightforward one, but one which I thought you'd be particularly suited for."

Woolrich pulled a large folder from a drawer and dropped it on his desk. Coop didn't like the look of it. And he didn't like the word *particularly* so close to the words *suited for*. He thought about swinging blades and death curses and a lot of other unpleasant things designed to hurt and/or kill him.

"What kind of job is it?" he asked.

"A simple theft," said Woolrich. "A local museum has a mummy on display. We'd like to have it instead of them."

Woolrich opened the folder and spread its contents across his desk. There were blueprints, photos of the interior and exterior of the museum, a list of employees with their schedules, and other useful information. Giselle picked up the papers and went through them. Coop stood next to her, trying to see while also trying to stay as far as possible from the murder forms. It's not that he was superstitious. It was more that around the DOPS, death seemed like something you could catch, like a cold or a bullet.

"Get in closer, Coop," said Giselle. "Don't you want to see?"

"I'm fine right here."

Morty held up the blueprints, checking for locks in and out of the museum. Giselle looked over the personnel information. Coop poked a fingertip at the photos, trying to ignore the death warrants and all the trophy heads on Woolrich's walls.

After pretending to study things for a minute, he said, "How soon do you want us to do it?"

"Sunday night makes the most sense. The museum is closed on Monday, so you'll have plenty of time to work."

"Which mummy do you want?"

"There's more than one?" said Woolrich.

"A whole roomful," said Coop.

Woolrich took the photo Coop had been studying and looked it over. He made a face.

"Well, that complicates things. Still, not a problem. I have a special consultant who'll be going in with you. An expert on Egyptian art and artifacts."

"In others words, an amateur," said Coop. "Goody."

Woolrich ignored him and set the photo down on the desk. "You can requisition any equipment you want, within reason. As I said, it's the end of the fiscal quarter, so we need to mind our budgets."

"Of course," said Morty. "An amateur going in with us and a tight budget sounds like the perfect crime."

"It looks like a fairly simple job to me," said Woolrich. "And I'm sure you'll find Dr. Lupinsky a great help when you're inside."

"I'm sure he will be, isn't that right, Coop?" said Giselle. She gathered up the papers from the desk and put them in her bag.

Coop sat quietly for a minute, thinking. "So, what's wrong with it?" he said.

"Nothing," said Woolrich. "It's a mummy."

"Why do you want it?"

"The thaumaturgic antiquities department requisitioned it. I'm sure they have their reasons."

Coop shook his head. "I've been down there. They have dead bodies stacked to the ceiling."

"It's true," said Morty. "Someone really ought to clean up the place."

"They don't want *any* dead body, they want a specific mummy," said Woolrich. "This mummy."

"They have plenty of those, too," said Coop.

Woolrich leaned his elbows on his desk. "Why are you being such a pest about things?"

"I'm just curious. Why are *you* giving us this assignment? Like you said, it looks straightforward. Someone could have covered it in an email. You only hand out the really big jobs."

"Not always," said Woolrich.

"Always," said Coop.

Woolrich sat back up and opened his hands. "Like you, I'm a humble servant of the DOPS. We go where we're told even if we don't necessarily know why."

"Don't mind Coop," said Giselle. "He didn't get to finish his breakfast. It makes him grouchy."

"Breakfast is the most important meal of the day," said Woolrich.

Coop got up. "Great. I'm going out for waffles," he said. "Who's with me?"

"Not so fast, Cooper," said Woolrich.

"Don't worry. You're invited. You look like a muffin man. Bran, am I right? It helps with the digestion."

"Let me rephrase. Sit down and *calm* down," said Woolrich. "This is an ordinary assignment of an ordinary theft. The reason I'm giving it to you is that I wanted to be here to personally introduce you all to Dr. Lupinsky."

Coop sat back down. Giselle gave him a look that practically left a bruise.

"Whatever you say. None of us knows much about Egyptian stuff, so maybe we could use some help. When do we meet him?"

"Right now," said Woolrich. He shouted at the office door. "Dr. Lupinsky. Are you out there yet?"

Oh, great, he's deaf, thought Coop. "I hope he has a monocle," he mumbled.

"And a pith helmet," said Morty.

Giselle said, "Shh."

The door to the hall opened and a five-foot-tall octopus walked into the room. That's what Coop saw at first. He glanced at Giselle and Morty. By the looks on their faces, it was clear that they were seeing it, too. Coop looked back at the octopus. This time, it looked to him more like a cat. A cat on top of an octopus. Coop closed his eyes, and when he opened them again, the knot of fear in his throat loosened a bit. Just a bit. He realized that the thing wasn't an octopus or a cat. It was a robot with a black-and-white television perched on top, and on the television screen, a thin, young cat paced back and forth. Even though it was obvious that the cat was a video image, Coop got the distinct impression that it was looking at him.

"What a cute kitty," said Giselle. "What is it? Abyssinian?"

"No," said Woolrich. "It's Dr. Lupinsky."

The robot glided into the room on its metallic tentacles. It used one to close the door behind it and held out the other to Morty. Morty looked pale, but eventually he put out his hand to the tentacle and shook it.

Giselle leaned across Coop and said, "Hi. I'm Giselle. Nice to meet you, Doctor."

The robot extended a tentacle to her and the cat sat up. A subtitle appeared across the bottom of the screen.

Purrrrrrr.

The tinny sound of a happy cat came from the television's small speakers.

"And this is Coop," Giselle said.

The octo-cat held out a tentacle to Coop. A subtitle appeared on the screen.

Pleased to meet you. I've heard a lot about you.

Coop shook Dr. Lupinsky's tentacle. "I haven't heard nearly enough about you, doc." He looked at Woolrich. "Why is there a cat on the television?"

A subtitle appeared.

I used to be a cat.

"Of course. It all makes sense now."

Woolrich twitched. "While studying some arcane magic texts, the good doctor transformed himself into a cat. When he died, his ghost entered the nearest viable object. The television. It's all very simple."

"No, it's not," said Coop. "It's all very weird. Why was he a cat? Some kind of mouse fetish?"

Woolrich shook his head. "He was studying Bast at the time, the Egyptian cat deity. The transformation was a mistake."

"Like the television was a mistake?"

"Exactly."

"And this is who you want us to partner with?"

The cat paced excitedly back and forth across the screen. There were more subtitles.

I understand that my appearance can take some time getting used to.

"Good call," said Coop. "No offense, doc, but I don't work with amateur crooks, robots, cats, or televisions. There's no percentage in it."

"That was yesterday," said Woolrich. "For this assignment, not only will you be working with Dr. Lupinsky, I'm putting you personally in charge of his well-being."

"You're fucking kidding me," said Coop.

"What was that?"

Giselle looked at the octopus. "He said, 'I'm looking forward to the job and working closely with Dr. Lupinsky.'"

Woolrich nodded. "Yes. That's what I thought he said."

Coop didn't feel so much like a drowning man as a drowning man wearing a chum tuxedo in a school of sharks. Sharks with tommy guns.

"Okay," said Coop, pulling himself back together. "Let's forget Robocat for a minute. The plans and everything you gave us are fine, but they're not the same as being there. I want to go to the museum and walk the layout."

"Naturally," said Woolrich. "Dr. Lupinsky can come with you."

"No, he can't."

"Of course he can. We spent a lot of money on his legs."

Lupinsky stood on the equivalent of his toes and did a kind of short, metallic soft-shoe routine. When it was over, Woolrich, Giselle, and Morty clapped. Coop shook his head.

"He can't come with us."

Morty leaned forward. "I think what Coop means is that while we're grateful for the doctor's expertise . . ."

Purrrrrrr, appeared on the television.

Morty went on: "As a member of the team, he isn't what you'd call 'low profile.'"

Woolrich gestured to Giselle. "That's why you have a Marilyn."

"I'll handle it," she said. "Don't worry."

"I wasn't."

"What about video surveillance?" said Coop. "Giselle can mess with people's heads, but she can't fool cameras."

"We've already tapped into their system. It will conveniently go down when you're inside." Woolrich reached under his desk and pulled out a small backpack. "You won't want to forget this."

"What is it?"

"The doctor's batteries. Do you think that's a nuclear television? No. It's old. And it takes D batteries."

Coop took the pack off the desk and weighed it in his hand. It felt like a cinder block. "Why can't the cat carry his own batteries?"

A tinny growl came from the television speakers. A subtitle appeared.

Grrrrrrr.

"Dr. Lupinsky isn't a pack mule," said Woolrich.

"I'm pretty sure we can agree that 'mule' isn't the word anyone is thinking when they look at him," said Morty.

Hissssss.

"Which isn't a value judgment," Morty added quickly. "In fact, we're all very fond of cats around here. Right, Coop?"

"I'm not," said Coop. "The neighbor's cat ate my hamster when I was a kid."

"You had a hamster?" said Giselle.

"It was my brother's. He abandoned it and I took care of it. Then the cat got in."

"Your poor hamster," said Giselle. "You never told me about it."

"It probably choked him up too much. That childhood stuff sticks with you," said Morty.

"I wasn't choked up. I just don't trust cats."

"He's not a cat!" shouted Woolrich. "He studied at the Sorbonne. He has a doctorate from Harvard. Right, Doctor?"

"He's gone," said Coop.

It was true. The only thing on the television screen was a grainy black-and-white test pattern.

"Look what you've done. Dr. Lupinsky?" called Woolrich. He looked at Coop. "Apologize."

"To an octopus?"

Morty frowned. "A minute ago you said cat."

"Woolrich said he isn't a cat."

Woolrich stood up. "Apologize now or you're fired and we both know what that means."

"I'm off the badminton team?"

"Jail."

"Do it, Coop," said Morty.

"Right now," said Giselle through gritted teeth.

Coop held up his hands. "Fine. Sorry, doc. Here, kitty kitty."

"Stop that," said Woolrich.

Coop looked around. He was outnumbered and the door was too far to run to and, anyway, he'd get lost and Giselle would never speak to him again.

"Hey, doc," he said. "Listen. Why don't you come along and help us case the museum? It can't hurt to have an extra pair of eyes."

The cat came back onto the television screen. It sat down and began cleaning its paws.

Coop looked at Woolrich. "What is that?"

"I think it means he accepts your apology," said Gisele.

"I wasn't apolo—"

Giselle shifted in her seat, discreetly kicking Coop in the leg before settling down again.

Coop looked Lupinsky over. "Do we have to take all of him? Can't we just wheel in the television?"

"You'll want all of him. Would you show them why, Doctor?" said Woolrich.

Lupinsky walked to the wall and kept going, strolling up it and across the ceiling. When he was directly above Coop, he reached down with a couple of tentacles and picked him up.

"Um," said Coop.

Woolrich sat back contentedly. "While Dr. Lupinsky's current situation can be problematic, it also gives him certain advantages. Wouldn't you agree?"

"Definitely," said Coop, dangling several feet off the floor. "Welcome to the team, doc. Can I get down now?"